I0592815

- ISBN: 978-0-6483291-4-5 (ebook)
- ISBN: 978-0-6483291-5-2 (hardback)
- ISBN: 978-0-6484370-2-4 (paperback)

❀ Formatted with Vellum

THE SHATTERED CITY

BOOK TWO — THE CREATURE COURT

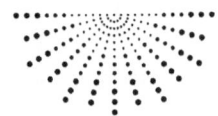

TANSY RAYNER ROBERTS

For Jay, who arrived halfway through.

CONTENTS

THE CREATURE
COURT CONTINUES

THE WORLD

Inglirrus

Camoise

The Green Isles

Atulia

Edore

Orcadia Stella

Isharo

Nova Stella

Ammoria

Zafir

Orcadia

Atulia

REYENNA

Tierce

LATTORIO

Aufleur

Barony of Diamagne

SILANO

Bazeppe

AMMORIA

© Jilli Roberts 2009

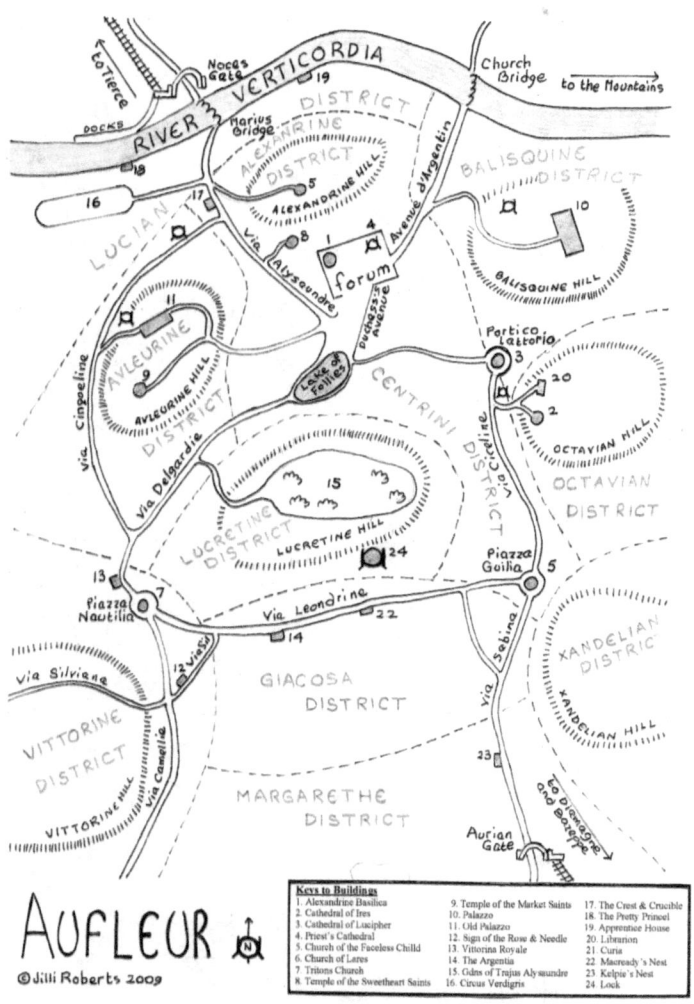

Keys to Buildings

1. Alexandrine Basilica
2. Cathedral of Ires
3. Cathedral of Lucipher
4. Priest's Cathedral
5. Church of the Faceless Childd
6. Church of Lares
7. Tritons Church
8. Temple of the Sweetheart Saints
9. Temple of the Market Saints
10. Palazzo
11. Old Palazzo
12. Sign of the Row & Needle
13. Vittorina Royale
14. The Argentia
15. Gdns of Trajun Alysaundre
16. Circus Verdigris
17. The Crest & Crucible
18. The Pretty Princel
19. Apprentiae House
20. Librarion
21. Curia
22. Macready's Nest
23. Kelpie's Nest
24. Lock

AUFLEUR

© Jilli Roberts 2009

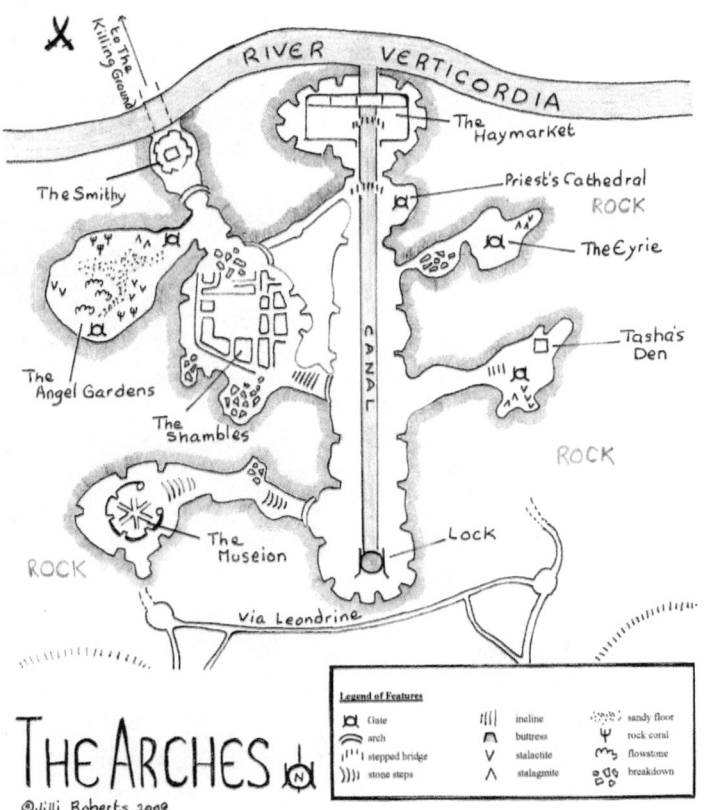

THE ARCHES

©Jilli Roberts 2009

PART I
NOXCRAWL AND
DUST DEVILS

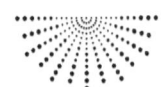

THE DAY AFTER THE NONES
OF FELICITAS (NEFAS)

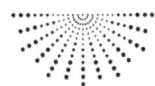

DAYLIGHT

*T*he silk was cool to the touch. It was a magnificent gown: flame-orange, trimmed with soft charcoal — black leaves of silk that tumbled from the Duchessa's shoulders to her knees. A perfect festival dress for the chief day of sacrifice, the centrepiece of the Sacred Games which would shortly be taking over the city.

It was the last fitting, and Velody was just managing to make the alterations — a stitch here, a stitch there — without her hand shaking on the needle.

There was no reason to be nervous. Sure, her entire professional career hung in the balance — a word from the Duchessa in the right circles could ruin her — and yet there were so many other things to worry about.

Velody could think of one person at least, if not an entire Court of them, who would laugh at her if they knew how anxious she was about this one everyday event. The world was so much bigger and more dangerous than she had ever known, and here she was fretting about the effect of a dropped waistline.

The slender, nineteen-year-old demoiselle who ruled the city of Aufleur gazed at herself in the mirror, lifting the weight of her long blonde hair. 'Should I bob it?' she asked idly.

Velody's own hair was bundled back in a snood. She still refused to have what most demmes these days referred to as 'the chop'. The very thought of it made her neck cold.

'The City Fathers would implode, my lady,' she said with a polite smile. 'But you would look exceptional.'

The Duchessa gave her an impish grin worthy of her age. 'I would, wouldn't I?'

The curtains in the room shifted as the door was opened abruptly. 'Ladies,' said the Ducomte Ashiol Xandelian d'Aufleur, striding through the room and hurling himself on the nearest floral sofa. He was dark, dangerously handsome, and held himself as if the city revolved around him.

Velody would not look. He was playing games with her, and she refused to allow him to put her on edge.

The Duchessa sighed dramatically. 'You will have to forgive the rudeness of my cousin, Mistress Velody. He was raised in the wild.'

'He does not disturb me, high and brightness,' said Velody, plucking pins from her mouth and ignoring the deep shiver that went through her flesh at the man's presence.

'Really?' the Ducomte said in a disappointed voice, kicking off his boots and putting his bare feet up on the arm of the sofa. 'I'll have to try harder, Mistress Velody.' He lifted his tousled head briefly, to examine the dress. 'I have to say, this one is an improvement over the other frocks you've laid in for the festival, gosling. Do you want the city to remember you as a worshipper of limp cabbage?'

The Duchessa set her jaw, looking older than her nineteen years. 'Most of my gowns for the Sacred Games have to be green, Ashiol. It is the colour of growth and renewal at the height of summer.'

'It makes you look like a salad,' he observed.

Velody hid her expression among the folds of the festival gown. 'My Lord Ducomte will not make the same comparisons when it comes to his matching tunics, I hope?' she suggested.

The Duchessa giggled. 'I wasn't going to mention that... yet.'

'Cruel demmes, the both of you,' said the Ducomte, letting his eyes fall closed. 'This is what comes of having a woman in charge.'

IT WAS EVENING, but the summer light meant that Velody would not have to walk from the Palazzo to her own shop in the Vittorine district in the darkness. The Duchessa's unfinished festival gown was wrapped in brown paper so she could carry it more easily. She had walked only a few paces when she felt the presence of the Ducomte Ashiol behind her, and slowed to allow him to catch up.

'A well-mannered seigneur would walk you home,' he informed her gravely.

'Indeed,' said Velody, unimpressed. 'This may surprise you, seigneur, but I am well able to take care of myself.'

'The streets aren't as safe as they used to be,' he told her, eyes dark.

'The streets were never safe,' she replied, pulling her wrap around her.

He did not offer to carry the parcel.

'Something bad's coming.' It was a different voice; Ashiol was no longer playing that odd game where they pretended to be vague acquaintances, the Duchessa's rude, flirtatious cousin and her humble dressmaker.

'From our enemies in the sky,' suggested Velody. She had felt it too — a dark shadow flickering at her throughout the day, the heavy weight of something to come, something more than the usual battles. 'Or your friends underground?'

'Both, I expect.'

They walked together in silence for some time, falling into step with each other. It was only a little over two months since they met, and he had become an essential part of her life. He had changed her world, quite literally, and Velody was still not sure how she felt about that.

The streets were clear of festival paraphernalia for once, though tomorrow was the beginning of the crazy season of Sacred Games — eight days altogether, then another seven of Victory Games later in the month. Victory Games, in a city that thought it hadn't been at war in decades. It was best not to think too hard about it.

That temple there, she saw it explode into pieces only a few noxes ago, shattered by a massive lashbolt from the sky, so fiercely bright that she had imprints of its shape on the inside of her eyes for hours afterward. When dawn came, the temple had discreetly reassembled itself, stones and dust moving back into place until it was pristine.

Oh, yes. This city made Velody's head spin.

DELPHINE HAD NOT EXPECTED THIS. It was more than a year since Rhian set foot outside the bounds of their house. But here they were, at the temple on the Lucretine, waiting to sacrifice their honey cakes. Almost like the old days.

Not quite like the old days. Rhian chose today because the Sacred Games had not started yet and there would be hardly anyone at the temple. She waited until almost dusk, and hid her face beneath her fleece garland as she walked along the streets.

That bastard Macready did not look surprised when Rhian suggested they come here today. Delphine hated him for being so confident. How had he with his lilting voice and easy ways talked Rhian into facing her crippling fear?

Delphine and Velody had struggled for so long, trying to find the right thing to say to coax Rhian into the world again. Glad though Delphine was (she wasn't that much of a sour bitch, surely?) that her friend was doing better, it burned that a stranger had wrought such a change.

'Wait for us,' Delphine said abruptly to him now as the last penitent emerged from the temple, leaving it empty. Macready shrugged and went to sit on the grass outside the temple. Why did he never get angry with her? She conveniently pushed out of her mind the few times she had seen rage in his eyes, because then she would have to admit that a spark of attraction shot through her whenever that happened.

'You are rude to him,' Rhian said as they stepped inside the cool temple. 'Why so harsh when he has been nothing but kindness?'

'I don't trust his kindness,' Delphine said. 'It leads to bad thoughts. Things! Bad things.' Rhian looked tense, as if her tall body and broad shoulders were the wrong size for the world. 'Why are you doing this?' Delphine blurted. 'Why now?'

'Velody says my father was a shepherd,' said Rhian. 'I don't remember him, but I should sacrifice on his behalf for the Parilia.' She looked apologetic, ducking her head low and purposefully, not adding what Delphine knew full well — the Parilia, festival of shepherds and fleece, was two days hence. But thanks to the Sacred Games, every temple in Aufleur

7

would be full of people then, all jostling and elbowing. This was the best Rhian could manage, for now.

The Parilia meant nothing to Delphine. She didn't even have to make garlands for it, as that work was better suited to the fleecers and spinners. Of all the hundreds of festivals celebrated in Aufleur, this was one she could happily ignore. She had honey cakes at the ready, though. Anything to preserve the old ritual of coming to a temple to sacrifice with Rhian. They were going through the motions, but it was a start.

Blurting the wrong thing was a hard habit to break. 'How do you know she told you the truth?'

Rhian looked at her in surprise. 'She's Velody.'

Ha, that was rich. Velody, who spent every nox on the roofs of the city, flirting with strange and dangerous people. Velody, who drew danger down upon them every day. Velody who sat Delphine and Rhian down and told them a fairytale about the city they were born in, how it had been destroyed in a battle so awful that no one remembered it had even existed.

Velody was not theirs any more, and Delphine did not believe a frigging word that came out of her mouth.

Rhian burned her offerings to the saint of shepherds and they emerged into the light of the early evening. 'I killed the Ferax Lord,' said Delphine, as if remarking on a new tisane she had learned about in the marketplace.

Rhian stared at her, and then tugged her away from the main portico of the temple, into the shade of nearby trees and well away from where Macready was waiting for them. 'The Ferax Lord,' she whispered urgently, two bright spots of colour on her cheek. 'The one who...'

'The one who invaded our home and held you prisoner,' Delphine said evenly. 'Who threatened Velody, stabbed her, and had Macready almost beaten to death. That Ferax Lord, yes. I killed him, and I'm not sorry.'

Rhian wore an expression that Delphine had not seen for a long time. The one where Rhian was the grown-up, the smart one who always knew what to do, until that awful day when she was hurt so badly she was unable to be that Rhian any more. 'You don't mean you actually... Delphine, you couldn't!'

'I didn't creep into his room and smother him while he was sleeping or spike his tonic, if that's what you think,' said Delphine, and the laugh that came out (because it was meant to be funny, really) didn't sound like it belonged to her at all. 'I — he was trying to kill me, and I had a... I had a sword.'

Should she be breathing this fast? It was loud in her ears. How had it happened? It was crazy. The ferax was one of them, so strong and powerful and Other, and she was just a person. One of the daylight folk, as Velody's Court friends said with such patronising airs. She was nothing.

'I don't know how I did it, but I was holding the sword and it just happened, and...' and she was crying now. How stupid — she never cried, and certainly not in front of Rhian, who had lost so much more than Delphine ever could. But now Rhian was holding her while Delphine sobbed into her best festival dress.

A hand touched her hair and it didn't belong to Rhian. 'It is how it has always been,' Macready said in his low lilt of a voice. 'I knew, lass. Your potential. It's like a glow around you. It's the brightest, best thing in the world. When it takes you, there is no chance. No sense. It was the same for all of us.'

Fury bubbled up in Delphine's stomach. 'No!' She was not going to accept it, not from him, not from any of them.

'What are you saying?' Rhian asked Macready.

'I'm saying that your lass here is a sentinel. Some are born to it, others are made. It happens often when a new Power is called, like buds bursting all over the city.'

'So,' Delphine said, making her voice cold. 'This isn't something I did, this is something that was done to me. By *Velody*.'

'Aye, well it's not as if she did it intentional,' said Macready, with that softness that came into his voice whenever he spoke about her high and mighty Majesty, Velody the Prim and Proper. Was he even aware of it? 'Just by being, she's set the cards tumbling in a long chain. The city calls new sentinels to honour her.'

'You talk about Aufleur like it is alive,' said Rhian, entranced by the idea.

Delphine wanted to hit them both. Repeatedly. 'I haven't been called by anyone, much less a city. It's ridiculous. I won't accept it.'

'Sword felt good in your hand, didn't it?' said Macready with a sly grin.

'Shut up.' Delphine had killed a person, and it made her feel awful, of course it did. She was not going to admit to that thrill of power, of how amazing it felt to have saved her own life and Macready's, to have done something so frigging mighty with her own hands. Never, never, never. Not to him, in any case. The last thing he needed was to become more smug.

'Is Delphine going to get into trouble?' Rhian asked. 'For — what she did?'

'That's the thing,' said Macready, his eyes boring into Delphine's. 'If she's one of us, sworn as a sentinel, then she did no wrong. She did her sacred duty. If she's just some demme from the daylight, every Lord and courteso will think it well within their rights to tear her into pieces.'

'I see,' said Delphine, swallowing. 'Isn't that a convenient stick to threaten me with?'

'What should we do?' Rhian asked.

Delphine was grateful for that 'we', but only a little. 'We go home,' she said firmly. 'We stop listening to silly stories. Velody may choose to play Court with the animals, but the rest of us have ribbons to make and flowers to braid and — oh.'

She saw him before either of the others did. A penitent, standing in the shaded portico of the temple. Delphine shivered at his presence. She felt Macready move behind her, just a little, so that he stood in front of Rhian, his hand ready to draw a sword if he had to.

Delphine wanted to be cross that he hadn't automatically moved to protect her — but she could not take her eyes off the man in the portico. He lifted his head up and smiled at her, and she felt her skin go creeping cold, all over. She knew him. He was the Orphan Princel, a theatre performer with a beautiful voice, who somehow glowed with beauty despite being on the skinny side, with an odd, knowing face and spectacles. There was nothing special about him... except that he was not just a performer. He had once turned into white rats in front of her eyes. He was Lord Poet of Velody's wretched Creature Court.

Poet bowed his head gracefully to them, and walked away from the temple.

'You don't think he heard?' Rhian asked in a choked whisper.

'Oh, aye,' Macready said, sounding grim. 'He heard, all right. We're in trouble, lass.'

VIA SILVIANA READIED itself for a street party as Ashiol and Velody approached. The various shopkeepers and families who were her neighbours set up a roast spit, and long tables

11

for food and drink. A small gang of flute demmes practiced badly on the street corner.

'Mistress Velody!' cried a friendly voice, and the red face of the local baker emerged from behind a lopsided festival drapery. 'We're celebrating this nox. Will you join us?'

'I'd be honoured, when my day's work is done,' she said politely. 'What's the occasion?'

'My boy, Giuno, takes his man's robe today,' said the baker with obvious pride. 'Glad to have you share meat and wine with us. And your man,' he added politely.

Velody felt a laugh stick in her throat at the thought that anyone might think Ashiol was her paramour, but she did not correct the baker. What other explanation was there for his regular visits? As long as no one in Via Silviana knew enough to recognise him as the Duchessa's cousin, there would be few questions asked.

'I like meat and wine,' said Ashiol with a gleam in his eye as the baker ran off to shout at some boys about oiling the spit. 'Is that goat I smell?'

'You're not invited,' she said firmly, unlatching the front door. They used it more now that Rhian was improving.

'That seigneur most definitely included me in the invitation.'

Velody hovered on the threshold, wanting to get rid of him rather than invite him in. 'Under false pretences. He thinks you're wooing me.'

Ashiol smiled, and oh dear, it did terrible things to her stomach when he smiled like that. 'I can woo.'

'I'd really rather you didn't.' Velody heard Delphine shouting from inside the house. 'Oh, hells.'

There was no getting rid of Ashiol now. He followed her to the kitchen, where Delphine was — surprise, surprise — having a shouting match with Macready.

'What's going on?' Velody demanded.

'Your lass is impossible,' Macready said, throwing up his hands in disgust.

'Of course she is — she's Delphine,' Velody said calmly. 'It's hardly worth shouting about.'

'Your little friend here,' said Delphine, deliberately stressing the word 'little', 'is trying to bully me into being one of his sword-swinging numbskulls, and I won't do it.'

'Poet knows who killed Lord Dhynar,' Macready said, addressing Ashiol and Velody more seriously.

Velody shivered. For a moment, dark shadows covered the world, shrouding all of them in blackness. She blinked rapidly, and the darkness receded. No one else had noticed anything odd. Ashiol was barking questions at Macready, who was getting defensive. Delphine looked as if she was about to explode.

'Do we have to get Delphine out of the city?' Velody asked in a low voice.

That got a reaction at least. 'Is that your answer to everything?' Delphine hurled at her. 'No, Velody. First you want to run away from all this, then you want to stay, and you expect us to fall in with whatever you decide. I have a *life* here. I'm staying put. And that life has nothing whatever to do with swords and rodents!'

She stormed off towards the stairs. Rhian sighed, and followed. 'I'll see if I can calm her down.'

Velody waited until Rhian was also upstairs and out of earshot. 'Is Poet a danger to us?'

'He's a danger to everyone,' Ashiol said darkly. 'You never know what's going on in his head. If he has this information on Delphine, rest assured, he will use it when it best suits him.'

Velody sighed, and looked at Macready. 'Would becoming a sentinel really make her safer?'

'That depends on your definition of the word "safe", so it

does,' Macready admitted. 'If she's one of us, then there are rules to protect her actions. If she's not...'

'You wouldn't really leave?' Ashiol interrupted.

'No,' Velody sighed. She had tried to leave. Had tried to take Delphine and Rhian away from Aufleur, and put the world of the Creature Court behind her. But that was before she fought and won against the corrupted shade of Dhynar Lord Ferax. Before she accepted her role as Power and Majesty of the Creature Court.

Accepting she belonged to them was one thing. Accepting that Delphine might also belong was altogether different. 'I'll talk to her,' she offered. 'If she won't see sense, I'll talk to Poet.'

'You can't negotiate with the Lords over tisane and finger sandwiches,' Ashiol warned. 'We're warriors. Animals. Offer the hand of friendship, and we bite.'

Velody gave him an impatient look. 'No one is getting bitten. Not today.'

DELPHINE WAS SO angry she couldn't see straight. She pulled dress after dress out of her wardrobe, flinging them on the bed regardless of the fact that Rhian was sitting there. 'I am tired of you making all the decisions,' she snapped, not turning around as Velody joined them. 'First you want us to hide from this Creature Court of yours, then you want to make friends with them, then we're running away and leaving our house, then we're staying here so you can do your duty by them. I'm done with it, Velody. This is my life, and you don't get to order me around.'

'How did you know I was here?' Velody asked.

Delphine flung herself around, staring. That was a very good question. 'I heard you come in.'

'Among all that shouting and muttering and clothes throwing? You must have very good ears.'

'I'm not one of them,' Delphine said, disgust dripping from her voice. 'You may enjoy running around pretending to be little brown mice and fighting invisible things in the sky and jumping off roofs but some of us are normal!'

'I didn't like this any more than you did when I first came into my power,' said Velody. 'But you can't fight it, not without driving yourself crazy.'

'I stuck a sword into someone,' Delphine said, feeling the fight go out of her. 'Anyone could have done it.'

'I don't think I could,' said Velody. 'Not even to save a friend. You're special.'

Delphine screwed up her face. She wanted to lash out and hurt Velody. It was the best way to make her go away and shut up and stop being all saintly and helpful. 'Is that what you think you are? Special? They're using you, all of them. Ashiol Xandelian threw you to the wolves so he didn't have to be their leader. The rest of them only pretend to worship you. It's the power they want. The minute you do something they don't like, they'll tear you to pieces. What are we supposed to do then, me and Rhian?'

Delphine saw Velody's face crumple, and knew she had hit home. 'Some of us have hopes and dreams and a real life right here at ground level,' she added, grasping the nearest frock. It would do, for a local street party. 'You should try it some time.'

2

THE DAY AFTER THE NONES
OF FELICITAS (NEFAS)

DAYLIGHT TO NOX

*V*elody came back downstairs to discover that Ashiol and Macready had left, thank the saints. With Delphine sulking upstairs and Rhian retreated back into her own room, the workshop was quiet.

Velody had work to do. The Duchessa's flame gown needed to be altered to fit perfectly, and there was a waist-coat waiting to be trimmed. These two projects had been her saving grace over the last few nundinae. When everything else got too much for her, when the darkness clouded her judgement, she could sit and work. Sewing made the shadows go away.

Velody noticed shadows on her hands sometimes, odd little blots that were gone as soon as she looked at them closely. Since she took Dhynar's ugly, corrupted shade into herself, those shadows appeared more often. Sometimes they were accompanied by stabbing headaches, or a heaviness to her shoulders. She snapped more, and retreated into dark moods when she was unhappy. Once, she thought she saw a black web covering both her arms, and jumped right out of her chair in horror, though her skin was flawless again when Rhian or Delphine asked her what was wrong.

Ashiol told her that being a part of the Creature Court meant madness and monstrous behaviour. Velody refused to believe that wielding animor would have such an effect on her. Every time she jumped at shadows or felt the uncharacteristically fierce anger welling up inside her, or heard Dhynar's laughter bubbling out of a corner of the room, she made herself work on the waistcoat, or the Duchessa's flame gown, allowing her dark thoughts and panic and even her animor itself to bleed into the embroidery stitches and the rich damask and tapestry fabrics she had used.

Thank goodness she had this. If there was only the Creature Court in her life, she would have gone mad by now.

Nox fell over Via Silviana, the sky darkening. Ashiol stood guard outside Velody's house as her neighbours worked on their street party. The music began, and the air filled with the scent of roasting meat.

There was no reason for him to stay. There were rooms waiting for him at the Palazzo, meat for every meal if he wanted it. He could rest and eat — the sky might have a battle to throw at them, but not yet, not for hours, perhaps.

Here he was, hanging around a demoiselle's door like a fool, because he did not want to be anywhere else. She had no need of his protection. Still, he loitered.

The crowd built up, friends and family and complete strangers toasting the boy who had come of age. It was an odd thing, to witness such merrymaking. Ashiol took his man's robe in a formal ceremony presided over by his stiff,

17

icy grandparents, with a sip of watered wine and gifts that befitted the son of the Ducal family. He and Garnet stole cups of beer later, and... but, no. He was not going to think of Garnet this nox.

He did not plan to drink, either, not with the sky on the verge of breaking open, but a group of laughing revellers planted a cup in his hand. There would be no harm in a mouthful or two.

Velody's friend Delphine ran out of the house to join the party. Ashiol turned swiftly away, not wanting her to see him. Hysterical demme — for all he knew she would start shrieking again the moment she clapped eyes on him.

He found himself near the spit, which was no hardship, and ate several slices of barely charred goat with his fingers before he caught sight of his own reflection in a shop window. He looked old, he thought, greasy fingers brushing against a thread of silver in his dark hair. No one lived to get old in the Creature Court, but that didn't mean they did not feel their years.

There was a flicker in the glass, and Ashiol blinked. No, not that. Not now. He turned and stumbled along the street, away from the window. But there were shops along the whole stretch, and he saw it in each of them. No longer just a flicker, or an impression.

Away from the crowd, where the tables and dancers trickled to nothing, Ashiol stood transfixed, his eyes locked on a face that was not his in the reflection of a closed-up haberdashery. Garnet, more than two months dead, smiled the smile of the morally righteous. 'Admit it. You missed me.'

This wasn't a flicker of a bad memory. This was a full-blown hallucination, and that was a very, very bad sign. Not now; he couldn't afford to lose his mind here and now. 'Dead is a good look for you,' Ashiol said, forcing his tone to be light. (Who exactly was he trying to fool here?) 'Or I should say, not torturing me is a good look for you.'

There were no words for this. For the sight of a man he hadn't seen in five years. Lover, brother, best friend. Madman. King. Garnet.

Garnet had always been pale; that shock of red hair over porcelain-light skin. Ashiol used to tease him that he was the one who should have been born an aristocrat, with looks like that. Garnet's eyes, though... they were not familiar. The light in them was wrong. Try as he might, Ashiol couldn't make them look real from any angle.

Not real, not here, that's why. Don't get fucking stupid.

'I like the new demme,' Garnet said now, his fingers flicking back and forth in an absent-minded pattern. He always talked with his hands, apparently unconscious of the way they moved and danced and told a different story to his words. 'Vel-o-dee. Can we eat her yet?'

'You created her,' Ashiol said. 'You sucked the animor out of a fourteen-year-old, you bastard. You used Velody's animor to build your power higher than me, higher than anyone. We're reaping what you sowed.'

He wanted to smash his friend in the face, to beat him, to finally let the hate take over. He didn't have to be loyal any more, didn't have to hold back.

Garnet's face was perfectly framed by the window, beside Ashiol's darker hair, skin tone, eyes. 'That's what kills you, isn't it? You finally figured out how I beat you — how I cheated — and you can't strangle me. Can't hurl yourself at me in one of those charming fits of rage before I put you into the ground, all over again.' The vision of Garnet brushed his lips against Ashiol's ear lobe, and for a moment he could feel the touch. 'Exactly how much do you want to bring me back, just so you can kill me all over again?'

Ashiol roared, the anger hot and scorching inside him,

and lunged. His hands collided with the glass, bruising badly. The cup he forgot he was holding broke into pieces, lacerating his palm.

He licked wine and blood from his hand, feeling the tremble of his skin against his mouth. When he dared to look again, there was no reflection in the glass but his own face.

Macready was waiting for Ashiol when he returned to the party. 'There you are, laddie buck. Are we taking to the sky soon?'

'Time enough for that,' Ashiol said grimly, dropping the broken pieces of his wine cup into Macready's hands. 'I need another drink.'

As many as it would take to forget the fact that he was losing his grip all over again.

VELODY DOZED A LITTLE, in the armchair. No point in going to bed. The air pressed around her like a storm was coming, and she knew enough to recognise that the sensation had nothing to do with the weather. She dreamed of Dhynar, of the corrupt taste of his shade, haunting the streets of Aufleur. Of the power she had wielded to chase him down. She dreamed he was still inside her, trying to tear his way out of her body, puncturing her skin from within, using teeth and claws to dig an escape route through her belly.

When she awoke with a gasp, the room was dark. The grate was empty — it was summer, after all. The sounds she heard were not the wailing cries of a ferax monster inside her skin, but a crowd singing drunken songs. The sky was going to fall, and the daylight folk were dancing and feasting. Why was she not surprised?

Velody opened the front door and saw a blaze of paper lanterns in the street outside. The party had grown — it now reached from one end of the street to the other. It may have started as a local occasion to celebrate one lad reaching manhood, but word had spread across the lower Vittorine and the breadth of Giacosa that there was a party, and the newcomers had brought further provisions with them. Tables lined the gutters, groaning with donated food. Half the city was on her doorstep.

She looked up, beyond the lantern light, and saw familiar streaks across the sky, a haze of green and then purple. The sky was not falling yet, but soon. Velody could feel the familiar spark of animor, colliding with her own. The Creature Court were here, nearby. That was a worry.

Delphine was there too, dancing in the crowd, going from hand to hand as if she had not a care in the world. Velody had always envied Delphine's ability to throw herself into the world like that. If the Creature Court were here, though, Delphine was in danger.

Roast goat. Someone had said something about roast goat. Velody followed her nose to the spit, where two lads were slashing strips off the beast, layering them up on platters for the crowd. She found a dish of the rarest slices, oozing blood, and ate ravenously, licking her fingers.

'Love a demme with an appetite,' leered one of the goat lads.

Velody wiped a smear of blood from her chin. 'Don't we all?' Fresh meat was a rare extravagance, and her body thrummed with it as she turned back to face the crowd. The music slid under her skin, and she could feel Ashiol's presence nearby. She could not see him in the crowd, but his animor sparked against her own, bringing mixed sensations of security and lust. *You don't want him*, she told herself sternly. *It's the meat making you crazy.*

That line of argument was no more convincing than it had ever been. Her only chance was to fill her mind with that other man — the red-haired lunatic whom she had not laid eyes on since she was fourteen, though he had been in her dreams often enough. Garnet. Ashiol's lover. The last Power and Majesty of the Creature Court. Thinking of him was the easiest way to push any desire for Ashiol Xandelian d'Aufleur out of her mind entirely.

Velody ate one last slice and went looking for Delphine. She found her friend in the midst of the dancing, spinning around young Giuno, who looked as if all his Saturnalias had come at once. Delphine looked healthier than she had in some time, her cheeks pink and her eyes bright. She grabbed at Velody's hand, ignoring her current dance partner. 'The uninvited guests belong to you, I suppose?'

Oh, *seven* hells. Velody had hoped that the animor she felt close by belonged to Ashiol, who could be trusted for the most part, but no.

Poet was here, his slender frame wrapped in a theatrical costume — bright diamonds of scarlet and gold satin, a gaudy hat, and bespectacled eyes that saw everything. He moved through the crowd as a cheerful dandy, flirting with demmes and boys equally. It was quite a pantomime, amusing if you didn't know how dangerous he was. He knew about Delphine. What was he going to do with that information?

'I like the dark one,' said Delphine.

Saints and devils, Warlord was here too. The warrior in bright Zafiran silks prowled through the crowd, every inch the panther he was in another life. Kerriden of the cheese shop simpered at him and he towered seductively over her, lips parted as if he was thinking about kissing her, or at the very least saying something terribly wicked. At least three demmes looked as if they were about to swoon.

Velody stepped away from the dance. Just one step, but Warlord's and Poet's eyes snapped to her. She felt naked. It didn't help that she knew that they both had very clear memories of what she looked like, out of her gown and slip. She took one more step back, and was overwhelmed by the power and scent of another of them, as a pair of female arms in long black gloves wound around her shoulders.

'Velody,' purred Livilla. 'We've missed you.'

Delphine had one eyebrow raised in a 'why is that woman pawing you?' kind of way.

Poet and Warlord let the dance draw them nearer. No, the dance was not in control. They were. The merchants and residents of the street eddied and swirled around them, in utter docility. Velody wanted to say something, but she couldn't think with Livilla's silk-sheathed hands caressing her neck, with the men coming closer, the thick atmosphere of so much animor clouding the air.

The sky. They should be in the sky, and soon.

Warlord nodded to her as he passed from one hand to another, circling around her to the tintinnabulation of the street musicians. 'We have not seen much of you lately, my Power.' He ate a tangerine with his spare hand, flicking peel to the cobblestones as he took small, fierce bites.

Where were her sentinels? Velody looked up and saw Ashiol watching her, not making a move in their direction. Of course not. Had she not told him to back off, to let her handle the Creature Court for herself?

She could handle them. They were gentle with her, since she proved her loyalty to them. She rid the streets of the tainted shade of Dhynar Lord Ferax, and the rest of the Court had tumbled into her lap like tame kittens. To a point.

'I have been busy,' Velody said, lips dry, lifting her chin to prevent her nervousness from showing.

'We are supposed to be what makes you busy,' Warlord said in that rich accent of his.

'Feeling neglected?' she shot at him.

Poet, closer than she had thought, laughed sharply. 'Always, my Majesty. Have you not realised yet? We require a great deal of attention.' His eyes went to Delphine, who lifted her chin and refused to look nervous.

'Yes, I can see that,' said Velody. 'Saints and angels, Livilla, get your hands off me.'

There was something deeply wrong with Livilla. Her eyes veiled a personality far more broken than Delphine or Rhian. Whatever her hurts were, they were old and scarred. 'Anything you say, Lady Power,' she purred now, stepping back as if delighted to be ordered around.

'Why are you here?' Velody asked.

'The mere pleasure of looking upon you,' said Warlord with his usual gentility. He took one more bite of the tangerine and threw it into the gutter, licking his lips.

'I am glad to have obliged,' Velody said, losing her nerve. 'But we have work to do this nox. Delphine — go into the house.'

'Nonsense,' her friend said, tossing her head. 'It's a party, Velody. I want to dance.' She seized the nearest hand, which was Livilla's, of all people. Livilla looked almost as startled as Velody. 'You'll do,' said Delphine, and dragged her into the drum beat and bells.

Velody blew out a breath in a huff. Did Delphine think Livilla was less of a viper than the other Lords because she had breasts? Livilla and Delphine danced against each other gloriously, eyes locked, teasing each other as much as their audience. It was the kind of dance that only happened when both participants wanted to win. Young Giuno and his friends stared in wonder, laughing and blushing.

For a moment, Velody was dazzled by the image of what the Creature Court could really be like if they all trusted each other — if she could trust them fully. If they concentrated all their energies on fighting their enemies instead of scratching and hissing at each other. It was a fine image, but they weren't there yet.

Velody moved on to the pavement, almost crashing into Poet. He looked far too pleased with himself. 'Don't trouble yourself, mouseling,' he said. 'I'll keep an eye on your lamb, protect her from the wolves.'

'Who'll protect her from you?' countered Velody.

'I was under the impression that the demme could more than protect herself,' Poet teased, though his eyes were dangerous. 'Dhynar found it so.'

'Dhynar was a fool, and no loss to us,' Velody snapped. She could say his name without flinching now, though the memories still flooded her, of the young Lord who challenged her so many times, who was not prepared to accept a female Power and Majesty. Dhynar died forsworn, and his shade trailed misery and death through the streets until Velody stopped him, consumed him. She could still feel him crawling under her skin. Above the noise of the crowd, she could hear the echo of his laugh.

The sky rippled above her. They could agree on that, at least. There was no time for music and sweetmeats when there was a city to protect. 'So sad,' Poet said mockingly. 'Our evening of slumming it with the peasants is over so soon?'

'I'd sympathise,' Velody replied. 'But no one invited you.'

'You wound me,' he sighed.

'You'll survive.'

'And wouldn't you feel terrible if I didn't?' His eyes danced at her, and then he whipped up into the sky, his garish robes flapping around him as he flew like a pantomime angel ascending to the stars above.

Velody jumped back and looked around defensively, but here was the blindness of daylight folk at close hand. Two chattering demmes had stood right behind Poet, and they did not even blink when he took to the sky. One of them broke off from their conversation when she caught Velody staring, and gave her an unfriendly look.

So, then. Could she turn into a mess of little brown mice in the midst of this mob, and have them not turn a hair? Every instinct told her not to try. The last thing she needed was her neighbours deciding to burn her as a witch.

The sky rumbled with a sound that was not thunder. There was a clash and the warm summer evening was suddenly cold, as cold as the Ides of Saturnalis. Velody breathed out, and saw steam. Across the street, she saw Maia from the laundry smiling up at Benedine of the hot food shop, shrugging her light summer shawl a few more inches off her shoulders. They did not feel the ice in the air. Velody looked around for the rest of them and saw Warlord standing in a small crowd of fruitsellers, charming them all effortlessly, a cup of wine in one hand and a demoiselle in the other. He met Velody's gaze and smiled at her, showing bright white teeth.

She tilted her head a little, giving him her best stern Power and Majesty expression. He lowered his head in an infinitesimal movement that might have been a nod, and then excused himself from his playmates, disappearing into the crowd.

Moments later, the silhouette of a panther appeared on a rooftop above their heads, and pounced on the sky as if he owned it.

Livilla prowled her way down the street towards Velody. She stopped only a few feet from her, looking her up and down as she always did, as if Velody was food. Given that Livilla's shape was the wolf and Velody's a horde of mice, it wasn't far wrong. 'Aren't you going to ask nicely?' Livilla said, arching her eyebrow.

'I didn't think I had to,' Velody said. She kept her voice

firm and confident, as if she was training a hound — *never let them smell your fear*.

Livilla laughed too long, and too loudly. 'You'll need us, I suppose, since your fellow King is deep in his cups.'

Oh, hells. Velody lost interest in Livilla, scanning the mob for Ashiol. 'Where is he?'

'How should I know?' Livilla kicked her shoes under a table and took to the air as Poet had, right in front of everyone. 'I'll be in the sky if you need me.'

Velody could still hear the Lord of Wolves laughing above her as she ran the length of Via Silviana, looking for Ashiol bloody Xandelian. Someone caught her arm and she spun around, ready to fight if she had to.

'What's wrong?' Delphine demanded.

'You need to get into the house,' Velody told her. 'No game-playing now. I mean it. Have you seen Ashiol?'

'No, and I don't care to. He's a boring drunk, no matter how well he can dance.' Delphine shrugged one shoulder. 'I was going in, anyway. It's freezing. What kind of summer is this, anyway?'

Velody didn't have time to think about what it might mean that Delphine could feel the chill from the sky. 'How drunk is he? Have you seen him?'

'You'll be taking to the sky without him this nox,' broke in another voice, a grumpy Macready.

'We'll see about that,' said Velody.

She found Ashiol leaning against a wall near the spice shop. His attention was wholly caught by the reflection of lanterns in the window opposite. Velody resisted the urge to ask if he might prefer a ball of yarn to play with. 'The sky,' she snapped at him. 'Now.'

Ashiol turned with a startled movement and half-staggered. Velody caught his arm to stop him falling, but it was more of a job than she thought. He had his dead weight leaning on her. 'Stop this right now,' she hissed at him.

'May as well tell the river not to flood in Martial, Saint Velody,' he said with a slur.

Her heart sank as she saw how glazed his eyes were, and caught the stench of his breath. He had been drinking more than wine. 'You knew the sky was throwing something at us this nox,' she accused. 'Why would you be so irresponsible?'

Ashiol laughed, and it was nothing like the laughter of Livilla. This was an empty sound. 'I don't need to be responsible any more, sweetling. That's what you're for.'

Velody shoved him off her, and this time he did fall, sliding carelessly into a heap at the side of the street. 'I should make you fight the sky anyway,' she said, but they both knew she wouldn't do that.

The air turned even colder, and when she looked up she could see a silvery pattern beginning to spread over the greenish clouds. She had wasted enough time down here. 'Macready, could you...'

'Way ahead of you, lass,' said the sentinel, tossing his brown cloak over Ashiol, and then hauling him to his feet with a grunt.

'Don't think I'm going to help,' said Delphine.

'My heart's broken, for I was counting on your kindness,' Macready shot back.

Velody tuned them both out, her eyes on the flickering silver strands in the sky. They formed something like a cracked snowflake, all jagged shapes and brightness. Other shapes flitted in front of the clouds — creatures from her own Court. She was needed there.

If Poet and Livilla could do it, why not?

Velody soared into the sky without a care for who saw her go. Her skin was chill with the frosty air as she sped higher, into the unknown. Every battle was different, and she hadn't seen spike patterns of ice like this before. She should learn everything she could about this new danger, but it was hard to clear her mind of her anger at Ashiol.

What did he think he was doing? She knew he wanted her to be Power and Majesty so he wouldn't have to, but she relied on him to be there, supporting her. There was still so much she didn't know about being part of the Creature Court, and Ashiol was the only one she could trust with that vulnerability. Without him, she was truly on her own.

The wind was freezing cold this high up, chilling her to the bone. Time to pay attention, before she got herself sliced to pieces. Velody gasped as ice blasted her from behind, showering her with tiny pellets that burned at her skin. She swiped them off, and felt another pair of hands helping her.

'Careful, Majesty,' said Priest, ever the polite seigneur. The large man, the only member of the Creature Court over forty, had not been at the street party with the other Lords, but he was here now. He dusted the last of the ice pellets from her back and hovered there beside her. 'These nodules are harmless enough, as long as you don't stay in contact too long. They're attracted by animor, and if too many cling to you at once it can drain your powers.'

'Good to know,' Velody said, shivering in her thin dress. Animor usually heated her from within, but right now she couldn't imagine ever feeling warm again. 'What else do I need to look out for?'

There was a cracking sound, and ice blossomed out of thin air. The sky splintered around them, and Warlord cried out nearby as white spikes burst through his chest. Velody saw his courtesi cluster to him, a cloud of cats and brocks and bats swirling around his agonised figure, but it was Livilla who blasted the ice spikes out of him, liquid heat pouring from her hands and through his ribs.

Velody was certain that would have killed him, but

Warlord shook it off. He seized one of the nearest brocks and bit hard into its body, taking enough blood from his courteso to return his strength. He kissed Livilla with his messy mouth before they flew their separate ways, hurling bursts of heat into the icy cracks in the fractured sky.

'Mind the frostiels; they hurt like hells,' Priest said in a grave voice. 'Oh, and stay warm.' He glowed white and Velody could feel a moment of heat rolling off him before he, too, plunged into the battle.

Velody concentrated, summoning her animor with as much heat as she could manage. She called to mind the balmy days they had enjoyed this summer, of sunshine on the side of the Vittorine, bubbling onion soup and flatbread baking on hot bricks. Her nest of blankets and quilts tangled around her as she dreamed of Garnet and battles and little brown mice.

When the sky broke into bursts of frostiels near her, Velody fought them back, forcing heat from her skin to seal every crack and chip. She ducked and wove, avoiding the stabbing spikes of ice.

Every attack drained more warmth from her skin, and she fell back, the darkness and cold overwhelming her. She could hear that laughter again, and she was briefly confused, unsure which dead man was mocking her — Garnet or Dhynar.

Oh, there was a potential source of heat. Anger. Velody flared up with it, letting all her resentment at what had been done to her flood through her entire body. Garnet stole her powers, prevented her from learning what she needed to defend the city against the sky, used Velody's own animor to fuel his reign of terror over the Creature Court. He tricked her into giving up a part of herself.

Dhynar had been so sure of her weakness, challenging her again and again, and ultimately destroyed himself, leaving her to deal with the guilt that she had not saved him, had not redeemed him, had not done enough...

Ashiol threw her to the wolves and was deep in his cups while Velody and the rest of the Court risked their lives to keep Aufleur safe.

Heat bloomed out of her skin, striking the nearest crack in the sky before it could shoot forth with frostiels or nodules. Velody's animor was so fierce that the crack melted into nothingness, sealing the sky closed. She turned on the next and the next, animor whirling from her fingertips. Somewhere along the way her body shaped and reshaped, into chimaera and then mice and then Lord form again. The only thing unchanged was the fire and steam of her animor. The sky boiled around them, and was still.

Finally, the last of the crack was sealed. The sky was silent and dark. Stars twinkled as if there had been no battle here this nox. Velody breathed, and no steam came from between her lips. She slowly became aware that everything hurt — her spine and ribs and skull — as if someone had been pounding her bones with a mallet. Somewhere along the way, she had lost her dress.

They were all looking at her, the Lords and Court, hovering in an uneven circle around her, in their naked 'people' bodies. They seemed impressed. Some of them were wounded, their skin scratched and punctured in places by those spikes of ice. Livilla licked a smear of blood from a scrape on the back of her hand and gazed thoughtfully at Velody.

Too late, Velody remembered her duties — to honour the Creature Court for their efforts. 'You fought well,' she said, finding her voice. Her throat ached as if she had been coughing up her lungs for hours.

'I'm not entirely sure we needed to,' said Poet slyly. He came forward, though, and she bestowed the ritual kiss of approval on him. Warlord was next, and Livilla and Priest, then each of their courtesi in turn.

They looked at her as if she had done something marvellous, instead of losing control. Velody found herself shaking, and it was all she could do to hold back the tears. 'You have earned your rest,' she told them, and then left, sinking too fast from the sky, stumbling as her feet hit the crest of the Vittorine. She felt cobbles bruising her soles, but kept walking.

She had no clothes, so she kept her animor blazing bright enough to light her way, and hoped it meant that any daylight folk awake this late would not see her, just as they had not seen Poet fly up from the middle of a busy street.

Halfway down the street, she found Crane and Kelpie waiting for her, serious and expressionless, not filling the air with whimsical chatter as Macready might have. Thank the saints for sentinels. Crane held out his cloak to wrap around Velody and the gentle touch of his hands made her break down, as she could not have done in the sky with the Lords and Court around her. Velody leaned into his chest, inhaling the scent of his skin and his shirt, and sobbed quietly. There was an awkward pause, and then he gently patted her back.

'Nest or house?' Kelpie asked a little while later. 'Home,' Velody breathed, and let go of Crane.

The party was over when they reached the street outside Velody's house, though tables and empty cups and bowls were strewn around as if there had been a battle fought here too.

'Do you need us for anything?' Crane asked, but Velody just shook her head and let herself into the house, alone. She went up to her bedroom, and pulled herself under the nest of quilts and blankets without even unwinding Crane's cloak from her shoulders. The blackness fell down around her, and she let it come.

3
PARILIA

SECOND DAY OF THE LUDI SACRIS, THREE
DAYS AFTER THE NONES OF FELICITAS

DAYLIGHT

*V*elody was still furious at Ashiol. She had not seen
him since the street party, nor did she expect to
— the Sacred Games were underway, and he would now be
swept up in the circus of ceremonies and sacrifices with the
Duchessa and her retinue.

Part of her *had* expected an apology for his appalling
behaviour, and when it did not come, she was surprised at
how angry she was. The dark shadows were back, clouding
her vision and making her hands shake.

It worried her that she had lost control in that battle,
allowing her animor to take over so completely. It made her
power a force to be reckoned with, and certainly made an
impression upon the rest of the Court, but Velody was used
to measuring every step that she made.

Sewing was an art of precision, of planning and counting
and making. This was her skill. Knowing what to do,
following the rules, creating something of beauty. Control.

Take the waistcoat she was stitching for Priest Lord Pigeon. Men's tailoring wasn't a craft Velody had spent much time on in recent months, though she had outfitted whole troupes of male masks and mummers back when she made theatrical costumes for the local musettes. She knew how to shape and cut the fabric, how to fit the garment, and there was even room for a little creative flair, in the buttons and the embroideries. It was good, she knew that it was good. Once again, the work made the shadows go away.

'And finished,' she said now, as she bit off the thread. The little brown mice that lined the mantelpiece, gazing at her with beady eyes, did not react. She was not sorry for that — talking to animals was one thing, but there were not enough sewing projects in the world to help her cope with animals talking back.

Velody wrapped the waistcoat in fine tissue and glanced in the direction of the mantelpiece. 'One of you, send word to Priest. I request an audience with him when he wakes.'

The Court mostly slept during the day, and Velody had taken to doing that too, after spending too long trying to juggle her nox and daylight roles. Mornings were for sleeping, afternoons for work, nox for the Power and Majesty.

A sound in the kitchen startled her. Rhian was upstairs, so who —

Why even ask? Velody's powers were not as sharp in daylight, but she could extend her animor to the other room, opening herself up to recognise the presence of the intruder. Crane.

Velody went to the doorway of the kitchen and looked at him. He was seventeen years old, the youngest of the sentinels, and unlike the rest of the Creature Court, strolled through life unaware of his beauty. When he turned his large eyes on her, it felt like they were the only two people in the world. He was nearly ten years younger than her, and Velody was pretty sure she could break his heart as easily as trimming an embroidery thread. Being Power and Majesty brought all kinds of responsibility into her hands, but this was one she did not want.

'I have your cloak for you,' she said.

Crane nodded. 'You weren't planning to visit Priest alone, were you?'

'You're as protective as Macready,' she accused.

'Protecting you is our job,' he said with that serene confidence of his. 'You can't push us away, or deny us. We breathe for you.'

And that, right there, was why Velody refused to get emotionally entangled with a seventeen-year-old. 'I don't want anyone to breathe for me. I certainly don't want anyone to be hurt for me. Not again.'

She had almost died once before, at the beginning of all this, and Crane gave his blood to heal her. It was not right. It made her sick to her stomach — not only that she had swallowed his blood, but that he had offered it so willingly. As if he was less important than her.

Yes, that was what Power and Majesty meant, she knew that, but it was a privilege she had no idea how to deal with.

Crane blew out a breath, impatient with her. 'You're too smart for this, my Power. The Lords and Court might be acting like kittens at the moment, but it won't last. They are playing you, and you need all the support you can to survive. The sentinels will not leave your back unguarded. Be sensible.'

She shook her head, smiling despite herself. 'You sound older than the rest of us when you speak like that.'

Crane's eyes flashed. 'I took my man's robe four years ago. I'm not a child.'

Velody bit her tongue, and went to fetch his cloak for him. That delay was enough to stop her pointing out that she had taken her woman's robe thirteen years ago, and to her he most definitely was a child — or at least far too young to be allowed to lecture her.

'Shall we go?' she suggested when she handed over the cloak.

There were a thousand things she could say and do to make him leave her alone, but few of them were remotely fair, and in any case he would only return, dragging Macready and Kelpie with him to prove his point. Velody had a headache just thinking about it.

Crane smiled as if she had given him a present. 'As you wish, my Majesty.'

The Arches, down below. The city beneath a city. It was supposed to be Velody's power base, the heart of the Creature Court. But she had barely set foot down there, allowing Ashiol's fear and the cautious attitude of the sentinels to sway her.

No longer. Velody had to discover for herself what hold this place had over her, and the power that lived under her skin. (She had something to prove to the Court, too, but she was trying not to think about that.)

She and Crane walked from the Vittorine to the Forum in the open air, and they found Priest waiting for them on the front steps of a cathedral. Velody had been here once before, at nox, climbing up through the structure to scream Poet's name into the sky, but she had never stopped to look at the cathedral itself. It was a prominent building, close to the Curia and the other temples that she knew well. The cathedral had a high cupola, and blue glass windows. Higher up, white shapes glowed out of the glass: winged birds of all shapes and sizes. It was beautiful, despite appearing abandoned. In all of her years working market stalls in the Forum, Velody had never noticed that there was a cathedral with stained-glass birds in its windows. Had anyone noticed?

Was this just one more thing that the daylight folk did not see?

'It was built in honour of Tanaquil, mistress of birds,' said Priest, bowing his head to her. 'But if that fair saint disapproves of my theft of her sanctuary, she has never told me so.'

'Does no one come to worship here?' Velody managed.

'Only my feathered friends.' Priest hauled the heavy black door open, and a flock of sparrows burst out from the darkness inside. Crane was trailing closely behind, of course.

The cathedral had no floor. This part, Velody remembered. They were at the top of a spiral staircase that led all the way down below. Odd light refracted through the mostly pristine stained-glass windows, though there were enough broken panes to let Priest and his courtesi out in bird form, should they wish.

'The Arches, milady,' said Priest with a flourish. 'My own private entrance.'

'I can see that,' Velody said, choosing not to mention that she had been here before. It might be some dreadful breach of etiquette. She allowed him to lead the way down the staircase. 'Couldn't ordinary — daylight people just wander down here by accident?' she asked.

'They could, I suppose,' said Priest, sounding amused. 'It's never happened. There is something about this particular cathedral that makes the daylight folk shudder, if they notice it at all. It precludes traditional worship.'

Live birds lined the banisters and window frames, staring through beady little eyes. Velody felt strangely naked in the face of their gaze. She continued down into the nave at the lowest level of the cathedral. It was imposing and beautiful and horrible, all at once. There was stained glass here, too, though it was hard to see the patterns as there was no light. Who would put stained glass in an underground church? There was also a finely wrought ceremonial throne on a vaulted altar, and enough seating for a hundred courtesi.

'I've seen daylight people walk past the cathedral above as if they couldn't see it,' said Crane.

Yes, that made sense. Velody nodded to show she had heard him.

'May I offer you refreshment, Lady Majesty?' Priest asked.

It was such a civilised offer, compared to the melodrama that accompanied every other encounter between Velody and the Creature Court. 'Thank you,' she said. 'That would be lovely.'

Priest drew her into a smaller cloister away from the grand nave and the sweeping staircase. This felt more normal, less like she was on display. Velody sat in a lavish tapestried armchair.

Crane did not sit, despite her meaningful look at him, preferring to stand to attention near the doorway, where his swords were within easy reach. Velody took his silent point. She refused to allow him to tell her how to be a Power and Majesty; likewise she had to respect how he chose to perform his duty as a sentinel. Besides, she had to admit that she felt safer with him standing there. She could not — should never — forget who Priest was, and what power he could wield. He was the oldest of the Creature Lords, and surely that meant something.

There was a touch of the kindly uncle about him. Not that Velody recalled any uncles of her own. Her memories of her childhood home — the city that had disappeared in the memories of all daylight denizens — were still patchy at best. She remembered the sisters she had shared a room with, though she had to work every time to remember each of their names. She would say them as a litany each morning — Amber, Thaya, Iris — to keep them lodged in her slippery memory. She remembered her papa's bark at the beginning of the day, standing there up to his elbows in bread dough. She remembered the tired crease in the corner of her mam's eyes.

Only a market-nine ago, Velody had woken up remembering that she had a brother, and spent the whole day stopping every now and then and saying his name aloud, marvelling at how familiar it suddenly felt. Sage with his strong arms, giving animal rides to his little sisters, striding out to work the docks every morning. Later, a shadow of himself, drinking heavily and spending the household shilleins on powders to help him forget that his leg would never be the same after a rope frayed and a crate of sandstone fell, crushing him.

There were still far too many gaps in her memory. She knew there had been an aunt, though she had no memory of her face or name. Perhaps there was also a rich uncle who stirred this response to Priest. Someone who paid for Velody's expensive coach ticket to the larger city. That, or she merely wanted a reason to hope Priest was trustworthy; that one of the Creature Lords might be on her side. It was foolish of her. They had underestimated Dhynar Lord Ferax, because he was young and thoughtless in his cruelty and held none of the innate violent power of Ashiol, or Warlord, or Poet.

Dhynar almost destroyed them all.

Priest sat opposite her, beautifully dressed as usual. Today it was a suit of green velvet with a cream silk cravat, fastened with a glittering brooch. She could feel his animor filling the room, more heady than any perfume. 'My Lady Power. To what do I owe the honour of this visit?'

Velody had carried the box layered with tissue all the way from the Vittorine. 'A gift for you, my Lord, in thanks for your honourable service,' she said now. It was a payment of a promised bribe rather than a gift, but her words made it sound prettier.

'Ahhh,' said Priest, with the satisfied sigh of a man at the end of an excellent meal as he shook the waistcoat out of the tissue and examined it. Velody had done her best work, enjoying the tailoring, and pouring all her stress and confusion of the last few months into the embroidered accents. It was a fine, deep mulberry colour with purple and gold trim.

'It is a fine garment, Majesty.'

'Fit for a Lord,' Velody said with a smile.

He nodded, squeezing the fabric into his hands. 'I can feel you in it. Your animor, pressed into every seam.'

Ashiol had told her that once — that he could feel her power in her handiwork. Velody didn't like the idea that her craft was influenced by what she still called 'the Creature Court thing' inside her head. But there was no denying that with the last two pieces in particular, something had flowed out of her and into the stitches as she worked. Even now, as Priest took the waistcoat into his arms, she felt lighter, as if a weight had been lifted from her lap.

Priest clapped his hands, and a courtesa entered. She was dangerously thin, and wore what could only be described as formal livery — an embroidered white vest with soft black cotton trews and shirt sleeves underneath. The courtesa set down a tray before Velody and began pouring a complex chilled tisane from several vessels. Scents of lemon, mint and honey filled the room.

'What is your name?' Velody asked her. She knew so little about the courtesi, and this was as good a place to start as any.

The courtesa glanced up in surprise at being addressed. 'Damson, my Power.'

Velody remembered her now; the gull courtesa who had been wounded first by Ashiol and then in skybattle. Priest had come close to losing her. 'Are you recovered from your injuries?'

A warm smile lit up the demme's face. 'Yes, my Power. My Lord took care of me.'

Priest was good to his courtesi, then. Velody regarded him thoughtfully as Damson placed the glass into her hands.

Resplendent in his green velvet suit, he spread his hands wide. 'I shared a little of my strength to bring her back from the brink. How could I not? The loss of a courtesa is one of the deepest wounds a Lord can feel.'

Interesting. Velody thought of Poet, who had lost a courteso recently. He did not seem to have taken it badly, but how could you tell what was going on inside Poet's head? He was all act and artifice.

A second courtesa entered, wearing the same black and white uniform as Damson. This one carried a plate of savoury dainties.

Velody took a tiny pastry stuffed with white cheese and herbs and bit into it. Delicious. 'You have been in the Creature Court so much longer than everyone else,' she observed, licking crumbs from her lower lip. 'You must have seen some changes in your time here.'

'None so dramatic as recent events, Lady Majesty,' said Priest with a sly grin. The third courtesa entered with a tray of sweetmeats and sticky cakes. Once Velody made her selection, the courtesa placed the tray close to Priest's elbow. 'Sadly I have no particular wisdom to impart on that score. I had twoscore years beneath my belt when I first set foot in Aufleur. Our Ashiol has been here longer than I, as have our Lords of Rat and Wolf.'

Forty. Priest had come here at forty years old. Where had he been before that? 'You were already a Lord then?' Velody asked.

'Aye, I belonged to the Clockwork Court in Bazeppe

once, in my youth,' he said, referring to the capital city of the duchy of Silano, far to the south. 'They had what you might call a surfeit of Lords, and I had no fondness for the politics they played. I travelled for several years and stopped in here on my way home — out of curiosity more than anything. Aufleur welcomed me with open arms, and who am I to deny such good fortune? Ortheus was a seigneur after my own heart. I made a home here.'

Velody had not given much thought to the other Courts, though of course they must exist. There had been one in Tierce, before it fell. She wanted to ask if there was any contact with Bazeppe now. Should there not be ambassadors between them? Ways of sharing information on the best ways to fight the sky? Or was it like the Creature Court itself: everyone so much of a danger to everyone else that they never got anything done? 'And Garnet?' she could not help but ask. 'Was his rule to your tastes?'

'Garnet was a lad with much to learn,' Priest said with a comfortable shrug, taking a violet cream from his tray. 'We got along right enough. I'm an old man, Lady Power — by Court standards, in any case. I'm not one for rebellion and petty politics. As long as I have my demoiselles, a full stomach and a sky to fight, I'm a happy man.' He eyed her empty glass. 'Would you like another? Or is there some boon I can provide for you, as my honoured guest?'

Velody took a deep breath. 'Show me where Garnet lived. Please. I'd like to see it.'

Priest paused, as if mulling over whatever secrets her voice had betrayed, and then bowed his head. 'As you wish, Lady Majesty.'

~

VELODY IGNORED Crane's disapproval as best she could. If she couldn't see the judgement in his eyes, she would not have to deal with it — and would not have to remind him yet again who was in charge around here.

They trailed through dank tunnels until the roof opened up into a wide concreted space, with a deep drain running through it. The walls were daubed with vivid images of the Creature Court themselves — warriors and animals fighting the sky. The murals were splendidly done, worthy of a temple ceiling or a Palazzo wall, and Velody could not help wondering who had painted them.

'The Haymarket,' said Priest. 'Centre of merchant activity and the storage of supplies, back when all of Aufleur were packed down here like rats.'

Velody had known this underground ruin was a functional city once, in the days before the skybattles were hidden from the daylight folk, but she had never thought about the practicalities of it — of merchants and food storage and other such everyday concerns. 'Garnet lived here?' she asked.

'This is the closest thing we have to a Palazzo,' Priest said cheerfully. 'All the Powers and Majesties have used this as a centre of power.'

Velody had never set foot here before today. 'Am I supposed to do the same?' she asked, forgetting that she was with Priest and not Ashiol — she should not be letting her uncertainties show so obviously.

'If it is your will,' said an acid female voice.

Velody looked up. If she did not know Livilla's Lord form was a wolf, she might have guessed cat. There was something about the watchful wickedness of the demme's eyes, the way she held herself.

Livilla posed at the top of a metal staircase. Her gown was short and all red bead fringe. With her harsh bob of black hair and chalk pale skin, she looked like a sketched fashion plate in the middle pages of a newspaper.

Not for the first time, Velody wondered where Livilla acquired her outfits. *I shouldn't be the leader of this patchwork army, I should be their tailor. I'd put her in emerald green and silver; hang pearl strands off that neck of hers until they brushed her ankles.* 'You live here?' she asked instead.

'I belonged to Garnet,' said Livilla, descending the stairs with a swooping grace. 'More than most. I lived in his rooms. My rooms, now.'

There was a challenge in her eyes, and in the strut of her walk. Velody lifted her chin, letting the animor bubble up in her blood. She could take Livilla. They both knew it.

Two lads appeared at the top of the stairs. Velody had done her best to learn who the Court were as well as the Lords, and she knew the names of these two though little else about them. The taller, older of the two was called Janvier, and he was a raven. He had black hair, and light brown skin. He wore feathers in his long braided hair, and a pair of ridiculously tight trews. His chest was bare. Either he put himself on display for Livilla's benefit, or he was part of her show. Velody suspected the latter. Livilla was certainly the type to select outfits for her courtesi and demand they primp their hair and fingernails before they set foot in public.

The other boy, Seonard, was younger and more defensive. Hair fell in his eyes, making it hard for Velody to judge his age, but she suspected he was at least a couple of years younger than Crane, if not more. He should be working an apprenticeship somewhere, or celebrating his man's tunic with his family like young Giuno. Not this.

The Creature Court offered a shadowy semblance of a life. Velody could see that now. Was she wrong for not escaping the city when she had a chance?

'It would not be much of a fight, should you wish to put her in her place, Lady Majesty,' said Priest, sounding amused at the possibility.

Livilla's head arched towards him. 'You're the new favourite, are you, old man? Ashiol will be heartbroken that he lost his position.'

'I don't have to put anyone in their place,' said Velody. 'We are all friends here. Allies. Our job is to protect this city from the sky. There is no place for petty rivalries.' She was going to make something of the Court. Something better than what it was. The first step was to rebuild them as a team rather than a tangled mess of rivals and enemies.

There was a short, strangled pause, and then Livilla started to laugh. Priest joined in with a deep, meaty sound.

'She's precious,' said Livilla. 'Don't you think?'

'There are worse vices than idealism,' said Priest, still chuckling.

'So glad I amuse you,' Velody said sharply. 'Livilla, I believe you had a question to ask, about your accommodation.'

There went that chin again, pointy with entitlement. 'Did I?' asked Livilla Lord Wolf, her voice utterly disdainful.

Moving from mortal shape to Lord form was no longer even a matter of thought. Velody made it happen, as naturally as breathing. She stood tall and straight, her skin gleaming with power. She could feel her blood sing. 'You were going to ask my permission to keep your rooms,' she said.

Livilla tossed her head. 'You would have me beg on my knees? I would rather die than lower myself to such an indignity.'

Saints and angels, it was as bad as talking to Delphine. 'I didn't suggest that you beg,' said Velody. 'Yet.'

Livilla stepped from the staircase and walked slowly

45

towards Velody, her hips swinging. The red beads of her dress shimmered in the lamplight. 'Tell me who killed Dhynar Lord Ferax, and I shall surrender my rooms to you.'

Velody smiled thinly. 'Dhynar fell in his attempt to betray and kill his Power and Majesty. It does not matter who wielded the blade; it was done in service to me. And I do not want your rooms, Livilla. I want the fealty you pledged to me on the third day of the Floralia. I want you to keep your word.'

'I have never disobeyed you,' the Wolf Lord said, baring her teeth in a snarl.

'Ask me for your rooms,' Velody said calmly. 'That is a direct order. Ask, or I shall take them from you, and more than that — I will take you apart. Chances are I'll have to do it to one of you at some stage, to prove that I am a worthy Power and Majesty. I might as well choose the first to rebel, the first to speak to me as if I were a *maidservant*.'

Velody's animor pulsed with frustration. These people confounded her. Why couldn't they be sensible? Why couldn't they accept that they had a job to do and get on with it, without all the silly blood and ritual and politics?

She would play the game if she must, but it made her skin itch. Changes had to be made.

'They said you were soft,' said Livilla, a smile taking over her face. 'I don't know what you are.'

A bloody good liar, Velody thought, loud enough to scream. 'I am Velody. I am the Power and Majesty that you swore fealty to. Would you be forsworn, as Dhynar was forsworn? Would you walk the streets in pain and corruption, a tortured soul doomed to destroy everything she touches?'

'That fate would only befall me if I died forsworn,' Livilla breathed. She was enjoying this, damn her. Her eyes sparkled, her breasts heaved under the stupidly skimpy frock. What the saints was holding those beads up?

'If you raise a hand against me and break the oaths you swore,' Velody said quietly, 'I will strike you down in an instant. I proved with Dhynar that I could conquer a street shade. I would risk it again, if I had to.'

'Such fire, from a little mouse,' said Livilla, and deliberately licked her lips.

Velody sincerely regretted that hitting the other demme over the head with a brick would be such bad politics. 'Make your decision, Livilla Lord Wolf. Fast.'

'Don't be rash in this, Lord Wolf,' said Priest with a smirk. 'You never did stand up to our last Power and Majesty, did you? Don't think this one will let you trade for your indiscretions by spreading your legs.'

Livilla's eyes flashed angrily. 'Garnet loved me!'

'Aye, perhaps he did,' said Priest with a hint of wistfulness. 'But you've no idea how to handle a Power and Majesty who has no love for you, who doesn't indulge your whims as our Garnet did. Look deeply into the face of this one. She's not impressed with your amateur dramatics.'

'Thank you, Lord Pigeon,' said Velody, taking back control of the conversation. 'I hardly need an interpreter.'

Livilla's perfect cosmeticked heart of a mouth twitched slightly. 'You won't hurt me, Velody of the Vittorine. You challenged your precious Ashiol because he gouged out Poet's stomach to prove a point. You're against wanton acts of violence.'

'So I am,' Velody said calmly. 'But apparently wanton acts of violence are the only way to make you people listen.' She had to be prepared to hurt Livilla, to win this fight, however much she hated it. She was going to remake this Court, one stitch at a time, so that none of this posturing was necessary. But to make that happen, she had to be prepared to be the kind of Power and Majesty they recognised.

She formed a blade in her mind, sharp and vicious. She

could do this. She filled her head with the image of slicing Livilla open, neck to belly, destroying that gorgeous sheath of red beading.

At least the dress wasn't white.

Velody held Livilla's gaze, showing her exactly what it was she was capable of doing, what she intended to do. Everything.

'You won't,' breathed Livilla. 'You're too nice.' She said 'nice' as if it was something sour on her tongue. 'Saint Velody.'

'Is that what you all call me?' said Velody, and gave a short laugh. 'Oh, you got that wrong.'

Blood, she couldn't do blood, not yet. Vomiting might damage her dignity in their eyes. It would have to be pain. Velody hurled her animor at Livilla, Lord Wolf, in a thousand agonising needles, and hated herself for it.

Livilla crumpled like a pierrot puppet with her strings cut. She made no sound as she fell.

'Once again,' said Velody. 'Is there anything you have to ask me?'

Livilla lifted her face, eyes wide and rimmed with tears. A nice touch, beautifully staged even through the pain. She opened her mouth, and no sound came out.

The two courtesi both tensed, ready to leap to Livilla's defence, but Velody turned her gaze on them, sharp and challenging. 'No,' she said.

The taller one, Janvier, placed a hand on the arm of the younger, Seonard, who was about to explode in frustration.

'Try harder,' Velody suggested to Livilla, not letting up the pain.

Livilla pressed her lips together, smearing her cosmetick. Slowly she rose, with great effort, knuckles white, body taut and defensive. She lifted her chin and stared at Velody in defiance. 'Power and Majesty,' she said, haughtier than any

Duchessa. 'May I please retain the rooms I shared with Garnet, for as long as you reign?'

'Yes you may,' Velody said, not wanting to draw this out now that Livilla had capitulated. She turned away as if this scene no longer held any interest for her. 'Priest, let us return to your nave for more refreshment.'

'As you wish, my Lady Power,' he replied with a bow.

'Excellent.' Velody walked away, her steps muffled on the concrete floor. She held her head high, pretending that she did not feel Livilla's eyes bore hatefully into her back. Velody had made an enemy instead of an ally today, but since when was that anything new?

'YOU DID WELL,' Crane admitted later, once they were in the city above, making their way back to Via Silviana.

'Better than you feared?' Velody asked. The light was fading from the sky already. Nox came all over again, as it always did. She had felt a brief glow of triumph for what she had wrought with Livilla, but now the darkness was back, wrapping around her like a cloud; it was all she could do to hold herself upright, not to hurl herself at Crane again and sob her heart out.

There had to be hope that she could change all this, that she wouldn't have to be monstrous every time she wanted something from one of the Court. But where to begin? With Ashiol pouring himself into a bottle to escape them all, she had only the sentinels to help her decide what to do, and how to behave.

'Better than I hoped.' Crane sounded so serious. 'But if Warlord had been there, you wouldn't have taken Livilla so easily.'

'Warlord and I have an understanding,' said Velody.

49

'His loyalty to Livilla is longer and older than any promises he makes to you.'

'Thank you,' she said, laying her hand on his arm. Even this brief touch made the dark thoughts lift off her, for a moment. 'I mean it. You work so hard, all of you, to keep me upright. To support me. I do appreciate it.'

Crane regarded her warily, as if he was waiting for the 'but'. 'It's what we're here for,' he said finally.

'I appreciate that, too.' Velody almost laughed at the look on his face. 'Is it so unusual, to be thanked for doing your job?'

'I thought you were angry at me.'

'Not right this second.'

He smiled then, as honest and true as if there were a lantern shining out from his face. *Oh, saints and angels.*

'You should get some sleep,' Velody said firmly when they reached her kitchen door.

Crane looked as if he was about to argue, then he bowed his head with a small smile. *Obedient. We'll see how long that lasts.*

Velody waited in the yard after he closed the gate behind him, until she could no longer feel his proximity heating her skin. Then she reached for a foothold there, a handhold here, and clambered up the side of her building to reach the roof. It was calm up here, and cool, and as good a place as any to arrange her cluttered thoughts. Velody lay on her back, the rough pattern of clay tiles digging into her spine.

The stars began to appear, one by one, as the sky gave way to nox. Nothing rained down upon them; not yet, in any case. Velody stared at her hand, making it glow brightly enough with animor that she could see every crease and callous, even the small scar from the time a knife had slipped when she was cutting cabbage. It was her, entirely her. And yet...

She shaped her thumb into a small, brown mouse. Its nose quivered, tickling her other fingers. She snapped back into herself, and the fur was gone. Just her ordinary thumb, same as ever.

Her body shuddered, from neck to ankle. She wanted to run in all directions at once. Wanted... something.

She flicked her thumb back into mouse shape, and let the mouse pull entirely free of her skin. It ran down her body, sniffing, and hovered near her stomach. Huh. Velody hadn't thought about that before. If she could control her mass, she could change her own human body shape, surely. Flatten the slight swell of her stomach, take an inch or two off her thighs. Delphine's dresses would hang better on her, when she borrowed them.

But, no. If something happened to some of her mouse shapes, Velody might need those curves. To make new thumbs, or something.

The skin on her hand was smooth where her thumb used to be. She called the mouse back, and took him into herself again, then moved her thumb back and forth.

Odd. She felt the presence of the wolf before it leaped from the baker's roof to her own. She stared at it. Not Livilla, she was certain. There was nothing of the Lord about this creature. But neither was it an ordinary wolf.

Velody reached out, pushing her animor against him. 'Change.'

He stepped back once, twice, his paws scrabbling for a hold on the tiles.

'Change,' Velody said again, and gave him a harder shove with her animor.

He shaped himself all at once, and sprawled on the roof: it was Seonard, the younger of Livilla's boys, all scowl and too-long hair. 'You oughtn't of done that,' he muttered.

'It's my roof,' she said calmly.

'Don't care about me,' he said, scratching the back of his head. 'You oughtn't of treated my Lord like that.'

'Did Livilla send you to me?' But she knew the answer to that already, from the shifty expression on his face. 'Your Lord swore fealty to me, Seonard. I deserve her loyalty, just as she deserves yours.'

'You're just some demme,' he protested.

'Your Lord is 'some demme' too.'

That made him angrier. 'Wash yer mouth out! She's a lady!'

Oh, don't laugh, don't laugh.

'What do you want from me?' Velody asked him.

The boy gave a shrug that seemed to encompass the whole world.

'I have no problem with Lord Livilla, as long as she holds to her oath,' Velody offered as a compromise that might allow him to retreat with some dignity. She had no wish to fight this boy and send him home bleeding to his mistress.

Seonard shrugged again, and made no sign of moving. He was worse than Crane for brooding silences.

'How long have you been in the Creature Court?' Velody asked finally. If she was to share the roof with him, she might as well get some useful information out of it.

Seonard lifted one shoulder, no longer bothering to even shrug properly. 'Couple a years.'

She had so many questions, though no reason to think he would answer them. Why would a child choose this life? Had it chosen him? Why Livilla, of all of them. Why did he think she was the one who could best offer him protection? This close, she wasn't even sure if he was old enough for his man's robe.

'Do you like it?' Velody asked instead, feeling ridiculous, like one of the formal patrons who had sometimes visited the Apprentice House, displaying as much knowledge about seams and hems as could fit on the head of a pin, but always being terribly polite about it.

To her surprise, Seonard gave her a wicked grin. 'Course I do. Nothing better, is there?'

'Nothing?'

'We're fighting the sky, aye? No one else gets to do that, just us, and we're rubies at it! Like chasing bolts of warlight across the sky, bam, wham, and bloodstars... you know they make this popping sound if you wrap animor around them, like in your hand? And iceblades, ha, if you blast them just right, they shatter into patterns. It's rubies, isn't it?'

Velody just stared at him. He looked so fiercely excited, like a child with a heap of Saturnalia parcels in front of him, and a mouth full of sugared raisins. 'Best job in the world,' she repeated.

Seonard nodded enthusiastically. 'Aye, course it is.' He paused, and when he spoke again it was in such a low mutter that she almost missed it. 'Wanted to say thanks.'

'To me?'

'You could have turfed my Lord out on her ear. Any other Power and Majesty would have done it, I reckon. You let her keep her pride when you didn't hafta.'

'I don't have anything against Livilla,' said Velody, which was almost entirely true. 'We're all on the same side.'

'Reckon we are,' said Seonard, as if he hadn't thought of it that way before. 'Aye, I'm off then.' He sat up straight. 'You try it, next battle. Hold the bloodstars in your hand and push the animor at them. They pop like sausages!' He laughed once, and then shaped himself into the altogether more sombre figure of the wolf. He trotted to the edge of the roof and leaped off.

Velody sat there for some time after he had gone. 'Like sausages,' she repeated in a murmur. She never would entirely understand the Creature Court.

Darkness fell more solidly around her, and there would be no battle this nox; she was sure of that now.

Still, she felt that shiver of a premonition she had spoken of with Ashiol days ago. She could not get over the thought that something was coming, something bigger and badder than she had seen before.

When Velody looked down at her hands, that spidery pattern was back, violently dark against her very pale skin. She felt a crushing weight on her chest, the air itself squeezing tighter around her.

Work, that was what she had to do. She would go below and finish the trim of the dress for the Duchessa, and when her needle finally stopped moving, she would feel better. More human. More herself.

Perhaps by the time morning came, she would be able to sleep without dreaming of dead men.

4

HELIORA

*H*ow did it start, for me?
I followed him home.

I was eleven and living on the streets (that is a story you will hear more than once, so many of us started out this way). I was a thief and a stray, and I put every spark of strength I had into pretending I was a boy.

Being a demme is all bad, on the streets. You get used up and thrown aside or you have to spend half your beggings on cosmetick so you can at least get paid to whore. I preferred stealing.

One day there was this lad, dark-haired and glowing. A complete shiny-blood; you could see it in his eyes and his swagger. He had no right to be hanging around Cinquilene — what the frig did he think he was up to? Only the dirt and the rats lingered here.

I could see bulge of his purse as he joked with his — companion? Manservant?

Wretched toff. I wanted to hurt him, wanted to wound him. Wanted to see his mouth gape in surprise when he saw his purse had been lifted by a sneak ten times faster than he was.

But I didn't steal it. Instead, I followed him home. I expected he would make his way to a fine Great Family house — high on the

Avleurine, or the Alexandrine, where the shiny-bloods gather to count their coin. Instead, he wandered deeper into the maze of slums and streets jammed between the Avleurine hill and the Lucian theatre district.

They were chattering all the time, those lads, though I only had eyes for the dark one, even then. The manservant was as full of himself as his master, and they cuffed and pawed at each other, sniggering as if they had some great secret.

An alley turned into a tunnel, and still I followed, down into the depths of a place I had never known existed, underneath the city itself. We walked down in darkness until we passed a ruinous heap and, beyond that, the quiet cobbled streets of a silent underground town, all empty streets and abandoned shops, like the breath had been sucked out of it.

The Shambles, yes, I know that now. At the time it was like I had stepped into another world. Which of course I had.

'Oh look, it's Tasha's cubs,' said a mocking voice, cutting through the cool air of the underground stone city. My boy (I already thought of him that way, pathetic but true) tensed as a lithe older lad leaped down from the roof of a ruined awning to land on his hands and feet as if they were paws.

'Get stuffed, Barthol,' said the red-haired manservant, doing his best to sound unimpressed.

'You're not anything,' said the older lad, sneering down at him. 'Not worth a centi, either of you. Someone should teach you respect for your betters.'

'There are two of us and one of you,' said my boy, dark and glorious. 'If you want to chuck your weight around, try picking on someone smaller.'

'Oh, I don't know,' said Barthol with a wicked grin. I saw them before the lads did — figures melting out of the shadows, a whole gang waiting to pounce. 'You seem small to me.'

I could do nothing — if the servant was less than a centi, then I was less than the dust on their shoes. I wasn't even sure why I cared, except I had followed a pretty fellow down a dark street only to watch him be beaten to death.

I've always had excellent timing.

The fight was brutal and ugly — six against two, fists and nails and blood. I could barely stand to look at the sight of it. I should have run away, should have clambered my way back up to the safety of the world I knew. I remember how it ended, though. There was a feeling that washed over the streets, of cold and despair. I shivered in my thin rags, and every one of those bloodstained boys hesitated and drew back.

He stepped into sight. A stately, wide-shouldered man wearing silks and velvets, every inch of his costume decorated with pearl buttons. His head was shaved, and shiny like a snake. Power resonated from him; not only the power that makes rich men cruel, but something deeper. He travelled with an entourage, and a dismissive flip of his hand made it clear that he intended them to obey even his silent orders.

They moved into action, three of them, drawing swords from their backs and advancing upon the spitting pile of boys.

I was awed. There was nothing but dim lamplight down here, and yet I swear I saw daylight gleaming from their blades. They moved in formation, so secure in their own power and competence. I had handled a knife half my short life, but I had never owned such a thing as those swords.

In that moment, I forgot the boy. I knew nothing but envy. I wanted to be like them, those coves and demmes with the shiny blades.

But I ran away. Of course I ran. I had never been brave, my first eleven years. I spent my whole life in hiding. I did not forget those soldiers, though, in their brown cloaks, silver sigils stamped into leather collars and straps. They wore their hair cropped close to their heads, even the woman. They were so strong and fine.

Three days later, the boy found me. I had stolen several apples and sat pressed against a stinking wall behind an old theatre in the

Lucian, determined to eat them one after the other before someone caught me. My jaw was sore and dripping with juices when a hand lashed out and slapped me, sending me sprawling to the ground.

When in doubt, cringe and whine. Let them hurt you as hard as they can, and hope they will stop before it gets too bad.

'You saw things you should not have seen, brat,' he said. Saints help me — when he spoke, he sounded like a cat purring in your lap. (It makes me laugh now to think how young Ashiol was then — never mind my tender years; he was such a baby!)

I glared at him from my place on the ground. I had dropped an apple, bruised it, and that made fury well up inside me, despite my fear. 'Can't help that, can I?'

'Thank you, courteso, I will take it from here,' said a clipped voice.

The boy Ashiol bristled at that. 'You're not my frigging Lord and master, Nathanial.'

The other man was older, with a steady jaw and clipped-short hair. He wore leathers with silver, and a brown cloak — one of those soldiers I had admired so much! 'And you're not mine,' he said calmly. 'I needed you to find her, but your part in this is done.'

Ashiol had a right sulk on him. 'Maybe my mistress would like to see her first...'

'Hands off, boyo,' said the soldier. 'The Power and Majesty takes precedence over your precious Lord. Any idiot can see she isn't Court. But she noticed us, and that means she's something else.'

Panic welled up in me. They knew I wasn't a lad. How could they know? I'd been binding my breasts since they started to curve, and I'd only had a couple of bleeding times. They shouldn't know so much. He leaned over me, the Silver Captain, blocking my view of the shiny boy. 'Would you like to learn how to use a sword, demoiselle?' he asked me.

Oh. Well. If he was going to put it that way...

~

IT WAS THE PARILIA, festival of shepherds, and the entire Basilica smelled of damp fleece and the entrails of sheep. Few were interested in a fortune-teller who used cards and crystals, not when there were bloodier auguries to be drawn. Heliora abandoned her Zafiran wig and costumes in her tent to go for a walk. Fresh air, and the summer sun. Nothing like the simple pleasures in life to remind you that you were going to die soon.

After some time wandering around, Hel ended up near the Lake of Follies. A grand Palazzo had once been built on this spot in honour of the first Duc d'Aufleur: an edifice so ornate and expensive that it all but financially crippled the city at a time when they were struggling to convince the population it was safe to live above ground. Then the skywar came back, and the Palazzo was crushed by boulders of ice and fire. The Duc's son bowed to the popular belief that it was his father's hubris that had brought the disaster upon them, and he hauled down the wreckage in favour of a decorative lake. It was said half the riches of that fallen Palazzo were still buried in the lake bed, and many a drunkard had drowned himself trying to prove that myth.

Of course, those of the daylight also thought that the skywar itself was a myth, or at least that it was a chapter of history that had been closed long ago. They all knew the stories, but they believed that the war had ended as mysteriously as it had begun.

Only the Creature Court knew the truth. The Kings, the Lords and their courtesi, the sentinels... and the Seer.

Not a day passed when Heliora did not wish she was as ignorant and blind as the rest of them. Imagine how blissful it must be to see only the everyday ugliness of the world. To not fear a burning, blazing, freezing, twisted death.

There were other stories about the lake. Babies would be named here in simple family ceremonies, and old men came to swear their sins away. The water was supposed to have cleansing properties, and half the city drank nips of it as a tonic to ward off the Silent Sleep. A useless tradition, if ever there was one. The Sleep was only a mystery to those of the daylight. If only they knew how miraculous it was how many of them actually survived each nox as the city was knocked down around them, only to rebuild itself at dawn.

It made Heliora shiver, to be this close to the lake. She had seen many futures where her death was within sight of this place.

A skinny fellow in spectacles sat on one of the wooden piers, his trews rolled up and bare feet dangling in the water. Heliora considered walking past, pretending she hadn't seen him, but a familiar voice called her 'coward' in her own head. So she walked out on to the pier, lowering herself on to the planking to sit beside him. He looked quite normal without his gaudy clothes and the theatrical cosmetick he often sported.

'Burdens weighing on your soul, Poet?' she asked him. 'Or is it something more fleshly that you need cleansed?'

'Sharp as ever, Heliora my dove,' Poet drawled, splashing her with his feet. 'You know me — always looking for somewhere innovative to hide the bodies.'

As if she could ever get a straight answer out of him. No, it always had to be riddles. 'Is the noxcrawl still bothering you?' she asked, shifting imperceptibly away from him so that her hip did not brush his.

Poet looked at her with a flicker of amusement. He was not fooled. 'Noxcrawl,' he repeated, as if he'd never heard of it. 'You have been paying attention, haven't you?'

'I know you were covered in it from a skybattle a few market-nines ago,' she said firmly. 'I know — saints, Poet, that muck can be lethal. If even a pin prick of it remains on your skin...'

'Not a prick,' he said without a hint of irony. 'Warlord and our precious Power and Majesty saw to that. If I had been any more thoroughly cleansed, I would have drowned three times over at the foot of this lake.'

Couldn't happen to a nicer cove, Hel thought to herself. 'If you were cleansed so thoroughly, why are you here now? Not getting paranoid in your old age, are you, Poet?'

'Nostalgic, perhaps,' he said with a wicked look at her. 'I feel calm here. It's a good place.'

Heliora shuddered. 'The lake smells of death.'

'That's what I like about it.' Poet smiled sadly. 'Some of my favourite people in all the world are dead, you know.' He pulled out a pocket watch with a long chain, toying with it between his fingers. It was familiar, though Heliora could not have said why. Clockwork was a rare sight in this city. 'Do you miss the old days, Hel?'

'Which old days?' she asked sharply. 'When the world was young and we were innocent? Those days never existed.' Her first memory of Poet was as a child, nestled into that fucked-up family Tasha had gathered around her. Tagging along behind Ashiol and Garnet and the others. Too young, too knowing, too broken. Just like the rest of them. 'I don't think about the past at all,' she lied.

Poet gave her a smug look. She hated the way he always seemed to know what she was thinking. She spent enough time inside her own head, keeping the voices and the futures at bay. The last thing she needed was anyone else poking around in there.

'Keep your feet wet,' she said, standing up to return to the Basilica. Where else did she have to go? 'You never know when the sky is going to throw something grotesque at you again. Anyone would think you deserved it.'

Poet gave her an aimless wave, and tucked his pocket watch away as she walked off. 'Stay as sweet as you are, Hel.'

Heliora reached the Forum by the time she realised where she had seen that watch before. It belonged to Garnet.

~

I NEVER WON MY SWORDS. I still burn about that. Sentinels don't get measured for swords until their seventeenth birthday; man's or woman's robe aside, you don't count as a grown-up sentinel until they're sure you've stopped growing.

A ridiculous system. I never gained another inch after my fifteenth birthday, and I know for a fact that Tobin grew three inches between getting his swords and the day he died; his reach was always a little off because of that. I wanted my swords more than anything, but the saints and devils that watch over the Creature Court had a different path for me.

I was a damned good sentinel. Cap and the others trained me well, gave me a purpose. Our job was to protect the Kings, to add to their power and glory. We had Ortheus, the Power and Majesty, and Argentin, the second King, his loyal friend. There were twelve of us sentinels, standing at their back, keeping them strong against the sky and against the Creature Court who were supposed to be just as loyal.

Meanwhile, I never stopped fancying Ashiol. They all knew it. A running joke — the little street brat who wanted the shiny courteso for her own. Even his Lord, Tasha, found it amusing, and she was never one to share her toys. I don't know if it was that I was too young or if Ashiol just didn't want me, but he put up a merry fight against my attempts at feminine wiles.

Oh, aye, I was a demme now. Cap insisted upon that. The Lords, Court and retinue could all see exactly who I was. Hiding anything about myself was an insult to them. I could shave my head and spin knives and still let my boobs stick out the front (when they weren't tucked away behind the leathers).

It was an odd sort of feeling. Freedom. Respect. All new tastes in my mouth. Then, the year I turned sixteen, everything changed.

MACREADY WAS GETTING TOO old for this shit. The thought of waiting around for a horde of babes in arms to come into their own as sentinels made him want to jump off a fecking bridge.

To be fair, most conversations with Delphine made him feel that way. It was a long time since a demme had got under Macready's skin like this. There was nothing easy about Delphine. She grated against him —every time he thought he was making progress, she slid away.

It reminded him of learning to fish in his gramp's favourite trout stream back home. Just when you thought you had landed a beauty, it slipped and slid right out from under your fingers.

Being a sentinel was not something you chose, not something you could walk away from. It was a sacred trust, and it burrowed into your heart like a mouse chewing its way into the walls of a house.

Macready was stuck. He hadn't walked away when Garnet started sending his people to their doom, when the Haymarket was awash with blood. He hadn't walked away when Garnet cut his fecking ring finger from his hand, in punishment for one drunken insult. How could he leave now, when the Court might actually have a hope of bettering itself?

So here he was, trying to save Delphine and turn her into a sentinel. Rhian sided with him at least, agreeing that a visit to the Seer sounded like a good way to sort Delphine's future out once and for all. She even agreed to step outside with them for the second time in the same market-nine, and that had been a master stroke, so it had. Delphine could not argue when she knew it cost Rhian so much more to make the trip.

Macready and Delphine had one thing in common, and that was their concern for Rhian. The lass grew nervous as they made their way through the crowded Basilica. She flinched when people brushed against her, and her friends walked on either side of her, trying to keep it from happening.

'Almost there,' Macready said, hoping to soothe. They circled a row of hot meat and cold pottage stalls until they finally reached the colourful, gaudy tent of Madama Fortuna.

A sign hung on the outside, declaring that the fortune-teller was not seeing customers today. A few offerings of centimes, tied posies and honey cakes had been left outside the tent. Ha, Heliora had a few satisfied customers, then. Good for her.

'Heliora,' Macready said against the tied door flaps of the tent. 'Are you there, my lovely? I've visitors for you.'

There was silence, and then a huff from inside. A slender hand slid through the slit to untie the flaps and let them fall open. 'I'm not working today, Mac,' said the Seer of the Court. She looked as much the urchin demme as she ever had, with her head lightly shaven and her bare feet sticking out from under a thin cotton tunic.

'Special occasion,' he suggested, and gave her a hopeful grin.

Hel gave him that suspicious glare, the one he liked to think was reserved all special like, for him alone. She stepped back to let him and the lasses through. The tent flap fell closed as they came inside the space, which was stuffy with incense smoke. 'Stray lambs?' Hel asked sarcastically.

'New blood,' Macready informed her.

That did interest her. Hel turned her strange, luminous eyes on Delphine and then Rhian, staring at them both until they glanced away, uncomfortable with her scrutiny. 'Not that one,' she said finally, dismissing Rhian. 'But you...' Her eyes widened as she took in everything about Delphine. 'Saints and devils. This is the one who —'

'That's not public knowledge, so,' Macready said sharply. 'Only the Kings and sentinels know it.' And Poet, feck it all. He had to get Delphine to accept her place as a sentinel before that bastard decided to use the information against her.

'Seer's privilege,' Hel said, eyes still fixed on Delphine. 'I won't tell. What a joke.' She laughed, high and loud. 'What a choice.'

'I don't think I like your tone,' Delphine said haughtily.

'I don't suppose you do,' said Heliora. 'It does upset people, when I mock the life and death situations they've got all tangled up in.'

'I didn't mean to kill anyone,' Delphine flared up. 'It just —'

'Happened?' said Heliora. 'Funny how it works like that the first time. I had headaches for ages, out of nowhere. I was living on the street so just figured I'd picked up something that was going to kill me. Turned out it was the other way around.' She and Macready shared a grin of old comrades. She still thought like a sentinel sometimes — he liked that about her. 'I didn't put it all together until after I followed one of the Court home and found myself caught up in their games. My first kill was five months in, and it took me a year to get over it. What a baby I was.'

'I don't get headaches,' Delphine said in a quiet voice.

That made Macready snort. How would she know, beneath the hangovers?

'It's different for everyone,' said Heliora. She dropped cross-legged to her carpet. 'I'm thinking of redecorating, Mac. What do you think? The Zafiran craze has to wind down soon, and I like to be ahead of the game. Maybe something Islandsish. I could be a redhead. Curls, cleavage, bit o' an accent. Do ye no think it's a bonny plan?'

'I promise to roll in my grave if you do, my lovely,' Macready said, pleased to see she still had some tease in her, even if she was butchering his mother tongue to do it. She'd been so serious lately. 'I'd have to strangle meself first, but that should not be a problem at all.'

'Excellent,' Heliora said shamelessly. 'I so look forr'd to that, so I do.'

'That's it?' Delphine burst out. 'Is that all you have to say? I thought you were going to help me.'

Heliora gave her an almost sympathetic look. 'I can offer you a cup of tea, I suppose? Though I'm almost out of the good stuff.'

Delphine looked accusingly at Macready. He put up his hands. 'What did you expect, lass? A book of instructions? Our Hel has a few tricks up her sleeve, but she can't solve all the mysteries of the universe at once.'

'I suppose you want me to look in the futures for her,' Heliora said, the humour draining out of her voice.

Macready blinked. 'I wouldn't go that far.' It wasn't the futures that bothered him so much as the after-effects. There was something not right about having to frig a lass to bring her back to her senses, especially when you were the one who had caused her to lose them in the first place.

She was choosy, Hel. Macready knew he was one of the few coves she had trusted with that particular task. Didn't make him any more comfortable with it, and he was sure as hell not going to do it in front of this particular audience.

'Prude,' Hel mocked him, though her shoulders relaxed more at his refusal. 'What do you want, then? A reading? I can tell what she is from here. I can taste it on her skin. Can't you?'

'She doesn't trust my word,' he said simply. 'More fool her.'

'Stop talking about me as if I wasn't here!' Delphine snapped. 'I know what Macready thinks I am. I think he's wrong.'

'I know what it is to be a sentinel,' said Heliora. 'You might not have been one a month ago, but it screams out of you now. You glow with it. Accept it, or it will drive you mad. That's how our world works.'

'Not my world,' said Delphine instantly.

Heliora's smile was deeply unpleasant. 'Time to get used to the idea that it is.'

'Who is this wench?' Delphine demanded of Macready.

'This, lass, is Heliora, Seer of the Creature Court. Our eyes and our voice. What she doesn't see isn't worth knowing about.' Macready exchanged glances with Rhian, and he was cheered by at least her encouraging smile. 'So, next step is to get Delphine some swords of her own, aye?' The sooner the better.

Delphine gave him the dirtiest of looks. 'I haven't agreed to anything.'

The Seer shrugged. 'It's only a matter of time.'

~

KISSING BOYS WAS EASY ENOUGH. *Boys who weren't Ashiol Xandelian, anyway. There were plenty of boys right there among the sentinels, and I kissed a lot of them.*

We weren't the slappers that the Creature Court were with each other (everyone knew Tasha frigged all her boys, sometimes at the same time) but the camaraderie in the sentinels still turned to comfort and shared body heat pretty fast.

Tobin was a sweetie, a couple of years older than me and the month I turned sixteen, I allowed him to rid me of my maidenhead.

Our fling didn't continue past that one time — we both liked our duties far more than each other, and besides, I only had eyes for one lad. The one who was busy frigging anyone and everyone in the Creature Court except me.

Somewhere along the way, we became friends, me and Ash. The game of trying to seduce him became exactly that — he would tease me, and I would mock him right back. Sometimes it made me love him more, sometimes it made me hate him. That was the year he frigged me for the first time, but I'm getting ahead of myself. By the time that happened, I wasn't a sentinel any more.

5

VICTORY OF JOY

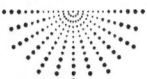

THIRD DAY OF THE LUDI SACRIS, FOUR
DAYS AFTER THE NONES OF FELICITAS

DAYLIGHT

*I*sangell was surrounded by maids pinning up the
overly elaborate gown she would wear at the ceremonies today. The colour was insipid and the corsetry far
too old-fashioned, but that was what came of allowing her
mother to have a say in so many of her frocks for public
appearances. At least she had Mistress Velody's flame dress
to look forward to, for the chief day of sacrifice tomorrow.

As if the thought of her mother had conjured her into
existence, Ducomtessa Eglantine bustled into Isangell's
chambers, like a puffed-up toad in taffeta, seething with
righteous indignation. Or gout. 'Isangell, we have to talk.'

'I am busy, Mama,' Isangell sighed, wincing as one of her
maids pinned the sleeves too tightly. 'The opening ceremonies begin in less than an hour, and we haven't even
started on my hair.'

'Out, all of you,' Eglantine commanded the maids. 'My
daughter and I must speak in private.'

To Isangell's frustration, the maids obeyed her mother, emptying the room faster than they ever moved for her commands. 'Mother, what do you think you are doing?'

'Servants talk, Isangell.'

'Yes, they also fix hair, which was what I was hoping for this morning. I wasn't aware you had an interest in idle gossip.' Isangell did not want to encourage her mother in this behaviour, but if she didn't allow her to speak her mind quickly, she would not be ready in time for the ceremony. 'What is troubling you?'

'Ashiol,' her mother said with great import. 'Do you know he has been ordering imperium from the kitchens? At break-fast time! Something has to be done about him, Isangell. It's exactly as it was before.'

'I have made my stance on my cousin perfectly clear,' Isangell sighed. Imperium in the morning was not a good sign, but she was damned if she would let her mother be right about this.

'You are entrusting the safety of this city to a drunkard and a madman,' Eglantine exclaimed. 'You must put aside this foolish notion of delaying your marriage and allowing your cousin to remain as your heir. If the City Fathers hear of his antics and suspect you are allowing your childhood loyalties to cloud your judgement, they would be honour bound to support one of the other Families to rise against you, and our family will lose everything.'

'I was not aware that any of the Great Families of Aufleur were completely lacking in drunkards and madmen,' Isangell said sharply.

'Don't be facetious. This is a serious matter. You were a child when Ashiol was last in this city. You know nothing of his reputation.'

Isangell sighed heavily. Why did everything have to be a

battle? Her mother was not in the least bit interested in her response; she was merely ranting to herself.

'... Roaming the streets, seducing women, and his — friendship with that country manservant was hardly proper at all. I always had my suspicions about them. You know Ashiol was questioned over the disappearance of the Zafiran ambassador's son. Nothing was ever proven but only because your grandpapa did his level best to hush it up...'

'Mama,' Isangell snapped. 'I have taken note of your concerns, but I have a busy day ahead of me, and I cannot walk into the Circus Verdigris looking like a half-dressed actress. For now you must leave and send my maids back in to me.'

'You will consider accepting a husband from one of the Great Families?' her mother rapped out, eyes gleaming.

'I will consider all options.' Damn it all. Isangell had been so relieved to find an excuse to put off her inevitable marriage, and not only because she had no wish to insult all but one of the Great Families in a single blow. The thought of juggling a husband along with her other duties was beyond irritating, never mind the fact that everyone would expect him to share her rule. 'But not today.'

'He is not the man you think he is, Isangell,' her mother said with the fervour of a fanatic.

Isangell was certain Ashiol was not the man her mother thought he was either, but she knew better than to say so at this moment, when she was on the verge of escaping the conversation. 'I shall think on it,' she said gravely, and was rewarded by her mother — finally — making her exit and sending the maids back in, scurrying and apologetic.

Not the best way to begin a day where every augury was a symbol of the city's fortunes. If Isangell's mother was an omen it would be a black crow, cawing its displeasure at the world. Eglantine always thought the worst of everyone, Ashiol especially.

Isangell had to trust that she could rely on her cousin to stand between her and the line of potential consorts, no matter how unreliable everyone — including Ashiol himself — said that he was. She had no other option, for now.

～

THE STREETS WERE thick with Victory banners, red-gold finery, and the buzz of Sacred Games. Everyone had been to one of the performances at the Circus Verdigris, or planned to, and they poured through the streets, fingers sticky with melon and mouths wet with cordial.

What a fucking joke. Ashiol wanted to grab the sticky revellers, demand to know exactly what victory they thought they were celebrating.

A long-ago war, so old that no one alive had fought in it. A myth passed down for decades. They knew to thank the saints and angels, to thank the devils themselves; they knew the war had been won, or at least had ended, and they gave offerings to the hounds of war on this day. *Don your red satin, watch a carnival act or two and suck down the sugar water. Pretend you know what it all means.*

'You didn't win anything,' Ashiol wanted to tell them. 'You didn't end the war. You just made it invisible. None of you see it, none of you know. But we fight it. We die for you, fucking ungrateful parasites that you are. Stop buying ribbons and fancies and look at the world around you. *See us.*'

They would think he was crazy. Many already did think that. The mad Ducomte. No one knew why the Duchessa Isangell had chosen him, of all her cousins, to stand at her side.

She was as blind as the rest of them. What exactly did she see in him?

Ashiol had made it through two days of Sacred Games so far without throwing a public tantrum. Judicious quantities of imperium assisted with that. He did his best to avoid reflective surfaces, and there had been no further hallucinations. Not yet, in any case.

Fuck, his mouth tasted foul. He needed another drink. Ashiol ran his hands over his face, almost — for a fraction of a moment — feeling the scars he had borne for five years. Scars he hadn't been able to see for most of that time, though there were days when he had looked at his hands and they crumbled under his gaze, crusted and broken.

He breathed, reminding himself that he had his animor back. He was whole again. Whatever else he had to deal with, there was that. This city pumped blood into his veins. He wouldn't leave Aufleur again.

He had been avoiding Velody since the nox he saw Garnet, and almost drank himself to death. She was probably still angry at him for not being sober enough to fight the sky with her. If he kept away, he wouldn't have to deal with her disapproval.

It was daylight, in any case, and that meant Ashiol's duty was to Isangell, not to Velody. He would do his best, for now.

AFTER THE PUBLIC ceremonies of the Victory of Joy, Ashiol returned to the Palazzo. He had a bath, changed out of the ridiculous festival finery, and drank a very precise measure of imperium before he joined Isangell in her rooms.

Isangell raised her fair head as he entered. 'Oh, you're here. Good. We need to consolidate the schedule for the rest of the Sacred Games.'

Ashiol winced.

'It won't be that bad,' his cousin chided him.

'Anything that requires use of a schedule is automatically bad.' He wasn't slurring. The trick was just enough liquor to make the situation manageable; not so much that he bumped into furniture.

'That's Felicitas for you. I couldn't keep track of all the ceremonies and traditions without a map and a timeline.'

'Do I have to sacrifice more sheep?'

'You're supposed to,' she sighed. 'I'm not sure that it's such a good idea.'

'I enjoy a good sacrifice.'

'Yes, and that's the problem — you enjoy it rather too much. It alarms the priests. You looked positively feral today, and there were complaints about — you know.'

'It was an accident.'

'Licking blood from your fingers is hardly an accident. It's not the best way to endear you to the people of Aufleur.'

He shrugged, lowering himself into one of her pretty wicker chairs. 'Surely my job is to make you look more respectable in comparison.'

'I wasn't aware my respectability was in doubt, Ashiol. Do you take nothing seriously?'

'Not if I can possibly help it.' This persona had held him in good stead — an indolent nobleman who took no responsibility. Last time he lived at the Palazzo, it made for a useful explanation every time he spent a nox on the rooftops, or battling the bloodthirsty politics down below.

Ashiol the wastrel, the drunkard, the addict, the debaucher. Such an easy façade, especially as it wasn't entirely a lie.

But here was Isangell, who had never seen him as a wastrel no matter what vile things were said about him between the adults in their family. She saw him as her big cousin, her hero, and now she expected him to be that.

It made Ashiol's feet itch, and his hair prickle. He needed to get out of here and kill something.

'Don't you get bored with the rigmarole?' he asked, placing his booted feet on the low glass table. 'Imagine how much you could get done if you weren't having to placate the city with a new ceremony every day.'

Isangell gave him another of those withering looks of hers. It was at times like this he recognised that she was, in fact, of the same ilk as his mother, who had always been able to see through him with a blink of the eye. 'Festivals are Aufleur. A fine Duchessa I would make if I didn't perform my role as guardian, priestess...'

'Figurehead.'

She sighed. 'And that.'

'Fifteen days of Sacred Games in one month,' he drawled. 'Are you sure we need all of them?'

Isangell didn't say anything for a moment. 'It is how it is,' she said finally. 'I would be letting everyone down if I didn't do my duty.'

'Ah, duty,' Ashiol groaned. 'If you're going to bring duty into it...'

AN INTERMINABLE HOUR LATER, Ashiol escaped up a twist of stairs and through a tiny window to leap on to the tiles that roofed the Palazzo. Just to breathe for a moment, he wasn't going to... Oh, he was.

Careful to crouch out of sight of any servants passing through the gardens, he stripped expertly, balancing his soft leather boots against the gutters before he pulled himself into the shapes that gave him his freedom.

The world on four paws was a fine one indeed. It was dizzying at first to be spread between several cat bodies, agile and sleek, heartbeats racing. But then Ashiol was himself again, and set out in a swarm to hunt. He wanted to taste blood in his mouth, even the tiny splash of a sparrow or a mouse.

Mice. His body thrummed with them. He wanted to lick, taste, bite. It made being around Velody fiercely difficult at times, his many selves warring with themselves as to whether he wanted to eat her or fuck her.

Both at the same time, if he could manage it.

Ashiol leaped from the Palazzo into the air, tangling and falling and then running over cool green grass through the formal gardens, in search of meat and fight.

The scent of them drew him in — mice, mice — and he spread out, his many cat bodies alert to the senses they needed. The smaller creatures smelled him coming, tried to scatter. But no one could pounce like Ashiol. A swipe of paw, sharp bite of teeth, and the bodies lay twitching.

Each of the cats enjoyed their meal, taking the warm carcasses apart with delight, sucking flesh from the bones, spitting wads of fur and tail into the grass.

The cats stretched, hunger sated at least a little. There were more needs to be met, after a morning of public ceremonies and far too long stuck indoors discussing schedules and rituals, after too many days without battle or the pulse of danger.

He needed to get laid.

The veins of the city lay open to Ashiol as he swarmed out into the streets. There were revellers, and food, and threads of panic, lust, joy, fear.

How did the daylight folk not go insane with so much inside their heads? At least those of the nox had animor to keep them contained.

His paws felt good on the cobbles, cool and proper. No need for boots in this form. Ashiol followed an easily remembered trail to a place not far from the Palazzo, to a familiar heartbeat that would be his if he asked for it. Easy.

The alley was narrow, between several townhouses belonging to the Great Families, but there was space enough for the cats that were Ashiol to trot three abreast. They reached the blank wall at the end of the alley and curled up, all of them, waiting. One cat remained on his paws, gazing expectantly at the narrow wall stones.

A door opened out of nothing, and Kelpie stood there. With the eyes of many cats, Ashiol saw human — familiar — home. She smelled like friend. The cats didn't care that she was glaring, that her rumpled tunic and trousers made it clear she wasn't expecting company, or even that she had told him to his face that she was not going to do this again.

Human. Familiar. Home.

Ever the good sentinel, Kelpie stood back to let him past, waiting until every cat was safe inside before she sealed the nest.

Each of the sentinels had a few nests scattered across the city. For the first time, Ashiol wondered what had happened to the nests belonging to the many sentinels who had fallen in recent years. Did they vanish? Had the sentinels who were left behind taken them over? He could not ask while he was cats.

'What's wrong?' Kelpie asked now, perching on the end of her bed, the only piece of furniture in the tiny low-ceilinged room. A tinge of fear swept through the room, just a little. 'An attack? I thought you were at the Palazzo all day?'

Ashiol gazed at her through the eyes of many cats. *Human. Familiar. Home. Sex.*

Kelpie tilted her head, and suspicion set in. 'Ashiol,' she said sharply. 'You cannot be serious.'

He leaped into her lap, one furry body rubbing against her stomach, begging to be scratched. Her hand came up automatically, and then dropped. 'You were gone five years without even a note to tell me you were alive. We are not picking up where we left off.'

The other cats joined them on the bed, rubbing up around her, watching her, tails swishing back and forth. 'You're a fiend,' Kelpie said, and now he could hear her wavering tone. Had he been human, he would have smiled at that evidence of indecision. 'If you actually wanted me, that would be something else, but you're just killing *time* —'

Ashiol shaped back into human form, male and naked and undeniably in her lap. The want that coursed through his body since he killed the mice was firmly evident. 'Kelpie,' he said in a low voice, 'I always want you.'

True, if not the kind of truth she had wanted from him five years ago. Kelpie stared at him for a long moment, calculating. Then she gave him a shove and he let her push him to his back on the bed. His cock was hard and jutting upwards, his eyes dark on hers.

'This is going to work a lot better if you don't talk,' she said as she straddled him, bringing her mouth down for a bruising kiss. She was angrier than he had expected. He wasn't sure why, even back in his human shape. Ashiol had never been hers, never belonged to anyone except Garnet, perhaps. If he was going to give himself completely to a partner it would be an equal, not a sentinel. She knew that, didn't she? It had never occurred to him that she cared one way or another.

Kelpie was still kissing him, fast and hard, and he ran his hands over her, feeling the tautness leave her body as they came together in the old pattern, bodies rough and clashing.

He helped her out of her trousers, peeling them to her knees and no further. She arched an eyebrow at him but went along with the haste of it, parting her thighs to take him inside her, rocking slowly as she descended on to him. He held her hips in both hands, burying his face in her throat, and only then did he smell it.

Someone else. Something else. A difference. 'You have a lover,' he grunted, teeth grazing her skin. 'Daylight?' No, not daylight. Not daylight at all. Ashiol was on the edge of figuring out who... but then the smell was gone.

'I don't — want — to talk about it *now*,' she gasped, her hips making little quick thrusts.

Ashiol sucked, and bit on her throat, working his way up to her ear. He wanted to complain, wanted to demand, but she would be justified in putting a knife between his ribs if he went all possessive on her.

Instead he concentrated on the intensity of the now, of Kelpie tight and hot around him, of the comfort of her hair, her neck, the fingers flexing against his shoulders, and that he knew exactly what she sounded like when she came. *Mine*, he thought furiously, and as if she had heard his silent declaration, she ground down harder on him, her nails digging into his back.

BLOOD STARTED DRIPPING from the sky a few minutes after dusk. Just a few drops at first, hardly noticeable at all.

Velody had worked through the afternoon, burying her anxieties and dark thoughts into the Duchessa's flame gown, which was to be picked up by a courier first thing in the morning. She had the windows open to relieve the stuffy summer heat that had been building since the Nones. Delphine breezed in through the workroom and slammed the windows down one after the other, her face wrinkled up in disgust.

'There's a smell out there.'

Velody, caught up with bead embellishments, had not noticed. But now that Delphine called attention to it... 'There is something in the air,' she admitted, without thinking about what that something might be.

There was a silence that lasted far too long. Velody looked up to see Delphine standing there, staring at her hand. 'Did you cut yourself?'

'No,' Delphine said in a strangled voice. 'It's coming from the sky.'

Velody laid the dress down and went to her. Sure enough, there was blood on Delphine's hand. Strange and watery, but the smell of it was unmistakeable. Velody's stomach reacted to it, the animals inside her skin craving meat, and more.

The blood was falling faster outside, droplets splashing into puddles. It was still — barely — light enough outside to see the redness of it. 'Wash it off,' Velody said quickly and drew the several bolts on the front door, shoving it open. The overhang of the porch sheltered her and she stood there for a few moments, gazing out as several passers by ducked in and out of the various shops along the street. Blood fell freely over their skin and they paid it no more mind than any other light shower of rain.

'Should I be seeing this?' Delphine asked in a very quiet voice.

Too late, Velody realised what she meant. The daylight folk could not see or smell the blood, but Delphine could. 'I'll send a mouse to summon Macready.'

'No,' Delphine said, too quickly. 'If I have to hear him tell me one more time how much that bastard ferax changed me, I'll have to stab him too.' She wrapped her arms around herself. 'I hate this.'

Velody felt an emptiness inside her. 'It's all my fault.'

'Yes,' Delphine said sharply. 'It is.' She pulled a linen wrap from the hook on the wall, threw it over her hair and ran out into the blood rain.

Velody almost called after her, but sighed and closed the door instead. Some things could not be apologised for. Besides, the sky was weeping blood. She should deal with that first.

A few minutes later, as the darkness closed in around the house, a horde of little brown mice streamed out on to the roof, drenched in blood as they scattered across the city in search of answers.

The blood did not hurt her, but she could feel it sticking to her fur, twitching against her nose. She couldn't smell anything but the blood, which was how she ended up surrounded by cats, black and silent, without warning. She shaped into Lord form, fast and fierce, glowing brightly as she floated naked only a few inches from the rooftop.

Ashiol changed a beat after her, hovering there with that look on his face, the one he always got soon after they had faced each other as cats and mice — as if he was reminding himself that he wasn't allowed to eat her.

'Is there a skybattle?' Velody asked. 'I've never seen the sky bleed like this.'

'Something's coming, not sure what,' Ashiol said. 'Best to be prepared.'

'How can we be prepared if we don't know what's coming?'

A third figure swooped past them and descended — Poet, in one of those fluttering white burnoose garments of his. 'Easy enough, lady Majesty,' he said with a florid bow. 'Just prepare for the worst. That's what we usually get.'

'So very comforting,' Velody said dryly. Her whole body was tense, her skin tugging towards the sky. The smell of the blood was everywhere, infusing all the other scents of the city.

Clouds had gathered overhead, making even the sky feel claustrophobic. There was a low rumble high up and deep down that made Velody's pulse shift just a little. 'Maybe it's just an ordinary storm?' she suggested, not really believing it.

'An ordinary storm,' Poet said in disbelief, shaking his head. 'No such thing.'

Velody turned her eyes to Ashiol. He stood with his mouth slightly open, head tipped back. The blood and rain splashed over his face, ran down his throat. How could he do that? It made her shudder.

Then he snapped his head around fast, eyes all but glowing silver. 'There,' he said, and took to the sky so fast the air seemed to crash into the space he left behind.

Poet laughed a short bark of triumph and took after him, following as close as he could. Velody took one deep, centring breath, and then stepped off the roof, the cool air scraping her bare skin as she flew. She had no idea what they were heading into, only that she wanted it. Days and days of close needlework, creating masterful garments, that was supposed to be what made life worth living. She had finally achieved her dream — making dresses for the Duchessa, the pinnacle of her profession.

But that satisfaction was nothing to the way that the sky made her feel alive.

6

VICTORY OF JOY

THIRD DAY OF THE LUDI SACRIS, FOUR DAYS AFTER THE NONES OF FELICITAS

NOX

*M*acready found Delphine in a seedy little Zafiran coffee house at the edge of the Vittorine. She looked thin and pale as she sat with her back to the window, resolutely not watching the blood fall from the sky.

Well now, was that not an interesting turn of events?

Delphine's eyes flicked to him and then away as she concentrated on her cup of fancy brew — the kind lasses liked to order, spiced and sweetened until it no longer resembled coffee itself.

Not that there was anything that could improve the taste of that much.

'How did you find me?' she asked.

'You're a bright beacon, lass,' Macready said easily, sliding into the booth opposite her. 'Wherever you are in the city, I can find you.' She stared at him in alarm, and he laughed. 'Or Rhian told me you often come here. One of the two.'

'I hate you,' she said without inflection.

'It's not me you hate.'

The madame of the house came over, skirts jingling, to pour a cup of plain and black for Macready. She had a few years on her but wore them well, and gave him a good view of her melons as she did the pouring. He flashed her a grin to let her know it was appreciated.

Delphine seemed less impressed. 'Did you want something in particular, Macready?'

'Just admiring the view, so I was,' he said innocently, and took a swallow of the coffee, which was only just hot enough to drink. Honestly, why did they not drink stewed dirt and have done with it?

'Yes, I could see that.' Delphine glared at the madame's back as she returned to the bar with more jingling from the sway of her hefty hips. 'Did you want something from me? I'm meeting friends shortly, I'd hate for you to scare them off.'

'No, you're not,' he said. 'Your demme Rhian told me you come here to be alone.'

Delphine raised her eyebrows. Macready raised his right back at her. 'You don't see the problem with you being here, in that case?' she said finally.

He swallowed some more coffee. 'Not really.'

'Go away.'

'You don't want me to do that.'

'Macready,' she said in frustration. 'How have you survived this far without being killed by a demme for being so damned annoying?'

'Natural charm?'

She blew out a breath, making a rude noise.

'Classy,' he observed.

Delphine did her best to ignore him after that, fingers clumsy on her cup, sipping, setting it down, fiddling with the too-short blonde hair that wisped around her ears. 'Why is the sky bleeding?' she burst out finally.

'Ah,' Macready said with a satisfied sigh. 'The Sight is falling upon you, then. We all have a touch of it. Not sure if it's ours entirely, or if it comes from so much time in orbit around their Kingships. But the world won't look the same to you again.'

'Make it go away.'

'Cannot.'

'I refuse to be stuck with it,' she said, her fingers drumming on the table. Big knuckles for a demme; they looked odd against her slender fingers. 'It can't just be like this forever, just because I —' She paused and glanced around, not finishing her sentence.

'It was no accident you struck that blow, lass,' Macready told her.

'So what, it was my destiny? What a stupid idea. It means I didn't have a choice.' Delphine leaned in, eyes wide. 'I made someone *die*.'

'It was you or him. Don't take an ounce of guilt from that deed.'

'I still think about him. I hear his voice in my sleep. I don't want to do this. I can't just run around stabbing people as a regular lifestyle.'

'If you listened to what I've been trying to tell you, lovely, you'd know that stabbing people isn't half of what the sentinels are. Not even a quarter.'

'I am not like you, Macready. I'm not.'

'No,' he agreed. 'Not in the least. But you could be better.'

'Better than a gin-soaked tart who doesn't see past her own nose?' she said bitterly.

Macready rolled his eyes, and did his best not to agree with her, though she was spot on about the nose. 'Better than me, you mad bint. You could be a better sentinel than me. You just have to take it into yourself.'

'I can see blood falling from the sky,' Delphine said hoarsely. 'I don't want to step any further into your world.'

'You're already here, lass. Nowhere to go but further in.'

'I'll run as far and fast as I can,' she vowed.

'No,' Macready said calm as you like. 'You won't. You feel more alive than you ever had before. This is better than gin, better than potions or powders. Better than sex.' *When it's good, when we have a Power and Majesty we can believe in, when the Kings love us as they should...* 'You need this, Delphine.'

'No, I don't. You're the one who needs me to do this, and I still don't know why.'

'Want me to show you?' he asked impulsively. She had a fair point, which hadn't occurred to him before now. It wasn't just the lass he was looking to save, in making her a sentinel.

She almost said no; he could see it in her eyes, in the tilt of her head as she opened her mouth. But then she paused. 'Fine, show me. It's not like I have anything else to do this nox.'

The sky was falling, and he should be with the Kings, but this — this was more important. 'That's my lass,' said Macready approvingly.

Delphine rolled her eyes. 'Oh, you wish.'

~

'I've been here before,' said Delphine, incongruous in her bloodstained dress against the grey sand on the ground and the bright sunshine in the sky. Macready couldn't take his eyes off her.

'The Killing Ground,' he agreed. Softly, softly. Get her used to the idea.

'Charming name for it.' Delphine swept her eyes around the arena, scanning the tiers of stone benches. 'I can't help noticing that...'

'It begs the question.'

'What the hells happened to the nox, Macready?'

He shrugged, looking up at the sky. 'It's always noon here.'

'That makes no sense.'

'Velody turns into little brown mice and flies naked through the sky — sense isn't exactly the main priority of the Creature Court.' Macready waved his arm, taking in the arena. 'Think of it as an anomaly.'

'I'm thinking of it as a way to sport a tan from Bestialis to Lupercal,' she said archly.

He laughed. Somehow she was always able to make the weird seem mundane. It was a good skill to have. 'Or that, lass.'

The blood spots on Delphine's dress faded slowly in the sunlight — vanishing like they had never been there, as the patches dried. Macready drew Alicity and Tarea, weighing both hilts in his hands. 'Care to try a little swordplay?'

'Is that why you brought me here? To show me how long your swords are?' She was laughing at him and half flirting, and that was seven hells better than morose, sulking Delphine. He liked her this way. Maybe a little too much.

'You cannot judge for yourself without laying your hands on them,' he teased back.

'Held one blade, held them all.'

As they bantered, he began circling her slowly.

Delphine reacted by moving with small steps, always keeping her eyes to his. Good lass.

Macready lunged suddenly, throwing one of his skysilver swords to her. Delphine jolted, but caught Tarea perfectly at the hilt. 'Stop that,' she said, wrinkling her nose as if he had waved some unpleasant market fish in front of her face. She tried to give the sword back straightaway.

Macready laughed, stepping back out of range. 'Does she not feel like she belongs to you?'

Skysilver, that was the trick to it. Didn't matter how fast it took you, being a sentinel, it was skysilver that drew you in and made you belong. It had a song you couldn't quite hear, a heat that connected you to the sky and the Court. If Delphine could only listen to the song of the skysilver, she would understand.

'No, she belongs to you, and I don't take gifts unless I know their price.'

'I only give away my lasses on very special occasions,' he said, face darkening a little as he remembered gifting Velody with his Jeunille after Dhynar's first attack. He had all four blades back now, and wouldn't lose them again in a hurry. 'Saints, lass, it's just play.'

'Is it?' Delphine weighed the sword thoughtfully and then extended her arm, the glowing tip dancing near his chest. 'You want me to give up everything good about my life to take part in this mad charade that's already swallowed Velody whole. That's not my idea of play.'

Macready still remembered the Silver Captain talking him through what it was to be a sentinel, detailing their rules and rights and responsibilities.

'We are their hands,' the old man had said on a cold day near Saturnalia, walking the bounds with his newest recruit. 'We do whatever we can to keep the bastards on their feet. We are their minds — the saints know, they can't do their own thinking. Half-mad, the bunch of them.'

Macready had chuckled at that one, not knowing then how true it was. 'If we are the hands and minds, Cap, what do they provide, the Lords and Court?'

'Hearts and souls, boyo,' the Captain had said. 'They're our reason for breathing in and out, and don't you forget it.'

Somehow, Macready didn't think the patriotic spiel was the right tack for Delphine.

Macready stepped forward deliberately, bringing Alicity up to counter Tarea. The swords made a small noise as they met, not quite metal on metal. The air took on that odd scent of steel kissing skysilver. Delphine stepped back — good distance work, he noted. He had no idea if it was her dancing that gave her that, or the sentinel soul inside her starting to emerge, but he was glad of it.

Any sign that he wasn't pushing the point because he fancied her rotten was a good thing.

'I can't fence,' Delphine insisted.

'You're doing fine.'

'I don't want to do fine.' She dropped Tarea so fast that Macready almost fell forwards, off balance. 'I don't want this, Mac. You said you were going to show me how special it was to be a sentinel. I don't see anything. I don't feel it. I'm not convinced.'

Macready was no Silver Captain, that was for sure. The old bastard would have had her in uniform already. He had been so sure he could do this, that he could sell it to her. But Delphine was a tough customer. 'This place is sacred to us. Every sentinel has walked this ground, practised their blades. Prepared for their destiny.'

'The Killing Ground,' she said, a false lightness in her voice. 'Have they all killed, Mac? Is that the special detail you're leaving out, of this little club of yours? And forgive me for being tactless, but this army of sentinels you like to wax lyrical about — so glorious, so loyal, so brave. Not exactly alive, most of them, are they?'

A sharp cut, that one. 'Not exactly,' Macready said. Damn

it, he should be better at this. Where were his reinforcements?

'I don't want this,' Delphine said again, sounding at least faintly regretful. 'I'm sorry, but I don't. Take me home.' She leaned down to pick up the sword she had dropped.

This time, when her hand wrapped around the hilt, heat poured out of it, and Macready's reinforcements made themselves known.

The grey sands rippled underfoot. The sunshine, just for a moment, became cold and false. Delphine shivered once as she straightened up. Her hand clenched hard around the sword, which was glowing fiercely.

Misty figures filled the arena. They fought, blocked, jumped, laughed. Training exercises, challenges, outright duels. The sentinels, the real thing. Macready hadn't seen this light show in years. Part of him had wondered if it was gone forever, if Garnet destroyed the heart of the Killing Ground even as he demoralised those of them who were left.

But here they were, large as life. Zyler and Rory, messing around with mock-blows and knife lunges, cracking each other up with their attempts at witty banter. Tobin getting in on the act, showing off for Heliora. Ilsa, so damned superior as she watched them, knowing her blade skills were better than any of them, but not bothering to demonstrate.

There was a younger, less battleworn Kelpie, holding Andronicus in a headlock because of some smart-arse thing he had said about demmes and sharp edges, beating him with the side of her hand until he yelled uncle.

Macready's heart stilled as it always did when he first caught sight of the ghostly Silver Captain, marching into the middle of it all, barking orders. No one could replace the old man. No one could even try.

'We were more than a gang, more than one arm of the Creature Court,' Macready said, his voice faltering. He could see his younger self, less battered around the edges, without the scar and missing ring finger. 'We were a family. We were strong and mighty, and we could be that again, lass. With your help, if we can resurrect the old spirit of what the sentinels were... we can make Velody great. We can do more than save the city by the skin of our teeth, we can make Aufleur fecking glorious.' There he was, heart on his sleeve, wanting her to understand what he was offering, and what he was asking of her.

Delphine's face was impassive as the ghostly sentinels around her danced their dance of blades and feet and hands.

'You'll have your own family back, too,' Macready said, almost as an afterthought. 'The memories of them. When you're a sentinel for real... once you accept it, the forgetting won't work on you any more. You'll remember everything you lost about Tierce and your childhood.'

In one fluid motion Delphine threw Alicity to him, hilt-first.

Macready caught his sword, troubled by the anger he could see in her face. 'Lass, I didn't mean...'

'I hate you,' Delphine said, and walked away.

He should go with her. A demoiselle on her own in the nox streets of Aufleur, without even a weapon? Dangerous and stupid. But Macready was stuck to the spot, eyes locked on the fading images of the family who had taken him in, twenty fecking years ago.

Only when the last of the ghosts had entirely dissolved did he run after Delphine — and by that time, of course, the lass was long gone. He'd spent enough time playing games with her. There was a battle that needed him.

DELPHINE WAS SO angry she could spit. How dare he? How dare he dangle her memories of her life before Aufleur as some kind of candied sweetmeat, to entice her to do what he wanted? Those were her memories, and he had no right to offer them to her.

It was still raining blood, and the sky was full of colours and shadows and bright, blazing moments of light. Delphine kept her head down as she hurried through the streets, ignoring it all. It was not her world. It was not her problem.

She kept thinking that right up to the point that she reached the yard behind her house, and found it full of monsters.

Delphine had blood in her hair, trickling down her neck with the rain. She was angry and tired, and she really did not need this. But she had little choice.

Poet, the Orphan Princel. She knew that one. He lounged on her back step, with a ragged boy sitting at his feet. The gorgeous dark one, whom Velody called Warlord, he stood with his back to the kitchen door, wearing a ripped red silk shirt the same colour as the blood that fell from the sky. He smiled at Delphine, the kind of smile she was used to from clubs and parties. *I want to fuck you, I want to hurt you, I want to show you what a worthless scrap of skin with tits you are.* That kind of smile. She knew well enough to keep away from those men, no matter how self-destructive she was feeling, but it was hard to do that when he was on your doorstep.

There were others in the yard, young men and a woman, dressed to match the Warlord. They kept to the shadows, but Delphine could feel their threatening presence.

'What do you want?' she demanded, giving them her best aristocratic accent. She could play the entitled demoiselle with great confidence, when she had to.

'We want to look upon the daylight demme who killed one of our own,' said Poet in that soft, lovely voice of his.

'Have you met Warlord? He was allied with Dhynar Lord Ferax. It is his duty to avenge the furry little bastard.'

Delphine wished Macready was here, and promptly hated herself for being so weak. 'If you have a problem with the Ferax Lord's death, take it up with your Power and Majesty,' she said coldly.

Warlord spoke next, his voice deep and rich. Power shone out from him, so that he glowed in the darkness. 'If you are not one of us, the rules do not apply,' he said. 'Our Power and Majesty cannot protect you. Nothing can.'

'And who says I'm not one of you?' Delphine flung at him. Macready thought so, and he was always right, damn it, though she wanted to believe otherwise. She reached inside herself, remembering how it felt to stand in the Killing Ground, how it felt to have one of Macready's skysilver blades in her hand.

She had not admitted to him or herself how skysilver made her pulse race, how it made her feel taller and sexier and more beautiful than she had ever felt possible. Here, in her yard, she glared at the terrifying man, filling her body with the memory of skysilver, of holding it and wielding it and being part of it. She felt the taste of it at the back of her throat.

The demme who wore Warlord's colours moved first, grabbing hold of Delphine and licking her roughly across the side of the neck. 'She's a sentinel,' she reported.

Delphine pushed her away. 'Excuse me — licking? Who said there could be *licking*?'

Warlord stepped forward now, fury pouring off him, and for a moment she felt him inside her head, touching the memory of how she had driven Macready's blade into the body of Dhynar. Delphine shook with it, and then Warlord released her, turning his fury on Poet. 'What kind of trick is this, rat?'

'She's the one tricking you, not me,' Poet retorted, backing up against the nearest fence.

'If I killed one of her sentinels, the Power and Majesty would have good reason to destroy me,' Warlord roared, and then shaped quickly into a large, black shape that radiated more power than he had as a man. Panther, oh, holy saints, it was a panther. Delphine had never seen one outside the Circus Verdigris.

Poet shaped himself too, into a horde of white rats, and streaked into the sky with the panther pursuing him.

The courtesi who remained in the yard looked warily at each other. Delphine cleared her throat. 'I'm going to go inside, then.'

Poet's lad moved aside from the foot of the step, to allow her to reach the kitchen door. Delphine unlatched it, let herself inside, and then closed the door hard, leaning against it.

A sentinel. It wasn't just Macready saying it now. It was them. She stood there for some time, working hard to erase every thought, every sensation that she had to do with the skysilver. She could damp it down, get rid of it; she could never think of it again.

Except, of course, that she now knew that she might need to summon those thoughts back at a moment's notice. Damn it all.

Delphine went to bed.

～

THE BEST FUN EVER.

Seonard's words buzzed through Velody's head as she fought the sky alongside Ashiol. The Lords and Court were there too, though she lost sight of Poet early on, and really she was paying attention to none of them except for Ashiol.

When the bloodstars crackled past her hair, she caught them in her chimaera claw and listened to them pop as her animor burned them. She amused herself by matching the pace of the bolts of warlight, blasting them into dust only in the last moment before they smashed the spire of a church, or a wrought-iron balcony.

It wasn't a battle, it wasn't even a dance. It was a game.

Velody was still grinning when she and Ashiol finally made it down. They landed on a flat roof on one of the temples on the Octavian, and Crane was there waiting for them, with a dress for Velody to slip into. Was this a usual service to Creature Kings, she wondered, or did he just not like her bare in front of the others? He had brought clothes for Ashiol too, which at least made it seem less obvious.

'Starting to enjoy yourself, are you?' said Ashiol, breathing hard.

Velody turned her smile up to him, before remembering that she was still supposed to be angry at how he had let her down. He timed his return well. She was too buzzed from fighting at his side again to start an argument about what had happened days ago. 'We're good up there, admit it. When you turn up.'

Ashiol ignored the dig. 'Not good enough. Took some damage.' He had a wound on his shoulder, a greyish slash that had puckered badly. Velody had her own little cuts and scratches, and her forearms were both warm with skyburn, but she found herself reaching out to his shoulder, wanting to heal the hurt. Ashiol flinched away and gave her an impatient look. 'I didn't mean damage to me. What difference does that make? The city took some blows. We can do better. Should do better.'

'Of course,' she said, frowning. She moved away from him, to the edge of the temple roof, and surveyed the china-pattern of the city beneath her, trying to see which buildings had been hit. It was not yet dawn, when Aufleur would repair the damage.

'My birds can give you a full report if you like, Majesty,' offered Priest as he landed nearly on the edge of the roof with his courtesi gathered closely around him.

'Yes, thank you,' said Velody, glad for the offer. This whole city was her responsibility, not just her personal family of broken monsters. She had to remember that. It was too easy to drop into thinking of it as a game.

She had controlled herself better in this battle, keeping her movements measured, not allowing the animor to push her own sensibilities and cautions out of her head. She wasn't sure if it made her a better warrior, but it sure as hells made her feel less like throwing up after the battle was over.

Priest sent his courtesi swooping across the city in feathered form. Velody dressed herself silently, not looking at Ashiol. He was in an edgy mood, and she didn't want to provoke him further. He dressed himself too, though it seemed more of an afterthought than a priority. His thoughts were elsewhere.

The gulls, plover and sparrows regrouped to perch on the head and arms of Priest, Lord Pigeon. 'The worst hit areas are around the Portico Lattorio, and some warlight flattened the far side of the Avleurine,' he announced after listening to the birds for a short while. He hesitated. 'There was also — half a street in the lower Vittorine.'

Velody swayed a little. That. She had never considered the possibility of that.

'It doesn't mean —' Crane said hesitantly.

'Don't talk,' she snapped, and took to the air, heading for the familiar green hill, covered in fine residences and surrounded by shopping streets. A black scar ran down the side of the Vittorine, charring mostly the pretty gardens. The middle of one street was torn up, the cobbles almost blistered. Via Silviana. Yes. Oh, it was.

Velody's eye followed the scar and the street, and she almost stopped breathing. One side of Via Silviana had been reduced to rubble. Her side. Her home.

When Velody's feet finally landed on the broken cobbles, beside the fallen sign of the ribbon, rose and needle, she was managing to breathe but that was the limit of her abilities. The shop was gone, beneath a weight of torn stone and battered roof tiles. 'Delphine!' she yelled. 'Rhian!'

Cool hands seized her from behind, pulling her in closer. 'It's not real,' Ashiol hissed in her ear. 'It won't last. The city will heal, it always does...' *Except when the battle lost is too grave*, was the part she had heard him add in the past. The lack of it now was no particular comfort. There was the Silent Sleep, which those of the daylight thought was a random illness. Daylight folk could die from damage brought down by the sky, when one reality crashed into another. There were always imperfections in the healing brought by the dawn — especially when it came to people, actual people. Bricks and mortar mended more easily.

'Macready,' Velody said desperately, shaking Ashiol off her, and ignoring Crane. Both of them were only interested in keeping her out of the broken house. 'Where's *Macready*?'

She saw a flash of hurt on Crane's face, and irritation on Ashiol's. Neither of them were any use to her.

'Here, lass,' said Macready, pushing his way past the Lords and Court who stood waiting for the kiss of approval from the Power and Majesty.

'They were both at home?' She didn't know. How could she not know? Delphine could be anywhere.

'Aye, I think so.' His voice was flat, as if there was something he was leaving out, some source of guilt.

'Is Delphine a sentinel yet?' Velody demanded. '*Will this*

hurt her?' She had only just thought of this. Delphine might not be of the daylight any more.

'It's early, lass; I can't say for sure,' Macready said, glancing around as if to check the reactions of the others. Too late, Velody remembered this wasn't common knowledge. She had blurted Delphine's secret in front of the whole Creature Court, though from the lack of reaction from Warlord and Poet, it was not a shock to any of them. 'I've survived worse,' Macready went on. 'Crane and Kelpie too. It doesn't take us the way it burns those of the Court.'

'But you're not daylight, either.' Velody said, turning back to the house. Dawn was lightening the sky, and with it, the city was recovering. The stones rolled back into place. The buildings stretched and arched back towards the sky. Roofs straightened. Glass unshattered, peeling back a piece at a time into the frames of windows.

'Only one way to find out, lass,' said Macready.

The bakery beside Velody's shop made groaning noises as it reassembled itself with its iron chimneys and smashed clay ovens. Impossibly, the smell of baking bread began to emanate from it. The world was being restored.

'Don't think too much about it,' said Ashiol, his body warm against her back. He wrapped his hand around hers, tangling their fingers together. 'Hurts the head.'

Velody wanted to lean against him and be comforted, but not yet, not yet. She pulled away from him and hurried towards her own house, grasping the latch of the wooden door that still wasn't quite assembled.

She ran through the workroom to the stairs, which were still cracked across the centre. For a moment as her foot passed over the gap she felt air, and then the security of a firm step. The house healed around her, the walls straightening and the floorboards cracking back into place.

Velody rushed into Delphine's room first. The window

was still broken, but the glass was filling the frame again, piece by piece. For one moment Velody saw a long broken beam crushed fiercely into Delphine's bed, but then the beam was intact again and up in the ceiling where it belonged. Velody reached out shaking hands to pull back the quilt, and saw Delphine curled underneath.

She muttered and blinked, then peered up at Velody. 'What's wrong?'

Velody stared. Bruises patterned Delphine's face, and down the side of her neck. Ugly blackish bruises that faded even as the sunlight fell through the whole window. They were still there but a paler purple once the room was fully lit, and Velody reached out her finger to touch.

'Ouch,' said Delphine, prodding her in return. 'Don't poke people's faces.' She stretched and rubbed her cheek. 'I must have slept oddly. Not as odd as you, obviously.' She held out her hand expectantly and Velody handed back the quilt.

She walked on unsteady feet to Rhian's room, though the bolts kept her out. She knocked, and when she heard a sleepy voice in response, relief flooded through her body. She leaned against the door for a few moments, composing herself. It was all right. This time, it was all right. They came through.

Slowly, Velody made her way back downstairs, finding her chair and curling up in it. The Creature Court were still outside, she could feel them, but they would have to wait.

Ashiol sat on the fabric cupboard, his feet on the table where her sewing machine rested. For once she didn't tell him to put them down.

Macready and Crane stood by the cold fireplace. 'Not so bad?' Macready asked with a false lightness to his voice.

'If she was really a sentinel she could be dead,' said Velody. Her hands were shaking. Delayed shock?

'Aye, maybe. Or she'd have died already, saving your life.

Or she'd have been with us, and safe. "What if" never led to anything of any worth. Just ask our Seer.'

'People do get hurt, though,' Velody said, staring at her fingers. She could see that dark web of shadows again, flickering over her skin, and she made fists to hide it. 'Not everything can be fixed. The Silent Sleep...'

How awful was it that she had never considered the consequences of that until she saw the wreckage of her own home, and thought Rhian and Delphine might be victims?

Would Velody's friends be safer if they were a part of the Court? Should they be setting up home in the Arches? Was living alongside Livilla and Poet less of a risk than living on the surface?

'Not everything,' Ashiol agreed. 'You were lucky.'

'I should have done a better job of defending the house.'

'You have a city to think of,' he said sharply. 'One house shouldn't matter. It can't matter.'

'And that's why you live underground, so you care about nothing?' Velody flared. 'How would you feel if it was the Palazzo that fell to the skybolts? If the Duchessa didn't wake up one morning, and you knew exactly why? How many cups of wine would it take to drown that one out?'

Ashiol's face darkened. 'I would be angry. Wounded. Lost. But you haven't lost anything.'

'Not this nox,' said Velody.

She went out into the street, performed the kissing ritual for the Lords of the Court perfunctorily, conscious all the while of Ashiol watching her, disapproving of how upset she was. How dare he? Of all people, considering his recent antics, he was the last who should judge her for how she felt.

When she had finally sent them all on their way to sleep through the morning, even Macready, Velody returned to her house. She found herself staring at every detail — every ornament or stray scrap of fabric, every wall and piece of furniture. She went into the kitchen and examined the spice jars. All was as it should be. All was back to normal.

The darkness overwhelmed her. Her animor roiled within her body, dark and awful and twisted. It had never felt this bad before. She stumbled from the kitchen, barely able to make out the familiar shapes of things in the work-room, they were so drenched in shadows. Something was wrong, really wrong with her.

She should have told Ashiol about the web pattern on her hands, about the dark thoughts she had been having. She should have told Macready. Somebody. She had been too embarrassed to admit, even to herself, that since she had saved the city from Dhynar's tainted shade, she felt as if her own power was dirty, polluted, stained. The only times she felt altogether sane were when she was fighting the sky, and when she was sewing.

Velody stumbled now towards the silk gown hanging ready for the Duchessa's courier. Every stitch had kept the darkness at bay. She laid her hands on the silk, inhaling a long breath, and felt calmness descend around her shoulders. That answered the question of whether she should stay on as a dressmaker as well as being Power and Majesty of the Creature Court. Obviously, it was the only thing keeping her in one piece.

AFTER THE COURIER took the dress to the Palazzo, Velody went to fetch fresh bread from the bakery. She felt a new lightness to her body. Her animor felt cleaner than it had for many days, and she was hopeful that she could make it work. She could balance the daylight and the nox. She didn't have to give either up. All would be well.

She had seen the bakery shattered only a few hours ago,

but every brick and stone was exactly where it should be. The scent of early baking still lingered, but there was none of the usual warmth and chatter pouring out from the double doors. As Velody came nearer, she saw that the doors were barred, with a brief sigil pinned up to warn customers away.

Velody stood there for a moment, not sure what to make of it. She glanced around, and saw the fruitsellers waving to her from the stall they ran on the far side of the road. She had last seen them deep into their cups with the flirtatious Warlord at the street party, laughing and dancing. They weren't laughing now.

'They say it was his boy Giuno,' said one of the dames, as Velody approached. 'Taken in the nox. The Silent Sleep. Poor lamb. The family's broken up.'

'The baker's on Havingale is open,' added the other. 'Get in fast, though; they'll sell out before noon, with the extra business.'

Giuno, who took his man's robe on the Nones, who danced with Delphine with a wide grin as if he was the luckiest boy alive.

Velody stood there for a long time, unable to move. Finally, she walked back to her house, numb all over. She made it back to the house before she started crying, but only just.

She expected the shadow of her animor to fall over her again, but it did not. She cried, she dried her eyes, and she continued with her day. Perhaps she was getting better at controlling it.

7

CHIEF DAY OF SACRIFICE

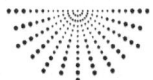

FOURTH DAY OF THE LUDI SACRIS, FOUR DAYS BEFORE THE IDES OF FELICITAS

DAYLIGHT

*I*sangell was tired. There was so much to be done, so many different ceremonies to prepare for, so many rituals to be learned. It all seemed easy when she was a child, when her grandpapa the Old Duc was sane and strong. Her grandmama took charge of every festival, smooth as a waterclock, always knowing what had to be done and what was to be done next.

The last few years had been a mess, all about hiding how badly Grandpapa's mind had degenerated, and then how ill Grandmama was. Keeping up the bare minimum was all they could do.

Isangell's first year of rule was in mourning, with no need for public appearances, just private meetings with the City Fathers and the Proctors. She had whole hours of peace to herself, to learn how the city worked, and who were the important people to please.

Now she must restore the traditions, every one of them,

and for every meeting on political issues, she had three with priests.

Isangell knew that it was important, that every ritual they performed contributed to the city's wellbeing, and yet it was hard to remember that halfway through an interminable season of Sacred Games when there was nothing to do but clap appreciatively when some over-muscled gladiator did something grotesque to a gattopardo or tigris.

Isangell really would rather not watch anything that involved the spraying of blood. Women were not permitted to commit acts of blood sacrifice, something for which she had always been grateful when the men of her family were called upon to perform their priestly duties. Women sacrificed wreaths and locks of hair, baked cakes with blood and swept the temples after sacrifice, but they did not hold a knife.

The Duc who ruled the city, however, was expected to slice open all manner of beasts in the name of auguries and sacrifice. It was quite a dilemma, discussed by representatives of the many temples and churches around the city for that whole year of mourning. Eventually it was decided that the Duchessa could select a man to act as her hand, drawing the necessary blood on her behalf.

A trap, of course. Almost before the priests delivered their verdict, the Duchessa was overwhelmed by a sea of letters of recommendation, offers and veiled threats from the various eligible menfolk of the Great Families. She had hoped that her public declaration that she would not marry for two years, and that each Family could present a single suitor to rotate the duties of her consort would calm them all down again, but it seemed to have made things worse. The relevance and social significance of every festival was weighed against the others, and various Family secretaries wore their pens down to the nub debating as to whether the

Lesser Quinquinatrus was worth more or less than the Matralia, and whether it was fair to allow Jordan Leorgette to accompany the Duchessa for both days of the Ludi Taurei when Darius Camellie had only been allowed to stand at her side for two hours during the interminable rituals of the Lares Vialibus.

It was enough to make Isangell scream. The only way to make them stop was to choose a Duc Consort once and for all. She wasn't ready for that, not yet.

She allowed each of the potential consorts from the Great Families to accompany her for one day of either the Ludi Sacris or the Ludi Victoriae, but that meant days left over, and certain days were obviously more important than the others... saints, she was even starting to think like those scorekeeping secretaries.

This, of course, was why she needed Ashiol. To his credit, he had done well, turning up when he should, standing at her side, making the more important sacrifices, and not showing any obvious signs of being either drunk or mad. Either her mother was wrong, or he was exceptionally good at hiding his weaknesses.

No wonder Isangell was tired. Thank the saints for the nettlebane that the dottore now prescribed on a regular basis, to shut the swirling schedules and timetables and rituals out of her mind for a few hours at a time so that she could sleep.

'High and brightness?' one of the maids called out. 'It's time to dress.'

The fire gown, adorned with crisp black tumbling leaves, was the finest yet that Velody of the Vittorine had made for her. It would only be worn once. Isangell might as well burn her gowns in the sacrificial grate. Tradition required that for every festival day, there must be a new baubled sheath for Isangell to wrap herself in for the latest display of decadence.

At least she was keeping the dressmakers employed.

Isangell let her noxgown slide from her skin, her eyes on the silken fire dress. It swayed in the fingers of the maids who held it ready, as if the flames it displayed were real, and it might dissolve into ash and smoke at any moment. She could almost feel the heat seeping out of the fabric into the air of the room.

She allowed the maids to help her into the soft corset first. They tightened the stays, not as narrowly as they would have done in her mother's youth, or her grandmama's. Waistlines were less prized than they once had been. It was all about the fall of the fabric.

Thank goodness she had been blessed with narrow hips.

Isangell breathed in as the fire dress was slipped over her shoulders. It felt like a heated embrace. Should silk be this warm? One of the maids brought a looking glass to her, and she found herself gazing at the shimmer of orange and black silk. She looked taller, older, in this gown. She turned slowly, noting how low the dress dipped in the back. Daring, but not too scandalous.

For a moment, the thought of wielding the sacrificial knife herself flashed through Isangell's mind. She had no idea where it came from, but she could almost smell the blood...

The familiar rustling sound of maids brought her back to herself and she stood straight-backed as they fussed around her with sandals and hair pins and cosmetick.

It was only a dress. She had to be imagining that the room was full of new shadows that watched her every move.

VELODY WAS NOT sure how it had started, but Delphine and Macready were arguing about her. 'It's a tradition,' said Delphine.

'Do you have any idea how many people turn out to see the sacrifices?' Macready countered. 'It's a riot waiting to happen, with melon slices on the side.'

'You would have to be there as sentinels anyway, with Ashiol on stage,' said Delphine. 'If Velody is there too, it makes it easier to keep an eye on them both.'

Macready's eyes narrowed. 'It's a fine turn of argument you have there, lass. We'd need all our sentinels on full alert for the two of them, and that's a lot of trouble just to catch sight of a frock we've all seen every day for the last month.'

'This is Velody's one chance to see that gown she worked her fingers to the bone to finish, as the city will see it, before it is torn off the Duchessa's body and discarded into the rag heap,' Delphine snapped.

Velody, who was amused at first by the two of them bickering over her plans for the day, thought it was perhaps the appropriate time to assert her own wishes. 'If any of the Creature Court wish to challenge me, they will be able to find a better time and place than a public sacrifice. If nothing else, there will be an audience of thousands ready to pelt miscreants with honey cakes.'

'You don't take this seriously enough,' Macready warned.

'Crane and Kelpie can watch over Ashiol,' Velody told him. 'You and Delphine can stand with me. It will be your chance to teach her what it means to be a sentinel.'

'That's not funny,' said Delphine, her expression turning flat.

'Speaking as the person who was just reminded that her life's work is to fill a rag bag, I find it hilarious.'

Delphine stood up with great dignity and flounced towards the staircase. 'I am not a sentinel!' she declared. Macready and Velody exchanged a look.

A few minutes later, Delphine's voice floated down from

her room. 'I am going to the sacrifice, though. Don't you dare leave before I'm dressed.'

~

IT WAS rare that one of these Palazzo farces allowed Ashiol to wear a costume he considered anything other than eye-scratchingly embarrassing. To ensure he did not eclipse the Duchessa's finery, he was allowed out in all black today, with only a few embroidered threads of orange and gold. He wore a chunk of honey-amber at his throat that matched the long trail of beads that fell from his cousin's headdress to wind around her neck.

The shoes provided for him were ridiculous concoctions: too tight, soles so thick you couldn't feel the cobbles beneath. Ashiol had swapped them for his favourite soft leather boots the second the tailor's back was turned.

Luckily few people paid attention to what the consort was wearing. Isangell was useful like that. All eyes went straight to her.

The Circus Verdigris was packed, racks and rows of people pressed into benches and scaffolding around the wide grassy arena. They were hungry for the show — for the Sacred Games that would fill the long hot day — but the performances of animals, gladiators, wrestlers and dancers would not begin until after the Duchessa's sacrifice had been made.

For the good of the city.

It felt alien, being out in the daylight, let alone blazing sunshine. Ashiol, used to dangers falling down on him from the sky, felt oppressed by the brightness. Or maybe he had miscalculated how much imperium he needed, to stay on his feet. He stood behind the Duchessa as she led the chanting song of summer and sacrifices, and wished he had brought a flask.

A sturdy lamb was caged beside Ashiol, its eyes already dull from the philtre it had been given by the priests. Ashiol had been doing this since he took his man's robe — he knew by rote the cuts he would have to make to bare the animal's innards to the sun. At least he was allowed to slash the throat first, one long cut to let its life's breath out before the real mutilation began.

No different to what he had done to Poet, and the others, more than once.

The sun was making him dizzy, and a vision overtook Ashiol for a moment. He imagined himself forming a long chimaera claw and carving the lamb up that way. The blood really would spurt.

Isangell's hymn came to an end. The priest brought out the lamb, managing to make it look somewhat energetic as they spread it on the altar. Isangell lifted her knife, letting the entire stadium see the sunlight glint from the blade, then turned and passed it to her cousin.

Rituals. Always controlling women, limiting how strong they could be. Ashiol had never thought about such things before Velody took her place over him.

He stood before the lamb, knife poised to strike. 'Next time, gosling,' he said conversationally in a tone low enough that only Isangell and the nearby servants and priests could hear, 'you should spill your own blood. New traditions. Why the frig not? Give them a real show.'

Isangell gave him an odd smile, as if she was contemplating the idea.

Ashiol brought the knife down in a killing stroke, letting the blood spray forward over the altar. Then the cuts, light and swift, careful not to pierce the vital entrails beneath.

Ashiol slid his hands inside the corpse of the lamb, feeling the heat of it infuse his skin. He drew out the entrails as he had been taught, letting them web and hang between his fingers. No obvious augurs of doom here — no maggots or blight.

He walked the bounds of the Circus Verdigris once, looping around the central altar and letting the blood drip from the entrails on to the grass, sanctifying it. When he returned, he handed the gory mess to the Duchessa, who carried a pale clay bowl in which to receive them. Ashiol painted a long stripe of blood on her face as the sacrificial 'kiss', and she returned the favour, dipping her finger into the squishy contents of the bowl once and daubing his forehead before taking the bowl to the fire to burn the entrails. There was that smile again. Perhaps the sunshine affected her too? He had never seen Isangell so relaxed around a blood ritual, like a cat waiting her turn to lick out the bowl.

The ashes were supposed to be baked into some kind of ceremonial cake, but Ashiol had little interest in that. He had done his part.

There were more hymns as he stood there, sun baking the blood dry on his skin. He could feel Velody in the crowd, her heartbeat strong and her scent drawing him in. Macready was at her side, and the blonde demme, Delphine. Her scent was stronger than ever before — was it true Macready was trying to turn the wench into a sentinel? Stranger things had happened.

Crane and Kelpie were further away, but Ashiol could sense them too.

Isangell came forward again, her fingers black with wet ashes, and drew a new smudge down between Ashiol's eyes, lingering over the touch. Around them, the priests sang their interminable song.

Bring on the fucking gladiators, Ashiol thought. *This is torture, and I should know...*

When the next chorus of voices raised in song, he heard the first scream. It was not here, not anywhere near the Circus Verdigris, but he felt the sound tear up from under the city as if it were directly connected to his veins. *Livilla. Livilla. Livilla.* He knew her voice before he even recognised the sound.

He searched the crowd for that familiar pulse and found one figure standing very still, her pale face standing out beneath long dark hair: Velody met his eyes and nodded slightly. She felt it too. He saw her turn and vanish into the crowd.

Ashiol touched Isangell's arm. 'I have to go.'

She stared at him, her disbelief evident. '*Now?*'

'I'm sorry,' and he almost was, but his mind was underground, racing after Velody, wanting to know what the hell those otherworldly screams meant. 'Is the ritual done?'

'Would you care if it was?' Isangell said impatiently. 'Oh, go.'

Ashiol took the bowl from her hand, marked her forehead with ashes in return, then bowed formally and withdrew from the altar. The crowd did not react until he reached the edge and they realised that he was actually leaving. Isangell threw up her hands and cried something to them. Something diplomatic, he expected.

Ashiol could feel Crane and Kelpie, moving in the same direction, but out of reach. It didn't matter. He tore away from the crowded Circus Verdigris, heading for the nearest cluster of buildings. There, in the narrow alley between a temple and a pie shop, he shaped himself into a small army of cats and scrambled for the nearest drainage area that led down below, taking the shortcut through the Killing Ground and Angel Gardens.

He smelled the blood before he reached the Haymarket, strong and pungent with the scent of wolf on it. A moment later, a wave of animor tore through the tunnels and he quenched as much of it as he could, without thinking.

Not Livilla. She was still alive, still screaming. Her pain bubbled up around him, clear and hot and angry as the dizzying rush of animor was released into the sky. Ashiol quenched what he could, and it made him faster, stronger.

When he reached the cool concrete floor of the Haymarket, Ashiol shaped himself roughly into Lord form, tall and glowing, and surveyed the scene.

Velody was there, skin glowing brightly, her eyes dark. She made for the stairs a moment before he did, and the sentinels fell in behind them all as they hurried along the balcony.

Livilla sat on the floor of her bedchamber, drenched in blood and keening like a child. The raven lad, Janvier, lay outstretched on her bed, recently dead. Ashiol could still taste his animor deep in his own body, like the opposite of an ache.

Livilla glowed with newly quenched animor, despite her misery. His demme. There was nothing of the calculated Lord about her now, not a hint of artifice. Her face was smeared with blood and tears and cosmetick, and Ashiol could see for a moment the scared, raggedy creature she had been when she first found the Creature Court.

She had the bloodsoaked body of her second courteso, Seonard the wolf boy, in her lap. He was limp and barely breathing. Nothing of him left, only flesh and bone, but Livilla still clung on.

Ashiol stood over Livilla, looking down at her. 'Let go of him,' he said, in a gentler voice than he would have used on anyone else.

'No,' she said, barely breaking out the words between cracked lips, her voice hoarse from screaming. 'I won't.'

He felt Velody's presence beside him, her hand brushing

his, the smell of her body overwhelming even the blood and animor that filled the room. 'What is she doing?' she asked in a small voice.

Crane volunteered the answer. 'She's trying to keep him alive, using her animor. He's — it's too late for that.'

'She'll kill herself,' Ashiol said roughly, and went to his knees. 'Livilla. Sweetling, you have to release him, or you'll follow.' He reached out, wanting to touch her, to brush the pain away, but she jerked back out of reach.

'No,' Livilla hissed between her teeth, pale and broken as she was beneath all the blood. 'Garnet's gone, Mars doesn't love me any more. My boys are all I have.'

Saints and devils, she had gone too far. She was clinging to the boy with everything she had, and Ashiol could feel her own power fading. Her heartbeat was as weak as a baby bird. Whatever she had done to him, however she had hurt and betrayed him, whatever she had become while he was gone, he was not going to let her die like this.

Mars had not stopped loving her, Ashiol knew that much. No one could. Damn her to the seven hells. She was the first demme he ever cared about, and seeing her wrecked like this only made those days clearer in his mind.

They were curled up like cubs in a bed, Garnet and Livilla, Lysandor, even the boy Poet, holding on to each other, sick and miserable, knowing Tasha was gone, and the connection between all of them would be broken too, and this was the last time, the really last time they would be a family.

He wasn't sure if it was a real memory, but it came from a place he had not thought about in so many years. It felt real.

Ashiol reached out his hand to stop Seonard's heart. He had to release the link between the courteso and his mistress, or she would die. Livilla's nails lashed out, striking him back, scratching hard to keep the hand away from her boy.

'No,' she said fiercely, and Ashiol felt her heartbeat

strengthen a little. 'I'll kill you if you try, Ashiol Xandelian. I'll bite your eyeballs out.'

'Livilla,' he said, his voice low and pulsing into her. 'You're not alone. Let him go. Don't fall with him. I need you here.'

'Lies,' she said, but there was a lilt in her voice. 'I can't,' she said again, and then she exhaled, and Seonard's body shuddered and escaped her hold. The animor struck like a whiplash, crashing into Ashiol's body, and Livilla's. Behind them, Velody shuddered with the impact of quenching, and she let out a small sound of protest.

Tears began to run down Livilla's face again and she released Seonard, letting him roll from her lap. Ashiol grabbed hold of her. Janvier's animor, and Seonard's, burned inside his blood. More than ever he needed to run, fly, eat, fuck. It felt like his skin was being flayed from his body.

Livilla pressed into him, shaking, needing him. 'Who did this?' she wailed.

Ashiol hadn't considered that question. He wasn't capable of rational thought right now. The animor was burning its way through him. 'You don't know?'

'I found them torn open, barely breathing,' she said into his shoulder. 'I'll kill them, Ash. Whoever it was. I will rip them apart. Those boys were *mine*.'

No one could understand the love between a Lord and their courtesi, the loyalty, the connection. No one who had not felt it. Velody would never know, but Ashiol remembered. Even when he hated Tasha, he would have died for her. When Mars was his courteso, he would have done the same, and even now the lingering sense of belonging to each other was there, never far away.

'I will help you,' he whispered into Livilla's hair. 'Whoever did this, I will help you kill them.'

Livilla shrugged him off, looking up instead to Velody, who stood awkwardly, watching them. 'I don't care what he says. He's not in charge any more. *You* are, Power and Majesty. Will you avenge my boys?'

~

VELODY BLINKED as Livilla stared her down so intensely. She had no idea what to say. What exactly did Livilla want in vengeance? Did she suspect one of the Court of doing this? It was hard to think rationally — to form any thoughts at all — with the scent of blood so thick and fresh in the room.

It made her hungry and revolted, all at the same time. She willed Ashiol to tell her what to say, but he gave her nothing, not even a look or a hint.

'This will not go unpunished,' Velody said, in as confident a tone as she could manage. 'I am sorry for your loss, Livilla.'

Seonard, whose eyes had lit up with such enthusiasm as he talked about the sky and the battles and sausages. Janvier... whom she knew nothing about, nothing at all. Velody had told herself she needed to pay more attention to the quieter creatures who crept along behind the Lords. They were all her subjects, not just the flashy and more dangerous ones. Now, for these two, it was too late.

Livilla's pain was like jagged glass, stabbing Velody from across the room. She had always thought Livilla was the kind of demme who felt nothing — but apparently not.

'I don't want your sympathy, Power,' she said now. 'I want your claws and teeth.'

Ashiol held Livilla with a gentleness Velody would not have expected of him, and then the Lord of Wolves was sobbing again, turning her face into his chest, clinging to him as if she were drowning.

Velody felt Poet's presence before she heard his step. Priest was there too, standing gravely near the doorway, eyes on Livilla.

Velody went to them both, speaking in a low voice. 'Who can have done this?' She felt safe to be ignorant in this matter, for once, as it didn't seem like Livilla or Ashiol knew either.

'Who do you think?' Poet said tightly. He had lost a courteso recently as well, Velody remembered. Not both, though, and it had been in battle, not like this. 'Which of us is not here, my lady Majesty?'

Livilla lifted her head at that. 'No,' she muttered. 'You can't think Mars would do this to me.'

'Aren't you the one who said he doesn't love you any more?' Poet reminded her. 'He's been busy, our Warlord. Two of Dhynar's courtesi have joined him already, and there are rumours...'

'Rumours?' said Velody. 'There's only a handful of us; the last thing we need is information being passed around in whispers. If you know something, say it.'

Poet glanced at Priest, who shrugged and spread his hands. 'We all neglected Dhynar's orphaned flock, my lady Power. Warlord took advantage. Word among the courtesi is that all four of them have vowed themselves to him.'

'But he already had three,' said Velody, thinking rapidly. She hadn't even wondered what had happened to Dhynar's courtesi, let alone asked after them. Some Power and Majesty.

What Velody did know was that Dhynar's four courtesi had been considered excessive. Poet had one courteso remaining. Priest had three — Livilla's were all gone. Warlord already had three, the greymoon cat, brock and bat. If Poet was right and Warlord now had *seven*, he was more than a force to be reckoned with — he was a danger to them all. 'I need to talk to Warlord.'

'If you can find him,' Poet crooned.

DELPHINE REFUSED to go running off with the others. She was not a sentinel, and the last thing she wanted was to come face to face with the two Lords of the Creature Court who had reason to believe otherwise.

So she sat through the games, turgid set pieces of gladiator against tigris, or historical battle re-enactments, and a team of fire-swallowers.

It being the chief day of sacrifice, there was a new blood sacrifice between each act. Without Ashiol standing at her side, the Duchessa should have summoned another man to play the consort. She did not. To the horror and titillation of the crowd, she slaughtered her own beasts, one after the other, with brutal efficiency.

By noon, with the hot sun burning down on them from above, the Duchessa's arms and legs were streaked with blood, though the flame dress still looked perfect and unmarked. Whatever fabrics Velody had used were worth their weight in gold.

It was the sixth sacrifice of the day. The Duchessa held a part-drugged dove in one hand, and a knife in the other. The priests around her were looking concerned. The crowd had stopped muttering in alarm and cheered her on.

The Duchessa stopped, and said something to the crowd that Delphine could not quite hear. Then she let the dove go. It lurched drunkenly away from her, and flapped its wings uselessly a few times before taking to the sky and making its escape. The Duchessa tipped her head up, watching it go with the apparent delight of a child, and she began to laugh.

Delphine shivered. The Duchessa spoke again, and this time Delphine heard every word.

'The Sacred Games are cancelled. There will be no more festivals in Aufleur. You should all return to your homes.'

Once she had finished speaking, the Duchessa bowed her head politely and stepped down from her dais. She was suddenly surrounded by lictors, who removed her quickly from the arena.

The air crackled around Delphine as the crowd muttered and complained and asked each other what she could have meant by that. Delphine squeezed her hands into tight fists. Something was dreadfully wrong, and the Duchessa was a part of it.

8

CHIEF DAY OF SACRIFICE

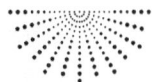

FOURTH DAY OF THE LUDI SACRIS, FOUR DAYS BEFORE THE IDES OF FELICITAS

DAYLIGHT

*V*elody went through the public baths on the way home. She had not touched Livilla or either of the dead courtesi, but the smell of the blood infused her skin and her hair.

Normally blood was a thing of excitement to her, though she hated to admit it even to herself. But whatever had been done to those boys was indescribable. Their blood smelled wrong, even as her own thrilled at the extra hit of animor she had quenched.

Crane followed, silently keeping an eye on her. There was so much Velody wanted to ask him, about Warlord, about what she should do. But he was her sentinel. She had to stop turning to him for answers. The answers were supposed to come from her. The Creature Court were looking to her for answers.

So few of us left.

Velody was damp and clean when they returned to Via

Silviana by the back alley. Mourning bells could be heard from the closed bakery next door, and Velody stilled for just a moment, remembering. Another dead child.

Her thoughts were full of blood and death, and she was not prepared for a kitchen full of flouncing Delphine in mid tirade. Rhian looked exhausted, as if she had been dealing with it for some time. 'What is going on?' Velody demanded.

'The Duchessa,' Delphine said, turning on her. 'If you'd stayed at the Circus Verdigris, you would know.'

'Something important came up.'

'More important than our livelihood? Than our life?'

'Calm down, Dee, she doesn't know,' Rhian said.

'Know what?' Velody asked, worried that Macready might have sent word ahead, that there might be more news of danger coming down upon them. More deaths? More to fear?

'The Duchessa,' said Delphine, her voice dripping with import, 'has CANCELLED THE SACRED GAMES.'

Velody just looked at her, and then turned and walked back out of the house. The mourning bells and the bright afternoon sun were infinitely preferable to Delphine's drama. 'Maybe I should live below,' she said to Crane, who had waited for her. 'Get away from this...' Mundanity.

Velody wanted to make dresses, she wanted to have a real life, she did. She craved those things. But there were days when they simply didn't matter. The scent of Seonard and Janvier's blood was still in her head — the glow of their animor sang in her blood. Festivals. Who cared about festivals?

'You should listen to her,' Crane said quietly. 'I can't remember a time when all the city festivals were cancelled. It never happens — the priests kept each of them going, even when the Duchessa was hidden away for her year of mourning. Delphine won't be the only one upset about it. Why would the Duchessa risk riots and protest? We should let Ashiol know.'

Velody stared at him. 'Are you serious? Livilla lost both her courtesi, Warlord might be on a bloodthirsty rampage, and you want to send a message to Ashiol about the Sacred Games?'

'It's all part of the same thing, Velody,' said Crane in that grave voice she liked and hated. 'Daylight and nox. When one thing breaks, it affects the other. When the daylight Duc died, we had sky massacres for days. If there's something bad going on with the Duchessa, it will come around to bite us, sooner or later.'

Velody nodded reluctantly. This was what it was, to be the Power and Majesty of the Creature Court. She could never assume that there was only one disaster at a time. 'Fine, but don't tell Delphine she was right. I don't think any of us could survive that.'

ASHIOL FOUND Heliora to be no help at all. She didn't bother disguising her impatience as he invaded her perfumed tent to rant about the death of Livilla's courtesi, and speculate who had done it. Who would dare?

He did not want to think it was true — that Mars might have done this to Livilla, of all people. It would mean that Ashiol knew none of them at all, that his history with the Creature Court meant nothing.

'I don't have any answers for you,' Hel said finally, her hands wrapped around a steaming cup of tisane. She looked unwell, but Ashiol pushed that out of his mind. He would deal with that later.

'You must be able to see something.'

Heliora twisted her face into an ugly expression. 'Why

must I? What have you done for me lately, Ducomte Xandelian? Why exactly should I give a flying frig that someone is running around killing Livilla's courtesi, or anything else to do with the Court?'

That took Ashiol aback. Hel had always been professional, above and beyond anything else. 'You're still the Seer.'

'Not any more, I'm not.' She set down her cup and gave him a hard shove, right in the middle of his chest. Surprised, he allowed her to push him out of the tent. 'I'm done, Ash. I quit. No more Seer. Go away!'

Ashiol could have argued, but the crazy look in her eyes made him think better of it. Obviously he was going to have to wait for her to get back what sense she normally had, before she would be of use to him again.

In the meantime, he could still smell blood on his skin. Time to do something about that.

Ashiol returned to the Palazzo, and made for the deep tiled bath in his rooms, not bothering to call servants to heat the water. Instead, he filled it from the pump and let his animor mist out of his fingers until the water steamed.

That was better. His muscles and his mind began to relax as the heat of the bath pressed around him. Ashiol closed his eyes, breathing.

Was this a direct hit on Livilla, or part of a larger, bloodier pattern? Impossible to know. He had to find out if Mars was guilty before the rest of the Court ripped him apart. He was so caught up in his thoughts that he didn't even bother to send for wine.

The door opened a little while later, and Ashiol knew it was Isangell without opening his eyes. She entered the bath chamber, her feet making a soft sound against the tiles.

'Would your mother be happy to know you were here?' he asked, dipping his head all the way underwater before surfacing. He could still smell the boys' blood, and between that and the extra pulse of animor, he was in no need of a drink.

Meat, though. He would need to eat something, and soon.

'Of course not. She'd probably try to have the lictors assassinate you.' Isangell sat primly on the ridiculous chair by the mirror. Ashiol had never used the thing. Four sticks of sugar and a puff of satin did not count as furniture in his world.

He shook water from his hair and then looked at her, really looked at her. Her hair was unbound, her feet bare, and she was still casually dressed in the same festival gown. She smelled faintly of blood and ashes, though her skin had been scrubbed clean. There was one dried spot of blood near her ankle. 'A little informal, aren't we?'

'I like this dress. I don't want to take it off.' Isangell plucked at one of the leaves of black silk, and smoothed her fingers over the flame-coloured skirt. 'I'm hiding from Mama,' she confessed. 'She was shouting so much, it gave me a headache.'

Ha. Anything that upset Aunt Eglantine was all right by Ashiol. 'What did you do, use the wrong fork at lunch?'

'No,' said Isangell. 'I cancelled the rest of the Sacred Games. And the whole Ludi Victoriae. The Mercatus can stay, as it's basically just a big market, but the cavalry parade from the second day is gone.'

The words sank in slowly, but Ashiol wasn't sure what to think of them. 'Are you serious?'

'Deadly serious.'

He felt laughter bubble up inside his chest. Crazy. Isangell was crazier than Heliora and then some. This was what they got for putting a nineteen-year-old demoiselle in charge of the city. 'What the seven hells do you think you're doing?'

'You're the one who said festivals were pointless,' she reminded him.

'I was teasing you. That's my prerogative, I'm not the Duchessa d'Aufleur...' Oh, holy shit, Aunt Eglantine was going to blame him for this. Ashiol was lucky the priests weren't banging down the doors of the Palazzo already, threatening to overturn the government.

In fifty years, no one had cancelled the Sacred Games. Or any festival, that he knew of.

'Silly Ash.' Isangell slid to the floor next to the sunken bath, all arms and legs and tangled hair. 'I'm tired, that's all. There was a ceremony practically every day this month. Cerialis will be calmer; I'm sure I will be able to cope again by then. There's only half a dozen or so.' She laughed, a wretched baby-giggle. It didn't sound at all like her. 'Then again, maybe I won't. Maybe they can all just get used to it. No more festivals.'

Ashiol had always been the black goat of the family. It was oddly charming to have been eclipsed by his baby cousin. And yet — no, there was something wrong here.

'That's not all,' Isangell said gravely, leaning down. 'I've made a decision about my husband.'

This was more alarming. 'You said you'd wait,' Ashiol said cautiously. The last thing he wanted to deal with was some clumsy Great Families oaf poncing around in scarlet and purple thinking that sharing Isangell's bed gave him power over anyone or anything. 'Weren't you going to parade the Great Sons around for a couple of years before you made your choice?'

'I don't want one of them,' Isangell said, smiling in a way she never had before. There was something of Livilla about it. Predatory. *Run away*, his inner cats yowled. 'I want you,' said the Duchessa.

Fucking hells. Ashiol stared at her in horror. 'Isangell, I am not going to marry you.' What an appalling idea.

'But it's perfect,' she said, sliding a little closer. Another inch or so and she would be in the bath with him, pretty silk gown and all. He would have to have a word with Velody. Putting demoiselles in flame- coloured frocks obviously brought out unwanted bridal inclinations. 'You already serve as my consort in all but deed. No one could protest...'

'I protest,' Ashiol snapped. 'We're cousins—' But yes, he deserved the derisive laugh that statement earned. Marrying cousins was a Ducal family tradition. One of many reasons why Aunt Eglantine ground her teeth whenever she laid eyes on him. She had seen this coming, right from the start.

What could he say? He remembered Isangell's birth, had bedded his first lovers while she was toddling around in ruffled robes. The whole idea was revolting. He couldn't touch her, not like that. As for the idea of making him share responsibility for the damned city... no, no, no.

'It's all right,' she said softly, reaching out a small hand to touch his wet chest. 'Don't you see? Together we can make this city what it's supposed to be...'

That was enough. Ashiol stood up, rivulets of water running from his nakedness as he climbed out of the bath, towering over her. 'If I wanted you, don't you think I'd have taken you by now?' he growled. Deliberate cruelty, it was the only way. 'Go back to your dolls and dresses, Duchessa. If this city is too much for you, give it to someone else. But stay away from me.' He pulled on his leather trews and black shirt, searched for his boots. Where the bloody fuck were his boots?

'You can't leave me,' Isangell said in a shaking voice.

He couldn't listen, couldn't dwell on whether he had shattered her. He had to push her away so hard that she would never try this stupid pantomime ever again.

'I won't let you leave me.'

'I can,' Ashiol said flatly. 'I will. You broke the accord between us, and that changes everything. I'm gone, Isangell.

You won't see me again.' He looked at her just once before he left. There were droplets of bathwater staining the orange silk of her dress. Her face was wet too, probably with tears. He didn't care, not now, not after this. Had she wanted this all along? Had the wide-eyed innocence all been some kind of act to get him to agree to a marriage? 'Give my love to your dear Mama.' For once, he was doing exactly what Aunt Eglantine wanted.

Normally he would leave by the windows, but not this time. He didn't even waste time looking for those damned boots. Everything in these rooms belonged to or had been gifted to him by his precious cousin, who swore she wanted nothing from him in return. Ha.

Ashiol, the Ducomte d'Aufleur, strode out of the Palazzo barefoot, by way of the main corridors. It was probably for the best that no one tried to stop him. His mood was murderous.

VELODY AND DELPHINE had given up speaking to each other, both far too cranky and frustrated. Delphine could not get over Velody failing to share her rage.

Velody sent a mouse to let Ashiol know what had happened, but she refused to take Delphine's melodramatics seriously. Rhian devoted all her attention to making sure Crane's soup bowl was never empty, as it was more rewarding than trying to make peace between the other two. Crane was quiet at the best of times, and knew better than to speak up when the demoiselles were all in this kind of mood.

Finally the door darkened and Ashiol strode in. He was a mess, with damp, straggly hair around his neck. He had hardly managed to button his shirt properly, and his feet were bare. Anger radiated from him, hot pulses that practically bounced off the walls. It made Velody want to lick his skin.

'Is the Duchessa really serious?' Delphine demanded of him. 'She can't mean to cancel all the festivals forever.'

Ashiol barely even glanced at her. 'We have to find Mars,' he said to Velody. 'Fast. Before things get out of control.'

'He's already killed two people,' Velody said. 'I'd say they were already out of control.'

'Oh, no,' he said grimly. 'Out of control is what happens when Livilla gets hold of him. She's crazed right now. We can't afford to lose another Lord.'

'So you lied when you told her you would avenge her boys?' Velody was surprised how much that offended her.

'No oaths were sworn,' said Ashiol.

'Are you sure it was Warlord?' Crane said unexpectedly. 'It doesn't seem right.'

'Nothing has been right about this damned Court for as long as I can remember,' Ashiol growled. 'We're crazy and we make each other bleed. What else is there to know?'

Velody looked at Crane. 'What are you thinking?'

The young man looked serious. 'For a start — since when does a Lord cut open someone else's courtesi, and not stick around long enough to quench them? I'm used to the Lords and Court making no sense at all, but... it's not selfish enough.'

Velody glanced back at Ashiol, who calmed down enough to take a seat at the table. Rhian put a bowl of soup in front of him the second he sat down. 'He has a point,' he grunted.

'If it wasn't Warlord, then where is he?' Velody asked. 'Doesn't he sleep with Livilla? Finding him shouldn't be that hard.'

Ashiol shrugged, glancing at Crane. 'He has his own territory down there. Doesn't he? Can't imagine Garnet welcomed him to break bread with him and Livilla that often.'

'Warlord and Livilla used to share the apartment below Garnet's, but there was some kind of fight a few months ago. After that, Warlord took over the Museion,' said Crane. 'It stood empty for a long time after Garnet took it away from you.'

There was something cold and horrible about Ashiol's face in that moment. 'Makes sense,' he said, and lifted the spoon to his mouth, eating without thinking. 'What's in this?' he asked after a moment.

'Vegetables,' said Rhian quietly. 'Herbs. Salt.'

Ashiol stared at it, as if wondering where the food was. Velody understood that much. Her craving for meat had intensified since she came into her powers. Pulses and nuts didn't cut it any more.

'He's not at the Museion,' Macready announced, appearing in the kitchen doorway. He took one look at Ashiol and relieved him of the confusing bowl of soup, slurping it standing up as if it was a mug of tea. 'Priest and Poet took the place apart down there. No sign of him anywhere in the Arches.'

'How is Livilla doing?' Ashiol asked.

Macready just looked at him. 'You really gave a frig, you'd not have fled the second you prised her talons from around your neck.'

'You go too far, sentinel,' Ashiol said in a dangerous voice.

'So sorry, my King. Did I forget to show you proper respect? I'm mortified, so I am.' More slurps. 'Is there anything you need from us, lady Majesty?'

'Where did Dhynar live?' Velody asked. If it was true that Warlord had taken over Dhynar's courtesi, might he not have taken over other things of his?

'He wouldn't be there,' Crane blurted. 'Lords don't move into the territory of a fallen Lord straightaway, it's not...'

'Not the done thing?' Velody said lightly. 'You may not have noticed, seigneurs, but your world has changed quite a bit lately. I don't think the old rules necessarily apply.'

'You're telling me,' Ashiol muttered. 'So, you intend to return to the Arches and hunt down our murderer?'

'Apparently I have nothing else to do, since the Duchessa cancelled a month's worth of Sacred Games and half my commissions will no longer be needed.' Velody stood up. 'You don't have to come with me.'

Ashiol just looked at her, and she smiled. He would follow her, of course. They all would. She was the Power and Majesty.

9

CHIEF DAY OF SACRIFICE

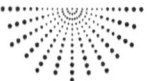

FOURTH DAY OF THE LUDI SACRIS, FOUR DAYS BEFORE THE IDES OF FELICITAS

DAYLIGHT

*M*acready walked through the Arches, following closely behind the two Kings with Kelpie at his side. It was a job and a half to get Crane to nest instead of coming along, but the lad was sleep deprived enough that they were able to bully him into resting.

'The Museion was mine,' Ashiol said in a low voice to Velody. 'Garnet kept Tasha's den after she died and he became a Lord. Lysandor and I went to Priest for a while. Then, when I became a Lord, I took the Museion as my territory. It stayed mine until... much later. Garnet took it from me towards the end.'

Macready and Kelpie exchanged glances. Oh, aye, they remembered those times. Dark days indeed.

'Couldn't you have taken it back when you returned to Aufleur?' Velody asked. 'You're a King, Warlord is only...' She swallowed whatever she was going to say, but they all knew she had thought it. Ha.

Getting the hang of the hierarchy now, aren't you, my lovely? Kings beat Lords, Lords beat Court, everyone beats the sentinels, tralala.

'I never even thought of taking territory again,' Ashiol said, bristling up like a broom head. 'I just wanted to run away from this fucking city. Still do.'

'Should I have territory?' she asked him, still keeping her voice low. 'Does it — make me look less powerful, to live only above ground?'

'It makes you unpredictable,' he said. 'Don't lose that, Velody. Once they figure you out, they will own you. All of them.'

IT WAS a while since Macready was down this end of the Arches. There were more collapsed tunnels around here, and steps crumbling away. They emerged into the covered court-yard where the Museion stood — a half-broken building shaped like a temple, surrounded with marble statues and smashed columns. Ashiol looked as if he was being pulled in a dozen different directions at once.

'It's beautiful,' Velody said, displaying a certain amount of tact.

'Plenty of beauty in the Creature Court,' Ashiol grunted. 'Doesn't mean much.'

'He's not here,' Macready felt the need to point out yet again as they stepped inside the temple.

'There's something of him,' Ashiol said, his dark head moving back and forth like an animal on alert. He darted forward, around heavy shelves that had once been piled up with fancy books. There were still some vases and other sculptures here and there — most of them chipped or broken. Forgotten antiquities. Rubbish, basically, though

Ashiol had never thrown any of it away, and it looked as if Warlord had made few changes.

The Kings both went very still. Macready could smell what they did, if he concentrated. Blood. It was a subtle tang after the massacre in Livilla's rooms. But once you knew it was there, it could be nothing else.

Kelpie made a noise, just a small one, which was odd for her. Ashiol dragged aside a heavy statue of an ancient warrior to reveal a splash of blood, not fresh enough to be wet, on the pale flagstones. He licked a finger and rubbed it roughly against the surface, inhaling the scent. 'Mars,' he agreed. His eyes went distant.

'What is it?' Velody asked.

'That scent,' Ashiol said, his head moving back and forth as he tried to work out the puzzle. 'There's something...' Then his eyes fell on Kelpie, and his lips curled back in the hiss of a displeased cat.

Macready tensed, ready to stand between them if he had to. What the hells was going on?

Kelpie folded her arms, looking unsurprised at his reaction. 'None of your business, Ash.'

'Oh, isn't it?' Ashiol advanced on her. 'What do you know, Kelpie? What have you been keeping from us? Where is he?'

'I don't know that,' she flung back. 'Why would I know?'

'Because,' he said, teeth bared, 'I know who your lover is now.'

'You're slipping if it took you this long,' she said defensively.

Macready stared at Kelpie, as shocked as if she had turned up to battle in a frilly frock. 'Oh, lass,' he said, and he wasn't careful enough to keep his voice neutral.

'Don't you dare judge me,' she flung at him. 'We don't always have a choice.'

Ashiol prowled around her, nostrils flaring. 'Are you saying he forced you?'

'No, I'm not saying that,' muttered Kelpie. 'I'm saying I didn't have a choice. And I don't know where he is. Warlord doesn't share secrets with me.'

'You might know something without realising it,' Velody suggested. 'Any hint of where he might have gone to hide if he was hurt...'

'Don't you think I would tell you if I knew?' Kelpie demanded.

'I have no idea,' said Velody, which was a fair enough call.

Ashiol turned away with an impatient sound and shaped himself into his swarm of black cats, slithering out of his fallen pile of clothes and converging on the patch of blood again. He licked at the stain, little rough tongues taking it in.

'How did I not know this?' Macready asked Kelpie in a low voice, but she silenced him with a quick shake of her head.

Ashiol lifted his many small black heads and sniffed the air, then took off in a rush.

Velody sighed, unbuttoning her dress to follow. 'Bring the clothes?' she pleaded to Macready before she shaped into her army of little brown mice, ready to chase after Ashiol wherever he went.

THEY CLAMBERED around tunnels and pipes, and emerged in a part of the upper city Velody did not know, though the tilt of the narrow alley suggested they were on the side of a hill. She shaped herself into Lord form, the glowing whiteness of her skin making her feel better about her nakedness. 'Where are we?'

Ashiol, casually human and unconscious of his own

133

nudity, placed his hands against the stonework. 'The Silver Captain had a nest here. But he's dead.'

'Does that mean anyone can get in?' Velody asked.

'It should mean that no one can. But a lot of rules have been broken lately... damn him.' He punched the stone with brute strength, not caring what it did to his knuckles.

'Are you angrier at Warlord for getting hurt, for going into hiding, or for sleeping with Kelpie?' Velody asked dryly.

Ashiol gave her a look that reminded her he was every inch an aristocrat. 'There's the small matter of him slaughtering two of the Creature Court's children.'

Oh, no. Velody was not going to let him get away with that. 'You don't believe he did it.'

'I don't want to believe it. But I was gone five years, and people change. Besides, it doesn't matter if he is guilty or not — the others believe it. They will tear him apart.'

'And we'll never know the truth,' Velody said, frustrated beyond all belief. 'What is your plan? For us to stand between half the Court and Warlord, to fight them? No. It will not be like this. However you have dealt with things in the past, it changes now. We are not going to lash out like frightened animals. When we find Warlord, we will discover the truth like humans. A fair trial.'

Ashiol stood in front of her, getting in her face, so she could feel nothing but his anger and his animor. 'And who will be the judge?'

'I'm the Power and Majesty,' she said coldly. 'Who do you think?'

'One way or another, this will tear the Court apart.'

'No,' Velody said decisively. 'If Warlord is innocent...'

'None of us are innocent.'

'Then someone else did this, and we need to know who, as fast as we can.'

'We're in agreement.'

'Yes, we are.' They were both still tense, facing off against each other. Violently in agreement. 'I don't believe anything in the Creature Court is as it appears to be.'

Ashiol's hands clenched and unclenched against the stonework. 'Send one of your mice to let the sentinels know where we are. I want to see if any of them can get into the nest of one of their fallen comrades.'

Velody ignored the fact that he had not said 'please'. 'Couldn't you just knock?'

Ashiol gave her a bloodthirsty look.

Velody took her place next to him, pressing her hands against the stones. 'Warlord,' she said, infusing her words with animor. '*WARLORD.*'

'Send the mouse,' Ashiol said harshly, behind her.

There was a long grinding sound and then the stones parted, opening up to reveal a small narrow space. A courtesa stood there, eyes bruised and wary. 'You don't have to shout,' she said. 'We heard you coming.'

Ashiol made a noise in the back of his throat and lunged forward. Velody caught his arm, fingers digging into his skin. 'Wait,' she said sharply. Possibly there was a layer of animor reinforcing those words too, or maybe she just getting better at being authoritative.

He snarled. 'Clara, where is he?'

The courtesa looked to Velody, and then stepped back, letting them pass. Ashiol held back enough to let Velody walk ahead of him. It was an odd space, like a room cobbled together from leftover boards and bricks. The ceiling had a deep slope to it, making the nest somewhat triangular. A courteso, the one whose creature was the brock, knelt beside a narrow bed, and Warlord lay upon it. There was no blood visible, but the room stank of it.

'What happened to him?' Velody asked.

Warlord turned his head weakly towards her. 'Your hands,' he said in a soft croak.

'He doesn't make much sense,' Clara said. 'He almost died. Lost a lot of blood. We brought him back...'

A slender young man, Warlord's third courteso, stood beside her. 'Maybe we shouldn't have,' he said gruffly. 'He'd gone so far. Not sure all of him came back.'

'Your hands,' Warlord said again, more forcefully. 'Yours. Velody —' He winced and closed his eyes.

'How did you get in here?' Ashiol asked.

'My master taught us,' said another voice. Velody's senses prickled and she turned her head to see two young courtesi in the entrance behind them. Grago and Farrier. Dhynar's men. The stripecats and slashcats. Blocking the only way out of the nest.

'Your master never listened to the sentinels,' Ashiol scoffed. 'How did Dhynar learn such a skill?'

Grago, the one who had spoken before, gave Ashiol an unfriendly look. 'Warlord is my master now. My secrets are his secrets.'

'Hands,' Warlord said again, agitated.

Velody went to him, sitting on the side of his bed. There was something very wrong about his eyes. It reminded her of something, and she fought through her collection of broken memories to the grandfather who had built the family bakery. A strong, grey-eyed man who suffered foolishness in no one, and drove Velody's mam, papa and older siblings to distraction, working them all harder than they thought capable. He never did less than that himself. She could see him kneading with those powerful arms, barking orders at everyone. One morning he woke up with his arm hanging limp at his side, and something wrong about his eyes. He would go whole days without speaking at all, just staring at the wall.

Velody had gone half her life without that memory, and now here it was. This was happening more and more, as her animor tried to repair the part of her mind that was broken when the city of Tierce was swallowed by the sky. 'My hands,' she said, and held them out to Warlord.

Would he recover? He was so young to be struck down thus. Surely the Court would kill him rather than let a warrior live with all that animor, unable to use it against the city. No wonder his courtesi had hidden him. Should she be angry at them for that disloyalty against the Court? All she could feel was sympathy.

'You did this,' said Warlord, his dark eyes holding hers, his hands squeezing her fingers for a moment and then going slack. He took a shaky breath and fell still.

'Sleep,' said Clara. 'He struggles to stay awake — we've been giving him poppy juice for the pain.'

'He doesn't need poppy juice,' Ashiol snarled. 'He needs blood.'

'We gave him blood,' said the brock courteso. 'We're not stupid. It didn't help. Only the poppy juice helps his pain.'

'Who did this?' Velody asked. A reasonable question, especially with the imprint of Warlord's grip tingling on her hands.

'We don't know,' said Clara. 'He was broken and bleeding when he came to us at the Museion, and the bleeding didn't stop. I've never seen anything like it.' The bat courteso put an arm around her, and she leaned into him.

'He told us who did it,' said Farrier, turning a glare on Velody. '*Her* hands. He said so.'

Ashiol opened his mouth but Velody cut him off, sending animor in a sharp stab directly into Farrier's stomach. He fell to his knees in a gasp of pain. 'Don't waste my time,' she said. 'If I had done this, I would *not have asked the question*. Your former master may not have valued intelligence, but don't tell me Warlord is the same.'

'The scents are mingled,' said Ashiol. 'Mars's blood smells wrong, but I still don't know how. The poppy juice could be masking something.'

Grago, still at the sealed entrance, tilted his head. 'The sentinels are here.'

'Let them in,' said Velody, her eyes returning to the stricken figure of Warlord.

'You are not my Lord,' Grago bristled.

Ashiol flashed his teeth. 'She is the fucking Power and Majesty, stripecat. Show some respect.'

Velody sighed. 'You can't just tell him to respect me, Ashiol. What are you, five years old? Grago,' she said helpfully. 'Respect me or I'll sew your balls to my tapestry.'

Grago made a disgusted noise and opened the wall.

'Nice,' Ashiol said in an undertone.

'You think I was bluffing? I've put great thought into the necessary technique.'

'What the seven hells is this?' Macready demanded as he and Kelpie marched into the nest. Velody looked at Kelpie, whose eyes darted to Warlord on the bed, though she did not move from Macready's side.

'You speak like that to your betters?' Grago sneered.

Macready barely gave him a glance. 'This is a sentinel's nest,' he thundered. 'This belonged to the Silver Captain. It was not designed to be the playground of the Lords and Court. It's *ours*.'

'Macready, stand down,' Ashiol said sharply. 'We have other issues to worry about.'

'More important issues, of course,' Macready said, folding his arms. 'Everything is more important than the sentinels, as ever.'

'Shut up, Mac,' Kelpie said tightly.

'You're just as bad,' he growled at her. 'Did you give Warlord access to this nest? Is that how he got in?'

Kelpie looked utterly devastated. 'Is that what you think of me? That I would dishonour our fallen?'

'I have no idea what you would fecking do,' said Macready.

'I'm sure Warlord will be more than happy to fight a duel with you over the matter, sentinel,' Ashiol said forcefully, his voice reverberating through the room. 'If he wakes up.'

Her hands. Velody tuned out everyone and everything in the nest, staring at the backs of her hands, then her palms. Her hands. What had Warlord meant? Was he crazed from his illness and wounds?

Her hands. She remembered the cobweb shadow that pulsed over her skin after the time she and Warlord saved Poet from the sticky black noxcrawl. She caught flickers of it occasionally, but thought she was imagining it. It appeared when she was angry, or afraid. It got worse after the battle with Dhynar's shade. She had thought there was something wrong with her, or with her animor. Was it something else? Had something crossed over from the sky? Was it still inside her?

She worked on her sewing, and every stitch calmed her, brought her back to herself. The shadows had vanished.

Her hands.

She couldn't have done it, couldn't have killed Livilla's courtesi, or hurt Warlord, without knowing about it. Could she? Velody already knew that she could not trust her own memory. Between Garnet's games and the loss of Tierce, her mind was well and truly jumbled, like a tin of stray buttons.

Her hands. She laid one palm on Warlord's chest and his eyes flashed open. His gaze held hers for a moment, and then he shuddered and fell still again. It was several moments before she was certain he was still breathing.

Velody filled her hands with animor, until she could all but see light streaming out of her fingernails, and then laid her hands on him again, using the power to see inside his body. He was full of shadows. Here and here she could see where his own animor had been ripped out of him by force. It was already beginning to heal itself, tiny fragments sparking back into life, but they were struggling. He had drunk the blood of five courtesi, and he still teetered on the precipice. The line between life and death was so very thin.

Velody flexed her fingers and gave him some of her own animor. One push at first, and then another, and she could feel it inside him, a slow burn to speed up the healing process. They were going to need him.

When Velody thought she had done enough, she looked around the nest again and saw chaos. The sentinels, courtesi and Ashiol were all arguing fiercely.

'Quiet, all of you,' she demanded. 'What now?'

'I want them out of here, all of them,' Macready said hotly. 'This is a sacred place and naught to do with your Court. Send them back to the Museion.'

'No,' Velody said crisply. 'I'm sorry, Mac, but Warlord is in no state to be moved.' She looked across at their angry, defensive faces. 'I have no idea what is going on here, but someone is attacking the Court. Livilla and Warlord are both victims. We don't have time to play factions or argue who is the most aggrieved. All of the Court is in danger, all of us are vulnerable. We need to hold together.'

'Pretty words,' growled Ashiol.

'You can't just choose to respect me when I agree with you,' Velody flung at him. 'Keep your mouth shut. I need you to think for once. If Warlord isn't behind all this, then who is?'

She looked to her sentinels next. 'You too, both of you — I need you with clear heads. You know these people better than anyone...'

Ashiol snorted. Kelpie glared at him. 'Something to say, my King?'

Ashiol's eyes were on Velody, anger flooding through every word. 'What are you suggesting? We all hold hands and vow to cleave to each other and the world will be well?'

'I know stamping your foot like a child is more tempting right now,' Velody said, trying to keep herself calm so that her fears did not overwhelm her. *Did my hands do this?* 'But you must be able to see that it doesn't help.' She looked to Macready and Kelpie. 'I want one of you to stay here, keep an eye on Warlord and his people...'

'No,' said Kelpie.

'Come now, lass,' Macready said in a low voice, hand brushing her arm.

She shook him off. 'No. You'll stand up for an empty nest but not for us? I'm sick of it, Macready. The world does not live and die for Saint Velody!'

Velody blinked, startled at the sentinel's venom.

Kelpie turned on her, eyes blazing. 'No one bothered to explain it, I suppose. Why should they? You have so much to learn about the Lords and Court, and we've long realised that we don't matter, not to any of you. But the sentinels are a sacred order and our duty — our only duty — is to stand at the side of the Kings. We protect you with our blades and our blood. But we are not your servants or your spies or your whores. Warlord has five fucking courtesi right here to defend his body. That is *their* duty. Ours — saints help us — is to defend you and Ashiol when Warlord or his courtesi or someone just like you tries to rip off your skin and drink you dry.'

Velody had no idea what to say to that.

Ashiol had no such qualms. 'That's enough, Kelpie,' he commanded.

'Not nearly enough, my King,' she retorted. 'In case you haven't noticed, there aren't a dozen of us to clean up after you any more. There are three, and we're doing our best.'

'You didn't seem to mind stepping outside your duties to romp in Warlord's bed,' he said harshly.

Kelpie's face froze over. 'Thank you for reminding me of my place in the Court, my King,' she said woodenly. 'A whore after all. Good to know.' She turned, and walked out of the nest.

Velody watched her leave. 'Go home, Ashiol,' she sighed. 'I don't have any use for you right now.' Without waiting to hear Ashiol's response, she went after Kelpie.

She didn't have to go far. Kelpie was sitting in a small miserable huddle against a wall, only a street and a half away. Velody joined her, crouching against the cool bricks. 'What did Garnet do to you?' she asked after a long pause.

Kelpie almost cracked a smile. 'That obvious, is it?'

'I know he used the sentinels — the whole Creature Court — in ways they should not have been used. I don't know enough of the details.' There was a long silence from the sentinel. 'I need to know, Kelpie. You might not like me, but I am trying to be different to Garnet. I am trying to make something of this Court. I need to know what mistakes he made, so I can avoid them myself.'

'He took our honour from us,' Kelpie burst out, as if it hurt too much to keep it inside.

'You mean your blades? Or something more?'

'That was the start of it. We couldn't fight, which made us weak. Toys for his amusement. Spies, dolls. He sent me to Warlord's bed. The joke was that I wasn't even a spy. How could I be? Warlord knew who had sent me. The only effect it had was to piss off Livilla.' Kelpie sighed. 'Garnet took our blood and our dignity — he liked to frig me because he knew Ashiol and I had something once. But Ash was just as bad, in the old days, even if I did choose to sleep with him. At least Warlord knew he was using me. He was almost nice about it.'

There were no words for this. Velody thought about Crane, about how eagerly he hovered around her, how much he wanted to please her. It was different, she knew it was, but it still made her cringe inside. Power imbalance could so easily turn sinister.

'It's not just about the frigging,' Kelpie said suddenly. 'We meant something once. Being a sentinel was glorious. Garnet took it away, piece by piece, and we let him do it. There's a bond between Kings and sentinels. We can't help loving them. They treat us like dirt, but it doesn't matter because we have our honour. We're warriors, with a place in the Creature Court, a place in the war against the sky. Our deaths matter.' She turned and met Velody's troubled gaze. 'Mac was so angry about them taking the Captain's nest. I barely even registered it. I thought, what does it matter? We've lost everything else. But it *matters*.'

Velody took a deep, shaky breath. 'Ash gave you back your blades,' she said carefully. 'But not your honour.'

Kelpie nodded slowly.

'I'll work on that,' said Velody. 'I want to make the Creature Court sensible and strong, and that means bringing back the parts of it that were good, the parts that have been lost. I need you to help, to show me the way.'

'I don't know where to start,' Kelpie said helplessly.

Velody almost laughed. 'Neither do I.'

'Is —' Kelpie hesitated, and then blurted it out. 'Is that blonde flapper of yours really going to become a sentinel?'

'If she's worthy,' said Velody.

Kelpie looked grim. 'I don't want to trust you. I don't even know how to hope for it all to be better.'

'Try trusting me,' said Velody. 'Working with me. For a short while, that's all. What do you have to lose?'

'Nothing,' said Kelpie, but it wasn't a happy answer. 'There's nothing left.'

They sat in silence together for some time.

VICTORY OF BLOOD

FIFTH DAY OF THE LUDI SACRIS, THREE DAYS BEFORE THE IDES OF FELICITAS

DAYLIGHT

*O*nly a few months ago, Ashiol was keeping farmer's hours — sunshine and hay — and had the world really made sense then? Once he returned to Aufleur, he moved effortlessly back into nocturnal life, so quickly so that it felt wrong to sleep when it was dark outside.

He awoke from an exhausted sleep to find himself in a narrow cot in Macready's smallest, mustiest nest, north of the city, with no idea whether it was day or nox. His mouth tasted foul. Ashiol ran his hands over his face, almost — for a fraction of a moment — feeling the scars he had borne for five years. Scars he hadn't been able to see for most of that time, though there were days when he looked at his hands and they crumbled under his gaze, crusted and broken.

He breathed, reminding himself that he had his animor back. He was whole again. Whatever else he had to deal with, there was that.

'If you're expecting coffee and pastries, it's the maid's day off, so it is,' mumbled a voice from a little way away.

'Fuck you,' said Ashiol. He sent his animor out to check the sky, and recoiled with surprise. 'It's morning.'

'You slept like a daisy once you swallowed that third glass,' said Macready. He had been resting in a battered chair, his feet up on a box.

'The sky was calm all nox?'

'Aye,' said Macready. 'Would I not have woken you if it got exciting out there?'

'Hard to tell.' Ashiol sat up on his elbows, blinking in the near-darkness. Sleeping so long was alien to him. 'Don't you have places to be?'

'Solemn duty to guard your person from danger,' Macready said, in that light voice that sounded exactly the same as the voice he used when nothing was actually wrong. 'More than ever now, given that we have a bloodthirsty maniac making their way through the Creature Court.' He paused. 'Well, *another* bloodthirsty maniac.'

'Dead courtesi, a Lord wounded and rambling,' Ashiol agreed. He was starving, but after Macready's crack about pastries, he wasn't going to mention it. 'If I didn't know better, I'd say there was a new Power and Majesty in town.'

'Funny,' said Macready. The box creaked under his feet. 'You have a point, my King. If it's not our Velody, not you...' To his credit he didn't pause too long after that suggestion. 'Which of them has got themselves a taste for blood? Livilla herself?'

Ashiol had considered that possibility. The mingled scents at the scene threw him into confusion, and there was something about that woman... she was not the Livilla-child he had once known, the demme he was able to read like a storybook. Not any more. 'Could be,' he admitted. 'She hasn't been right for a long time.'

Macready laughed shortly. 'Are we only considering the suspects who might not be sane? I think I've spotted a flaw in that plan.'

Ashiol's stomach growled. He might be able to skip breakfast but the creatures inside him could not. 'Let's go.'

They were at the arse-end of the Alexandrine, right by the river, and it was only just beginning to get light. Ashiol stopped at a hot food bar and eyed the unappetising selection of cold pulses and pickled eggs.

'Not open yet,' the dame told him, sniffing against her sleeve.

Ashiol glared at her, and fished a silver duc out of his purse. 'Wine, meat. Buy it elsewhere if you have to. There's another of these in it for you if you don't make me wait long.' He threw himself on the nearby bench, impatiently.

The dame scuttled down in the direction of the docks. When she was gone, Ashiol saw a look he didn't like on Macready's face. 'What?'

'They all act like nobles,' said Macready, seating himself with deliberation. 'We forget, I think, that you really are one. You breathe it.'

'That has nothing to do with blood in the Haymarket, and Warlord flat on his back,' said Ashiol.

'Never said it did.' Macready helped himself to one of the dry rolls from the counter, since there was no one to stop him. He started to whistle, a slightly offkey rendition of something undoubtedly filthy. 'You were hard on Kelpie yesterday,' he offered some time later. It was almost a relief after the whistling.

'She deserved it,' Ashiol growled. *Don't go there, Mac. Seriously. You'll regret it.*

'For falling into bed with Warlord? She's hardly the first to have done that.' *Hypocrite*, went unsaid.

'For keeping secrets from her Kings,' said Ashiol.

Macready laughed. 'And considering how well you took the revelation, can you blame her for keeping quiet?'

'You knew, did you?' Ashiol accused.

Macready gave him that look he pulled out on special occasions, the 'I have half a decade on you and don't you forget it, laddie' expression. It never failed to make Ash want to thump him. 'I didn't know it,' he said finally. 'But I'd have kept her secret if she wanted it so. Were you listening to her words at all?'

'That she had no choice,' Ashiol said bitterly. 'Whatever that means. Is Mars supposed to have forced her?'

'Not in this lifetime,' said Macready. 'I think Garnet gave the order.'

Garnet, always back to Garnet. Ashiol stared into the distance. The dame hurried back with a basket, her cheeks red with the exertion. He should be able to talk about Garnet without feeling like the walls were about to fall in on him, crush him into fragments and dust on the ground. 'Made a habit of that sort of thing, did he?'

'Aye,' said Macready, eyes flat. 'He sent us spying, since we didn't have blades to make ourselves useful. Wouldn't put it past him to put Kelpie in Warlord's camp. If it annoyed Livilla, drove some distance between her and Warlord, all the better. Feck, he'd have done it to prove he could. Liked to show the sentinels who was boss, so he did.'

Ashiol's throat was dry. 'Where's that wine?' he snapped as the dame passed him. She fussed behind her counter for a and then emerged with a platter of sausage and oysters, with a dusty bottle of red wine that she poured into chipped cups.

Macready had obviously caught a flicker of contempt on Ashiol's face. 'You'll give that poor hen the second duc,' the sentinel warned, gulping from the cup nearest to him. 'Or I'll throw you in the river, King or not.' He made a face. 'Too early for this.' Didn't stop him refilling his cup.

The oysters were fresh, at least. Ashiol was swallowing the last salty morsel when a brown mouse skittered across the floor and up the side of the bench. Its eyes glowed for a moment and Kelpie's voice said, 'Get your sorry selves to the Palazzo. We'll meet you there.'

'Interesting,' said Macready.

'Where the hell is my coat?' said Ashiol.

ASHIOL GREW MORE and more tense as they walked up the road to the Palazzo. He didn't want to be here, not since Isangell turned into some kind of seductive harpy. He hesitated, as they rounded the crest of the Balisquine.

'Waiting for Saturnalia, are we?' Macready mocked.

Ashiol couldn't explain why he didn't want to take another step towards the Palazzo. *Damn you, Isangell, why did you have to screw everything up?* He gritted his teeth and continued on.

'Ay-aye, we're not the only beggars up early,' said Macready.

There was a crowd gathered at the Palazzo gates. There were often people hanging around, but this was different. Robes, veils, garlands... Priests, for the most part, and several people with scholar bands around their arms. Ashiol had a horrible feeling that he wasn't going to like whatever this mob had in mind. 'Let's go around the other way,' he suggested, but it was too late.

'It's the Ducomte!' cried one voice and then more. The crowd moved frighteningly fast.

'Feck,' said Macready. They backed up, but it was too open here, no narrow alleys to disappear into. 'What's going on?'

'Isangell cancelled the Sacred Games,' Ashiol said in a low

mutter, only now remembering. 'And every other festival this month.'

'That'll be popular,' said Macready. 'No touching the Ducomte,' he added in a bark, drawing his steel sword to keep the mob at bay. 'Stand back!'

'Please, seigneur,' cried one, and many others added their pleas to the chorus. 'You must beg the Duchessa to let us perform the ceremonies.'

'She won't listen to me,' said Ashiol, but they drowned him out with their cries.

'Please, Seigneur Ducomte, we can't miss another day... there are four days left of the Ludi Sacris. We must be allowed to complete the rituals.'

'It's one circus,' Ashiol said, raising his voice so they could all hear. 'Give her this. She's a demoiselle; let her have her way and she'll roll over like a kitten in a few nundinae.'

This caused ripples of panic to surge through the crowd. 'Seigneur Ducomte, we don't have nundinae to spare, there's the Mercatus to think of, the Equitum, the Ides, Ludi Victoriae...'

'Enough!' Ashiol yelled. He was tired and his head hurt. 'I can't help you.'

'If not us, Seigneur Ducomte, think of the city, you must save the city...'

Ashiol rolled his eyes at Macready. 'Like I don't already get enough of that.'

'I wouldn't laugh at this number of frightened priests,' said Macready. 'But I'm a commoner, so what do I know.'

Where are you? Ashiol heard Velody's voice in his head, clear and familiar.

Quarrelling with priests. You?

Around the back.

Why hadn't he thought of that? *I'll be right there.*

Ashiol and Macready found Velody near the merchants'

entrance at the back of the Palazzo gates. She sat on a slab of stone, with Crane and Kelpie on either side of her. They looked troubled.

'I received this for you at the house,' Velody said without ceremony, as Ashiol approached. 'I was lucky to spot it among the commission notes.' She handed him a pretty piece of card ringed with gold — the kind of formal invitations that the Palazzo servants sent out to members of the Great Families. It was Isangell's stationery all right, even stamped with her seal, but it wasn't her spiky handwriting, inviting him to tea with the Duchessa.

It was Livilla's.

Ashiol could have run, could have shaped himself into cats, could have flown through the corridors faster than any of them. But he needed his sentinels at his back. This was not a time for haste. Whatever Livilla wanted, whatever performance she was planning in that evil little bobbed head of hers, she would wait for her audience to arrive.

They marched in through the servants' entrance and strode along the familiar halls, heading for the Duchessa's rooms.

Livilla, here. Fuck. Livilla, who had kept a pet kitten because 'it reminds me of you, Ash', and then drowned it in a fit of anger when she felt he and Garnet were neglecting her. Livilla, who was now more like Tasha than he had ever believed possible. Petulant, destructive, powerful. Livilla, who was grieving and broken for the loss of her courtesi.

He had most assuredly been neglecting her, and this was his punishment.

The sentinels and Velody followed Ashiol as he looked from room to room. No sign of Isangell, but he could smell Livilla's recent presence here. There was cigarette ash on the carpet.

'Where would Livilla take her?' Crane asked aloud.

'No,' said Velody. 'Where would the Duchessa take Livil-la?' Ashiol looked at her, momentarily baffled. 'A scandalous-looking demoiselle comes to her,' she explained patiently. 'Claiming intimacy with you. Assuming they are acting in a civilised manner, where would the Duchessa choose to take her?'

'What makes you think they are acting in a civilised manner?' Kelpie said scornfully.

'They're both women,' said Velody. 'From what I've seen of Livilla, she likes to put on a show. She wouldn't just... pounce. She would play for a while first. Especially if she's doing all this to get Ashiol's attention.'

It was a horribly accurate assessment. Ashiol went back out into the corridor. He headed to the old Duc's rose atrium first, knocking aside pots and green fronds to check it was empty. If not there, then where? 'Which way is the walled garden?' he barked at a passing servant, not trusting his own memory. The maid scurried along ahead of them, leading them back out of the building and across the grounds that spilled down the far side of the Balisquine, past the glassy pools and fine statuary, past the scented lawn to the high hedge he remembered, and the polished, antique wooden door set into the hedge.

Ashiol sent the maid away and pushed open the door with both hands.

The walled garden was their grandmother's favourite place. The old Duchessa would invite her grandchildren for tea there only when they had been especially well behaved (for Ashiol this was almost never). As a child, Isangell yearned to hold dolls' tea parties there, and was never allowed.

It looked exactly the same as he remembered from his childhood. There were no fancy topiary animals or gleaming statues or scalloped beds as in the rest of the Palazzo grounds. No colour, just green herbs in the beds, neatly trimmed lawn, and jasmine vines climbing the walls. Simple. Calm. For a moment, the old Duchessa was alive again, sitting there with her giant teapot, passing the almond cakes. But no, she wasn't here.

Instead it was Livilla, dressed in a long white morning dress as if she was a daughter of the Great Families, all pearls and pale green accessories. She wore gloves, and even her cosmetick was muted. They had been right, damn it. Livilla was putting on a show.

She was alone, despite the table being set for three. As Ashiol came down the grey stone steps, Livilla dropped a sugar cube into her own teacup with a tiny splash. 'You're here,' she said, sounding pleased with herself. 'I knew you loved me really.'

'Where is Isangell?' Ashiol demanded as Velody and the sentinels crowded in behind him.

'Oh, Ash, it's too funny. The one demme you actually care about also happens to be the most important person in the whole city? That's the kind of thing people write ballads about.' Livilla tilted her head to one side. 'Someone should write a ballad about me. Don't you think?'

'I'm not going to ask you again, Liv.' He imagined breaking her open to get the truth. He would if he had to, she knew that. Would she push him that far?

'Here's the really funny thing,' said Livilla, in her sweet-as-teacake tone that didn't fool him for an instant. 'You came back for her. Not for us, for the Creature Court, not to stand at Garnet's side where you belong. Not to save the city. You came back here to play courtier to the pretty daylight Duchessa. What exactly does she have that we don't?'

'Apart from a soul?'

Her expression changed. 'Cheap shot, my King.'

'What have you done to her?' Ashiol roared. He felt a cool

hand on his arm and knew it was Velody. Her calmness drove him crazy at times, but still managed somehow to make him feel... less like shouting.

'Let me try,' Velody suggested, and walked over to Livilla, seating herself in one of the fancy lace-metal chairs. 'We found Warlord,' she said, those calm grey eyes of hers holding Livilla's. 'He was attacked. We don't know how yet — he wasn't able to tell us much. But we don't think he was the one who took your boys from you. You have both been victims here.'

Ashiol wanted to challenge her. Who was she to say that Warlord was innocent? There were so many possibilities. Velody's words were having an effect on Livilla, though, so he kept his mouth shut. For now.

'Are you sure?' Livilla said in a baby voice, small and vulnerable.

'Yes,' said Velody.

Ashiol admired her ability to lie like that, to make it sound like the world was a sane place, and she had an assured place in it. He almost believed her, and he knew she was making it up.

'Will he be all right?' Livilla asked, sipping her tea. So very civilised.

'We hope so,' said Velody. 'But he will need some time to recover. His courtesi almost lost him,. They gave him blood; it should be enough.'

Livilla started to cry, tears blobbing down her face as if she were a child. Her whole body shook, and she tried to put the cup down, but it slid off the table and spilled on the grass. Velody comforted her like she was Rhian or Delphine, hugging the viper and murmuring words of kindness to her. Demmes. Ashiol wasn't sure he understood them at all. 'Do you think he still loves me?' Livilla wept into Velody's shoulder.

'I don't think he has changed,' said Velody in a moment of pure diplomacy. She pushed Livilla's long black fringe back out of her eyes. 'Where is the Duchessa?'

'We were having tea, but she ran away,' said Livilla, using that little demme voice of hers, the one that always made Ashiol want to slap her. 'I don't think she liked me very much.'

Ashiol turned to throw orders at the sentinels, but Macready held up his hand. 'Do you hear that, my King?'

It was a soft sound, barely there at all, but when Ashiol paid attention to it he could tell it was a demoiselle singing. He nodded abruptly and turned around, leaving the walled garden.

Beyond the jasmine hedge was the ridiculous maze, everything that Grandmama's garden was not. A veritable zoo of topiary animals, bright and exotic blooms, hedges of twelve different varieties and heights.

Yes. Isangell. He could hear her singing.

Ashiol followed the path around, two rights and then a left, the pattern repeated. Here, nearly at the centre, was the avenue of saints and angels, glowing in the finest Atulian marble, and black basalt from the mines of Stelleza. There were alcoves along the edges and there — that one — that was where Ashiol had kissed Garnet for the first time, an awkward question of a kiss, half-expecting the other boy to thump him.

Gone, he's gone. He was gone long before he died. Move on.

What the hells was wrong with Isangell? Why was she singing? What had Livilla done to her? Ashiol rounded the corner into the centre of the maze and saw her, finally. His throat rasped dry.

Isangell sat in ladylike fashion on the back of a giant topiary snail. She still wore the flame-coloured festival dress from the previous day, her feet hanging bare and her hair tangled in its matching garland. Her eyes were... not right. No, not his gosling. He was the crazy one, everyone knew that. *Please, let it not be happening to her too.*

Ashiol would strangle Livilla in cold blood if she was responsible for this.

Isangell broke off her song when she saw him, and gave him a searching look. 'You have returned, cousin dear. Was I so terrifying?'

'Isangell,' Ashiol said in a quiet voice. 'You should come inside.' Had he done this to her?

'But then I won't be able to see the stars,' said Isangell, tilting her head to one side. 'I want to be here when they all blink out.'

'It's morning,' said Ashiol. 'We can't see the stars.' Daylight, they were supposed to be safe in daylight, nothing bad happened here.

'Can't you?' said Isangell. 'I can see them. Every single star. But they're going to go out soon.' She giggled, and that was not Isangell's laugh. Nothing like it. Not crazy, perhaps. Drugged.

Ashiol turned on Livilla, who was busy looking innocent. 'Potions, yes? Some of your fucking party powders? Tell me right now what you did to her.'

Livilla laughed. 'That's the amusing thing, darling. I didn't do a damned thing to your honey cake. She was broken when I found her. I like her like this, though. Far more entertaining than the dried-up little virgin I was expecting.'

'Why don't I believe you, Liv?' said Ashiol.

Isangell slid off the topiary snail and tumbled to the ground with a cry. Ashiol reached down to pull her to her feet.

'No,' said Velody sharply. 'Don't touch her.'

'What?' Ashiol demanded, his hands hovering only inches from Isangell. 'What is it?'

'Look at her back.'

Isangell stood up on her own, made a slow, teasing pirouette and then sank into a curtsey. 'My dressmaker!' she said delightedly. 'Ashiol, have you stolen my dress-maker? She's very lovely. If you want to marry her, I won't mind a bit. I'll throw may at your wedding. And sugared violets.'

The flame-coloured festival gown dipped low enough at the back that the thick black spiderweb inked across Isangell's skin was clearly visible. It flickered as Ashiol looked at it.

He knew what it was. Not the family complaint, then, nor potions and powders. Noxcrawl. The fucking sky had taken Isangell.

THE WEBBED pattern on Isangell's back was dreadfully familiar. 'My hands,' Velody said in horror, remembering what Warlord had said to her. She had feared that she was losing control of her memories or her body, but this... she had not seen the possibility of this. 'Ashiol, I think this is my fault.'

Ashiol turned to her, the anger radiating out of him. 'What have you done?'

The Duchessa giggled like she had been swallowing ansouisettes or party powders by the dozen.

'I made her a dress,' Velody said, the words coming out slowly as she thought about it. Everything was beginning to make sense, the horrible truth of it. 'The dress she's wearing. I think — it's poisoned with something from the sky.'

'It's noxcrawl,' said Ashiol dismissively. 'That much is obvious. When did you touch *noxcrawl*?'

'Poet,' said Velody. 'He was covered in the stuff. He half-

157

drowned himself in the lake to get rid of it. Warlord and I helped him... it was a month ago.'

'The lake should have cleansed it all,' Ashiol said impatiently. 'Even if you got some on you...'

'I saw webs like that, on my hands. Shadows, sometimes.' Velody stared at the dark, spreading pattern across the Duchessa's back. Her skin flushed with heat as she admitted it, finally. 'Darkness out of the corner of my eye. I thought it was normal, that it was the animor inside me. But I've been seeing shadows for some time.'

'You should have told us, Majesty,' Macready said in a pained voice. 'That's not an everyday complaint.'

'Why hasn't it just swallowed the Duchessa?' Crane broke in. 'When — when the Captain died...' and he broke off.

'He's right,' Kelpie said, her words coming out flat and hard. 'Noxcrawl doesn't work like this, all slow and sinister. It just *takes*.'

Ashiol seized Velody's arms, gripping her cruelly between his hands. 'What else, then? Why is this different?'

'I don't know,' she said angrily. 'I don't know what's important, I only know what you tell me. Let go!' But she did know. She had some idea now, at least. 'Dhynar,' she admitted, all in a rush. 'When I swallowed his tainted shade, I don't think he truly left me. Whatever he had twisted into, at the end. I kept hearing his voice, his laugh.' She didn't want to look into Ashiol's accusing eyes. 'I thought it was *normal*. I've always had strange dreams, and you told me that animor turns us into monsters. I thought it was part of the process.'

Ashiol stepped close to her, too close, his eyes roaming over her as if she was a slice of roast goat straight off the barbecue. He licked his lips, and Velody felt how dry her own were. She let him touch her, a brush of his palm over her arm, and then her shoulder. He leaned in as if he was going to bite out her throat.

Velody stood still, and let him.

His mouth stopped short of her collarbone, and she could feel his hot breath against her skin. Then she felt something else — the slow invasion of his animor sliding against hers. He was exploring inside her. Their only contact was between his mouth and her throat, but she could feel him everywhere.

Noxcrawl, Ashiol said inside her head. Velody's body ached all over, where he wasn't touching her. *It was here, I can taste the trail of it. And you have the stink of Dhynar's shade all over you.*

'Charming,' she said aloud.

Ashiol took her hands, lacing his fingers between hers. 'Here. It's concentrated here. Velody, what did you do?'

She could deal with anything if he kept his voice out of her head. If they all did. 'I worked,' she said, and felt her lips crack and tasted the iron tang of blood on them. 'I sewed. It made the darkness go away.'

'Ah,' said Ashiol. 'And you never thought to ask where the darkness went?'

The dress, *oh*, that beautiful dress. Velody reached out with a strand of her own animor and touched it tentatively, tasting it as Ashiol had tasted her. Now that her power was alive instead of being pushed away, the taint was obvious. The Duchessa's dress reeked of spoiled animor, of the seething noxcrawl and the death of Dhynar. 'Oh, saints,' she whispered. '*Priest.*'

Livilla turned to her at that, and all pretence at civilisation melted away. She curled back her lip and growled, her teeth sharpening as if she was going to shape herself into the wolf she was. 'What?' she said.

'I made a waistcoat,' confessed Velody. 'I used it like the Duchessa's dress, to make the shadows go away. I didn't *know*.'

'Priest,' snarled Livilla. 'You promised him the waistcoat

that nox, when you made your oath to me. You think *Priest* killed my boys?'

'I didn't say that,' Velody said quickly.

'It's not Priest,' Ashiol cautioned her. 'It's the sky. It's always the sky.'

'Then let the sky stop me from plucking every feather from Priest's demmes in retribution,' said Livilla. She unhooked her dress, letting it fall to the ground. She was naked underneath, and she glowed.

Velody had to stop this, before it became a bloodbath. 'No,' she commanded. 'It is not your place to stop Priest, or to hurt his courtesi. This is not the time for vengeance.'

Livilla growled again. 'There is always time for vengeance,' she said, and shaped herself into two slender wolves, running away through the gardens.

Velody stilled, forcing herself not to look at Ashiol as if he might have the answers. She had to be the one to provide answers. She was the Power and Majesty.

'I suppose,' said Kelpie quietly, 'we should thank the saints that there has been no massacre here in the Palazzo, too.'

The Duchessa moved, and they all flinched. 'I like you,' she announced to Velody with an adoring smile, and lay her head on her shoulder. 'You make such beautiful frocks.'

11

HELIORA

*R*aoul the Seer was an odd fish. On the streets we'd have called him 'touched' and left him to his own devices. In the Creature Court, he was everything. Ortheus (all hail the Power and Majesty) demanded that we treat Raoul like some kind of precious flower. The Seer spent most of his time in the Angel Gardens, wandering around the overgrown weeds and herbs like it was some kind of paradise, talking to the dead.

I'd only been a sentinel for a few market-nines when I saw Raoul lose himself in the futures for the first time. He went from a quiet, mostly sensible exchange with Ortheus and Argentin to a full-on panic attack, babbling about everything he could see. Once he ran out of words, he ended up flat on his back, his whole body convulsing. Argentin leaned over him, murmuring, and it was only afterwards I realised what he was doing — his hand pressed into Raoul's crotch, methodically bringing him off.

When the Seer gasped his release, the futures released him as well. I'd known that the Court were all tramps and tarts, but that was the first time I'd seen how casual they were about frigging, like it was as ordinary a need as catching your breath.

Raoul liked shiny things. Beads and baubles, necklaces. The

161

first bracelet I ever owned was a gift from Tobin — his embarrassed way of thanking me for our awkward tumble. It was a thin, simple chain of silver and I treasured it because I had never had anything special like that. Only things I'd ever held before that glittered were stolen, and on their way to be swapped for shilleins.

I wore my bracelet for three days before Raoul spotted it and put on that odd smile of his. Our Power and Majesty cleared his throat, and looked at me. Obeying Kings is what sentinels do.

I handed it over, and Raoul danced away happily with my bracelet gleaming on his wrist, along with the dozens of other pretties that he owned.

~

RAOUL WAS the Seer of the Creature Court for nine years. He used to be a clever fellow by all accounts, but consulting the futures for so long had left him simple in the head. Most of the time, anyway. When the futures hit him, or he delved deep into them at Ortheus's request, his voice took on a new timbre, an adult cadence. He became Ortheus's friend and equal in those moments, not his pet.

Nine years turned him into that. Next month I will have served the Court as Seer for ten.

~

ONE DAY I walked into the Haymarket to see Raoul standing on the metal railing. I think he was waiting for an audience. Or waiting for me. He swayed, and I said nothing, too afraid that any word uttered by me would make him fall.

He didn't fall. He stepped into oblivion quite intentionally. The sound as he hit the concrete was sickening. I ran to him, not sure what to do. He took several minutes to die, as I stood around and watched him breathe his last. Others came, and stared, and kept their distance. No one offered to share blood with him, to make it *unhappen. As he choked and wheezed his way into death, my eye was caught by the gleam of silver, that one thin bracelet among so many baubles, the thing I hated him for.*

The first thing I hated him for.

THE COURT LOOKED *at me oddly for days afterwards. I didn't know why. Witnessing death wasn't such a rare thing to any of us. The sentinels all but stopped speaking to me. Ashiol was unusually nice, letting me hang around and pester him instead of rolling his eyes or going off with Garnet and Lysandor like he usually did.*

I had no idea what that son-of-a-bitch had done to me until it was too late. Simple-minded? That bloody Seer had known exactly what he was doing when he ruined my life.

This is the thing I never told anyone about Raoul's death: for days afterwards, my dreams were full of him, and not just images of him falling to his doom. I could hear his thoughts, a steady rattle in the back of my head. Sometimes I even thought I could hear other voices, other Seers, chattering away in there.

You understand why I kept this to myself.

THE HEADACHES WERE GETTING WORSE. Heliora could hardly sleep and when she did, the dreams dragged her out of sleep, gasping and sweating, her head full of the Lord and Court, and a bloody heap of corpses.

When she was awake, the voices in her head were louder than usual, drowning out everything else. The only thing that calmed her was the tea she had bargained from Poet. She had almost run her supply down to the last leaf.

Perhaps she wasn't going to die with Ashiol's hands around her neck, or beaten and abandoned in an alley by

Poet. Perhaps she was just going to burn out. Seers had gone that way before, she knew their stories. If she didn't sleep soon...

Heliora was going to have to ask Poet a favour. Damn it.

She was practised at going unnoticed in the Arches. In her young days as a sentinel, it was just what you did. You kept your steps quick and quiet, choosing back streets, shadows and stillness. You picked a time when they would be sleeping. Morning was best. You avoided crossing the path with the bratlings of the Court or their overblown Lords and masters. It didn't make her feel any less safe to know that one of them was murdering the others — the Creature Court had never been a happy family.

She stood finally in front of the old grocer's shop in the Shambles, and knocked quickly before she could change her mind.

There were footsteps, and when the door finally opened, she was faced with Poet in a pair of silk pajamas, peering over his spectacles at her.

'Bringing your messages of doom in person now, are you?'

'I come in supplication,' Heliora said, not hiding the irritation in her voice.

He smiled delightedly. 'Excellent. Will there be bowing?'

'No.'

'Sexual favours?'

'Definitely not.'

'Shame, you'd look good on your knees.'

She brushed past him to the stairs. 'With a charming patter like that... it's a good thing you're an actor of some repute, or you'd never get laid.'

'Don't go up there,' Poet said suddenly.

Heliora turned, curious. 'You don't want me here?'

'You were not invited inside.'

She tilted her head at him. Usually he had at least the façade of manners. 'What is it you don't want me to see?'

An impatient voice came from above. 'Master, you're not supposed to open your own door...'

Heliora caught a flash of a familiar face and a shock of white hair before Poet waved the courteso away with an impatient gesture. 'Lennoc,' she breathed. 'Saints, you got the *brighthounds*.'

Dhynar had four courtesi when he died. The Creature Court — or Ashiol, at least — suspected all four had been taken by Warlord. But they were here. 'You have been spreading rumours that Warlord is starting some kind of mad rebellion with seven courtesi under his belt. Do you have the darkhounds and the cats too?'

'Upstairs,' Poet said grimly. 'Now.'

Heliora shot him a mocking look but proceeded up to the intense warmth of his sitting room. 'Should I be worried that you're so keen to make the others fear Warlord, while you build your own power base? Are we talking actual machinations here?'

Saints, was he the killer? Did it even matter to her if he was?

'Sweet as ever, Seer,' drawled Poet. 'This supplication thing really isn't working out for you.'

'It doesn't come easily,' she admitted, turning to face him. Now was as good a time as any to make her request. 'I need more tea.'

Poet laughed as if that was the last thing he had expected her to say. 'That's why you came to me? Addict.'

'Apparently,' she conceded. 'It's the only thing that helps me sleep. The dreams are... bad.' The headaches too, though she wasn't going to admit that particular weakness to him. He might be a murderer, but he was also her salvation.

'Tea's no good for that,' Poet said. 'Drink too much and it

will have the opposite effect — keep your mind awake too late.'

Damn it, of course it had been too easy a solution, once she got past the humiliation of begging for what she wanted. Heliora slumped her shoulders, sinking into his couch. She had slept soundly enough here once before. It might be the safest place in the Arches, since Poet was unlikely to slaughter anyone where their blood might spatter his nice furniture.

Lack of sleep had obviously rendered her insane.

'Don't lose heart, petal,' Poet said, sounding amused at her. 'I have more than one interesting substance to share with you.' A shelf above his stove yielded a small glass vial. 'A couple of drops of this in your evening milk will have you deep under for a whole nox — or day, if you prefer.'

Heliora looked at him, resisting the urge to snatch. 'What is it?'

'Do you really care? Its name is something long and complicated in Zafiran. On the street they call it Oblivion.'

'Sounds like the kind of potion that's hard to give up,' she said warily.

Poet shrugged. 'What do you care? You'll be dead by Saturnalia. Hardly time to form a habit.'

His words were a knife to the gut, but it was a fair point. 'What do I have to do for it?'

Putting herself in his hands — she hated that. But Heliora had known when she came here she would be trading favours with him. She just hadn't known how great a favour... At least she had something over on him. 'I take it keeping quiet about your brighthound is worth something?' she offered.

'Oh, Heliora,' Poet breathed. 'You're going to have to come up with something better than that.' He held the vial tantalisingly out of reach. 'Lucky for you, the first taste is free.'

HELIORA WAS DROWNING. Every time she closed her eyes, she found herself in the Lake of Follies, fighting against the futures until her mouth and lungs bubbled up with water and she slid down underneath. The water was layered with rose petals so thick that no light shone through from above. The blackness was terrifying and inviting.

It was over. There was something comforting about it being over.

Heliora awoke, not for the first time, on Poet's couch, the taste of lake water and rose petals still cloying her mouth. She heard movement and the clink of a spoon against a cup. When she arched her neck up to see who was there, she recognised another of Dhynar's former followers. Shade, the darkhound courteso.

'Good morning, Seer,' Shade said politely, and presented her with a cup. 'My Lord said you might like this when you awoke.'

She took the tea, inhaling its comforting fragrance.

'Thank you. How long did I sleep?' It had been early morning when she came to Poet.

'Most of the day,' said Shade.

The Oblivion worked, then. She would have to keep up the supply, no matter what it cost her. Dreams of drowning were better than the state of living death she had been walking through in recent days.

The tea was too hot, but Heliora sipped it anyway, enjoying the way it burned tartly against her lips. 'Why him?' she asked. Perhaps inappropriate for so early in the morning,

167

but the question had been on her mind since she first saw that Poet had taken in Dhynar's former courtesi. 'It's not just the Lord who gets in first, or the one with the strongest arm. Why did you and Lennoc choose to come to Poet, of all of them?'

He would be their third master. A better question might be why they had chosen the boy Dhynar as their second when both Shade and Lennoc were older, wiser, more accustomed to sanity.

'He has a sweet voice, and he promised many things,' said Shade, but there was a flatness to his words that suggested he was not being entirely truthful.

'Oh, he has a sweet voice all right,' Heliora agreed ruefully. What was she doing here? Putting herself in Poet's hands again. She was as bad as these courtesi, choosing the wrong master. At least Ashiol made sense to her. Poet was a blank page. 'Are you sure you can pay his price?'

'I don't think I'll pay as high a price as you, demoiselle Seer,' Shade said politely, then turned and left the room, leaving Hel staring after him.

Damn. He had a point.

She was hungry in a way she rarely was, her stomach clawing at her. She needed something. She rose and went to Poet's stove, finding nothing but the warm kettle. No food smells. What did they live on down here, moss and mushrooms?

Obviously Poet liked his meat fresh-caught and still wriggling, but that was no help to her. Heliora opened a cupboard and found a few apples. She took one and bit into it — still a little too green, it burst sharply on her burnt tongue.

The door opened and she jumped as Poet came inside. Ridiculous, to feel guilty for taking an apple without asking. Still, he smiled at her as if he planned to eat her for supper. Her caution was hardly unwarranted.

'Thank you for the tea,' she said, taking another bite defiantly.

Amusement flickered over Poet's stupid, schoolboy, open face. How did he manage to look so wholesome and innocent? Those ridiculous spectacles of his. Heliora had to keep reminding herself that he was a monster.

Had he killed Livilla's two boys? Did she care?

'Did you sleep well?' Poet asked. Oh, so polite.

'Yes. You were right about the Oblivion.' Heliora took another bite of the apple, sucking down the sour juices, not wanting to stop or give him any sign of how unsettled she was.

'You will be wanting more, then?'

'Yes,' Heliora said fast, before she could come to her senses. 'We have not yet discussed payment.'

'Ah, there's the problem,' Poet said with a smile that was almost sad. 'I have no needs you can provide.'

Fear stabbed her — the thought that he had been teasing, that he wouldn't allow her any further doses. She wouldn't show him that fear, though. 'Please,' she scoffed. 'You're the same as the rest of them. You need food, sex, power. You're not special, Poet.'

'Am I not?' he said, smirking. 'Food and water are all I need to keep going, but that's boring and oh so easy to get hold of. Sex does little for me, and you're hardly my type. Power... well, you have me there. I do like power. But I'm at a loss as to what you could give me that I couldn't just take.'

'Is it more fun to take?' Heliora challenged, then wished she hadn't asked him that.

'Always,' said Poet, eyes hard on hers.

She was at a loss. People *always* wanted what Heliora had to offer. They wanted her futures, her visions. They wanted affirmation of their own desires. The Seer had currency, damn it, and he was mocking her to pretend otherwise. 'You're lying,' she said finally.

'Is it so hard to believe that I'm a satisfied person?' Poet sat on the couch, easy and relaxed. 'Garnet wanted to use you, to get validation of his insane rule. Part of him thought he could control the future if he could control you — so of course he wanted your visions. Wanted to frig you, too, I wouldn't wonder. Whereas our darling Ash... you gave both up freely to him, whether he wanted them or not. What is it that you think you can offer me?'

'I don't believe that you're immune to wants,' Heliora said, stepping closer to stand over him. 'I think you're trying to torture me. Making people squirm might even be above food and frigging on your list of needs.'

'But not power,' Poet said softly. 'Never above power. Top of the list every time.'

That was what he needed, then. What he wanted. Heliora had to give him something (or take something from him) that was worth more than the power he held over her with the Oblivion. She moved, straddling his lap experimentally.

Poet laughed openly at her. 'So predictable.'

'Hush,' she said. 'I'm concentrating.' It was a long time since sex had been anything but an end result for her. A cure for being lost in the futures. This was far from recreational, but it was different.

Poet was watching her with curious rat eyes, like she was a song lyric he wanted to learn, but didn't entirely like.

Heliora didn't want to kiss him, at all. She sat poised on his lap, waiting for some reaction, but he did not move. She wanted to make him moan, or at least twitch. She wanted to prove that he wasn't made out of Shambles stone, cold and dry.

'Never mind a price,' she said calmly, wriggling her hips a little. 'How about a bet? I can do anything to you, and if you make a sound, you supply me with Oblivion between now and Saturnalia, no cost.'

Poet leaned back against the cushions of the couch. 'You're very sure of yourself.'

Heliora gave him a biting smile. 'I'm very good.' She had played these games before, when she needed to distance herself from someone. Ironic that she was now using them to draw Poet in.

'What's my prize?' Poet asked. 'This is what we come back to, Hel. You have nothing that I want. Nothing worthy of a wager.'

'If you win, I will speak the futures to no one but you,' she said, voice shaking only a little.

He laughed at that. 'Doesn't that go against the duties of the Seer?'

'I don't give a frig about duty, or Ashiol or her high and mighty Power and Majesty,' Heliora spat. 'I'm dying. I want to get a decent nox's sleep.'

'You're not dying, petal,' he chided her. 'You're going to die. Two separate things.'

She gave him a dirty look. 'Think how much it would annoy Ash if you won.'

There was something unrecognisable in Poet's eyes. 'Fine.'

'Any last words before silence begins?' she asked as she slid off his lap to her knees.

'Wait,' he said, and she glanced at him. 'You said you could do anything to me. I don't fancy having pieces sliced off.'

'I thought you liked that sort of thing.'

'Not when someone else does it.'

Caught off guard, she laughed. 'No blades,' she agreed. 'Maybe nails, maybe teeth. I won't draw blood.'

Poet nodded amiably. 'Silence starts now,' he said with a smirk. The reason for the smirk was evident as she unlaced his trews. He wasn't even hard. Maybe it was true — sex did little for him. In which case, she was embarrassing herself for no gain.

Poet made no sound as she touched him, a soft stroke of her fingertip, then her palm cupping him gently. She sucked on her fingers to trail wetness around his shaft, coaxing his body into wanting her.

Weak after all, she decided as his cock began to harden under her touch. She risked one look up and saw amusement, detachment. Nothing else.

When Heliora wasn't messing around with Ashiol, most of her lovers had been sentinels. They were saner on the whole than the rest of the Creature Court, and enjoyed frigging without the distractions of animor, blood and the power struggles which took up so much of the time of the Lords, Court and Kings.

With Rory and Tobin, even her brief liaison with the Silver Captain (damn, that man could kiss like he knew how), Hel was able to drown herself in the sensation of being herself, not just the Seer. The Heliora who might have stayed a sword-monkey, had she not been called to a higher purpose. More recently, on occasion, there had been Macready, reliable though hardly romantic. It worked for both of them — calm and grown-up and uncomplicated. She rarely thought of him when he was not there.

Heliora had never been angrier than the day Raoul died and the powers of the Seer transferred to her. Bloody man, what was he thinking? How had he thought she was the one?

Then Garnet took their blades away, and the sentinels started dying. Her world had crumbled — or her illusions about it had.

Heliora closed her lips around Poet's half erection, feeling him grow in her mouth. It was eerie how silent he was — not even his breathing had changed. He honestly thought that he could get the better of her. Perhaps he hadn't realised that power was a very individual thing. Some people gave power during sex, some people took it.

More fun to take, Poet had said. Heliora grasped his shaft, squeezing in gentle pulses as her mouth coaxed him harder. She would show him what taking really meant.

Possibly it was the most perfunctory blowjob in the history of the world, but that was not significant.

The point of the exercise was not to make it particularly good. It was to make him cry out.

Finally Poet jerked in her mouth, once, twice, and the heat of him flooded her tongue as he spilled easily into her. She raised her eyes to his, only just manageable from this angle. He was smug, and silent.

She swallowed.

Images hit her fast and frenetic, snatches of a broken childhood, the smell of oysters and seabreeze. White rats spilling out across a city alley. The shudder up her arm as she plunged a walking stick through the body of a man. A top hat, falling to the floor. The smooth gold chain of a pocket watch. A blowsy woman in a red gown, drunk and leaning over a backstage balcony, howling about her betrayal. Mermaids and pearls, mermaids and pearls. And then a man, sleeping in tangled sheets, his face hidden, but she didn't need to see his face to know exactly who he was.

'No,' Poet roared, standing up in a rush, knocking her over. 'You can't have that!'

'Too late,' said Hel, wiping her mouth. 'I took it.' She had his secrets now, the parts of him he most wanted to hide inside himself. Knowledge was power.

'That was not yours to see,' Poet said, shaking with anger.

Heliora stood up slowly. 'You're the one who assumed I was offering sex because I had my mouth around your cock. Still think no one can touch you, Boy?' She used the name deliberately, knowing it had meaning to him.

'Get the frig out of here,' Poet snarled.

'I won the bet,' she reminded him. 'You cried out.'

He turned and went to his stove corner, crashing through cupboards until he came up with a vial. It glittered, full of the silver liquid. 'Take it. That should do you a month. If you're still alive halfway through Cerialis, I'll send you another.' His voice was terrible, face paler than usual. 'Don't come back here.'

Breaking Poet was a strange, unreal thing to have done. It made so little sense. And yet she knew him now, in a way she never had before. Boy. Baby. Orphan Princel. Poet.

She knew he had not killed Livilla's boys, that he knew nothing of their deaths. He genuinely believed that Warlord had done the deed. It was a small piece of what she had taken, but it was important to know.

He was a murderer — she could still feel her hands closing around an old man's throat from the memory — but not today.

And, oh yes. She knew who he loved most in the world, and why he had hidden that for so long. He really was still a frightened boy, wanting to be looked after. She would never be scared of him again.

Heliora took the vial. She said nothing. No reason to thank him. She had earned her prize.

She went downstairs and let herself out of the little grocer's shop. She had brought no lamp this time, so the narrow streets of the Shambles were a dark maze as she made her way towards the upper world.

She came up in the wrong place, a street she didn't know, far from her home in the Basilica, and broke down crying, leaning against a wall as her body was racked with sobs.

It wasn't Poet's memories that lingered with her now, it was the look on his face when he realised she had seen them, all of them. His whole story, laid out in a single swallow.

She was as much a monster as any of the Creature Court. It wouldn't be just the futures she needed to blot out next time she used a drop of Oblivion.

She had to pull herself together. Had to stop being a ridiculous demoiselle about this. She had done what she needed to do, got what she wanted. *Breathe*, she had to breathe. She had to get back her control. Only then, away from him, calming herself with steady breaths, could Heliora come to terms with what she had learned.

Garnet. The man in the bed was Garnet. Did that make a difference? Did it matter? Garnet was dead. Why did he blaze inside Poet, so brightly? What were the futures trying to tell her?

Hel was so weakened and distracted that the mere thought of the futures summoned them into her head. They hit so hard that she almost threw up in the street. All thoughts of Poet flooded away.

Heliora could see a thousand worlds unfolding in front of her, so many possibilities, and she could not see the pavement under her feet.

She had no one to help her, no one to make it stop, and all she could do was hope this wasn't the day that the futures broke her.

Minutes, hours later, she came back to herself, a huddled figure in an empty street. She pulled herself slowly upwards, hanging on to the wall, shaking wildly and trying not to let herself fall. The end was coming, spiralling towards her, black and promising beyond all those futures. She had to make a choice, and soon.

In the meantime, she had a vital message for the Kings of the Creature Court.

1 2

VICTORY OF BLOOD

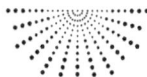

FIFTH DAY OF THE LUDI SACRIS, THREE DAYS BEFORE THE IDES OF FELICITAS

DAYLIGHT

*a*shiol's animor flashed hot and violent against the inside of his skin. He wanted to hit things, break things.

'We're not allowed to play in here!' Isangell teased as Ashiol led the way to the Eyrie, a ruined tower on the side of the Balisquine. 'It's haunted.'

'That it is,' said Ashiol grimly. The Eyrie had been Saturn's territory, another of the Lords who came to a bad end. Not that any of them died in their sleep.

Kelpie was right. If Priest and Isangell were both contaminated by the sky, there was every chance Isangell could also be turned into a weapon. He needed her to be kept away from anyone she could hurt, and he could not count on the sentinels to guard her. Not now that they had rebelled against duties that did not directly involve the Kings.

'Isangell,' he said in a more gentle tone. 'I need you to go into that room.' He pointed to one of the few intact rooms, at the top of a crumbling staircase.

'But I want to stay with you,' she purred, snuggling against him.

Ashiol gave Velody a helpless look, and she moved into action. 'There are more dresses for you, high and brightness. Just inside the room.'

'I like this dress,' Isangell pouted.

'Didn't you say you wanted to bob your hair?' Velody added in a moment of brilliance. 'They're waiting for you, right in there.'

Isangell squealed with delight and darted inside.

Ashiol pushed the door closed with a satisfied clang, and infused the wood with his animor. He couldn't do much to affect the steel lock, but the wood quivered under his touch and artificial branches sprouted free of it, holding the door tightly in place. It would never contain one of the Court, but his cousin was — in physical form at least — still human.

'Let me out!' cried the Isangell-thing from within the cell.

Ashiol turned away, ignoring her. He heard her outraged screams for the entire time it took them to climb down the long staircase, to the base of the tower, and then along several winding tunnels.

'Can Livilla take down Priest by herself?' Velody asked as they came out into the Arches.

Ashiol shrugged one shoulder. 'She won't. She's mad as hell, but not stupid. She likes others do the heavy lifting.' He stretched his animor out in all directions and found Livilla nearby in wolf form, her tongue lolling out as she hid from them.

'More likely she'll follow us and wait until we have Priest at our mercy before she bothers to get involved,' he added, particularly loudly.

'Do you think Priest is working alone?' Velody asked.

'He has his three courtesi,' Ashiol said, though he didn't think much of them. 'Warlord's down, and we mostly know what Livilla's up to. Then there's Poet.'

'Would Poet side with Priest if he was crazy?' Ashiol just looked at her. 'You know what I mean,' Velody said crossly.

'I've given up guessing what Poet might do.'

They followed the canal path along to Priest's cathedral, imposing and silent. Ashiol smashed the doors open with such force that they broke from their hinges. Whatever was happening to Isangell, they could deal with it later. Priest (if it really was Priest) was carving a bloody path through the Creature Court. Stopping him had to be their first priority. 'Search the place,' Ashiol ordered, and the sentinels spread out, checking the ante-rooms and climbing the high stairs into the upper reaches of the cathedral, skysilver blades at the ready.

'No sign of any birds,' Macready finally called down from above.

Velody started in on those bloody questions of hers again. 'Where else would he go? How would he keep his courtesi safe?'

'You're assuming that there's any of Priest left at all,' said Kelpie, the first of the sentinels to return from above. 'Nox-crawl is liquid evil. If the sky is inside him, he'll have little say about what his body's up to.'

'Poet,' said Ashiol, dispirited. 'If there's any of Priest in there, and he needs help, he would go to Poet.' *Or to me*, was what he did not say aloud. Priest had always been the one who valued civility above strength. The one Ashiol had the hardest time thinking of as a monster.

If Priest fell to the sky, what would be left of the Creature Court?

Someone took his hand, sending a warm charge directly

into his bloodstream. He looked at their linked fingers first, and then at Velody.

'Heliora,' she said.

'Yes,' he replied. Finally, a useful suggestion. 'Heliora.' It was that, or wait for the bodies to pile up.

THERE WAS no sign of the Seer at the Basilica, and Ashiol was too twitchy and irritable to wait. Velody brought him back to her house instead. She was sure there had to be a way to find Priest which didn't involve walking over every square inch of this city.

Ashiol had an idea now, at least. As the sentinels clustered in the kitchen where the food was, he dragged Velody into the workroom to find a map, and any scraps she had left of the waistcoat she made for Priest.

She brought him all the spare pieces of the damask and velvet, even the embroidery threads she had used and the satin of the lining. Ashiol dropped most of them to the floor, but kept hold of a few scraps, pushing them into Velody's lap. 'There,' he said, guiding her hand to the council map of festival locations in Aufleur. 'Find him.'

Velody tried, she really did, but she couldn't even feel the difference between the velvet scraps Ashiol kept and those he had discarded, let alone get a sense of Priest's location from the paper. Ashiol kept insisting she try again. She was close to pretending she felt something, just to shut him up.

Crane passed her a cup of mint and lemon, and a spark passed between them as their hands touched. He smiled shyly at her, and retreated.

'That!' Ashiol declared.

Velody held her cup closer to her. 'What?'

He pointed a finger at her. 'You fancy him.'

Heat flamed on her cheeks. Crane had stopped in the doorway to listen. 'I do not. What has that to do with anything?'

'No, it's good. Come back here!' Ashiol motioned briskly to Crane, who stepped back in Velody's direction. 'Kiss her.'

'No one is kissing me!' Velody protested.

Ashiol seized both her wrists, jolting hot tea out of her cup. 'You're holding back. No matter how powerful you think you are, there is always more inside, untapped. You need to access parts of your animor that you don't even know how to reach, and the best way to do that is desire. Touching. Kissing. Sex.' He could have been discussing the weather, or the wines of Atulia.

'I'm not doing that, and certainly not in the workroom,' Velody hissed at him.

Ashiol smiled. Not a nice smile or a desirable smile. The kind of smile that made Velody glad, so glad she had made that oath to Livilla, to keep herself from falling into bed with him. *Cats eat mice.* 'Would you rather kiss Crane, or me?' he dared her.

Velody turned in a moment, seizing Crane by the collar and pulling him down to her level. Their mouths came together, clumsy at first, and then Crane apparently decided to make the most of it. He knew what he was doing. He pinned her to the chair, far more in control of this kiss than he had been the last time, a million years ago on a rooftop.

Velody kissed Crane back, hands tangling in his golden hair. She felt the animor uncurl within her body, heated and thirsty. She needed this. He was here and it was easy... A fine excuse, to make out with a boy because it might make you more powerful.

She could already feel the difference — her animor came alive with every stroke of lip or tongue. Something deep and powerful rose up inside her when he braved himself to brush a hand against her breast. Saints. No wonder Kings could take power from each other when they coupled. No wonder... everything.

Velody reached out one hand, and Ashiol tipped the velvet scraps and threads into her palm. Heat ran from Crane's mouth to her wrist, as if his kisses were all over her skin, under her skin. She felt for a moment as if every mouse shape danced inside her body. Her fingers tingled with every stitch she made on that waistcoat. All that hand-sewing, because she wanted to keep her fingers busy, because that was the way that the best tailors worked. She might have saved the Court a lot of heartache and fuss if she had only used the dratted sewing machine.

Velody was hardly even paying attention to Crane, only to the sensations, and heat coursing through the animor beneath her skin.

The whole city opened up to her; the paper map rustled with a wind that came from nowhere, and Velody broke off the kiss to stab her handful of velvet scraps down on to the map. 'There,' she said.

Crane was breathing fast and loud, or was that Velody? Her heartbeat was like a drum in her head. Did Ashiol care? Was he paying attention? Was she an utter wench for enjoying the thought that he had been watching?

Velody pulled her eyes from Crane and saw that Ashiol had his nose buried in the map. She should have known. He had been part of the Court too long to be moved by something as innocent as a kiss. (Not that the look in Crane's eyes right now was remotely innocent.)

'The Circus Verdigris,' Ashiol said, leaping to his feet, bright with energy.

Velody remembered that first time he came to her, high

on animor and clutching a handful of rose petals. Mad, he had been mad with power, so desperate to find the mythical King who would take his place and save him from being the Power and Majesty.

He stared back at her now, impatient. 'Come on, then. You too, sentinel. Let's go.'

Velody followed without pausing to think, catching up her long silk coat on her way out through the kitchen door, with the sentinels at her heels.

IT WAS DARK. The sky did not yet show any sign of throwing a battle at them. The Circus Verdigris was abandoned yesterday by order of the Duchessa, and no one had bothered to pick up the debris. Velody could see discarded melon rinds, garlands and banners littering the grass and the seating area. She could also smell blood, from the moment they came near it.

Priest, though. There was no scent of Priest.

A wolf had been tracking them since Via Silviana, and now watched them silently as they descended into the grassy arena. The sentinels all had their skysilver blades bared.

The scent of blood was richer here. Velody inhaled it giddily. Her stomach growled. Had she eaten today? She couldn't remember, but whatever she might have consumed, it was not enough. Meat. She needed meat.

'Here!' shouted one of the sentinels. Ashiol followed the cry in that loping run of his, as if he had forgotten he was not yet in the shape of cats. The other sentinels followed. Velody stayed stock still. She heard a low sound, a tiny moan, and ran lightly across the grass in the opposite direction to the others.

He was a small, crumpled figure beneath a tier of seats and a makeshift scaffold. Velody pulled away rubbish and a broken bench to get to him. He lay with his eyes open, shuddering, his whole body drenched in blood. For a moment, Velody thought it was Seonard, the wolf boy, but Seonard was dead. This was Poet's lad. Zero, they called him. She did not even remember what his creature was. Something rodenty, though not rats or mice. She would have remembered that. She extended her wrist to him, only just able to reach underneath the seats. 'Drink.'

He flinched, expecting a killing blow rather than a lifeline.

'Drink,' Velody said again, and braced herself as he reached for her, his teeth making a first, unsuccessful bite. The second time, he broke the skin. She felt the blood fill his mouth, and his tongue flick over the wounds. It hurt more than usual.

She turned her head and saw, further along, a body lying on the grass. Moonlight gleamed on his bright white hair. Lennoc. What was he even doing here? The wolf crouched nearby, sniffing at the body, but making no move to help.

'He's still alive,' Velody said, unable to move with Zero latched on to her wrist. 'I can hear his heartbeat from here.' She could hear everything. Her animor was alert to the whole area. '*Help him.*'

The wolf shimmered, and shaped itself into the bare body of Livilla. She sat back on her haunches, her face wary. 'Look at you,' she said in a musical voice. 'Giving your precious King's blood to save Poet's courteso. No one saved mine. Why should I bother?'

'Because you're a human being,' said Velody, gritting her teeth.

'That's assuming rather a lot.' Livilla went, though, sliding

183

her whole body over Lennoc. She sniffed his neck, licked it for a moment, and then began to laugh. 'Oh, my. So many secrets, I don't know where to begin.'

Lennoc groaned and muttered something that Velody could not hear.

'Don't blame me, darling,' said Livilla. 'Apparently we're all saints these days. It's the new mode.' She lay her throat over him, and moaned with every appearance of pleasure as he bit her.

Ashiol appeared with the unconscious body of Shade in his arms, and the sentinels with him. Crane went to Velody, ashamed at having left her alone, and helped her remove her wrist from Zero's greedy mouth.

'Priest is long gone,' Ashiol reported. 'No sign of Poet either.'

'Took him,' Lennoc said, when he drew back from Livilla with a blood-smeared mouth. His shirt was ripped, and a long ragged wound on his chest slowly began to close up as new strength coursed through him. 'Priest took him.'

'I take it Poet is your master now,' said Ashiol, sounding grim.

Lennoc wiped the blood from his mouth and licked the smear from his hand. 'If he's still alive, he is.'

'Not very good at keeping your masters alive, are you?' Livilla drawled. She leaned back on her elbows on the grass, looking amused.

'Nor you your courtesi,' said Lennoc.

She hissed at him between her teeth, suddenly furious. 'Watch your mouth. *Courteso.*'

'Where has Priest gone?' Velody asked, getting to her feet, only a little light-headed. 'Where did he take Poet?'

She did not ask why. The sky that controlled Priest now needed no motive but to distract and damage the Creature

Court. To make them weak. Velody was determined that whatever happened, they would be stronger than before.

Lennoc looked at the ground. 'Lord Poet said that if Lord Priest really wanted to rip the heart out of the Creature Court, it might be a fine idea to kill the Seer.'

Ashiol growled.

13
VICTORY OF BLOOD

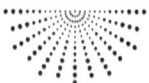

FIFTH DAY OF THE LUDI SACRIS, THREE DAYS BEFORE THE IDES OF FELICITAS

NOX

*D*elphine had decided that the world was crazy. The Duchessa was crazy — why else would she destroy everything that was good and right about the city by closing the festivals? Velody was crazy, and so was her Creature Court. Rhian was seven kinds of crazy, and not even for the usual reasons.

When a bedraggled bald fortune-teller you hardly know turns up raving on your doorstep, it's not *normal* to drag her in, sit her down and feed her soup.

'It's all right,' Rhian assured the demme, who was wild-eyed and shaking. 'Come on in. We were just sitting down to supper.'

Delphine folded her arms and watched as Rhian made the Heliora comfortable. 'Why did you come here?' Delphine asked bluntly. The entire time in that dratted tent, she had got the impression that the demme was laughing at her, like she and Macready had private jokes together.

'Nowhere else to go,' said Heliora, warming her hands on the soup bowl. 'I can't — it doesn't —'

'Don't worry,' Rhian soothed. 'You're safe here.'

'The broken mirror won't mend itself,' Heliora said, urgently, as if it was the most important message in the world. 'You must tell the Kings.' She pulled her palms away from the bowl — they were reddened from the heat of it, and she didn't seem to know why. 'Ashiol. He has to know.' She gripped the edge of the table to stop herself swaying.

'He doesn't live here,' Delphine said bitchily. 'Try the Palazzo. What do you think we have, a magical Ducomte-summoning charm?'

The demme was shivering now. Possibly because she had left her hair at home. 'The broken mirror will not be mended,' she said again, and started crumbling a piece of bread, arranging the crumbs in neat lines.

'We should send for Ashiol?' Rhian suggested.

'He's a little busy saving the world,' Delphine said airily. 'Besides, how would we send for him?'

There was a soft thud as the smelly old tomcat that had been hanging around the house since the Creature Court breezed into their lives leaped on to the table, and stretched. Delphine glared at it. 'We remember that I'm not a sentinel, yes? Your tricks are no use with me.'

This was all Macready's fault. He had happily gone trip-trapping off with the others like the good dog he was, and left her here to deal with this. What were they supposed to do if the so-called Seer snapped and went for a potato cleaver? Delphine wasn't a trained sentinel...

Stupid thought. She wasn't a sentinel at all. She didn't want to be. She wanted to braid flowers. Being a part of the festivals, of the complex rituals of the city had always been important to Delphine. She had long since tossed away any ridiculous notions of being a high-class dressmaker.

Everyone needed garlands. Her work mattered to more people than Velody's frocks.

Delphine knew every festival, every day by rote. In a few days' time, the Sacred Games of the Ludi Sacris were supposed to reach their crescendo with the public circus. Boatloads of new and exotic animals were imported for that special day, and only the best performers were allowed to strut the arena.

Poppies. The circus meant poppies: orange and gold and scarlet, strung on glossy white ribbons. Delphine should be working on them now. Rhian should be sending her runners to the docks to ensure the best blooms. But according to a statement from the Palazzo, reprinted in the city broadsheets and passed even faster by word of mouth, hemming a ribbon for the sacred circus was against the Duchessa's word of law. Delphine wanted to scream and tear at something. Rhian was ridiculously calm, as ever. Of course she wouldn't fuss. But how could the rest of them not care?

The obvious reason. They might blithely take a public garland or buy one of their own or maybe even not bother, and the world would keep turning. Velody's new friends were so oblivious to the ways of daylight. How could they not understand that this was important?

The city felt dead, with the festivals closed down. Every corner should be draped with banners and sigils announcing which performers would be performing in the games each day. Children should be playing with toy javelins and hurling discs, or begging their parents for the bright striped circus candy that was only sold on barrows during the Sacred Games.

There should be songs and smiles and holiday baskets. What was the point of protecting a city if it was already broken?

Rhian tried to wrap a blanket around Heliora's thin

shoulders, but the Seer grabbed out at her wrist, hanging on too tightly. 'Roses,' she said unexpectedly. 'Why do I always see roses when I look at you?'

'I work with flowers,' said Rhian. 'At least, I did,' she conceded in response to the rude noise Delphine made. 'And I will again, once the Duchessa's senses return,' she added, firmly detaching Heliora's hand from her wrist without her usual shudder at human contact.

'Assuming they don't all dry up while we're neglecting them,' Delphine huffed. She had hemmed a dozen ribbons today, to prove that she could, the stupidest outlaw act she had ever performed. Then she hid her silks and pulled out a lopsided knitting project, just to be doing something with her hands.

'This is how it happened before, with Tierce,' said the Seer. 'I knew I wasn't going to make it past Saturnalia, but it never occurred to me until now that maybe it wasn't just me. Maybe all of Aufleur will go. That makes sense.' She didn't sound particularly upset.

'How considerate of us to keep you company,' Delphine said bitterly. 'What do you mean, this is how it happened with Tierce? What do you know about Tierce?'

It was still just a name to her. Velody tried to explain how her memories were coming back, the more time she spent among the Court. Delphine's own memories remained hidden, and she was content for them to stay that way. There was nothing wrong with having a blank spot where your childhood was supposed to be. Not when it was what you were used to — how things had always been.

Rhian hungered for any stories of Tierce that Velody could share. Delphine did not. When Macready tried to bribe her with her lost memories she felt nothing but rage that he thought her price was so damned cheap. Still, the idea of this little wretch knowing more about their city than she did was unbearable.

'I saw it all,' said Heliora, hugging herself. 'Usually it's the futures that come upon me. But when it happened, I saw the *now* in a way I never have before. I saw every blow of the final battle. They turned against each other. The city didn't work any more, didn't heal, couldn't hold it together. One by one, the Shadow Court was swallowed by the sky, and when the last of them was gone, the sky ate the city whole.'

'The Shadow Court?' said Rhian. 'They weren't creatures then, the Court of Tierce?'

'Oh, they were creatures,' said Heliora with an unpleasant smile. 'Greater, darker, more fierce creatures than anything you've seen here in Aufleur.'

'So,' said Delphine, her voice strangely loud in the kitchen. 'What you're saying here, basically, is that we're doomed.'

'Oh, yes,' said Heliora with a firm nod. 'That was never in question.'

This was the last time Delphine would allow Rhian to feed soup to ragamuffins. Seriously, it was time they started making use of the sturdy bolts on the kitchen door.

'I have to go,' Heliora said, on her feet all of a sudden.

'Don't,' Rhian said in alarm. 'Wait for Ashiol...'

'I can't wait, I have to — oh, I can hear him laughing!' And the crazy Seer was running for the door.

'Let her go!' Delphine said impatiently to Rhian. 'She doesn't belong here. We're not part of this!'

Rhian put her hand out to grasp Heliora's arm, but the Seer shook her off and ran out of the kitchen door. Delphine was shocked to see anger or fear — something quite feral — shining out of Rhian's eyes. 'We have always been part of this,' Rhian said fiercely. She swept out of the kitchen and up the staircase, half- running to get away from Delphine.

Delphine heard the back gate creak. She flung the door open, expecting to see the Seer again, but it was Macready, looking rumpled and bloodstained.

'What's wrong?' she asked with a catch in her throat, wondering whose blood it was.

'Eh, nothing like that, lass,' he said. 'We've had word that Priest is hunting Heliora, our Seer. I wanted to warn you two to keep your heads down and your door barred... what is it?'

Obviously her dismay was all over her face. 'She was just here,' Delphine confessed.

'Oh, lass,' Macready said in a sigh and made for the gate, then out into the alley at a fair lick.

Delphine ran after him. 'I told you I wouldn't make a good sentinel.'

'Aye, well I believe you now,' he said sarcastically, hurrying to the corner and looking in all directions. 'No sign of her. What frame of mind was she in?'

'Raving.'

'Wonderful,' he sighed. 'You may as well get back to your ribbons.'

'And what's that supposed to mean?' she snapped. 'Our whole city is falling apart — in a real way, not a "building gets broken, building fixes itself" kind of way. Your precious Ducomte knows the Duchessa, but he doesn't give a damn about anything that's real. None of you do. My ribbons pay for the food that you all help yourselves to when you breeze in and out of our lives. It's not all about mad Seers and exploding skie!'

'Aye, well you might have a point if it were not for the Pigeon Lord trying to kill off people I know, one by one,' Macready snapped. 'I don't think we've got our priorities in the wrong order, worrying about that. In any case, you're *part* of our world now.'

'Because I picked up a sword?' Delphine scoffed. 'It was a

fluke. I am not a sentinel. I don't even know what that means.'

He held his hand out to her, looking all battle-worn and adorable. No, not adorable. Scruffy. 'Come with me. There's a fight to be won this nox, and Velody needs all the sentinels she can get.'

Delphine stared at him, so furious that she thought she was about to explode and take the sky with her. Why was it so hard to walk away from him? He smiled his stupid smile, and his hair was all curled up at the ends, and she didn't care. Not at all.

She wasn't going to take his hand. Delphine folded her arms. 'I'd rather die.'

A scream cut through the streets around them. 'Hel!' said Macready, and ran towards the sound.

Only later, Delphine realised that she had not hesitated to follow.

MACREADY FOUND Heliora at the mouth of an alley that led out on to Via Camellie. She shook wildly, foam flecking her lips. As he took hold of her he could feel her bones jutting through her skin. When had she last eaten a meal? She was all but vanishing under his hands.

'Hel,' he said urgently. 'Come back to us, my lovely.'

'Everything's breaking,' she forced out through a throat that barely seemed functional. 'It won't mend.'

'We have to get you inside, sweetling. Away from Priest. The sky wants your blood.'

She laughed horribly, clinging to him. 'Not enough left to tempt it.'

Macready scooped her up in his arms and carried her back to the house. Delphine stayed at his side, watching him.

She opened the gate for him, which was something. 'Can't help yourself, can you?' she said. 'You just love rescuing people.'

Macready carried Heliora into the kitchen and sat her down. She stared uselessly into the distance, not reacting to him. 'Nothing wrong with that, is there?'

'That depends on how you look at it.' It was obvious that Delphine very much did think there was something wrong with it.

Macready left Heliora in the chair and drew Delphine into the workroom, speaking in a low voice. 'How do you feel when you finish one of your garlanding commissions?'

She gave him a hard look, her narrow sapphire eyes cutting into him. 'Tired.'

'Is that all?'

'Satisfied,' she said grudgingly. 'I love being busy, I hate having nothing to do with my hands, and it is *killing* me that our bitch of a Duchessa has screwed with my business.'

Macready nodded. 'Imagine that same satisfaction, only the work you have done was for the good of the whole city. You've been a part of something that saves lives and sanity and the very bricks holding us up. Something so essential that it makes you glow to have been part of it.'

'And then they pat you on the head, the Kings, and say good dog. Only they don't,' Delphine scoffed. 'I've seen — they hardly ever notice you except when they need something. You all walk around with this air of vitality, like your work is so important.'

Macready gave her an odd look. 'It is important.'

'No more than anyone else's job.'

'Delphine, you braid silk and *flowers* for a living.'

She stared razors at him. 'You're a frigging maidservant, Macready, and that's worse. You're not going to turn me into one too!'

'You had the right of it all along,' he said angrily. 'You're not one of us, not if you think that way.'

Delphine made an irritated gesture at him, like he was speaking the obvious. Macready went back to the kitchen and found it empty. 'Shite!'

So much for keeping the Seer safe.

'Some sentinel,' Delphine observed.

1 4

VICTORY OF BLOOD

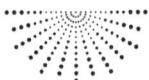

FIFTH DAY OF THE LUDI SACRIS, THREE DAYS BEFORE THE IDES OF FELICITAS

NOX

'*A*shiol, wait!' Velody hurried along the main thoroughfare that was Via Alysaundre, a step behind Ashiol and some way ahead of the rest of their group. It was late enough that there were few people around, who paid no attention to a bloodstained mob with bared swords, a wolf and several hounds at their heels. Even the boy had shaped himself into animal form — a small gang of weasels.

'I'm going to tear that bastard limb from limb,' snarled Ashiol.

'Priest or Poet?'

'Both.'

'You know Poet,' she chided him. 'He wouldn't have seriously meant to put Heliora in harm's way.'

'Would he not?' Ashiol raged. 'You don't know the first thing about the Creature Court, Velody. Don't start pretending that you do.'

'I am the Power and Majesty,' she said furiously.

Ashiol snorted.

'You never said we were going to kill Priest,' she tried, barely keeping up with his long strides.

'I thought that was implied.'

'This isn't his fault. Are we going to murder the Duchessa, too? Just so I'm clear on the order of events.'

'I'm not enjoying this,' he snapped at her. 'Isangell isn't responsible for a bloodbath. Priest, or whatever the hell is walking around inside his body, is *killing us*.'

'So we create our own bloodbath. Lovely.'

'Did you think being Power and Majesty was going to be easy? That there would be no hard choices to make?'

'You're not giving me a choice!'

'No one forced you to be part of this world, Velody. You chose us. You stepped up to be our Power and Majesty. Maybe it's time you started behaving like it. Sky falls, we fight it. Danger comes, we fight it. Something tries to destroy us, we destroy it first. What the hells else can we do?'

Ashiol stopped suddenly. They were at the arched entrance to the Forum. The Basilica was lit up from within — the only public building which was open all nox.

'He won't be in there,' said Velody. 'Too many witnesses.'

'Heliora might be. If she's not, we have to find her before he does. She doesn't even have a fucking sword.'

The sentinels and the others were close to catching up with them.

'I'm not going to kill anybody,' Velody said quickly. 'You can't make me do that.'

'So your battle with Dhynar Lord Ferax was a one-time deal? Good to know.'

'He was already dead,' she said, stung by his words.

'Dhynar was trailing pollution from the sky. He was tainted. He broke the rules. Any of this sounding familiar?'

'I won't kill anyone,' Velody said again. 'Not in cold blood.'

'But you're happy for us to kill on your behalf — for your sentinels to kill on your behalf.' He raised his eyebrows, looking scornful. 'Not even sentinels.'

Anger flared through her. 'You put me here because you thought I could be something different. Something better than what you had before. Stop being angry at me for not being Garnet, or Tasha, or whatever standard it is you hold me to. Help me be *Velody*!'

There had to be a solution to all this. Some way of bringing everyone through it alive.

'We've gone as far as we can with you being Velody. You can't handle this world. You never could.'

She was furious and tired and hungry and beaten down, and this was the last thing she needed. 'You're wrong.'

Ashiol was gazing across the Forum to the lights of the Basilica. 'I was wrong before. You should go back to your seams and hems. I'm taking over. Follow me or get out of my way.' He stepped down into the darkness, and a figure rose up out of the Forum to confront him.

'That's hardly the way for a King to speak to his Power and Majesty,' said a familiar voice, rich and deep. Warlord.

Priest was a murderer. Poet was a fool. Livilla was a basket-case. Velody would not. Stop. Yapping. Ashiol wanted to burn the lot of them. Where the hells was Garnet when you needed him? Garnet would have killed Priest already and be looking around for a celebratory fuck.

Now here was Warlord, on his own two feet, dressed every inch like a Zafiran prince, in gleaming red silk robes with gold embroidery. He still looked like death warmed up; his courtesi stood nearby, as if ready to lunge forward and catch him when he fell. Still, it was an improvement.

'Cats,' Mars said in his deep voice, looking over Ashiol's

shoulder to Velody. 'They're fiends for lashing out when you kick them. And their scratches last a long time.'

'I am so sick of talking in metaphors,' said Velody.

Mars smiled with bright white teeth. 'Aren't we all?'

'Let me pass,' Ashiol advised. 'Or I'll push you over with my little finger.'

'Not yet. It's rude to turn your back on a lady.'

'Ashiol is right,' said Velody, sounding defeated. 'I don't know how to find Priest, or stop him. I don't know how to fix this whole unholy mess. Thanks to the Duchessa, *in her infinite wisdom*, I don't even have any hems to sew. Maybe he should be the Power and Majesty.'

Ashiol turned and looked at her. He could take her, in a fight, if he had to. Velody had more animor, more raw power, but he had years of dirty tricks behind him. He had been a match for Garnet, most days. He could take it from her. He could make her whimper.

'I will say this,' said Mars, pretending that he was only speaking for Velody's benefit. 'Ashiol is a better leader than he thinks he is. But no one can match him when it comes to being stupidly loyal. He has never broken an oath in his life. He swore to serve you as Power and Majesty, and if he says otherwise now, it's just words. That's how he's made.'

Ashiol turned and glared at him. 'I can break an oath any time I like.'

Mars shook his head slowly. 'I don't see it.'

'How is he following me by walking away?' Velody demanded.

Mars chuckled. 'I didn't say he wasn't complex.'

'Giving away all my secrets,' Ashiol said in a low voice.

Mars met his gaze. 'You came for me, when I was hurt and in hiding. You brought Velody to me, so she could heal me. We were friends once. I hope we can be again someday.'

Friends. Yes. Ashiol had missed that. Silently, he reached

out one arm, and Mars clasped it. The Panther Lord's animor felt weak still, but it was returning.

'The time for playing mind games, for pitting Lord against Lord, is over,' said Mars. 'We need you both. Power and Majesty, Kings. We are fighting for our survival now.'

'Some of us were always fighting for our survival,' remarked Ashiol.

Velody didn't look uncertain. She looked strong, and ready. Like someone you could count on. 'Let's find Priest,' she said. 'We can discuss what to do with him after that.'

'Oh good,' muttered Ashiol. 'More talking.'

VELODY COULD NOT QUITE BELIEVE that it took Warlord to broker a peace between the two Kings. She was glad of it, not wanting to expend more energy in fighting Ash. Then screams rang out across the Forum, and there was more reason to be glad of it.

'Hate to interrupt this touching scene,' said Kelpie. 'But I reckon we've found Priest.'

Ashiol moved the fastest, all but flying to the wide doors of the Basilica. He couldn't get through, for the crowd of people flooding their way out of the building. 'Round the back!' he yelled to the others, but that door was full of merchants and customers scrabbling their way out as well. Some of them were wounded, or streaked with blood. All of them were terrified.

Ashiol really did fly this time, up to the domed roof, and broke one of the high glass skylights to get inside. The other Lords and Court, some in animal form and others glowing bright as day, followed him in. Velody shaped herself into Lord form and lifted Crane and Kelpie up into the air and through the skylights.

199

Inside, the Basilica was a wreck. Stalls and tents were overturned. Hot food bars lay cracked open. Most of the vendors and customers had fled the scene. Bodies lay dead or bleeding on the ground. Priest had been here. Priest and whatever monster the sky had put inside his skin.

'Saints and devils,' breathed Crane. 'What has he done?'

Velody couldn't answer. There were no words for this. The Creature Court were supposed to be above and beyond the daylight folk. They didn't slaughter them for their own entertainment. They didn't play these games with anyone but each other. True, the message that they were supposed to protect the daylight folk often got lost along the way, but this... This was more than neglect. It was sport.

'Priest!' thundered out an angry voice.

'There's our boy,' said Kelpie, her blades bared as she headed towards the sound of Ashiol's voice, ignoring the wreckage and the death around her.

They found the rest of the Creature Court in a cleared space, where several tents had been torn up and cast aside.

'Have you been looking for me, king of cats?' boomed the voice of Priest. He appeared in his usual stately glory of velvets and silks, the new waistcoat gleaming over his portly stomach. It made Velody sick to look at it. Her hands, as Mars had told her, over and over. Her fault.

Priest was surrounded by birds — the gulls, plovers and sparrows of his retinue.

How could they go along with this? Courtesi served Lords, yes, but surely they knew by now that their master was not the one driving this cabriolet?

'What the hells do you think you are doing?' Ashiol raged.

'Isn't it obvious, my boy? I'm looking for the Seer.' Priest tilted his head thoughtfully to one side. 'Slippery little thing, I can't find hide nor hair of her. I'd demand you produce her, but if you had possession I doubt you'd have that shocked look on your face. She'd have seen this coming, and told you everything.' He laughed. 'Clever creature that she is, she's a challenge to find.'

Heliora's tent was in pieces, her belongings scattered across the Basilica floor.

'Priest,' Velody said now, trying to sound calm and assured as she stepped forward to stand at Ashiol's side. 'This isn't you. This isn't what you want. The sky is controlling you, but you don't have to let it.'

Priest laughed a big belly laugh. 'My dear demme. You surely don't think that you're dealing with Priest any more? He's long gone.'

'Who are you, then?' Velody asked.

Priest smiled. 'Ask the dust, my sweet. When the dust falls, you will all die.'

'What does that even mean?' Velody demanded. 'When the dust falls?' If this was not Priest, what was he? A dozen people of the daylight lay dead, and more had been wounded, for no reason but being in this creature's way. It made no sense.

'Where's Poet?' Velody asked.

Priest smiled expansively. 'Lost another Lord, have you? How careless. You'll hardly have any remaining by the time we arrive.'

Velody turned her eyes up to the birds that still flocked around him. Priest smiled as he followed her gaze. 'A pretty retinue, but they have outlived their usefulness.' He held up a hand, and one of the gulls burst into a mess of blood and feathers. A sparrow next, and then a plover. The other birds shrieked pitifully and rose up to flap against the domed Basilica roof, but there was no way out.

'Stop it,' Ashiol roared, enraged. 'You'll cripple them. And —'

'Myself?' Priest said with a smirk. 'I am well aware whom

I am crippling, little King. Flesh and meat bodies mean little to me, I assure you. We are dust. We will not be denied, nor slowed. Mourning the meat left behind is your distraction, not ours.'

One more bird exploded into a mess of guts. Velody's vision tunnelled darkly down into itself. She changed without thinking about it, shaping herself into the fearsome chimaera. Ashiol was faster, and he reached Priest first.

Priest held up one large hand, and Ashiol's body froze in mid-air. Priest flexed his fingers, and Ashiol changed: from glowing Lord form to winged black chimaera, then a horde of cats. Lord — chimaera — cats — over and over, like it was some kind of game.

'You didn't think I was limited by Lord Pigeon's powers, did you?' taunted Priest.

Velody could not move. Her clawed feet scrabbled uselessly in the air. She wanted to scream, wanted to tear the creature limb from limb. The thing in control of Priest was toying with Ashiol, and then it would move to her, and how could she defeat it if she could not move?

Priest smiled at her. 'Wait your turn,' he chided, and made a slashing motion with his hand, making Ashiol twist and scream with pain as he hovered in the air.

Velody closed her eyes, hating herself for being so weak, but why should she watch Ashiol's pain if she could not move to help him?

She could hear other sounds in the Basilica. There were Crane and Kelpie, helping the last few stallkeepers and wounded daylight folk to make their way to the exits. Poet. They had found Poet. She opened her eyes and saw the Rat Lord being lifted gently out of the wrecked remains of Heliora's stall. His wrists and ankles were shackled with skysilver, and he was battered and bruised down his face and half his body.

'Sentinels to the rescue,' he said through swollen lips as Crane unchained him. 'Aren't you useful little helpers.'

'This is your fault,' Kelpie snapped. 'Kill the Seer indeed.'

'I thought it would be a fine distraction,' said Poet, spitting blood. 'Not to mention a bright beacon to lure in our Ashiol. I wouldn't worry about Heliora, she can take care of herself.' He tried to stand up, wobbled, and then sat down again in a hurry. 'Well, that was fun.'

Velody could not hear them now, their voices drowned out as Ashiol's screams filled the huge space. Priest made a casual gesture and Ashiol's long black wings tore free from his chimaera body. His body sagged, finally silent as blood fountained from the stumps.

The sentinels and Poet ran for cover as Ashiol was thrown in their direction. His body made a crunching sound as he hit the floor.

'Your turn now,' said Priest with a polite smile, turning his attentions to Velody.

PAIN, the pain was everywhere and then it stopped. Ashiol could not even scream now. His raw throat had nothing left, and he could feel nothing but numbness in his limbs. He managed one choking breath, but it would be far easier to float away and leave the rest of it behind.

He heard the scrape of a knife and smelled blood. Kelpie's blood. Automatically, he opened his mouth to suck, but there was nothing brushing against his lips.

'I wouldn't,' said Poet's voice nearby. Fucking Poet. What did he know? 'Making him mortal while there are bits missing? Not the best plan.'

'Then what?' cried Kelpie. 'What can we do?'

Ashiol felt a gentle touch against his forehead. Poet's

hands. 'Let him die?' said the rat. Then he caught his breath in a sound like a gasp. 'Can you hear that? Whose voice is that?'

'Believe me,' Crane said in a low mutter; 'it surprises none of us that you are hearing voices.'

Ashiol was not only numb now, but cold. How could he be cold, if he could not feel his body?

Poet was giggling maniacally now. 'Oh, I've changed my mind!' he howled. 'Let him live. He's going to get such a kick out of what comes next.'

There was a wet sound, and Ashiol felt a pressure against his side as if Poet was lying near him. He could feel the vibrations as the little rat breathed exhaustedly.

Ashiol breathed, one more time, and the familiar scent of Livilla flooded through him. He opened his eyes and saw her stunning naked body fill his vision. 'This is what we are, now,' she said in a soft voice, crawling over his broken chimaera body. 'Apparently. Who'd have thought?' She leaned down to press one kiss on his brutish mouth, then arched and twisted her neck. She already had one bite mark raw against the pale white skin. Ashiol growled quietly. He could smell her blood and he wanted it, but she was still too far away.

'It won't be enough,' said Crane. 'Not for this. Maybe if she was a King...'

'I think,' said the voice of Mars, surprisingly close, 'you should never be surprised at what Livilla can do, when she puts her mind to it.'

The blood came, after that. Ashiol closed his eyes and opened his mouth and let it drip inside him. He tasted Livilla and Mars first, then each of Mars's courtesi in turn. Then Livilla again, so fucking sweet he wanted to drink her dry.

It felt as if an eternity had passed, and then Ashiol was breathing without difficulty, his body still wrecked and sore all over again, but human and in one piece. Livilla and Mars were on top of him, kissing messily; blood was smeared everywhere and her legs were tangled around his waist. It seemed rude to interrupt.

Ashiol moved eventually, his palms touching his own torso. There were jagged, barely healed lines across his body, puckered new skin and scar tissue where there had recently been smooth lines, but the animor of the two Lords had done its work.

He turned and saw Poet lying beside him, wet with Ashiol's blood, paying attention to none of them. He had a stupid grin on his face.

'Where's Velody?' Ashiol asked, though his throat was still too damaged to produce more than a sound or two.

'Up there,' said Crane, sounding broken.

Poet laughed weakly. 'Of course she is.'

IN CHIMAERA SHAPE, Velody was invincible. Power coursed through her muscles, bolder and brighter than anything she felt when she was in human form, no matter who she was kissing. Chimaera was strength and spirit and there was nothing the sky could do against her when she wore that skin.

She could not move. Slowly, invisible hands lifted her high in the air, above the thing that wore Priest like a cheap suit.

'One King down,' the creature said with a friendly smile. 'Only you left.'

But it wasn't true, she knew it wasn't true; she hadn't felt the burst of Ashiol's animor demanding to be quenched. As long as he was alive, there was hope for everything else. 'I won't let you do this,' she said, the words pouring off her unfamiliar chimaera tongue. She wasn't sure what language she was even speaking, but he understood her well enough.

'Do you really think you have a choice? Power and Majesty. Such important words you people use, to make yourselves sound grand. You are nothing compared to sky and dust.'

From here, so high up into the domed roof of the Basilica, Velody could see Ashiol's fallen body. Could see the sentinels, and the Lords...

Could see that Livilla and Warlord were giving their blood to save his life. Though no one had compelled them.

'Oh, you have no idea,' she said, relief and pride filling every inch of her chimaera skin until she was ready to burst. 'I got it right. This is *my* Creature Court, the way it's supposed to be.'

'You have taught the creatures to be weak like humans,' the thing inside Priest said dismissively. 'It is of no matter.'

'You think humans are weak?' Velody demanded, and then gasped because his invisible hands were squeezing her so hard that there was no air in her lungs,. It might not be pride she burst of after all. 'You have no idea what we can do.'

She thought of Crane, of his sweet face and the look in his eyes when he kissed her. The way her animor had responded to him. She thought of Ashiol; of how close they had come once to frigging on the kitchen table; those dark eyes of his, and clever fingers, and the sleek hard lines of muscle in his body. He was not dead. Livilla and Warlord had saved him.

There was hope for everything now.

She thought of another young man, a lifetime ago, clumsy and earnest and, oh, long-dead. Cyniver fell when Tierce was swallowed by the sky, but she remembered how alive he had been once, the most human person she had ever known.

No matter how powerful you think you are, there is always more inside, untapped.

All she had to do was let herself lose control.

Velody's animor exploded out of her, blasting in all directions. The invisible hands fell away, burned by the brightness, and then she had Priest flattened to the floor, her teeth bared, claws ready to kill. 'No more,' she snarled through her beast's throat. 'No more blood, sky creature. Just this.'

She was dark rage and blinding hate, and she could take him to pieces as easily as breathing.

Priest had a distant expression on his face as he regarded her. A thick black web of noxcrawl crept up his neck, patterning over his chin. 'Be my guest. My message has been delivered. Your Court is broken, and ripe for our conquest. I have done my work.'

'Not quite,' Velody said, and tore handfuls of animor out of his chest. She had meant to save him. She didn't want to believe that it could be this simple, that it boiled down to blood and death and sacrificing one Lord to save the rest of them.

But her claws dragged more than animor out of his chest, and there was no way to separate out what belonged to Poet or Warlord, let alone Seonard or Janvier. Velody dug deeper, and blood sprayed out with the animor.

Priest laughed, and it was worse somehow than the time that a blood-drenched Poet had been laughing hysterically, on the brink of death... and there was no reason for her to be thinking about Poet, surely.

Except that he was there. White rats poured all around her, covering Priest's twitching and bleeding body, and when he shaped back into a Lord it was unmistakeably Poet, a thinner and paler Poet, his hair spiky and his face stained with Ashiol's blood, now pressing his hands hard against the wound in Priest's chest.

'Where have you been?' Velody gasped, shaken back into her own Lord form, glowing but human-shaped.

'It doesn't matter. Doesn't matter what he did to me. I'll heal.' His eyes were intense and bright without those odd round spectacles he usually wore. 'Priest was my Lord once, and he was a good one. He *is* one of the good ones. He gave me a safe place to hide when I needed it. Velody. If you are really the Power and Majesty, the one we swore our oaths to, the one who was going to change everything, if any of that was true and the bright happy future is going to happen, then *you have to save him.*'

'I don't know how,' she said.

'Start figuring it out, little mouse,' Poet said, his voice light but meaningful. 'None of us have faced this before. You get to be exactly as ignorant as the rest of us! But I've seen the future, and he's in it, so think fast.'

'Blood,' Velody said a beat later. It always came down to blood, didn't it? 'Crane!'

'I'm here,' said a voice. Crane came to kneel next to Poet and drew his knife to make a neat slice in his arm. Barely even wincing, he let a few drops fall into Priest's mouth.

Priest bucked and made awful sounds. The noxcrawl web glowed fiercely on his skin and then faded from black to grey.

'He's bleeding more,' Poet said, squeezing his hands harder into Priest's chest. 'Velody.'

'I know,' she said. 'We have to wait.'

'He can't wait.' Poet gave her a stern look. 'You're supposed to save him. What good are you if you can't save all of us?'

Velody held her hand out to Crane, who gave her his skysilver dagger. She sliced her own arm and splashed a few drops of her King's blood — Power and Majesty's blood — against Priest's lips.

'Don't let him touch you,' Crane warned, but Priest had already grabbed Velody's arm, dragging it down to his sucking mouth. Velody let him have two sucks and swallows before she drove the heel of her hand hard against his forehead, pushing him back and disentangling herself. Her wound burned where he had touched her.

Poet kept holding Priest together for minutes afterward, then finally drew his hands away from his chest. The skin sealed over, pink and raw. 'That went well,' he said brightly.

Velody rocked back on the floor, so tired she could barely form words.

'Don't fret,' said Poet, patting her on the shoulder. 'This future is better than anything that doom-laden Seer has ever come up with. Everything's going to be all right now.'

Velody stared at him. He appeared different. More peaceful, almost happy, for all that he looked as if he had rolled around in Ashiol's blood. 'We thought he had killed you. Or that you had joined him.'

'So sweet. You were worried.' Nothing could wipe the smile off Poet's face. He stepped back, still in his own cheerful world.

'Oh, a fine happy ending,' Kelpie said, nodding towards the group of courtesi who had been Priest's birds. The three of them clung together, miserable and hurt. Damson, the gull courtesa, was bleeding from one arm, and another courtesa was missing part of her foot. 'Tell them how bright the future is, Poet.'

'Where's Ashiol?' Velody asked.

'He's alive,' said Crane. 'Not moving so much right now.'

'My Power,' murmured Priest from the ground, sounding his own self. 'Please...'

'I know I'm just a sentinel, and my opinions are worth so much hogshit,' said Kelpie, 'But can I suggest we get that garment off him?'

Velody swapped knives with Crane and used his steel dagger to slice the seams of the waistcoat, already torn open by the chimaera claws. For a moment it felt as if the threads were crying out in pain, and then they were silent. The rich tapestry fabric fell away from Priest in pieces. The shirt underneath had rotted away, as if he had been buried in it for months. The skin of his belly was bloodstained but there were no scars or marks where the wounds had laid open.

Priest seemed normal, but how could she be sure he was free of the darkness? Velody wasn't even certain that she was. Something still roiled and burned inside her.

'I appear to have missed some events of great import, my dears,' Priest said now, surveying the trashed Basilica, the bloodstained floor and the many wary faces.

'Murders and mayhem,' said Warlord, who stood holding Livilla's hand. 'Nothing out of the ordinary.'

Priest saw his courtesi clinging together and extended one hand to them. 'My sweet birds.' They did not come to him, and his face shifted into displeasure. 'Have you stolen my demoiselles from me, Power and Majesty?'

'You may have done that yourself,' said Velody. If it was true that he did not remember, she did not want to be the one to explain to him what he had done.

Priest looked at each of their faces, and settled finally on Poet. 'You, my boy. You will not spare me the truth.'

Poet sat on the rough ground of the Basilica floor, leaning back on his elbows. 'No, old man,' he said in a voice that had fondness in it, oddly enough. 'Nothing will be spared. Not today.'

Velody left them to it. She walked on shaking legs to where Ashiol lay still in a pool of his own blood. He met her gaze and then sighed, and closed his eyes.

'Will he be all right?' she asked.

'It's Ashiol,' said Kelpie with a sigh. 'He's never been all right. I don't see why he'd start now.'

15
PERFORMANCE OF THE MASKS

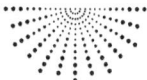

SIXTH DAY OF THE LUDI SACRIS, TWO DAYS BEFORE THE IDES OF FELICITAS

DAYLIGHT

*D*elphine searched up and down the side of the Balisquine hill, finally spotting the overgrown ruined tower among a clump of scratchy bushes. She scrambled down the slope towards it, almost losing a shoe in the process. Damn that Ashiol Xandelian to the seven hells and back.

'What are you doing here?' demanded a sharp female voice. The sentinel Kelpie stepped into view.

'What are you doing here?' Delphine countered, teetering on the broken steps that led into the tower.

'I asked you first.'

'I'm doing a favour for the Ducomte,' Delphine said, folding her arms.

Kelpie scoffed. 'Since when do you play nice with Ashiol?'

'You may not have noticed in your little Creature Court bubble, but the Duchessa took away my livelihood,' Delphine said firmly. 'The sooner she gets better, the sooner she can bring back the festivals.'

'You plan to blackmail her while she's possessed by a devil from the sky? Excellent plan.'

Delphine made a face. 'I felt bad, okay? He's all banged up and he said you sentinels have refused all duties that don't involve bodyguard duty.'

'You're not a sentinel, then? Good to know.'

They stood there for a few moments, sort of staring each other down. 'So why are you here?' Delphine asked finally.

Kelpie blew out a breath. 'Same reason as you. He cares about the damned Duchessa, and I'm a soft touch.'

This was Delphine's chance to ditch the chore she never wanted to take on in the first place, but somehow she wasn't willing to relinquish it to Kelpie and have the ratty sentinel be all bitchy and smug about it.

'I guess we're going in together,' she said finally.

'Looks like.'

It was dark and clammy and smelled bad inside the tower. Delphine stepped gingerly around the muck on the floor. Kelpie made a snorting sound and pushed past her. The door to the cell swung open.

'Oh, frig,' Kelpie said with feeling. The door swung further back, and the words *TOOK THE LADY HOME* were visible in bright red lip-paint. 'Livilla's got the Duchessa.'

ASHIOL SLEPT UNTIL PAST NOON, and even then there was a ghastly pallor to his skin. Velody went to him the second his eyes opened. 'How do you feel?'

'Like I was hit by a cabriolet,' he muttered. 'Or possibly a train.'

'Can you sit up?' She was worried about the damage he

had taken. He had received enough blood to recover, but his arms and chest still bore the marks.

Ashiol tried, grunted with pain, and then tried again. This time, he managed to get into a seated position. 'I'm fine.'

'You're not,' she chided. 'You should have healed faster than this.'

'Sorry about that.'

'Don't be a thimblehead.'

He looked around. 'Am I in your bed?'

Velody had hoped he wouldn't notice. 'The workroom is full of sentinels. I made them bring you up here.'

'Nice.' There was a different tone in his voice now, all dark and promising. Velody found herself backing away out of reach.

Possibly she should have backed all the way down the stairs and out of the house. Instead, she asked, 'Would you like soup?' in what she hoped was a matronly way.

'I'd rather have a measure of imperium,' he replied.

'I think there's an inch left in the brandy bottle,' she said, but didn't move. 'How much does it hurt?'

'On a scale of one to having your wings ripped off? Call it a seven.' Ashiol glowered at her. 'If you're not going to fetch the brandy, you could at least give me blood.'

She shuddered, remembering how much of him had leaked out on to the floor of the Basilica. 'I'm not sure I have any left.'

'Come here,' he said, with a certain light in his eyes. 'I'm sure I can find it.'

Velody very clearly saw herself climbing on to the bed and kissing him until neither of them could breathe. A very, very bad idea. 'I'll fetch the brandy,' she said, and ran.

When Velody returned with the brandy bottle, Ashiol was asleep again. His breathing was less troubled than before, and the sunlight played on his eyelashes as it patterned across the bed. It was so rare to get a chance to observe him without being observed in turn — watched, and judged. She sat beside him, loosely cradling the neck of the bottle in one hand, and straightened the top quilt over him.

Strong hands wrapped around her wrists, and she realised too late that he was not asleep at all. His dark eyes held hers as he drew forward the hand that held the bottle, and uncapped it with his teeth. She tipped the bottle up and he drank, all without letting go of her wrists. They both released the bottle at the same time and it rolled to the floor with a thunk.

There was a wet smear of brandy near his mouth, where it had dripped. Velody was not going to lick it off. That would be an entirely misleading thing to do.

'My animor is weak,' Ashiol said. 'I need to heal.'

She opened her mouth to ask what he needed, and then stopped because it was a stupid question. He needed Court blood, or he needed someone to wake up his animor. Just as Mars and Livilla had done for him last nox.

Velody didn't want to give him blood. Or rather, she did. The thought of it made her pulse race, and she wasn't ready to question that particular desire. Instead, she gave in to a different one. They were already close enough to kiss. She moved further on to the bed, letting him draw her in by his hold on her wrists. 'Heal yourself,' she told him, and brushed her mouth against his.

A kiss should be enough. A kiss, mixed with a healthy dose of the craving they had for each other. She could already feel his animor burning more fiercely than before. As long as they stopped at kissing, it would all be fine.

Ashiol groaned and buried his mouth in her neck, his slow sucking kisses moving down towards her collarbone. His hands moved from her wrists to her waist, and then to her breasts. Velody pressed her fingertips against his chest,

215

and ran her nails around to the muscled curve of his shoulders. She slid her hands up his naked back, relishing his human shape and the heat of his skin.

His breath caught as if she was hurting him, but he found her mouth again before she could ask if it was too much. His hands were busily working on ridding her of her dress.

Velody could not stop thinking about his chimaera form, ripped so badly, of the sight of blood pouring from his wing sockets. If he could survive that, he could survive anything. She felt his animor strengthen now with every touch, and it made her slide forward to press her body against his chest so they could be touching in as many places as possible.

The raw scars on his chest flared hot, and then cold. Velody ran her tongue along them, tasting his blood and skin and animor as Ashiol dug his hands into her hair. Power passed between them, until it was no longer possible to tell what was hers and what was his except that they were both so much stronger than they had been moments ago.

He unlaced her dress and pushed up the chemise she wore underneath to give himself access to her stomach, trailing kisses across the warm curve of her skin. Oh, they had gone so far beyond kissing now. She fell on her back and he pressed his body over her, like a cat worrying at his prey.

It would be so easy to just part her legs and let him in, but this wasn't healing now, it was foreplay, and they could not do that. Worst of all, he did not know why.

Velody grasped his hair, pulling his head up and away from her. 'Stop. We can't do this.' The weight of his body was still a reminder of everything they had been doing. He was so very, very naked. No one had ever in all their life been as naked as he was now.

Ashiol gazed at her, his eyes nox-dark and scorching. 'You still think I'm going to use this to steal your animor?'

'No,' she breathed. *Hells, yes you would, in a hot second.* 'But

I made a blood oath to Livilla she could... watch us, if we ever. And she's not here.' For one horrible moment she imagined Livilla leaping out of the wardrobe with a pair of opera glasses.

Ashiol just stared at her. Velody wanted him to kiss her again. How weak was that? If she was this desperate for a warm body, she should pounce on Crane who was both desirable and safe. There was nothing safe about Ashiol.

He rolled off her suddenly, head in his hands. 'A blood oath,' he repeated. 'You swore a blood oath to Livilla.'

'A while ago. It made sense at the time.'

Ashiol stared at her through his fingers. 'Do you know how rare it is for two members of the Creature Court to *not* have sex, sooner or later?'

Velody started relacing her dress, wanting very much to be covered up while they had this conversation. 'To be fair, you never mentioned that aspect of the Creature Court when you dragged me in. It was a notable omission.'

'I take it you haven't become an exhibitionist since you became our Power and Majesty?'

Velody stared at him, aghast. Was he seriously suggesting that they invite Livilla in to watch them? 'No, actually,' she said sharply.

'Well then,' he said, shaking his head at her, 'I suppose we have to behave.'

Yes. That was most definitely what they were going to do. She was not going to become an oathbreaker on his behalf. No matter how good his hands and mouth felt upon her skin.

Velody could still taste him, and he knew it. He smiled slowly, and she felt his animor spark hard against her own. Oh, saints. She wanted him so badly that it scared her.

One moment Velody genuinely cared about Livilla and the oath, and the next she did not. What did it matter if tainted shades trailed polluted animor through the streets of the city? She couldn't think, couldn't breathe. She wanted to feel his hands on her breasts again, to feel him slick and hot inside her, and it wasn't enough that she could feel his strength returning and she knew that he was as healed as he needed to be.

Ashiol spotted her insanity a mile off. He caught her closer, mouth ravaging hers, hands tugging at her dress to get her naked all over again, and there was no way that her human body could resist him. With a cry of frustration, Velody shaped herself into a horde of mice, scattering her bodies over the quilt and the floorboards.

He started to laugh, his whole body shaking. *That bad?*

Shut up, she sent at him. *Get out of my bed.*

Ashiol threw back the covers, stretching his devastating body. He pulsed with strength, animor rolling off him as if he had it to spare. The faintest of scars ran over his chest in a pattern that had seemed so ugly before. 'You might want to stay in mouse form until I've gone,' he advised her. 'For both our sakes.'

It would be undignified to bite him on the ankle. Velody gathered her many mouse bodies and scampered out to the landing, where she waited patiently until he was gone.

'Act like you're meant to be here,' Delphine hissed. Head up, casual smile, relaxed shoulders, snooty expression.

'I've been here before,' Kelpie insisted. She wasn't doing too well at the 'look like you're supposed to be in a Palazzo' routine. Her cloak smelled like it hadn't been washed — ever.

'With your master, you mean? The Ducomte isn't here to wave you past the lictors this time. Maybe you should be my maidservant.' Delphine was already building up a posher accent, as she did when hanging out with Villiers and Teddy and that set. It felt as natural as breathing.

Kelpie gave her a disgusted look.

They made their way to the Duchessa's rooms without incident. Delphine had the bright idea of seizing some hat boxes they had found in a foyer, so no one gave them a second glance. She thought it would be pretty obvious that Kelpie wasn't a milliner's assistant, but no one seemed to notice the leather coat or the swords on her back. Perhaps that was part of being a sentinel. People didn't see you any more.

Another reason to avoid it at all costs.

Kelpie motioned Delphine into a pretty sitting room. Livilla, thin and bitchy as ever, glanced up at them as she ashed out a cigarette in a tulip bowl. 'Oh,' she said, amused. 'You're here. Excellent. It's been so dull.'

'What have you done with the Duchessa?' Kelpie demanded.

'I haven't done anything,' Livilla said, arching both her eyebrows. 'Don't speak to me like that, sentinel.'

Delphine eyed the other woman. Oh, she thought she was so special. 'Why did you bring her home?'

'Just trying to help. Velody has taught me the error of my ways. I healed Ash, didn't I? I'm on the side of the saints and angels now.'

'I don't believe that for a second,' snapped Kelpie.

'Believe what you like.' Livilla lit another cigarette, and this time Delphine noticed that her hands were shaking. 'Maybe I'm trying to do my bit to prevent further tragedies.'

'Where is the Duchessa?' Delphine asked. 'Since you're keeping such a close eye on her.'

Livilla shrugged carelessly. 'She's in her bedchamber. Apparently I'm not welcome in there.'

'Imagine that,' Kelpie said sarcastically, only a beat before

Delphine said, 'Hard to believe,' in the same tone of voice. They looked at each other, startled to have been thinking the same way.

Kelpie went to the adjoining door and knocked lightly on it. 'High and brightness?'

'Oh, she's not answering,' Livilla said dismissively. 'She didn't react well to my interrogation at all well.'

'Interrogation?' Kelpie tried the door, which didn't budge. 'What have you done, Livilla?'

Livilla shrugged. 'Apparently all is forgiven where Priest is concerned. Fine and peachy. But the thing that killed my boys is still inside that sweetling. I wanted answers.' She stared defiantly at them both. 'I didn't hurt her. Not even a little.'

'I expect you want a medal for that.' Kelpie flipped a wicked looking knife out of her belt and slid it into the lock as if it was butter. The door clicked open, and Kelpie went in. Delphine followed at a more cautious pace. Livilla trailed after them both, her eyes glittering.

The Duchessa lay sprawled out on a bedspread made from silk finer than Delphine had ever seen before. Would Velody be prepared to make frocks from stolen sheets? It was a tempting thought. 'She's still wearing the dress,' Delphine said aloud.

The flame festival dress from the day of sacrifice was crumpled, but as vivid as ever. The same could not be said for the Duchessa, who was horrifically pale. She looked drugged to Delphine, who had more than her share of experience with potions.

'Ashiol thinks that the dress is what has made her run mad,' said Kelpie. 'Like Priest's waistcoat.'

'Easy, then,' purred Livilla. 'Let's take it off her.'

'Worth a try,' agreed Delphine. 'It fastens at the back,' she added, having watched Velody work on the dress for long enough. 'We'll need to roll her over.'

The Duchessa's skin was clammy and cool, but rolling her on one side did not make her stir. It was definitely more than sleep keeping her down in that particular chasm. Delphine felt for the soft buttons, remembering how Velody had tucked them behind ruches of fabric to hide them and allow the dress to fall smoothly from the shoulder blades. Her fingers slid over the first button and she tugged it open, then the next. The Duchessa cried out.

'What did you do, stick her with a pin?' Kelpie asked.

Delphine tried to peel back the fabric. 'It's attached to her skin. It's actually — fixed there.'

'It can't be.' Kelpie leaned over and took hold of a handful of gown, yanking on it sharply.

The Duchessa punched her in the face.

It wasn't much of a punch, but it shocked the hells out of Kelpie, who fell back on the cornflower-coloured carpet, one hand cradling her nose.

Livilla laughed like a sucking drain. 'Oh, I've changed my mind. She's not a silly aristocratic waste of space. She has style.'

The Duchessa turned and looked at her, eyes so dark they were nearly black. Livilla stopped laughing.

Delphine was close enough to see the spidery lines of a web tattooed across the Duchessa's milky skin. The lines were actually moving, creeping from her back over her shoulders and wending their way up her neck. 'I don't think she wants us to remove the dress,' she said hesitantly.

The Duchessa turned to her. 'We are the dust,' she said, the words torn from her throat as if they did not belong. 'You cannot stop us. Not Kings, nor Lords and Court, nor...' And she smiled, a thoroughly nasty smile. 'Sentinels. Not even you.'

Delphine's throat went dry. 'I'm not a sentinel,' she said, just to make things absolutely clear.

'I am,' grated Kelpie. She had one of her knives out and was holding it steadily, the tip only inches from the side of the Duchessa's neck. 'This is skysilver. The Duchessa is mortal, and this will glide through her, not making a mark. But you — I'm pretty sure it will do some damage to whatever the hells you are. I'm good with it, in case you were wondering. I've been accused of artistry in my time.'

The thing inside the Duchessa laughed. 'You thought your skies were treacherous before, Creature Court. You were wrong. We are coming to break your city into pieces. The dust will fall.'

WHEN A SNOTTY STEWARD called Armand attempted to show a party of City Fathers in to see the Duchessa, it fell to Delphine to look respectable and make the fast explanations. After all, Kelpie was in her leathers, and Livilla was... well, Livilla.

'The Comte de Leondres, Baronne Mauricel Nantes and Seigneur Giovannius have an *appointment*,' the steward said in a scandalised tone.

'The Duchessa is indisposed,' Delphine replied in her haughtiest manner. She had whipped on a shawl to make her dress a little more Palazzo-respectable.

'I am not sure who you are, demoiselle, but I should like to hear from the Duchessa herself if I am to make further changes to her schedule!' Armand looked harried.

'I am Dame Delphine, personal secretary to the Duchessa,' she told him firmly. She had never questioned where her aristocratic accent and general sense of entitlement came from, but it helped to talk her way out of all sorts of scrapes.

'You will *not* disturb my mistress while she is in such a delicate condition.'

Oops, possibly 'delicate condition' was the wrong phrase to use. The last thing they needed were rumours of a Ducal pregnancy. Still, it sparked up a gossipy gleam in Armand's eye before he returned to his default state of 'huffy and offended'. 'The Duchessa does not have a personal secretary,' he protested, at least having the discretion to speak quietly so that the ministers could not hear their discussion.

'She does now,' Delphine shot back, arching her neck and looking down her nose at him. Ha, he thought he could beat her at this game? 'She hired me this morning, in the presence of the Ducomte Xandelian. He will vouch for me. As will Lady Camellie and her daughters,' she added, using one of Velody's recent clients and her own knowledge of Great Families gossip to best effect.

'Interesting how the Duchessa became indisposed so soon after your appointment,' hissed Armand. 'How convenient for you, Dame Delphine.'

Delphine sighed. This idiot wouldn't let himself be fooled easily. She would have to go to greater effort. 'What exactly is it that you think I might be trying to hide here, Seigneur Armand? What is the greatest fear of the Palazzo servants since the Duchessa made her announcement about cancelling the Sacred Games?'

The reign of the mad Duc had ended only a little over a year ago. It was unlikely any of the servants and ministers had forgotten in a hurry what it had been like.

Armand's eyes widened painfully. 'Our lady is not...' His voice broke on the words. Interesting. He genuinely cared about the Duchessa. That should come in handy. 'Is not seriously unwell?' he added in a rush of a whisper.

'No,' Delphine said gently. 'Her dottore does not believe this current malaise is anything more than exhaustion, caused by her devotion to her new duties over the last few months. But you understand the need for discretion. Rumours that this is more than a brief illness could be greatly damaging to our lady's reputation among the City Fathers.'

Armand was buying it, nodding repeatedly. 'The Ducomte knows of this? And Lady Eglantine?'

Oh, hells. One sniff of the Duchessa's mother, and the game was up. 'The Duchessa is desperate to conceal her exhaustion from Lady Eglantine,' Delphine said hastily. 'She is worried that... her mother will use this as an excuse to usurp some of her duties or...' *Think, Delphine, think.* What were the most common rumours about the Duchessa and her mother? 'Or that she will push a marriage upon her sooner than she wishes. If we can buy her a few days of rest, she will be grateful to everyone who aids her in this endeavour.'

If they needed more than a few days then... well, Ashiol bloody Xandelian could come and personally kiss the arses of the servants. Delphine would provide the lip balm.

Almost all the lines of suspicion had been erased from Armand's face. Delphine used her blue eyes and pretty face as shamelessly as she dared, along with a deep confiding tone. 'Only the Duchessa's most trusted servants are to know the truth, Armand. I need you to assure me that this will go no further — although perhaps you can let me know who else we will need to bring into our confidence.'

Oh, and he was sold. Really, Delphine should twist men around her finger for a living. She was bloody spectacular at it.

'If I can help the Duchessa in any way, I shall,' Armand promised eagerly.

Thank frig for that. 'Please, convey our lady's apologies to the ministers and arrange a later appointment.'

Armand nodded. 'After the Ides?'

'The very thing,' said Delphine, as if she cared what date they picked. 'The Duchessa shall be returned to her usual self by then.' If Kelpie hadn't knifed her or anything.

Armand swept away, planning far better excuses to the City Fathers than Delphine could ever have come up with. She returned to the others exhausted, as if she had been dancing all nox.

The Duchessa sat with her back against the pillows on the bed, her body stiff and her eyes glowing black. Kelpie perched near her, the gleam of her skysilver knife reflecting patterns against the silken wall hangings, and her nose bruising up nicely.

'So,' said Delphine. 'What do we do now?'

'I'm thinking of slicing that dress off her,' Kelpie muttered. 'Piece by piece.'

The Duchessa preened, stretching her neck. The black web pattern reached almost to her chin. 'Do you really think the dress still has an influence over me? I am becoming.'

'Becoming what?' Kelpie asked.

'True,' the Duchessa said sweetly. 'Real. *Here.*'

'We could just kill her,' Livilla said. 'Listening to anything from the sky is dangerous. That's the first thing we are taught as courtesi. Never let your guard down, never take your eyes off them, do whatever damage you can. Killing her makes the most sense.'

Kelpie looked impatient. 'Yes, I can just see you explaining that to Ashiol.'

'Ashiol hasn't done me any favours lately. None of you have.' Livilla lifted one slender shoulder, looking just as weary as Delphine felt. 'My boys died, and no one cares but me. I want revenge.'

The Duchessa laughed, a low and deliberate sound.

'Shut your face,' Livilla hissed. 'They were *mine.* You had no right.'

'It's not like she did it,' Delphine said, losing sympathy for Livilla as quickly as she had acquired it.

'Don't be an idiot,' said Livilla. 'If the thing inside her is the same thing that was inside Priest, then that's what murdered my boys.' She leaned in, staring at the Duchessa. 'Noxcrawl doesn't have a voice. It doesn't have needs or wants, and it sure as frig doesn't have a sense of humour. You are not noxcrawl. You're something else, something from the sky.'

The Duchessa smiled cruelly. 'Nothing but dust.'

'Shut up. If you can't say anything useful, hold your tongue.'

'We could cut it out,' Kelpie said, as if seriously considering that option.

Livilla smiled. 'Her tongue? Good *plan*.'

Delphine was really not used to being the most sensible person in the room.

IT WAS dark by the time Ashiol returned to the Eyrie to find it empty, and a message scrawled on the door in Livilla's bright cosmetick. TOOK THE LADY HOME. That was all he fucking needed.

He made his way back to the Palazzo. Apparently he was never going to get away from this place. Armand, that limp lettuce leaf of a factotum, gave Ashiol an oddly deferential nod of the head as he approached the Duchessa's rooms. There was a story there, but damned if he cared what it was.

He could still feel the sensation of being wingless, and it made him pause several times to check he still had arms. That, and he was distracted by thoughts of Velody, her swollen mouth and big grey eyes; the heat of her skin under his hands.

There were several reasons why he had needed a drink or two before he got to the Palazzo. Luckily all the bars in the area had a tab running for him. He kept forgetting to carry money.

In Isangell's rooms, Ashiol was greeted by the sight of Livilla and Delphine tangled on the couch like kittens, both fast asleep. Strange bedfellows, indeed. Kelpie was alert and sitting on the edge of Isangell's bed. She gave him a look that wasn't friendly. 'Come to clear up this mess?'

'Got here as fast as I could,' he said glibly. Kelpie looked about as bad as he had felt earlier, before Velody had helped him heal himself. Her hair was all over the place, and she was badly bruised across the face. 'You didn't have to come here.'

'Shut up, Ash. You don't know anything.' She looked him over. 'You're all right now?'

He nodded impatiently, his attention on Isangell. She was sweating, her skin shiny and damp as she muttered in her sleep. The noxcrawl web had made its way over half her face. Someone had bound her to the bed.

Kelpie, probably, though he recalled that Livilla was good with knots.

'Do you know how to fix this?' Kelpie blurted. 'We can't keep standing watch over her. They're going to find out.'

'Yes,' he said heavily. 'I know how.'

A few drops of Kelpie's blood would drive the noxcrawl from Isangell; turn her back into the mortal she was supposed to be. But the thought of it revolted him. Priest belonged to the Creature Court, at least. This was part of the life he had signed up for. But Isangell... Ashiol had never wanted his world to touch her. Had never wanted his rosy daylight cousin to be tainted by the nox. Look at her now.

Not only her. They had all been ravaged by the sky one way or another, and in broad daylight. Hel — what the saints had happened to Hel? No one had seen her since she ran away from Velody's house. Ashiol had half forgotten about her while everything was such a mess, but looking down at Isangell's vulnerable body, it was Hel he was thinking about. She was so certain she was going to die. The last Seer had taken his own life. Might Heliora go that far?

He had never known the sky to have so clear a voice before. To steal into their daylight lives. The Creature Court were hurt and wounded, and none of them could trust each other any more.

Except Velody. For some reason, they all trusted Velody, even the ones who didn't like her. She was on their side, and that meant that it wasn't only the enemy's rules that were changing.

The sky, always been something to be battled and feared, to protect yourself from. Something to fight. Ashiol had never seen the sky as an intelligent foe. The thought that there might be a mind behind the attacks, some kind of guiding force enjoying the damage it did to them... it sickened him.

Ashiol sat on the edge of the bed. 'You. Wake up. Now.' Isangell was sluggish to respond, her eyelids fluttering open, and that made him angry all over again. 'What are you?' he demanded.

She smiled a sleepy, un-Isangell smile. (Thank fuck at least that the wench who had tried to seduce him was not actually his cousin — was it too much to hope she would remember none of this?) 'We are the worst thing you can imagine, son of Ducs. You are the last of your kind, because we shall make it so.'

'Don't listen to it,' Kelpie said. 'It's trying to poison your mind. It's been working on the three of us all day, trying to turn us against each other.' She managed a wavery smile. 'Luckily we didn't like each other that much to begin with.'

Ashiol glared down at the creature inside his cousin. 'Why her? Why this body?'

'Only she had the power,' said the thing inside Isangell.

'She has no power of the nox,' he raged. 'She has nothing you need!'

The not-Isangell giggled, and stretched her body.

'I'm going to need your blood,' Ashiol told Kelpie. Kelpie rolled up her sleeve without a word, without even a pause. That was loyalty.

The Isangell-thing twisted, and pulled against her bonds. 'Do what you like to the meat,' it howled. 'We are dust and you cannot deny us. We will swallow you!'

Kelpie let blood trickle down her wrist, into her palm, then knelt over the Duchessa in businesslike fashion. 'We're tough,' she said grimly, and pressed her bloody hand over Isangell's nose and mouth. 'We come with gristle.'

Ashiol had to look away. He was usually immune to the casual horrors of the Creature Court. But the sight of Kelpie forcing her own blood into Isangell's mouth was more than he could stand.

There was a commotion in the other room. 'I don't know who you trollops think you are, but I demand to see my daughter *right now*.'

'Holy fuck,' said Ashiol. 'Aunt Eglantine.' Now they were in trouble.

16
PERFORMANCE OF THE MASKS

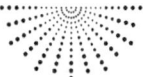

SIXTH DAY OF THE LUDI SACRIS, TWO
DAYS BEFORE THE IDES OF FELICITAS

NOX

*V*elody napped in her chair for an hour or two, but not enough to feel rested. There had been a lot of that lately. The daylight adventures were harder on her than the nox.

She awoke in darkness, and slowly realised that Crane was there, seated on the other side of the workroom. 'I don't think I can do this any more,' she said quietly.

'Of course you can,' he said, as if he never had any doubt. 'You're doing so well.'

'The Creature Court has been haemorrhaging people since I started this,' she said. 'Don't any of you blame me for that? I'm supposed to be your leader.' The very idea was laughable.

'The Lords barely even used to speak to each other,' said Crane. 'I think they were afraid to. Poet would never have begged for Priest's life when Garnet or Ortheus were in charge. He wouldn't have thought of it. He just would have mourned, afterwards. They would never have hesitated to believe Warlord was responsible. More of them would be dead, without the changes you have made.'

Velody wanted to argue with him, to point out her mistakes, but then she remembered Livilla and Warlord using their blood to save Ashiol. 'You think I make a difference?' she asked finally. 'Because they're not afraid of me?'

'I think you're the only chance we have to act like human beings instead of pawns and performers,' said Crane. 'If you can't see the difference you've made, you have to trust that we can see it.'

'I don't think I trust anyone,' said Velody. Least of all herself, after what her hands had wrought. 'Not any more. There's no ground under my feet.'

'Trust me,' said Crane. Oh, so certain. So young. What would she do without him? 'We are doing better than we were. You are our salvation, Velody. We couldn't survive another reign of Garnet. Keep going.'

She reached out wordlessly and took his hand, squeezing it for a moment. The moment passed. Perhaps he was expecting something more of her, but she had little to give.

Besides, she was needed elsewhere.

Velody left Crane downstairs and went slowly up to her bedroom.

Shivery darts crossed the sky, flickers of light and colour. Sure signs that something was waking up out there. She didn't know what kind of battle it would be — a light cloud skirmish or something far more epic and bloody.

'I don't care,' she told the mice that lined themselves up on her mantel, gazing at her. 'Really, I don't. I need sleep more than I need to prove myself in battle all over again.'

But she climbed out the window anyway.

～

ASHIOL EMERGED from Isangell's bedroom, his hands still damp from a frantic visit to Isangell's washstand to remove the evidence of blood. 'Aunt Eglantine, how are you?'

Isangell's mother was almost purple with rage. 'Ashiol, what game is this? Get rid of these drabs and bring me my daughter.'

Delphine mouthed the word 'drabs' as if she couldn't quite believe it. Livilla was amused, which was a good thing considering she was quite capable of killing Eglantine with a hat pin if the urge took her.

'She is sleeping,' said Ashiol. It was true, he hoped; the last thing he had done before slipping out here was to push a large vial of nettlebane at Kelpie and suggest she pour half of it down the Duchessa's throat. 'She didn't want to admit it to you, Aunt Eglantine, but she has been unwell.'

'So Armand informed me,' Eglantine said in a chilly voice.

(*That rat*, Delphine hissed to Livilla).

'She will be perfectly well,' Ashiol said defensively. 'The dottore said she only needed a few days' rest...'

'Ah, the mythical dottore,' Eglantine said between her teeth. 'Isangell has been attended by the same dottore for years, and he knows nothing of this new condition. Exactly who do you think you are, to take these matters upon yourself, boy?'

Ashiol could hear every epithet she left unsaid. He had heard them from her lips before. He knew what they saw — all of them, the whole family — when they looked at him. They saw the feckless black goat of the Ducal family, who had been exiled once for his chaotic and unreliable behaviour. Tidied away to the country, where he could do no more damage to the family reputation with his wicked ways. The drunk. The addict.

'I am the Duchessa's chosen consort,' he declared, infusing his words with animor. It would have little effect on his aunt, who was the most daylight creature he had ever known, but it gave him extra strength and resonance.

Aunt Eglantine went redder in an instant. 'You are *not*,' she bellowed. 'You dare presume...'

'I am not the one who presumes,' Ashiol thundered. 'You cling to the hem of your daughter's skirts in the hopes that we — the rightful Ducal family of Aufleur — do not remember that you have no power here. You married a man who was never Duc, and his family have allowed you to remain here entirely at Isangell's charity with your honorary title and borrowed wealth. You may have your spies and toadies here in this Palazzo, but you are not and never shall be Xandelian.' A speech along these lines had been bubbling under his skin for some time now.

There was no explosion. Eglantine twisted her mouth as if she had sipped a tisane with too much lemon. 'You really are Augusta's son, aren't you?' she said.

'Never doubt it,' Ashiol grated.

'I trust my daughter will make room for a discussion with me on the first day she is able to resume her public duties.'

'I am assured so,' said Ashiol. Was that it? Was she actually going to let him get away with this?

'Well, then. I shall take my leave of you, Seigneur Ducomte.' *And may you choke on it*, her icy tone suggested.

'Phew,' said Delphine, when Aunt Eglantine had finally sailed out of the parlour. 'That went better than expected.'

'You're telling me,' said Ashiol. He didn't know whether to be relieved or suspicious that she had backed down so quickly. What would her next move be?

'You are rather glorious when you shout, my cat,' said Livilla with a slow smile.

'Nice to know.'

Kelpie came out of the bedroom. 'Dragon gone, is she?'

'Oh, she'll be back. But that's a mess I'll leave for the Duchessa to sort out.' Announcing he was to be Isangell's official consort was something of a political disaster. But with luck Eglantine would be so horrified by the whole concept that Isangell politely letting her know it wasn't true would be enough to keep her quiet.

'You're the best cousin ever,' said Kelpie. 'She's breathing well enough now, if you're interested. The noxcrawl isn't visible anywhere on her skin. Which is for the best, considering.'

Ashiol nodded. The sky was calling them. He had been aware of it for some time, but Eglantine distracted him.

'Considering what?' said Delphine, alarmed. 'Does it never stop with you people?'

'Not while the sky is black,' Livilla said. 'I think I'll sit this battle out, Ash.'

'I don't think you will,' he said in a low growl. 'You're the only Lord who is entirely in one piece right now, and you're coming with me if I have to drag you by your hair.'

Livilla shivered deliciously. 'Well, if you put it that way, sweetling.'

By the time Ashiol and Livilla made it into the sky, the battle was underway.

It felt different now that Ashiol had heard the voice of the creatures — the intelligence, damn it — beyond the frostiels and screelight. The skywar wasn't a natural occurrence like thunder and lightning, it was real and malevolent. Every blow or strike or ripple of light felt personal.

He had known this, or part of him had. The Court had

always told stories of it. But he hadn't entirely believed. Now he had proof that devils inhabited the sky. Real devils, not monsters of myth. They were coming, and they had nothing less than the destruction of Aufleur in mind.

A silvery bolt of iceblaze lit up the sky near them. Ashiol chased it, pouring animor into the centre until it exploded into dust.

Velody was there, streaking brilliantly across the sky, calling commands to each of the Lords, directing them to one sector or another.

'Keep an eye on Livilla,' Poet yelled as he swooped over Ashiol's head. 'She let the Octavian catch fire!'

Ashiol turned, surveying the city below. Fucking hells. Flamebolts had hold of the librarion and were spreading to other buildings on the Octavian Hill. Poet was right — Livilla was the only Lord in that part of the sky.

He soared to her, body glowing with animor. 'Livilla, what the frig?'

She was dressed like a matrona again, in the same modest gown she had worn to take tea with the Duchessa, a rope of pearls hanging to her knees. What kind of maniac danced the sky in beads? 'Ashiol darling, you can't expect me to catch flamebolts. I have my hair to think of.'

He growled under his breath. 'Put the fire out. Move it!'

'Who died and made you Power and Majesty?'

Ashiol hesitated to go chimaera, just for a moment, unsure what he might find when he reached for that shape. Then, realising his weakness, he threw himself into his chimaera form, black and powerful and edged with claws. And yes, wings, back where they belonged, barely even aching as he swiped out at Livilla.

'Such a bully,' she said, eyes flashing with animor, but she turned and arced her body over the river where it curved behind the Balisquine. She dipped down then soared up again like a swan, and a trail of river water followed her in a fan-like tail. Livilla dropped down over the Octavian and the water exploded over the flames, drenching the buildings in a haze of light and animor.

Livilla had always been an artist in the sky, when she wanted to be.

'Good enough, my King?' she asked archly when the flames were dampened.

Ash returned to Lord form and kissed her once on the cheek. 'Where did you get that stupidly respectable dress?'

'Stole it from a nun.'

'That explains a lot, really.'

Livilla raised her eyebrows. 'Go see to your own patch of sky, Ash. I can handle this.'

'I know you can,' he said. 'You're damned good at this, Liv.'

Her whole body glowed at the compliment. Acting like Velody continued to have pleasing benefits. Ashiol wasn't sure if it was enough to make him do it more often, but it was interesting.

'About time someone noticed,' said Livilla smugly.

DELPHINE STOOD on the grass of the fancy Palazzo grounds and watched Ashiol and Livilla turn themselves into cats and wolves, hurling themselves into the sky.

Kelpie drew her skysilver sword. Delphine could feel the hum of it, the glow that made it different to a sword made of ordinary metal. She liked to pretend that she couldn't sense such things. 'Are you coming along?' Kelpie asked.

Delphine shook her head once, quickly. 'I'm not a sentinel.'

'If you say so,' said Kelpie with an odd sort of smile. She ran off into the darkness.

The sky was not just dark. It was pink and green and scarlet and there were shapes up there, dancing silhouettes that could kill or maim.

Delphine stared at her feet as she walked down the Balisquine. On the Avenue d'Argentin, she hailed a noxcab and flirted the cabriolet driver into giving her a ride all the way to the Vittorine, even though he didn't usually go that far.

There was a lamp lit in the kitchen. She never knew who to expect in the house these days — and wasn't remotely surprised to see that it was the puppy sentinel, the boy who looked at Velody as if she was all the saints and angels rolled in together.'

Sorry,' he said. 'Did I startle you?'

'It would take more than you to do that after the nox I've had,' she said, and pretended she was Rhian by putting the kettle on. 'Shouldn't you be sentinelling it up? I hear there's a party in the sky.'

'Velody didn't want me,' he said, staring at the table. 'She went out the window rather than take me with her.'

Oh, the darling baby. Delphine had been heartbroken at least three times by his age. She got a little bit tougher every time. 'Isn't that what they're always like, the Kings?' she said, finding cups. 'So busy saving the city, they don't have time to check whether they bruised anyone else along the way.'

His chin went up at that, and he looked offended. 'I'm not feeling sorry for myself or anything.'

'Pardon me for breathing,' she said. It was going to be hard to get through this conversation without laughing at him. 'I'm still learning about this sentinel thing.'

'Macready thinks you'll be good at it,' said the puppy.

Delphine turned away, because she didn't want anyone to

know that it felt good to be told that. Stupid, so stupid. 'Macready needs his head read. And boiled. And removed.'

The kettle sang, finally, and she scooped spoonfuls of dried mint and lemon into the cups, poured water over them. The puppy accepted the cup with thanks, but didn't drink.

'Tell me something,' she said.

'If I can.'

'Velody said you told her about Tierce. The city that disappeared.'

Obviously that wasn't what he had expected her to ask about. 'Yes, that's right.'

'Your family lived there?'

'My brothers. They moved there for work. I visited once, at Saturnalia. Years before it was swallowed by the sky.'

'Did it —' And she wished the tea was cool enough to drink, so that she could hide her face. No such luck. The puppy was looking at her as if he could see inside her skin. No wonder Velody had jumped out the window. 'Did it have yellow walls?'

She hadn't told Macready, or Velody, or Rhian. But Delphine had been dreaming of a city with yellow walls, of voices and hands and familiar things. Every time she woke up, she ached for what she had lost.

'Yes. Most of the buildings were sandstone. Not like Aufleur.'

'Oh.' And now she wished he would leave, so she could cry or something. Drink. Was there any drink in the house?

'If you're remembering,' the puppy said earnestly, 'it's probably because you're becoming a sentinel. Like Macready says. The rules are different for us...'

'Yes, I know. Shut up. Drink your tea.'

～

238

VELODY ONLY SAW the flamebolt when it was too late — as it smashed through the top of an elderly Avleurine tenement. She darted down towards it and found Poet distracted, standing on the roof of the old, abandoned Palazzo at the crest of the hill. A cluster of darkhounds and weasels gathered around his ankles, making their allegiance clear. The brighthounds knelt before him, their slender heads bowed in supplication. Not one of them was fighting the sky.

'Here she comes!' Poet announced theatrically. 'Will you bow to her too, liar?'

'What are you doing?' Velody asked him. 'We have a city to protect.'

'Finding the truth, lady Majesty.' Animor poured from Poet's fingers, scorching the hide of the poor brighthounds. They made a keening noise, but did not cry out.

Velody pushed Poet hard, forcing him to stop. 'What do you think you are doing? The sky is falling and you stand here playing power games? What can possibly be so important?'

'The truth,' Poet said with a cruel smile. 'Tell our Power and Majesty the truth, Lennoc Lord Brighthound.'

Velody turned and looked at the cringing brighthounds. They looked no different to her. 'Lennoc?' she said quietly.

The hounds met her eyes with a placid expression, and shaped themselves into glowing Lord form. His hair had already been white, but now he was fierce and uncompromising. He stood silent, his face and body under tight control.

Lennoc was a Lord.

'See,' Poet crowed. 'Ask him how long he has been clinging to my coat-tails, pretending to be less than he is. Oathbreaker,' he added in a sing-song voice.

'I broke no oath,' Lennoc protested, that accusation at least spurring him to speak.

'Did you not?' said Poet. 'Whose animor bestowed this exalted status upon you, my pretty? Livilla's children? The damage that the devil inside Priest inflicted on me, on Warlord?'

The new Lord, still glowing, looked only at Velody. *If he is this helpless already, how will he manage in the Court?* she could not help thinking.

'Dhynar,' Lennoc admitted finally. 'I quenched my master when he died. I have been a Lord since then.'

Shade reacted first, bolting into his mortal form in an instant. 'Since Dhynar?' he raged. 'You could have kept us together. Grago and Farrier — you could have looked after us!'

'You think I'm strong enough to hold three courtesi?' Lennoc yelled back.

'We were your brothers!'

'All very touching,' said Poet. 'I suppose you will run to your brother now, will you, Shade? Since you would prefer him as a master.'

Shade looked from Lennoc to Poet and then shook his head. 'I am no oathbreaker. You are my master and protector. I owe him nothing.'

Poet's smile was a deeply unpleasant thing.

Velody walked to Lennoc, seeing the pain in his eyes. She didn't blame him for being afraid. How could she? The Creature Court ate its young. 'You will serve me now as Lord?' she asked quietly.

Lennoc flinched as if expecting a punishment from her. 'Aye, lady Power.'

'Then we shall speak no more of this.' Velody turned on Poet, glaring. 'I appreciate your disappointment at losing your courteso. But a new Lord strengthens our Court. You should be glad of it.'

'Glad,' Poet said, eyes wide. 'He swore an oath to me as

courteso knowing he was a Lord. I should kill him now and let him die forsworn.'

'I repent,' Lennoc said instantly. 'I have regretted it every day. My Lord — Poet, I am sorry. I —' He looked at his feet, ashamed. 'We have always been looked after. I did not know any other way to be.'

'Have you no weaknesses, Poet?' Velody said. 'Such a magnificent specimen you must be. Not a single flaw.'

'Weakness begets weakness,' Poet retorted. 'If your Lords are made of dainty glass, Majesty, your Court will shatter and there will be nothing left for the rest of us.'

'The battle has not ended,' she told him, not letting on how much his words stung. 'I want you all in the sky. No matter your alliances. We have a city to defend. All of you owe it to me to dance the sky and keep the city safe. If you cannot accept Lennoc's repentance, Poet, that is your curse. Not his.'

'You are less likeable today,' Poet sighed and then took to the sky. Shade shaped himself back into darkhounds and followed, along with Zero's weasels.

Velody looked at Lennoc. 'If I can manage the newness of all this, so can you,' she said sternly.

He nodded. 'I will not let you down again, Majesty. May I make my oath to you as Lord?'

'Find me after the battle. If we are still alive, you can swear your oath.'

Lennoc nodded his head once and took to the sky, a bright glowing beacon. Another warrior to fight the demons. A sharper weapon to combat the sky.

It should concern Velody that she was thinking of the Creature Court as things rather than people — but she did not have time for that kind of weakness. Right now, there was a battle to fight.

∾

THE BATTLE LASTED the whole nox, growing fiercer even as the first lightness of dawn began to change the colour of the sky. They were all exhausted, beaten down by the relentless fight. Except Velody.

Ashiol had his own sky to fight, but he still could not take his eyes off her as she dodged the fierce bolts of warlight until she found one that glowed more deeply orange than the rest. She caught it, pouring all her animor into her hands and muscles, seizing hold of the burning thing until she could feel the heat through to her fingertips. Then she hurled it hard against the other bolts, cracking several open and sealing at least one gaping maw in the sky.

Ashiol still felt uncomfortable in his chimaera form, as if it was not entirely stable. His wings felt false, and his claws and teeth were a fraction slower than he was used to. There was an ache deep in his muscles that suggested he was not healed as well as he had thought. He struggled for a while with a cloudweb that left icy patterns in the air around him, and finally shattered it with a roar from deep inside himself.

For a moment, the sky surrounding him appeared to be made up of snowflakes, or the shards of a shattered mirror.

Finally, the sky calmed. Ashiol descended on the grass of the gardens of Trajus Alysaundre and took his naked human form. In that at least, he felt at home. Velody collapsed next to him, gasping air down into her chest. He knew that feeling. The air at ground level always tasted fresh and good after the harsh tang of being so high above the city.

He felt alive and half-dead and starving all at the same time. Velody rolled over, shifting her body on the grass, and looked directly at him, her dark eyes locking on his own. She looked starving too. Possibly not for meat.

Ashiol pounced, his hard body pinning her to the grass.

She tipped her mouth up to his as if it was easy, as if there was no reason in the world not to, and they kissed deeply, their skin sparking against each other.

He had always known that he wanted her, but this... damn Livilla and her games.

Ashiol broke off the kiss with a grunt of frustration. The sky was alight with pinks and golds for another reason that had nothing to do with war or danger. 'Safe for another day,' he said. 'Not from each other, obviously.'

'No,' Velody said, wrapping her arms tighter around herself, as if she could conceal her nudity from him with her equally bare limbs. 'Not from each other.' Local mice and cats surrounded them, peeping at the two naked humans with undisguised curiosity. Velody sent one and then another off in search of the sentinels.

Clothes would be good. If Ashiol was not allowed to lick every inch of her body, he would far prefer her to be clothed.

'Look at that,' Velody said suddenly.

Ashiol followed her gaze and saw the ruined remains of a temple that had obviously met the wrong end of a bolt of warlight. He could see the recent scorch-marks, and now that he was paying attention, he could smell the remains of the bolt — it was sour, like old lamp-oil.

'Isn't that the Temple of the Mater Matuta?' said Velody in a small voice.

'Yes,' he said, still not quite believing what he saw. 'It's dawn, and it isn't healing. The city isn't rebuilding itself.'

'The city always heals itself,' said Velody. 'You taught me that.'

Ashiol wanted to scream and swear and break things and throw thunderbolts at the fucking sky until it broke forever. Instead, he said, 'I know,' and nothing else.

What the hells else was there to say? The rules had changed again, and he had no idea why. He had to find

Heliora. When the world fell apart, she was always the only one with the answers.

Ashiol and Velody sat in silence as the sky lightened from dark to daylight, and the temple remained in pieces. Not a stone moved.

17
HELIORA

*N*ot long after the Seer Raoul's death, Ortheus called a
formal Court at the Haymarket. I was in attendance
with the other sentinels, standing at attention. I had no idea I was
the subject of the Court until he called me to kneel before him and
hand over my knives. I did so, chilled that he might be blaming me
for the Seer's death.

But he wasn't. He took my blades, placing them carefully out of
reach, and then he told me to look into the futures for him. I didn't
believe it at first. But they all stared at me like I was a prize peach,
succulent and ready for the biting. I denied it, protested, but
Ortheus just sat there calmly, shiny-headed old bastard that he
was, and made his demands.

I wanted to run. I searched their faces for some sign that it
wasn't true. Finally, as a last resort, I looked inside myself... and
the futures tumbled out so fast I could barely stay upright.

The futures are a white hot pain, a jumble of too much knowledge all at once. That first time, they flashed through my mind like
an oil fire. I thought my head would explode, or my tongue would
crumble to dust, I was so dry from the gabbling.

I was a Seer, I was alone, I had lost my family of sentinels, I would never get my swords. All so unfair. I thought this even as the futures dragged me deeper. I had no way of pulling out.

Finally, it seemed, I had done enough or said enough to please my Power and Majesty. Ortheus waved a hand and suggested that Tasha allow one of her boys to 'quiet the bitch'. (Let us not mistake the fact that this was a show for the rest of them, and like it or not, I was intended to be the star act.)

Tasha had never liked me. She could have easily chosen Lysandor, whom I had no grudges against, or Garnet, who disliked me as much as I hated him. She chose Ashiol to hurt me. This was her one chance to ruin any hope I had that he might choose me as a lover of his own volition.

She took the choice from him, and I'll never know if he might have loved me if our history was different.

He kissed me first, I remember that, even though I was mostly gone by that stage, howling random futures to the cavernous chamber, so swamped in the futures that I was barely aware of my body. His mouth hot on mine was almost enough to bring me back from the brink — I shuddered and stopped talking as his tongue slid into my mouth.

I couldn't hold on to reality, though. It was slipping away like a shadow at dusk. The futures pressed in on me, shrieking and screaming for attention. I watched every person of that Court die a hundred times before I came, gasping, my back against the wall of the Haymarket, my legs wrapped around Ashiol Xandelian's waist and a deep almost-pain throbbing inside.

Our first time together, and I had pretty much missed it.

HELIORA CHOSE her hiding place carefully. For all he pretended to have returned to them all, she knew that Ashiol had kept himself away from those places that actually reminded him of what it was like to be part of the Creature Court, when they were young.

Tasha's den had not been anyone's territory for a long time. Once her golden cubs became Lords and Kings, they moved away from the home they shared as children. Hel didn't care a flip of her hand about Tasha, but this dusty old den reminded her of that time when the Creature Court was something new to her, bright and irrepressible.

It reminded her of the very young Ash, the boy who dodged every attempt a certain young sentinel brat made to drag him into her bed. Of Garnet before he was broken by power. Lysandor, too soft-hearted for his own good. Even the children, Livilla and Poet, before the Court hardened them and turned them into just another couple of monsters.

It was a good place to sleep. For once, she wasn't dreaming of the futures. Heliora was lost in a haze of Oblivion, and it was the past that was choking her.

Someone grabbed her shoulders, shook her awake. 'Hel. Heliora. Wake the fuck up.'

She gasped and lost her hold on that sweet drugged warmth. She shuddered with cold even though he was there, already wrapping a blanket around her shoulders. The air was cold, and she could feel the scrape in her lungs.

'How long have you been here?' Ashiol demanded. 'I've been looking for you all day.'

Heliora leaned into his heat and rage. 'Don't know. How did you find me?' The first drop of Oblivion had been so good. She took more the next time, and then again. It was so long since she had felt real peace.

'One of Mars's courtesi saw you come down here. Apparently we all help each other out now. For fuck's sake, Hel.' Ashiol held the vial between finger and thumb and, oh, saints and devils. It was almost empty. No wonder her body felt slow, as if she hadn't moved in days. One drop and then another... it had been so very easy. 'We needed you,' he accused.

'Someone always needs me,' Hel said between sore, cracked lips. Real life was much harsher than dreams. She wanted to crawl back into her slumbering state. How much was left in the vial? She had to get it back off him. 'I need not to be needed. Or something.'

'Do you have any idea of what's been happening to the Creature Court, to the city?' Ash demanded.

Heliora laughed. 'Of course I do. How could I not know? I've seen it all, and I'm done with it. I don't want to see anything else.' Dust. Her thoughts were full of dust.

For a moment she had thought he was concerned for her, but no. It was his precious city, as ever, that he was thinking of. 'Is there worse coming?' Ashiol asked. 'Is there, Hel? We need to know.'

Fuck you, Ashiol Xandelian. 'There's always worse coming,' she flung at him. 'No wonder Raoul threw himself off the balcony. Don't you listen? I said I'm done. I can't hold on until Saturnalia, I'm done now. I can't keep Seeing what is to come — not and stay in one piece.'

Poet — why were her thoughts sliding away from him like he was something for her to be ashamed about? She poked at that strange thought and then memory hit her square in the chest. She used her gifts to steal his thoughts and memories, to intrude upon his darkest past. She had never done that to anyone before. 'I'm too broken. You need a new Seer.'

A look crossed Ash's face — sympathy? Pity? Heliora wanted him to care, wanted him (saints, talk about embarrassing) to take care of her, but she sure as hells didn't like that expression on his face.

'You're just tired,' he said finally.

She laughed, long and hard, the sound of it scraping her

throat. 'I'm squeezed dry, Ash. I can't do this any more. Not for you, not for that sweet-faced Power and Majesty of yours. I may as well climb the steps in the Haymarket and be done with it.'

That got his attention. Yet another thing to not be proud of. *Watch me not care.* 'Don't say that, Hel.'

'Why not?' she demanded. 'None of you give seven damns about who the Seer is. You want your prophecies in a neat paper parcel tied up in string. The city's about to be torn apart. I've seen it a hundred times over. I don't want to be here for it. Go tell your Creature Court that, and leave me alone.'

Ashiol was quiet for a moment. 'Can it be changed? Can we change that future?'

'The future can always change,' she said sullenly. 'You know that. I'm sure you can play the hero; it's what you do. I just won't be there to throw the victory garlands.'

She saw him play the hero, in the many futures. Saw him fall, saw him swallowed by the sky, saw Velody swallowed by the sky. She really didn't want to be here when that happened.

So damned tired.

'You're prepared to give me hope about the future,' Ashiol said quietly, one hand reaching out to stroke her hair. 'Even though you believe that hope is false. But you won't allow yourself even a little.'

'I don't have a future,' she said flatly, willing herself not to lean into his touch.

'That's bullshit.' His voice was strong and familiar and did more to bring her out of the Oblivion haze than anything else. 'Who's to say that your life is over? Raoul made that choice for himself. We don't know if he took that leap because of something he saw or something he didn't see. Just because the futures are closed to you does not mean you're going to fucking die. Maybe it just means you don't have to be a Seer any more.'

Heliora knew. Of course she knew. She still had Raoul's voice rattling around in the back of her skull, echoing her own thoughts and despairs. He threw himself off the balcony because of the empty future, because it was his only way of taking control.

Ash's idea was like a shock of cold water. It had never occurred to her — because perhaps it had never occurred to any other Seer — that the futures being closed to her did not mean her own death was imminent. 'Have you ever met a former Seer?'

'I've known one who jumped off a fucking balcony, and one who hasn't yet. Not enough for a pattern, is it?'

'Maybe,' she said numbly. Hope, oh hope. She wasn't sure how to deal with that. All those voices of former Seers running around in her head, and she had never asked any of them how they died, or if they had walked away from being the Seer. 'I've been seeing visions,' she confessed. 'Not the futures. Something else. I saw Garnet.' She would not tell him that she saw Garnet inside Poet's memory. If there was a scar there, she had no reason to show it to the world. But the other vision, the one in the alley — that worried her.

Ashiol looked as if she had ripped a piece of his skin off. He had always held his emotions and his anger out for anyone to see — she sometimes thought that was why Garnet had been able to hurt him so badly. 'Me too,' he said finally. 'I think the sky is trying to drive me mad again.'

'That makes two of us,' she sighed.

Ashiol wrapped his arms around her, until she felt warmth actually returning to her flesh. 'Hel,' he said some time later. 'I have to ask you something.'

To do her job. Of course. It had always been the Court first, with Ashiol. 'You can ask,' she said.

'The city isn't healing itself.'

She nodded. 'I was trying to tell you earlier, but I couldn't find the words. Macready and the others thought I was raving. There's a mirror in my head, and when it's broken, it won't mend.'

'But how? Why?'

She leaned back, away from his touch. 'You know why they took over Priest. To cause havoc and pain to the Creature Court. To make you turn against each other. To kill you, one by one. Have you not thought to wonder why they also took over the body of the Duchessa?'

'Isangell? She didn't get a chance to do much apart from screwing things up for the priests, and trying to seduce me.'

Caught by surprise, Heliora laughed. She hadn't known the part about the seduction. Ashiol looked like someone tried to feed him month-old cabbage ends. 'They chose the wrong body if that was the task they were after.'

'Damn straight.' He was giving her that intense look. 'The priests. Is that it?'

Heliora nodded slowly. 'In all the futures where the festivals were cancelled, the mirror would not mend. All this time, we thought the daylight folk were useless, playing games with their honey cakes and ribbons. But what if they were fighting the sky in their own way?'

'Aufleur only heals because of the daylight festivals?' Ashiol frowned, thinking it over. 'So what now?'

What could she tell him that he didn't already know? 'The dust is coming, and the city can't heal itself. All the rules you thought you could rely on are gone, Ash. When they get here, the city's going to bleed, and there's not a damned thing you can do to stop it.'

Now Ashiol was the one moving away from her, his mind calculating the next move, thinking of anything but her. 'No,

TANSY RAYNER ROBERTS

I don't believe that. Now we know the problem, we can fix it. The damned sky won't win, not this time.'

Heliora leaned against the wall, sighing. 'No,' she said. 'It won't win. Not against you. How could it?'

～

I'M NOT STILL in love with Ashiol. That would be one humiliation too many, thank you.

～

IT WAS business as usual at the Basilica that afternoon. If you knew what to look for, you could see what was missing. Who was missing. Heliora's belongings were salvaged by some of her kinder neighbours, who had no idea that she was the reason a madman chose to rampage through their place, killing, maiming and wrecking. The smiles were falser than usual, but Heliora's fellow merchants carried on, doing what they always did: taking shilleins from customers.

Ashiol told her about this, after he broke the news of what Priest had done. Heliora had not seen this coming at all, and it was a strange thing to feel so outside reality. He offered to come with her as she retrieved her belongings, but she refused.

Breathing was harder than it should be. The thoughts kept crowding around Heliora, harder and faster than the futures. She sat on the steps outside the Basilica, a laden swag at her feet, looking out over the Forum. She still had her position, rent paid to the end of the season. She could buy another pavilion. But the thought of telling even one more fortune made her stomach cramp and her head hurt.

She couldn't come back here, not after this. She couldn't bear the Arches either, or any of the territory down below.

Now that the Oblivion was leeching out of her system (no more, she had given the last of the vial to Ashiol to be sure of it), she wanted nothing but to curl up in a ball somewhere quiet.

'Haven't you heard? We're saving Aufleur after all. No need to cut and run.'

Heliora looked up, and saw Poet haloed in the late afternoon sunshine. He was dressed in his fine city clothes, the ones he wore to play the stagemaster of the Vittorina Royale: a long coat, top hat and a cravat tucked neatly around his throat. A sack sat at his feet, paper masks spilling out of it. Heliora stared at them. 'You're saving the city with costumes and trinkets?'

'Apparently so. A little cat came to visit me, said that he needed to raid the wardrobe room of my theatre. I have no idea what he's on, but I'm prepared to enjoy the show.'

A show. Was Ashiol planning to recreate the missing festivals himself? The thought would be comical, if Heliora were not numbed with grief and guilt. 'What do you want?' she asked.

Poet drew a watch on a chain out from his pocket and looked at it exaggeratedly, then flicked it back and forth between his fingers. The face was cracked, and it was blood-stained, but he looked at it as if it was the most beautiful thing he had ever seen. 'Retribution. True love. Cherry tart for tea.'

She closed her eyes, and wished him away. Instead, she felt him swoop closer, and smelled the wool of his coat as he sat beside her on the step. 'Go away, Poet.'

'Not yet. I want something from you.'

Heliora remembered the feel of him hard and urgent in her mouth, of the memories and thoughts she had stolen from him, just to prove a point. She squeezed her eyes tighter shut, because that wasn't something she ever wanted to think about again. 'I'm not going to tell anyone about what I saw.'

He was silent, and she risked a look at him. His face was oddly serious. 'It's not the world's most shocking secret, you know. A lot of people loved Garnet. But I would prefer to be considered unique.'

'I shouldn't have taken it.'

'No.' Poet's mouth curved into a soft smile. 'You shouldn't. Isn't it sad? You were looking for blackmail material, and instead you found an old hurt, long dead, of no relevance to anyone. Though I did well enough at hiding it when Garnet was alive. I would hate to slip now.' He flipped the watch back and forth again. He seemed casual and relaxed, but then he had always been an excellent actor. There was a light in his eyes that was unfamiliar, a tense excitement.

'Why are you so stupidly cheerful?' Heliora asked.

'Because you gave me something, when you stole a peek at my memories. Did you know, O Seer, that you can give your visions to other people?'

She stared at him. 'I'm not dead yet.'

'I don't mean your whole job, dear heart. But you did give me a vision of the future, when you swallowed me down. It's quite a party trick you have there.'

'Apparently you are unique,' she said finally.

'I suppose if you could transfer visions by sucking a fellow off, Ashiol would have his eyes permanently crossed by now,' Poet smirked.

'What did you see?'

His face closed over. 'That's for me to know. But it's a lovely future I glimpsed.'

'Just the once?' This had never happened before. She wanted to wring the details out of him.

Poet's eyes shone behind his spectacles, and he was no longer playing the fool. 'I saw something, when you were taking my memories. Then again in the Basilica, when that fucked-up sky devil was inside Priest, and Ashiol's blood was everywhere and the world was ending. I heard a voice, and saw a flash of the future. A good future.' He tucked his watch away carefully. 'How do I get to see it again?'

'I don't know,' she said. 'I don't know how you got it in the first place.' First Ashiol, and now Poet. Was everyone a Seer now? Heliora wanted to say something useful. She owed him, after all — though from the look on his face, she had repaid him already in some way she couldn't fathom. Whatever he had seen, it had made him happier than she had ever seen him. 'The other fortune-tellers I met — I never knew how much they really saw truth in the cards or the crystal, but I think some of them did.'

'Cards don't interest me,' Poet said dismissively. 'I want my vision, not some old haddock in a spotted veil telling me what she thinks I want to hear.'

'Some of them used drugs to see visions,' Hel said. She'd never bothered about such things; her issue was holding off the damn visions, not pulling them closer. 'Others swore by particular types of music, or dance rituals, to fall into a trance.'

'That sounds more my sort of thing,' Poet said, gazing intently at her. 'Music. I can do music. What else?'

'Mirrors,' she told him. 'There's something about mirrors. Some people think they can be window between worlds — if you look long enough, and take the right kind of potions.' She was starting to suspect this was not the best advice she could be giving him. 'I'm not recommending the practice...'

Poet leaned forward suddenly and kissed her. Not the usual sort of kiss between a man and a woman. A sudden, dry brush of the lips, like a mark of honour. 'Don't die yet,' he said when he drew back. 'I have so few friends left.'

She felt breathless again. 'Is that what we are? Friends?'

'Silly fish. What did you think we were?' And then he was up, practically capering, swinging his sack of masks over his shoulder. 'Take care of yourself, Hel. The future's going to be fine, no reason to fear it.'

Hel sat on the steps for some time after he was gone. Had Poet finally cracked, or was there actually something to look forward to?

She had nowhere to go. She picked up her swag and started walking. Her long skirts swished around her as she left the Forum, heading south towards the lower Vittorine. There was no reason why Velody should take her in, but there was a demme there with kind eyes who had fed Hel soup and asked no questions. Heliora thought of roses whenever she saw her, and it made her oddly calm. A house with a roof and stout walls, and perhaps there might be a corner where she could curl up to sleep.

NATURALLY, the door was not opened by the rose demme at all, nor Velody, but by the sulky blonde who disliked Heliora from the start.

'May I speak to Rhian?' Hel asked.

The blonde snorted, but allowed her inside.

ONE THING *I am grateful for — I stopped being a sentinel before Garnet became a King. Serving Ortheus and Argentin was an honour and a privilege. Serving Garnet would have been seven hells. He used the sentinels as his private playthings, and there was nothing any of them could do to stop him. He couldn't go too far, though, not with Ortheus still Power and Majesty.*

Ashiol and Lysandor became Kings too — it was better, some-

how, the two of them curbing Garnet's excesses. Then Ortheus died, and Argentin, in the same battle. Garnet quenched them both. Seers swear no oaths. That's part of why they treat us well — baby us and give us anything we need. We have no obligation to serve the Power and Majesty. But there is an expectation that we shall. I never looked into the futures for Garnet, not once. I didn't trust him. Didn't trust whom he might thrust up my skirt while I was vulnerable.

After he exiled Ash, there was nothing left for me in the Court. Reading fortunes for shallow courtesans and dames was far less degrading than unpicking the seams of my brain to please the ego of a madman.

If the sky is trying to send Ashiol mad with visions of Garnet, then he's not the only one. They know he is the thing that scares us most — all of us. It scares me that the sky knows us so well.

18
CIRCUS OF BEASTS AND SONG

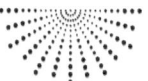

SEVENTH DAY OF THE LUDI SACRIS, ONE DAY BEFORE THE IDES OF FELICITAS

NOX

*V*elody dressed herself in a long peacock-silk gown that a client had refused to pay for, months ago. She couldn't remember why — perhaps the cut was not daring enough. It was unfashionably modest for the current season, falling past Velody's knees and covering her up to the neck, though the arms at least were bare.

It sent a message, or was intended to do so. She was not going to play the Court's games on their terms any more. If it took dressing like a musette matrona to do it, then she would.

Ashiol wanted Velody to hold Court in the Haymarket. Poet pressed for the Shambles square. She was not happy with either option, not least because they had suggested them. She eventually chose the Gallery, between Mayor's Bridge and the tunnels leading to the mouth of the Arches.

The Creature Court came as summoned, a little after dusk, primped and arranged in their usual finery.

Warlord stood with his five courtesi; Poet with the two who remained to him, Shade and the boy Zero. Priest's three demmes stood nearer to him than to any other Lord, but there was a distance there, too. None of them were close enough to touch, or be touched. Velody did not blame them for being wary. All were damaged by the noxcrawl's attack on them; one limped, and another stood uncomfortably, as if there were something wrong with her arm. All three were painfully thin.

Livilla and Lennoc stood apart from the other Lords, their lack of courtesi quite evident.

Ashiol was waiting near the bridge when Velody arrived with the sentinels at her back. Heliora was invited to join them, but preferred to stay with Rhian, who made up a cot for her in the corner of the workroom. Delphine had reacted with an incredulous laugh to Macready's suggestion that she come along to the Court, and refused to budge.

'You swore an oath to me,' Velody said now, to the Lords and Court. There would be no pontificating or booming voice amplification. If they wanted to hear her, they would have to make the effort. 'Because you were willing for the Creature Court to change. You hoped for something more than what you already had. This is what you chose. We face a crisis you have never seen before. The city is not healing itself. The buildings destroyed in skybattle stay as rubble. The corpses stay dead. We won't survive many more noxes of skybattle. There is little time in which to act, to prevent us following the fate of Tierce.'

'I'm bored,' Livilla said out of nowhere. 'When are you going to punish bright-hair over there for pretending to be a courteso? When do we see Priest crawl? We're only here for the blood sport.'

'There will be no punishment, and no blood,' Velody said simply.

Livilla was furious. 'We were attacked from within. My boys were slaughtered. Where is my justice?'

'The attack did not come from within,' said Velody.

'Like hells it didn't.' Livilla took two steps towards Priest, teetering on her spiky black heels. 'He has Janvier and Seonard's blood on his hands. My *boys*.'

'The threat came from the sky, as it always does,' Velody insisted. 'Priest was a victim too. We cannot afford to lose more strength by squabbling and punishing each other.'

'Speak for yourself,' Livilla sneered. 'I demand recompense.'

'That is not —' Velody started to say, but Priest interrupted with a lift of his hand.

'Dear Majesty, my fellow Lord has a point. I may not have willingly sinned against you all, but my hands were indeed responsible for cruelties visited upon others. If there is any way I can make recompense, I wish to do so.'

'Are you going to compensate all of us for the inconvenience of being attacked, threatened, tortured?' Poet said dryly. 'Not sure you have enough blood to give, old man.'

Livilla folded her arms. 'You took my courtesi from me. I want yours.'

'Ridiculous,' said Warlord. 'No Lord has ever been asked to give a courteso to another, like borrowing a pair of boots. Loyalty does not work like that, Livilla.'

'Don't be so quick to dismiss it,' said Poet. 'How many Lords had a courteso killed in front of him to prove a point? This is a far less monstrous suggestion.' He seemed in an odd mood, fidgety and bright-eyed.

Ashiol was silent. Velody looked at him out of the corner of her eye, willing him to react in some way, to give her some clue of what she should do or say in response to all this. He gave her nothing.

One of Priest's demmes, the sparrow courtesa with a

damaged arm, stepped forward. 'I would go, Power and Majesty.'

Priest looked wounded, but said nothing.

'You are under no obligation,' Velody said gently, not entirely sure if that was true.

'I —' and the courtesa glanced back at Priest, not meeting his eyes. 'It is for the best, Majesty. I should like to serve Livilla Lord Wolf, if she will have me.'

Priest bowed his head, accepting the loss. 'What is your name?' Velody asked the demme.

'Bree, lady Majesty.'

'Livilla, Lord Wolf, will you take Bree as a willing servant under your oath, to compensate for your loss, and agree to speak no more of the matter?'

Livilla seemed confused by the sheer reasonableness of the offer. Perhaps she had been expecting more of a fight? 'I lost two,' she said, regaining some of her usual edge.

'Accept the gift freely given,' Velody snapped. 'It is the only one you shall be offered this nox.'

Livilla hesitated, then held her hand out to draw Bree towards her. They stood there as if they had no idea what to do with each other.

'Does anyone else feel they have been wronged?' Velody asked.

'Why, do we all get demmes?' Poet sniped. He held up his hands in his own defence as Velody glared at him. 'As ever, I want only to serve, Power and Majesty. My motives are as clear as ice.'

'I remain weak,' said Warlord unexpectedly. 'In the Creature Court we have never spoken of weakness except in insult. But I have not recovered fully from the attack upon my person, and the recent battles with the sky were further drains upon me. I am tired, and my dreams... It will be a long time before I feel the usual strength in my bones and flesh. Assuming I ever regain that strength.'

'What would you ask of me, dear fellow?' Priest asked, sounding genuinely regretful.

Warlord lifted one hand to indicate he had no real idea what to ask for. 'Under ordinary circumstances I would ask for blood, but you understand why I hesitate to do so on this occasion.' They must all feel like Priest was still polluted. Velody did not blame them for that, especially after what had happened with her hands and the garments she had made.

'Indeed,' Priest said with a weak smile. 'Would you settle for the offer of a favour to be repaid at a time of your choosing?'

Warlord considered it slowly, and then nodded. 'Aye, that would be sufficient. Your offer is generous, old friend.'

'As is your forgiveness,' replied Priest.

They bowed to each other. It was faintly surreal to Velody. She had to bite her lip to stop herself grinning like a loon. 'Priest Lord Pigeon,' she said. 'I would ask your courtesi if they wish to continue in your service. Given what happened during your time under control by the noxcrawl, I would not blame them for choosing to step away from your service, regardless of past oaths. I would ask you to release them of all obligation.'

Priest breathed out slowly and then nodded his head. 'My demoiselles, I free you from —'

'No,' said the gull courtesa, Damson. She looked wan and walked with a limp, but there was anger in her voice. 'I will stay with you, my Lord. I am loyal.'

Priest glanced to the other courtesa, a very thin demme. 'And you, Fionella? I would not blame you for walking away after what my hands did against you.'

Velody winced, remembering the bursting sound as Priest attacked the birds, one by one.

'I will stay,' said the courtesa of plovers. 'My Lord.'

Priest bowed his head to Velody, relief evidence across his face.

'There will be no further punishment, Priest, Lord Pigeon,' said Velody. 'Continue to serve as you always have, and all will be well.' She glanced across the gallery to where Lennoc stood alone 'Likewise, Lennoc, Lord Brighthound, there will be no punishment for your actions. Assuming this will be the last time you tell a lie to this Court, in thought, word or deed.'

Lennoc bowed low. 'Aye, lady Majesty. I vow to serve as Lord to the best of my ability.'

'Come then, and take the oath,' she invited.

Lennoc came and knelt before her, speaking the words of the official oath to serve Velody as Power and Majesty. He had given it once as a courteso, but he was a Lord now, with far greater responsibility to the Court.

Poet's face was flat in a false smile as the man who had lied to him gave the Lord's oath. Velody did not think she had to warn Lennoc to watch his back. Instead, she thanked him for his oath, and then turned her attention to the rest of the Court. 'I ask you all to trust me, and to keep the oaths you made. We have a city to save, and I need all of you. Even if it means putting aside your ideas about how it is the Court are supposed to behave. The only way we can win against the coming invasion is to open our mind to new ways to fight the sky.'

She had their attention, at least.

'Ritual,' Ashiol spoke up. 'Ritual is important, Majesty. We have our rituals... and the daylight folk have theirs. We have always been so disparaging of their honey cakes and ribbons. The game of saints and songs. But it was all a lot more important than we imagined.'

Delphine should most definitely have come to this Court, if only to hear Ashiol admitting she had been right all along.

'The noxcrawl chose Priest to cause havoc and pain amongst the Creature Court,' Ashiol continued. 'To hurt us from within. But it chose Isangell because only she had the power to cancel the festivals. To call off the Sacred Games. As soon as she did that, the city stopped healing itself.'

'Easily solved,' said Poet lightly. 'Ask the Duchessa nicely to bring them back. Problem solved, let's have tea.' He was doing a good job of pretending he had not already been brought in on the plan Velody and Ashiol had devised. He had provided the costumes and masks, and was now feeding her straight lines. It was best not to wonder why he was being so obliging.

'I can do that,' said Ashiol. 'But we've already missed most of the Sacred Games.' He looked at Velody. 'We can't get those days back.'

'No,' she said. 'But maybe we can still give the city what it needs.'

There was silence, and then Poet struck a pose. 'Are you saying, lady Power, that it's time for us to put on a show?'

'Yes,' said Velody. 'I thought you'd like that part.'

THE MORNING DAYLIGHT streaming in through Isangell's bedroom window was not something to be celebrated. She was up half the nox conferring with her ministers and proctors, not to mention the various priestly representatives who managed to talk Armand into giving them an appointment.

Ritual was important. Variations of that sentiment had been drilled into her head, over and over again. She must never again do such a foolish thing as cancel the Sacred Games for her own amusement.

Assuming that was why she did it. She had no recollection of the action, nor the motive.

The morning light felt hot on her skin, and she rubbed uncomfortably at her neck. If only she had some idea of what had happened. Her mother and Armand were no help at all, and Ashiol, whom they both claimed should be able to supply some if not all the answers, had not been seen for more than a day.

Apparently she hired a new secretary during the time she did not remember, though no one knew where the dame in question was now.

The more Isangell pushed for answers, the more she felt the concern of Mama and Armand. Did they fear as much as she did that she might have fallen victim to the family complaint? If there was even the slightest possibility that she was losing her mind, the question of her heir became so much more urgent.

No more holding the sons of the Great Families at bay. She would have to marry, damn it all to the seven hells and back.

Isangell stepped into her sitting room and was about to ring for her maids when she saw a curtain fluttering. 'Ash?' she said suspiciously. 'Come out here where I can kill you.'

'That's a popular desire,' drawled her cousin. His foot appeared from behind her sofa, waving to let her know where he was. 'I thought it best to catch you before your day starts.'

'Don't even pretend you've been trying to get in touch,' she accused. 'Every lictor and servant in the Palazzo has orders to detain you on sight.'

'Eglantine took back the reins of power, did she? I thought she was unlikely to stay cowed for long.'

Isangell crossed the room with as much dignity as she could muster while wearing a short and fluffy silk noxgown.

She firmly lifted one of his booted feet from the side of the sofa, letting it drop to the floor. 'My orders, not my mother's,' she said crisply. 'I want to know what happened to me. If I am to believe Mama and Armand, I hired an army of strange women, had three nervous breakdowns and besieged myself in my rooms. Why don't I remember anything since the chief day of sacrifice?'

'Believe me,' Ashiol said, holding her eyes with an intense gaze, 'you don't want to know.'

'Not good enough. I'm not just your baby cousin, I am the Duchessa d'Aufleur, and I need to know anything that might affect my rule.' She stared him down, determined that her lip would not quiver, not even a little, though it took great courage to ask her next question. 'Am I going mad?'

Ashiol's face changed in an instant, reflecting surprise and then horror. Oh. He hadn't even considered the possibility. Why was that so comforting where her mother's platitudes had been insufficient? 'No,' he said, seizing her hands firmly in his own. 'You're not going mad. I'm sorry you thought it, but no one else can ever know the truth.'

'What truth could possibly be worse than that?' Isangell demanded. She hated being shrill, but some situations called for it. 'If you have any respect for me, you must speak.'

To her surprise, Ashiol actually paused to consider her words. His face was so serious. If the answer was worse than succumbing to the family complaint, it must be very bad indeed.

'You were attacked by an outside force,' he said finally, not sounding like her Ashiol at all. 'Like a — cold, or a fever, only with malicious intent. For a few days, your mind and body were not your own. But it's over now. You are free of it.'

'Attacked,' Isangell repeated. 'By whom? A malicious cold? That makes so little sense.'

'I'm not sure how else to explain it,' he said.

'Try,' she said between her teeth.

'There is another world, above and beneath the one you know. Battles being fought for the city every nox. Heroes. Devils. Saints and angels. You weren't supposed to get caught up in all this. Those of the daylight are usually immune.'

'Immune to what?' This was all impossible, surely. 'Ash, you sound like the crazy person my mother has always said you are. Was I drugged? Hypnotised?'

'I think the word for it is... possessed,' he said reluctantly.

And oh, it was true; she could see it in his eyes. There had been something inside her, a mind other than her own, and Isangell felt her skin prickle all over at the thought of it. 'Are you part of this other world?'

'Yes,' he said in a rush, as if relieved to be confessing at last. 'Yes, I am. You don't understand how serious this is, Isangell. The Sacred Games have to go ahead.'

Not him as well! 'Believe me, I know. Twenty separate ministers and priests have spoken to me over the last day. The Mercatus and other festivals will go on this month as planned, and they have all agreed to draw a line under the Ludi Sacris. I don't need you to tell me I shouldn't have cancelled the damn thing, I need you to tell me what made me do it.'

Ashiol was so angry, so certain. Not a hint of the rakish philanderer he pretended to be. He looked like a warrior, as if he was finally standing up to his true height after slouching for decades. 'You can't draw a line under the Sacred Games, no matter what the priests say. You have to stage the closing circus today, or the city is doomed.'

Isangell's mouth had fallen open. 'Are you insane?' she demanded.

'Only nearly.'

'The whole idea is ridiculous. The priests of the city are

barely speaking to me, we don't have flowers or animals or performers...'

Ashiol laughed hollowly. He sounded just short of despair. 'Well,' he said, 'I can provide the animals.'

OF ALL THE things Ashiol had thought he would never do, taking Isangell to the Killing Ground was top of the list. He had to weigh up which was better — bringing her through the streets of the city, or down through the Arches.

Today, all of the Lords and Court were supposed to be on the same side. The idea was patently ridiculous, and yet Velody was in charge, and that made a difference. Today, this once, perhaps the Creature Court could be trusted to do what was necessary instead of what suited themselves.

Ashiol had not taken a swallow of imperium all morning, and he was starting to feel the lack of it.

He chose the Eyrie, to avoid them being recognised in the streets above, and led Isangell through the mess of tunnels that led under the city until they came out in the Arches. His cousin was fascinated by this relic of history. It was all he could do to draw her on through the maze of narrow, shabby streets in the Shambles, to the Killing Ground itself, without her stopping to ask a million questions about how the people of Aufleur had truly once lived here, underground.

Isangell coped with the tunnels and the dirt, clambering about in her day dress through the darkness. But when they walked through the Smith's forge and the harsh sunlight burst around them, Ashiol thought for a moment he might lose her.

'Oh,' Isangell said faintly. 'Oh, Ash — is this what you meant? About things I couldn't understand?'

This was the least of it, but he knew better than to say that now. Baby steps.

'We need you as witness to the circus,' he said. 'And to close the festival — you opened the Sacred Games, before everything went to seven hells. Only the daylight Duc can close them.'

Isangell's hand rested on his arm, clenching and unclenching against the cloth of his shirt. 'Let me know what I have to do, and I will do it,' she said, every inch the cool and poised Duchessa.

Ashiol had never been so proud of her, or so scared for her.

The sandy arena was bright and gaudy for once, filled with flapping tent cloths and pavilions. Poet had called in every favour he could from every musette company in the city, and Ashiol had to admit, he had come through for them. If only the damned rat wasn't enjoying himself so much.

Ashiol led Isangell to the tiered seats, and made her comfortable on the velvets and cushions that had been laid out for them. 'Remind me again why I trust you,' she said, her voice faltering.

'Because in your heart you know I speak only the truth, gosling,' he said, settling her on the high tiered seats. 'And I would never hurt you.'

She gave him an exasperated look. 'What do you need of me?'

'What you would normally do at a circus. Take fright at the beasts, tap your foot to the songs, marvel at the saints and devils. Hide your face as they pretend to kill a dummy version of you, in the name of some saints-begotten tradition no one really remembers. At the end, when they call for their patron's ovation, give it to them. Then you can speak the closing song, I can wield the knife, and there's a nice drugged lamb ready for the sacrifice. All as usual, only without the crowds.'

'And this will save the city.'

'We can hope.'

It was the first time Ashiol had ever seen the Creature Court united in something other than battle. It could work. It had to work. If the city would not heal itself, they were all doomed.

'I see we're not the only audience,' Isangell noted.

Ashiol looked up and saw Heliora crossing the grounds, looking unlike herself in a borrowed dress, her shaven head thick with stubble. She had a sombre Rhian on one side of her, and a boldly dressed Delphine on the other. Ashiol frowned. He had not known Velody intended to bring them here. It seemed like a bad idea.

All three demoiselles bowed with due deference to the aristocratic visitor, and chose seats a few tiers below Ashiol and Isangell.

The sunshine blazed over them with little actual heat. Isangell's small hand lashed out and clutched at Ashiol's knee. He resisted the urge to shake her off. *It was the noxcrawl; she wants me no more than I want her*, he reminded himself.

'Is that a rat?' she squeaked, sounding like the child he remembered, just for a moment.

It began. As Ashiol watched, one white rat skittered across the dry sandy stage. Then another, and another. A small horde of them converged upon the simple cloth of blue silk and silver stars that lay in the centre of the arena.

Poet did love to play the showman, and today was no exception. The rats shaped into the man with a flash of light that had to be one of his stage tricks, and when he stood before them in Lord form, it was with the blue and silver cloth neatly draped around him like a toga. 'Demmes and seigneurs, dames and boys, milady sweet,' and with that he nodded graciously at the Duchessa with a scorching look that put a little colour in her cheeks. Oh, hells no. Ashiol found himself growling under his breath. Poet was getting no closer to Isangell, that was for damned sure.

'Welcome to the circus of the nox, a cabaret of bloody battles and daring adventure such as you have never seen before. Believe your eyes if you must, but listen to your heart. It beats to the rhythm of our song.' Poet grinned toothily. 'The song of the monsters of Aufleur.'

There were more fireworks and sparks after that, and a parade of animals. An odd mix of creatures to be sure — panthers and stripecats were hardly out of place in the arena of an Aufleur circus, but it was rare to see domestic cats, with birds and mice alongside them, weaving together as if they were not natural enemies, predators and prey. Ashiol remembered that their grandfather the old Duc had been trying to get wolves to perfom in his own circuses for years, but no one could tame them to any satisfactory results. The old Duc had not had Livilla on his side.

'Why are there no beast-handlers?' Isangell asked in a whisper.

Delphine, overhearing her, giggled.

'Demmes and seigneurs,' Poet announced with great flair as the animals cleared the arena once more. 'May I present our first bout of the evening — the gladius and the slashcats!'

Ashiol wondered if Mars was up to a sword fight with his own courteso, then almost swallowed his own tongue when he saw Crane stride out in the leathers of a gladius, steel sword bared. How had Velody talked him into this indignity?

'He's pretty,' Isangell said approvingly.

Rhian turned in her seat and presented the Duchessa with a basket of fresh flowers. 'For your favours, milady,' she said clearly.

'Oh, thank you, demoiselle.' Isangell took the basket with pleasure and selected a crimson camellia, tapping it thoughtfully back and forth. 'The favours are the best part,' she confided to Ashiol. 'I was rather sorry to miss out on it this year. At least, I think I was. If only I could remember.' She blew a kiss to Crane and waved the camellia at him. 'Someday you'll have to show me what kind of show you can put on when not working at the last minute, Ashiol.'

'Oh, it would be a marvel to behold,' he muttered sourly.

The fight was to be staged, of course. The steel sword made Crane's part in that easy — it simply would not leave a mark in the bodies of the three silver slashcats currently pacing back and forth on the sands. It would be harder for Farrier who would have to rely on actual restraint, never an easy thing in Court form. If he could resist the urge to bite Crane's throat out, all would be well.

The fight was swift and dramatic, with plenty of over-telegraphed moves. The cats snapped and slashed at Crane, playing with him. Ashiol was swiftly bored, his attention drawn instead to the audience, and their reactions.

Delphine watched the sword, her head tilting imperceptibly with every flash of the blade. Saints, was Macready right about her? It seemed impossible that a little wench like that could make the transition into sentinel, especially at her age.

Isangell made a small noise and hid her face in Ashiol's shoulder when Crane 'dispatched' the slashcats, one after the other, with dramatic thrusts of the sword. A moment later her nails dug fiercely into his arm as the slain slashcats shimmered and shaped themselves into a fit naked man, the sword still lodged beneath his ribs. He rose, and he and Crane bowed to the audience. Delphine and Rhian cheered and threw rose petals.

Isangell looked faintly stunned, and then hurled a

camellia to each of the young men. 'Will it all be like that?' she asked Ashiol quietly. 'This is not like any circus I have ever attended.'

'This is just the beginning,' he promised her.

The traditional circus for the final day of the Ludi Sacris began with "beasts and song". Velody and Poet took this quite literally for the first half of their show. Poet sang two of his musette numbers, a comic and a tragic. Livilla sang too, her voice throaty and vulnerable, as her new courtesa performed a choreographed dance of sparrows around the arena.

Warlord the panther took on Kelpie and won, pinning her to the sands and licking her face until she rebelled against the role she had been given, and kicked him in the balls. Ashiol held his breath at that point, waiting for him to savage her in retaliation but instead Mars shaped himself mortal and kissed her messily, half-carrying her off stage before his mouth left hers.

Isangell fanned herself. 'Can we hire these people for the next set of Sacred Games?' she asked breathlessly.

'Ask me again after Cerialis,' said Ashiol. 'We'll see how many are still alive.'

The back of his neck prickled. The everlight of the Killing Ground made it timeless, but it should be late afternoon. They only had a couple of hours to make this work.

'I'm not stupid, Ashiol,' Isangell said quietly. 'I know this isn't just a circus.'

'I hope it's the best damned circus Aufleur has ever had,' Ashiol said. 'We need it to be.'

ISANGELL'S HEAD hurt from the bright sunshine. She was out of her depth. She did not know who any of these people were, but she could not shake the feeling that she was the least important person here.

The acts blurred into each other — men and beasts and swords and songs — and Ashiol watched the whole thing so intently, as if it were about to fold up like a paper bird and fly away.

'Is this what you've been doing all this time?' she asked him. 'When they all thought you were — drinking and carousing?'

'Not this,' said Ashiol after a long pause. 'This is new to us. But the Creature Court, yes.'

Creature Court. The words had an extra reality to them the way he spoke them aloud, as if there were a hundred layers of meaning that she could never comprehend. 'So my mother was wrong all this time,' Isangell said, rather pleased at the idea. 'She insists that you're crazy, or broken, and that you can only bring misery to our family. But all this time, you've been fighting to protect us.'

'Oh no,' Ashiol said, his eyes on the grey sand. A beautiful demoiselle was dancing, so lightly that she seemed to walk on air, and her arms fluttered like the wings of a bird. 'Aunt Eglantine had the right of it, all along. Broken. Crazy. Dangerous.'

She did not like the chill tone of his voice. 'But all this —'

'It's not usually a pretty play,' he said hoarsely. 'It's death and power and rivalries, and...' He broke off and closed his eyes, as if the very sight before them was alien to him. Wasn't Isangell supposed to be the one who felt out of place here? 'Your mother fears me for good reason. You'd all be better off if I never returned.'

'I don't believe that,' she said, determined to prove her loyalty to him.

'You were too young to remember last time. Before I went away.'

'I wasn't a child!' She had been fourteen. Ashiol was older and mysterious and the grown-ups were always worried about him, but he was charming and he danced with Isangell and her friends at parties, when he turned up. Then one day the grown-ups weren't just worried about Ashiol any more, they were afraid for him, and he was locked away in his rooms. then he was gone — back to Aunt Augusta and Diamagne — and Isangell didn't see him again for five years. 'You were sick,' she said uncertainly. 'And they sent you away.'

He looked so bleak. 'Is that what they told you?'

Isangell was a demoiselle of the world now. She could absorb new information. 'Was it the drink?'

'It was the Creature Court.' Ashiol was staring at the arena, but Isangell didn't care what the latest act was. She was watching him. 'I lost it all. Purpose, power, love. I tried to hang myself. Made a botch of trying to fall on a sword. I would have done anything to make it stop.'

Isangell's hands were curled so tightly into the basket that she could feel the wicker biting into her palms. It hurt, but she did not care. 'But you didn't succeed.'

'No. I did not succeed.'

'And now?'

Ashiol turned to look at her, really look at her, and his smile lit up the world. 'And now I have something to live for again.'

19

CIRCUS OF BEASTS AND SONG

SEVENTH DAY OF THE LUDI SACRIS, ONE DAY BEFORE THE IDES OF FELICITAS

NEARLY NOX

*V*elody's skin felt tight all over. Poet had raided the entire backstage of the Vittorina Royale to clothe the Court for this production. Her own role in the performance was to be mercifully brief, which was for the best considering she had to spend so much time getting everyone else in the right places.

She wore a scarlet frock that smelled of cigar smoke and brandy and mothballs. She also wore a high crown made from bamboo and silver paint, and (against her better judgement) a long, fair wig made from silk and horsehair. It scratched horribly.

Impersonating the Duchessa was a step too close to impertinence for Velody's comfort, but Poet had insisted. The 'sacrifice of the Duc' was essential to any traditional circus, and if ever tradition had been important, it was today.

As Poet rightly said, the only person to play the Duchessa in this scenario was Velody. She still felt uneasy about it.

Readying herself, she rounded the billowing corner of the tents they were using as dressing rooms, and came upon Poet. He sat on a stool by himself, gazing into what looked like a small compact mirror. As Velody stepped closer, she saw that it was the broken glass of a pocket watch.

How odd. She had never seen such an object in Aufleur — there was too much superstition about clockwork. The proctor of the Vittorine had once tried to replace the water-clock in the Piazza Nautilia with one made of gears, and the people had risen up against it, claiming it was ill-fortune.

A pocket watch, though. Her grandfather in Tierce had owned one like that — on a gleaming brass chain. She had not remembered it until that moment. Sage, too — there was a memory about her brother Sage and clocks, but she could not hold on to it. 'Poet,' she said now. 'I'm ready.'

He flicked the watch closed and put it away in a pocket. That odd smile was back on his face — the one that said he had happy secrets. 'Stage fright?' he teased, pulling out the cosmetick pens to wipe a line of bright scarlet across Velody's mouth.

'Hardly,' she said, which was not entirely true. 'You seem to be having fun.'

'Well, it's inspiring, all this Creature Court camaraderie. It's giving me all sorts of ideas for the new season of the Mermaid Revue.'

'Glad it's proved useful,' she said dryly.

There was a full-length mirror beside them, set up so that each performer could check their costume before they went out onto the stage. Velody looked at their shared reflection, and Poet's eyes flicked over hers before he straightened her hem. 'You'll do,' he said.

She moved away from the dressing tents. When she looked back, she caught gazing into that mirror, as if he expected to see someone other than himself staring back.

Crane passed Velody as he came off stage. 'You look terrible as a blonde,' he said.

'That's what they tell me,' she replied, straightening her wig. Just a few more acts and it would be her turn to go on, and this whole sorry mess would be over.

Ritual is important, she reminded herself every time she started to feel silly. *Ritual is everything.* After all, this had been her idea.

It would be over soon.

ASHIOL COULD BARELY TELL who was who beneath the masks — the arena was full of false saints and devils in bright costumes. There were not as many mimes, tumblers or dancers as usual at these events, but that was hardly surprising. The Creature Court had to play to their strengths.

One particularly garish scarlet devil proved his identity by bursting into a flock of bats, his costume falling empty to the sands.

Isangell said nothing, sitting there with her eyes on the arena and her hands folded tightly around the basket of flowers in her lap. The silence between them was palpable after his revelations. Still, it was best she knew. He should have told her long ago, back when she first asked him to come back to the city.

Still. If he had never come back, he would not have his power again, would not have a place in the Court. They might not have Velody as Power and Majesty, and hope for the future. All those things.

The sky over the Killing Ground was a paler blue than usual. That was so many kinds of wrong. It was always day in the Killing Ground; it never changed.

Heliora, still seated below him with Rhian and Delphine, turned and looked directly at Ashiol. Her face was grim.

Oh, fuck. It wasn't going to work. They were wasting their time. The sky was going to throw everything it had at them this nox, and the city was not going to heal.

HELIORA WANTED TO SCREAM. It was almost fun at first, watching the Creature Court perform an elaborate pantomime of costumes and morbid humour. She could feel how much they were enjoying themselves. They spent their whole lives in the shadows and the nox; how could they not relish a chance to play themselves in front of an audience, however select?

But it wasn't going to work. She could feel tight pressure building up in her ears. A storm was coming, and not the kind of storm they were used to.

We're coming, and you cannot stop us. The dust will fall.

Poet sang an operatic ballad of clowns and dead demmes, surrounded by a cabaret of grinning devils and horrified saints. It was grotesque and brilliant, and Heliora could not stand to look at him. She knew too much about him now, knew why he still clung to the theatre even though the Court had taken hold of him so early.

His broken childhood and fractured teen years were piled up in her head, along with the voices of Seers past, and the futures that were always digging at her for a way through. It was so damned noisy inside her head. *We are dust. You cannot stop us.*

The climax of the gruesome pantomime came when a false Duchessa stepped out from behind the tent cloths, artificial golden hair blowing in the breeze that whipped through the arena.

That wasn't right at all. There was not supposed to be wind here. This was the Killing Ground. The sacred space of sentinels. Nothing moved here, nothing lived. Sand and sunshine and emptiness was all it had to offer.

A retinue of sentinels gathered around the false Duchessa. Not Macready or Kelpie or Crane, but sentinels long dead, so pale and translucent that Heliora could not bear to look at their faces.

Perhaps it was they who stirred Velody's cornsilk wig and the hem of her gown. Ghosts all.

'I always hated this part,' Isangell confided to Ashiol. 'They would bring in some aging clown playing Grandpapa, and the fellow couldn't resist playing it for cheap laughs. When Grandmama was Regenta, I swear they brought in the same man in a padded dress.'

Ashiol had forgotten about the sacrifice of the Duc. This wasn't right. Even play-acting at killing Velody made his skin go cold. 'Poet,' he muttered beneath his breath. 'You go too far.'

MACREADY WAS CONVINCED this was madness, so it was. A fine day indeed when they had to resort to this kind of pageantry. Were their lives not colourful enough?

He played the game at Velody's behest, dispatching animals with false kills when called upon (though the lad Crane made a better show of it; the young cove was relishing his chance to playact). This was too much, though.

It didn't fecking matter that steel couldn't hurt those of the Creature Court when they were in their full power. Macready was a soldier, and using real blades for a circus went against everything he had been trained for.

'Aim for the heart,' Poet informed him with a twist of his

mouth that suggested he was enjoying this all far too much. 'The lack of blood is a shame, but Velody refused to have her throat bitten out in public, bless her.'

Macready wanted to refuse to do this, but he didn't trust the rest of them to do it properly if he walked away.

Duty was a bitch, some days.

THE ENTIRE CREATURE Court were on show, some as animals, some as people. Heliora chewed her lip as Velody-as-the-Duchessa made her slow promenade around the circle of sand and then stood in the centre, surrounded by dead sentinels, ready for the slaughter.

It was a fine ritual, but it wasn't ritual enough. It wasn't real enough.

'It's getting dark,' Rhian said in a low voice, wrapping her shawl more closely around herself.

'No,' said Heliora. 'This is the Killing Ground. The sun never goes down here. It's always daylight.' But Rhian was right. The colour was draining out of the sky.

Heliora looked down to the arena where Velody stood waiting for her mock execution. Macready was there now, his steel sword bared and ready for the final blow.

'Oh, saints, devils, frig it.' She had seen none of this. Surely all the rules of the Creature Court and sentinel history being broken was worthy of a vision or two. Had the Oblivion dulled her powers so much?

Macready slid the steel sword harshly between Velody's ribs, a killing thrust if ever there was one, and darkness fell.

VELODY DID NOT FEEL the bite of steel as Macready ran his sword into her, just the usual numbness of metal ignoring the reality of her body. But then the Killing Ground went black, and her chest burned bright and fierce. 'Oh, saints,' she gasped, and fell to her knees with the shock of it. 'Mac!'

'What, Velody?' His hand still on the blade made it move inside her and she cried out.

She felt Macready move nearer, and another jolt of the sword. 'It's stuck. Are you — feck, you're bleeding.'

Velody choked as blood filled her mouth. It was all so fast. The pain shot through her body. She could feel his hand shaking on the hilt, and she was cold all over. 'Don't move the blade,' she gasped. 'I'll bleed out faster.'

Everyone around them was noisy, protesting the darkness, but none of the Lords and Court had realised Mac and Velody's predicament.

'Can you shape?' he asked.

'I don't think so, not if steel cuts me...'

'Try it, for devil's sake.' Every time Macready's hand shook, the pain burst through her senses all over again.

Velody closed her eyes, reaching past the pain and the reality of the sword hard and scraping inside her body. She shaped herself. Becoming the mice had become so natural to her now, like breathing. She scattered across the sand, a horde of little brown creatures, all breathing, none of them bleeding. Safe.

The city hit her like a skybolt, crashing into her hundreds of little minds and overwhelming her completely. In that moment, she saw not just the futures, stretching out in many different flickering directions like ribbons on a parade float, she also saw one very particular future, glowing like a beacon.

Velody watched with her many beady little eyes, fascinated by the vision. So that was it. That was how it had to be.

That was how it ended.

WHEN SHE CAME BACK to herself she was lying on the sand, naked and gasping and Velody again. The sun was bright, blazing down on her in that sinister Killing Ground way.

Velody rolled and found the gown she had been wearing as the false Duchessa. She stared at the fabric in her hands for a moment, and then someone was helping her slide it over her head. She gazed at Macready, who looked devasted.

'I'm all right,' she told him, grasping his hands. 'Really. No damage. I need Heliora. Where is our Seer?'

'Hel!' Macready yelled, too loudly, and Heliora ran forward from the tiered seats.

The Seer looked smaller than Velody remembered her. That might have something to do with Ashiol coming up behind her, tall and glowering in that dark, threatening way of his that Velody recognised as concern. 'I'm here, Majesty,' said Heliora.

'How do you do this every day?' Velody gasped. 'My head feels like it's going to break apart like a melon.'

'Are you in one piece?' Ashiol asked, eyes roaming all over her. He leaned in, as if perhaps he could smell whether she was hurt or not. 'We're going to need you in the sky.'

'Did it work?' Macready blurted. 'Will the city heal now?'

'I have no idea,' said Ashiol. 'We haven't closed the games yet. Hel?'

The Seer shook her head once. 'I can't tell. I can't see anything, Ash.' The panic in her voice was evident.

I saw it. Velody had no idea why she had not spoken the words aloud, but... she had seen the answer to that question, and so much more. She had seen everything. She knew what she had to do. For once, she wasn't hovering on the outer edge of the Creature Court, lost in the sea of tradition and hidden knowledge and rules no one had told her about. She could finally be Power and Majesty, could finally embrace what that meant.

Had this happened to Garnet? Had he known?

Ashiol was talking, something about how they were going to have to trust that the circus had restored something to the city. 'Velody bled all over the sand; we shouldn't need to bother cutting a lamb's throat. Isangell, do it now!'

The Duchessa was speaking then, old rote words flung to every edge of the arena, and Velody felt it; she could feel the city closing in upon itself, the unbearable rightness of the sacrifice and the festival, and everything being as it should be.

'That's it,' she whispered. 'We did it.'

'You did it,' Ashiol said, giving her an odd look, and then he drew her to her feet and kissed her. It was a gentle kiss, not their usual lunging and grabbing, and when it was done, her blood was all over his shirt.

Ashiol turned, then. 'Delphine, Rhian, can you escort the Duchessa back to the Palazzo?'

'They are not yours to order, Ashiol,' Velody said, not quite letting go of him. 'They are not part of this.'

'You shouldn't have invited them then,' he snapped, threading his fingers impatiently through his hair. She wanted to push his hands away, and tidy him up.

'We'll do it,' said Delphine. 'Look after yourself, Velody,' she added in a rush, as if embarrassed. Then she turned and gave the Duchessa a small curtsey. 'We haven't formally met, but I believe I'm your new private secretary.'

Rhian smiled. 'All of you, look after yourselves,' she echoed, and was it Velody's imagination or was she looking directly at Macready? 'Look after each other.' Rhian went to join Delphine and the Duchessa.

Velody closed her eyes. It was still there, that beacon future, bright and fierce. She could see everything. It all made so much sense that she ached with it. 'Heliora should go with them,' she said.

Ashiol looked at her as if she was crazy. 'Why?'

Because that's where she is when the sky breaks open. 'The Duchessa may be a target again, when the battle comes. The nox knows her now. Neither Rhian nor Delphine are experienced in the ways of the Creature Court.'

'I may as well be useful,' Heliora agreed.

Swords, they were going to need swords, too. Velody looked up and saw Crane watching her steadily. He knew there was something going on with her, even if no one else did. Velody just gazed at him, their eyes locked together, hers silently pleading. Crane broke first. 'Come on, Heliora. You know you've been dying to play sentinel again. I'll show you how it's done.'

Heliora laughed suddenly. 'Are you going to share your swords with me, pretty boy?'

'I wouldn't go that far.' Crane gave Velody one last meaningful look before he and Heliora went over to join the Duchessa's makeshift retinue.

Thank you, thank you. I'm sorry.

Velody looked back to Ashiol. He didn't seem to know what she was up to. He looked a he always did — sexy and hungry and ready for battle. 'We should go,' she said.

Ashiol nodded once and turned to the untidy stage tent. 'Lords and Court! Attend your Power and Majesty. The circus is over... but we have an encore to perform.' He turned back to her, eyes glowing. 'Together,' he said, almost boyish in his enthusiasm.

If only that were true. 'Together,' Velody agreed, tasting the lie on her tongue.

20

CIRCUS OF BEASTS AND SONG

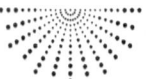

SEVENTH DAY OF THE LUDI SACRIS, ONE DAY BEFORE THE IDES OF FELICITAS

NOX

The sky was a bright, angry red. Velody, with Ashiol at her side and the Lords and Court at her back, emerged from the tunnels into the city above to find that nox had fallen early and the moon was rising, full and perfect, glowing with scarlet light.

'Hard to see how that could be a good omen,' Poet said in a quiet voice.

'Never seen it like that before,' said Warlord.

'There are no cracks,' Livilla said. 'No points of weakness. Apart from the colour, the sky looks *quiet*. Where are they going to come from?'

'Everywhere,' Priest said. He spoke so rarely now that it was easy to forget he was there. Velody noticed that the other Lords were still reacting uncomfortably to him, unwilling to entirely believe that he was the same man he had always been. 'They will take our sky apart and start on the city, brick by brick.'

Lennoc just stood there, glowing in his unfamiliar Lord form, and said nothing.

'If we can just get through this nox,' Velody said in a steady voice. 'The circus did its work, we'll have the protection back and the city will mend itself at dawn.' She didn't know how she managed to sound so confident, but someone had to be.

'Also there will be fairies who leave cakes on our pillows in exchange for our baby teeth,' Ashiol growled. 'So that's all right, then. Here it comes.'

The sky began to crumble, from edge to edge. The moon brightened in the darkness. *Now.*

A long tearing wound sliced across the sky, and dark shapes bled out of it.

Velody called the Creature Court into the sky, and not one of them hesitated to answer her battle cry.

This is how it starts, and this is how it ends.

THE SKY WAS ANGRY. That was just fine with Ashiol because he had gone so far past angry.

Fucking fucking fucking Aufleur. This city had been biting and gnawing and chewing at him since he was a boy, destroying any chance he might have had at a normal life, and what did he have to show for it?

Another battle. A red moon. Fine dust pouring out of cracks in the sky, drifting on the breeze with an odd kind of beauty to it. Velody. Always Velody, floating there in the sky beside him, brave and uncompromising as she watched the dust fall. Damn her to the seven hells too.

The dust scattered in wide arcs across the sky and then shaped itself into arms, legs, muscles, blades. A living foe.

'Frig me sideways,' Poet said in wonder. 'Devils. After all this time. Devils.'

Ashiol said nothing, but an old conversation with Garnet filled his mind and his memory. Always Garnet. *Why do we always have to fight lights and fire and — all this insubstantial shit? Why don't we ever get people to fight? Real enemies — warriors with faces to smash in, veins to bleed, swords to duel against? Where are the fucking devils?*

Someone had replied: *Be careful what you wish for.* For the life of him, though, Ashiol could not remember which of them it had been.

'They could as easily be angels,' Livilla breathed. 'How can we tell?'

'It doesn't matter what they are,' Velody said, 'we have to fight them, force them back. Or we lose everything.'

Game on. Ashiol hissed low in his throat, the sound of a cat faced with an enemy far larger and more fearsome than he. *Game fucking on.*

∾

FIGHTING the sky had never been like this before. Velody slashed and burned her way through the army of dust devils, her chimaera form glowing with dark animor. Her blood felt hot and pounded inside her veins as she battled.

'We're not getting anywhere,' Poet yelled from nearby. His hands and feet, glowing white in Lord form, dissolved the devils when he hit them, but they would simply reshape themselves elsewhere.

The dust felt hot to the touch, and made Velody's chimaera skin itch where it brushed against her. She let out a cry, the animor exploding in a burst of light from her throat, and the nearest devils vanished under her assault.

There were always more.

She blasted a second group of them, who clustered around Poet. He emerged looking unflappable, as usual. 'Much obliged, lady Majesty.'

'Always a pleasure,' Velody said, the words coming strangely out of her thick chimaera body. She could see Ashiol and Warlord fighting more of those things, surrounded by Warlord's many courtesi. Livilla and Priest were further across the sky. Lennoc was doing well on his own, his slender brighthound bodies darting quickly back and forth, never letting themselves be caught.

The devils stopped. All of them. A momentary pause, but it was noticeable. Their faces (if you could really say that those were faces) all turned inexorably in one direction.

Velody whirled around to see what had caught their attention, and saw two figures on the roof of a temple high on the Avleurine hill. Kelpie and Macready, both with skysilver swords flashing.

Warlord moved first, a dark streak across the sky, but then the devils moved, all of them converging at once upon the two sentinels.

The devils were faster.

MACREADY DIDN'T REALISE the fecking devils were coming for him and Kelpie until it was too late and they were on top of them. He fought with sword and knife, the skysilver carving up the devil figures, though the dust kept reshaping into new bodies. The air was filled with howls and cries that didn't seem to come from fecking anywhere.

Kelpie went down first, under a wave of glittering bodies. Warlord swooped over them, blasting the devils back into the dust they came from.

Macready stepped back, once and then again, until he was standing right over Kelpie, protecting her from the hordes.

One of the devils seized Kelpie's fallen Sister, waving the sword in something like triumph, and another dragged her knife right out of her hand.

The devil holding the sword seemed harder somehow — leaner and sharper and more real. Macready feinted and lunged at him, and the tip of Tarea met resistance instead of gliding through an insubstantial body.

Feck it.

Velody was yelling at him from somewhere. 'They want the skysilver!'

'It makes them stronger,' he yelled back.

But then the dust came down around him, thick and fast, and there was no holding on to his blades, not when he could not see or breathe or...

He let go. He hated himself for doing it, but damn it all. He wasn't the Silver Captain. He wasn't going to die, not here. He relinquished his blades and let the dust take him.

For a moment, he couldn't move; there was just heat and dryness sucking the moisture out of him, and his head was full of that bastard Garnet and the pain in his finger as it was severed from his hand...

SOME TIME LATER, Macready coughed, and lifted his head from Kelpie's chest. She was breathing too, but barely, the sound ragged and scraped. He looked up and saw the Creature Court close around several solid, real devils who no longer looked as if they were made only of dust and moonlight.

'Where is my bloody sword?' Kelpie demanded through a throat that could barely produce a sound.

'Gone,' said Macready. Both his skysilver blades. Both hers. 'They're gone, my lovely.'

He would have preferred to lose another finger.

THE STREETS WERE bright and cold — too cold for the month of Felicitas, despite the eerie red light that made it look like there were fires somewhere. It was so long since Isangell had walked the streets like an ordinary citizen. Most of the last year was spent in private mourning for the old Duc, her grandfather; running the city behind closed doors with her ministers and priests, allowing half a dozen fair-haired priestesses to perform her ritual roles in public.

Perhaps it would be better if she kept up that tradition. Though the memory of seeing the false Duchessa take a sword through her chest still chilled her. Everything went dark in that moment, but part of Isangell had reacted viscerally, had felt something hard bite into her flesh.

There were some duties she would rather not personally fulfil.

This Creature Court, these people of Ashiol's, they frightened her. The young man with the swords acted with the assurance of a soldier twice his age, but there was only one of him. When Isangell went out, it was usually with at least a quadrigo of lictors.

Ashiol's eyes slid away from Isangell as soon as his people started talking about the sky. It was as if he could not stand in two places at once — could not be whatever he was to them and his daylight self in the same body. Could not care about her and the animals in the same thought.

She had seen so much today. Isangell did not want to think about this new knowledge, about the worlds of strange illusion Ashiol had opened her eyes to. She wanted to block the images of the crazy circus from her mind, to forget entirely about men who shaped themselves into beasts and birds and bats. If at the same time she could forget Ashiol telling her how he had tried to hang himself, that would be more than acceptable.

There was not enough nettlebane in the world for this. Isangell's head ached.

It should not be dark this early; the hour was not approaching sunset and yet it was dark, the only illumination coming from that terrible crimson full moon hanging over-head. The old Duc had always been frightened by full moons. The first undeniable sign of his failing mind was one Ides, when he attempted to personally draw every curtain in the Palazzo, to keep the bright moonlight out. Isangell still remembered that look of weary comprehension on her grandmama's face, as if she had been waiting her entire marriage for this moment, the first of many partings from her husband. The beginning of the end.

Isangell was accompanied by demoiselles, at least. Ashiol had not gone so far as to spit in the face of propriety, even if they were not exactly the kinds of maids and ladies-in-waiting to which Isangell was accustomed. The blonde demoiselle spoke well, as if she was used to being among the Great Families. The other tall and quiet demoiselle, Rhian, had rougher hands and a rougher accent, though she seemed in all other ways respectable.

Then there was the one they called Heliora, who looked like a street drab, and must have had the pox recently, to do that to her hair. The others listened to her instructions, and there was a strange power about her.

Isangell felt as if she had known this demme in another life; her voice seemed so familiar. Perhaps it was something she had dreamed.

The young soldier stopped suddenly, drawing the lighter

and more silvery of his swords with a hiss. 'Stay back.' His entire body was composed as if he faced some dreadful creature, though there was nothing but air between him and the street.

'I see nothing,' Isangell protested, but stopped when Heliora reached out a commanding hand, gesturing for her to halt. Heliora peered at the air before the soldier's sword as if it personally offended her.

'We are not supposed to see it,' said Rhian in a low voice.

Delphine made an odd noise in her throat. 'I see it,' she whispered. 'Oh, saints, it's true.'

THEY JUST HAD to get the Duchessa home to her fancy Palazzo and then they could go home, all of them. Delphine could pull a blanket over her head and wait for Velody to return and tell them that, once again, the city had been saved in that odd invisible way they were supposed to believe in.

Delphine was so far from believing. Yes, there was a strange magic to these people; she could not sit through that whole ridiculous circus and accept that it was stage trickery that turned that creepy Poet from a horde of white rats into a man (it took every strength she had not to scream at that part of the show; it still made her shiver to remember being trapped in his dressing room).

What Delphine did not believe was that this battle of theirs was as dire and serious as they all seemed to think. She convinced herself it was a game to entertain them, to keep them from clawing each other's eyes out. Really, if today proved anything it was that they would be better off channelling their energies into musette melodrama.

This small gang charged with accompanying the Duchessa now made their way through the Lucian district, circling the Alexandrine hill to make the most direct way to the Balisquine and the Palazzo.

Crane of the puppy-eyes stopped, up ahead of them, drawing that sword of his like he knew what to do with it. While her ladyship and Rhian wasted time speaking of what they could not see, Delphine was too busy being over-whelmed by the fact that she could.

Saints, she was one of them, she really was; there was no denying it now in the face of *this*.

The creature was big, taller than Crane, shoulders wider than those of any man Delphine had ever seen. Its body was formed from a powdery dust the colour of moonlight (ordi-nary silver moonlight, not the blood red light that filled the sky this nox), and its face... Delphine gasped as the *thing* bared sharp teeth in a mouth entirely the wrong shape, below a nose that resembled that of a stone gargoyle rather than any actual person's.

If there were saints and angels in the world, then this was a devil.

'I can't see it,' said Heliora, her voice ragged and miser-able. 'I can't see anything any more. I'm not even a sentinel any more, I'm *nothing*.'

'Believe me, it's not pretty,' Delphine said sharply. Oh, help. It was true. If she could see that... thing, then she really had been contaminated by the world that had swallowed Velody up.

Macready had been right, damn him. Heliora might not be a sentinel, but Delphine was.

Crane stood between the demmes and the devil, sword and knife at the ready. The creature he faced did not have any weapons. That was good, right?

The glittering dust swirled, losing the devil shape to form a cloud that wrapped itself around Crane. He coughed and fell to his knees.

'No!' It was Heliora who moved; Heliora who couldn't even see what he was fighting. She slammed into Crane from behind, and his choking cry expelled some of the devil dust from his lungs. He toppled to the cobblestones, limp but —

'Breathing?' Delphine cried out. The puppy was so young.

'Breathing,' Heliora confirmed grimly. 'For now. Flapper! What do you see?'

That would be her, Delphine supposed. 'A devil,' she said, struggling to find her voice. 'There's no other word. It was a devil and it turned into dust and he breathed it in.'

Heliora did not disbelieve her for a second. It was oddly exhilarating, to be trusted. 'Where is it now?'

'I don't know.' Delphine looked around wildly and saw a gleam just for a moment, swirling into a narrow alleyway. 'I think it's gone.'

Heliora looked critically down at Crane for a moment and then reached under his cloak, unbuckling the leather straps of his sword harness.

It was the Duchessa who spoke first. 'What are you doing?'

Heliora gave her a look like she had spat in her drink. 'What does it look like I'm doing?' She buckled the harness on to herself, the steel sword hanging down her back. She was too short for it, but the sword didn't actually scrape on the ground.

Delphine felt relief that she was not being asked to take up the blades, closely followed by a prickle of resentment.

Heliora picked up the fallen skysilver sword and slid that one home too, looking satisfied with herself. 'We're going to need to get him to safety,' she said, kneeling down beside Crane and relieving him of his knives. 'Come on, boyo, open those eyes of yours. Are there any nests nearby?'

Delphine felt Rhian slip her hand into hers, squeezing it gently. She squeezed back once, and found herself exhaling in a rush when Crane opened his eyes. 'The Duchessa,' he murmured.

'Screw the Duchessa,' Heliora said impatiently. 'Sorry, your Ladyship. But if there are any more like that out here, we're not going to make it to the Palazzo. We need a nest, Crane. What do you have?'

His voice was hoarse and cracked, like he hadn't tasted water in days. Swallowing devil dust would do that to you, Delphine supposed. 'Not mine. But there is one, three streets away. Harder to secure than if it belonged to me...'

'We'll take it,' Heliora snapped, and rose to her feet. 'I'll lead. You —' She looked at Delphine and Rhian. 'You look strong enough to help Crane walk,' she said to Rhian. 'Good shoulders. And Macready thinks something of you,' she added to Delphine.

Oh, thank you very much. 'I'll help him,' Delphine said quickly, knowing how much Rhian hated to touch anyone, men in particular.

'I can,' Rhian said quietly. At Delphine's look of surprise, she said, 'He's Crane,' in a voice that trembled only slightly. There was so much else to be brave about right now.

Delphine nodded, and slid one arm under Crane's. Rhian took the other, and they pulled him to his feet. He was weak as a kitten, leaning against them.

'Keep her Ladyship where you can see her,' Heliora said crisply, and set off ahead with her borrowed swords swinging.

The Duchessa stepped gamely enough in behind Heliora. Rhian and Delphine brought up the rear, with Crane half-collapsed in their arms. He muttered quiet instructions to them, and they wended their way to a narrow street lined with shops and tiny piled-on-each-other apartments.

'Where is everyone?' the Duchessa said, the first words

she had spoken aloud in a long time. 'Shouldn't there be people in the streets?'

Delphine wanted to laugh at the fact that the Duchessa genuinely seemed to not know. Had she ever walked the streets of her own city after noxfall? 'That depends,' she said, not losing the chance to make a point. 'It was supposed to be the last day of the circus — if all went as usual, there would be dancing and rioting until dawn. Perhaps they all have better things to do.'

Perhaps the sky has already eaten them all. Perhaps they know better than to step outside when the moon is the colour of blood.

'Here,' croaked Crane, gesturing at a blank wall. In that instant, the devils came down upon them, all in a rush.

The devils were clearer this time, shapes of dust and dirt and moonlight that moved towards them in a rapid, whispering swarm. Delphine dragged frantically at Crane and Rhian, pulling them hard against the nearest building, the wall that Crane had indicated. 'Come here!' she screamed at the Duchessa, who gave her a bewildered look but joined them.

Heliora did not move. She stood in the middle of the street, skysilver sword gleaming in the near-darkness as the devils — four of them, no, six — swirled straight at her, surrounding her. Their false maws gaped horribly, the dust forming sharp points of teeth. A hideous noise filled the street — howls and cries that just made the blood run cold — though the devil sounds did not seem to come from their mouths so much as from everywhere. A vicious wind whipped down the street, rippling their dust shapes.

Not one of the devils even glanced in the direction of Delphine and the others, even though Crane had been their focus before...

'The swords,' Delphine said suddenly. 'Saints, the swords.'

'Skysilver,' Crane gasped, most of his weight slumped

against Rhian. 'They want the skysilver; it's drawing them. Stop her. She can't fight them, not like this.'

'Heliora!' Delphine screamed above the tearing wind and the howls of the devils that filled the street. 'Throw your blades away! They want the skysilver!'

HELIORA:

I could have done more, I should have done more, I knew what was coming, and I couldn't stop it. I failed them all.

Maybe this is how it always was supposed to be.

It will be different for you. I might not be able to see beyond Saturnalia (it was closer last time, I didn't see a thing beyond Bestialia) but I know who you are. I have made my choice, just as Raoul chose me.

Velody changed everything when she stepped into the Court as Power and Majesty. She has no idea how much she changed everything. But you...You will be the Seer that the Court has never had, and always needed. I am glad, in many ways, I will not be there to see it.

I'm not convinced they deserve you.

HELIORA HESITATED ONLY for a moment as the devils converged upon her, their dust-shaped bodies glowing with Ideslight. She took Crane's skysilver dagger and threw it hard. It bounced and clattered against the nearest wall and one of the devils turned around whip- fast, consuming it with one harsh snap of teeth. Its body solidified. Not just dust and air now, it glowed as if in Lord form, fierce and powerful.

Not good. This was not good.

'The sword too!' the Delphine bint screeched behind her, and Hel could hear Crane's low croak agreeing with her.

What would the devils do with the sword? She couldn't risk it. What strength had she given that one by giving up the dagger? Hel's fingers tightened on the hilt of the sword. She lashed out with quick flicks of the blade, forcing them to keep their distance. 'I won't let you have it,' she yelled into the noisy air.

The devils smiled.

As a sentinel, not a Seer, was Heliora's thought as they swarmed around her, blocking out the crimson moonlight.

21

CIRCUS OF BEASTS AND SONG

SEVENTH DAY OF THE LUDI SACRIS, ONE DAY BEFORE THE IDES OF FELICITAS

NOX

*A*shiol knew that they were losing the battle. How could they not? The sky kept pouring out more dust, glowing with the red Ideslight of a full moon. The stolen skysilver from the sentinels had made so many of the devils solid, and no amount of animor, no chimaera claws or Lord blows could damage them. He fought still. They all fought, though they had no bloody idea how to end this.

The glowing skysilver demons were more interested in Velody than the rest of them, and damn it if the Creature Court weren't working as a team to protect her. Ashiol had never seen that before.

Priest, Poet, Lennoc. Even Mars and Livilla. Had they even realised what they were doing?

Ashiol's chimaera claw was caught between two solid devils. He shaped back to Lord form to slide free, but one of the devils slashed at him, and he felt blood run down his thigh as the pain bit deep.

Ashiol exploded into cats, each of his small black bodies throwing itself out into the sky, scratching and hissing.

(Scream, he heard a scream. Not Livilla, but another voice so much a part of him that he couldn't not hear it, even if it was impossibly far away. *Oh fuck, Heliora, what's happening, what's happening...*)

Ashiol shaped himself back into Lord form, blasting animor out of every pore of his body, and the devils barely fell back. In one instant he felt pain — a searing burst of pain and fear — and knew it didn't belong to him.

Hel!

ISANGELL HAD NEVER FELT MORE blind in her life. She knew this was serious, that it wasn't just the final act in their circus pantomime, but she could still see nothing of what they were up against. The shaven-headed demme with the sword set her chin, stalwart as if she faced some terrible foe. Isangell had no idea what happened to the knife, but she saw it vanish.

Then the demme with the sword — Heliora, Delphine had called her Heliora — cried out once, and the sword in her hand vanished as well. So did half of her skin.

Beside Isangell, Delphine screamed and hid her face. The wounded soldier let out a noise as if he was gutted himself. Rhian — the one Isangell thought of as being the most sensible — pushed the rest of them away and ran forward to catch the bleeding demme as she fell.

There was no light in her eyes as Rhian lowered Heliora to the ground. She looked as if she had been flayed, the flesh under her missing skin bright red and weeping.

'They're gone,' Delphine was saying, over and over, clutching at the soldier as if he were keeping her upright and not the other way around. 'They're gone, they're gone. Why didn't she drop the frigging *sword?*'

'I don't know that I could have,' the soldier rasped. 'Or would have. She didn't want to give in to them.'

Rhian was crying hard, clutching the body to her, blood drenching her dress. She said something, and Isangell had to step closer to hear her, much though she didn't want to be anywhere near that thing. Body. She had never seen anyone killed like that. Death was a calm figure in a coffin with thick cosmetick to hide the horror.

Rhian's eyes burned with a fierce intensity. Isangell had not known this particular demoiselle long, but there was a strangeness about her which did not fit. 'The Queen must be sacrificed,' Rhian said in a voice not entirely her own.

'No,' Delphine breathed. 'Not you too.'

Not just blind but deaf, dumb, speaking an entirely different language. Isangell looked from one to the other, wishing they would make some kind of sense to her.

A demoiselle had died defending Isangell from something she couldn't even see — how could anything make sense?

'Rhian's the new Seer,' the soldier said flatly. 'Ashiol's going to slaughter us for this.' His legs collapsed under him, and he slumped to the ground.

THE BATTLE RAGED AROUND THEM, and Velody wanted so desperately to speak to Ashiol. Would she get that moment, before it was all over? She had barely had a chance to think about what she wanted to say, but the words welled up in her. She could not send them to him — could not give him any clue what was going to happen next.

You've got it wrong. Ashiol, you've got it wrong about the Crea-ture Court. They don't hate each other, they don't work against each other. They never had to be like that. They can be a family. It's going to be all right. They'll take care of each other. It's what they've been doing all along.

They don't need me for that. And neither do you.

The devils centred their attention on her now, and Velody found herself hemmed in with the entirety of the Lords and Court hovering between her and their attackers.

This is how it's supposed to be.

The voice in her head was now not her own.

Velody saw Ashiol fall, struck down from behind, and tried to reach him, but the devils kept hurling themselves in the way. They had to be fought off, one by one.

The dust kept pouring through from the sky above. Hard devil hands slammed down around her, holding Velody fast, and she hissed, lashing out with her animor until the devils fell back.

You know what you have to do. Her vision, the one that had overwhelmed her in the Killing Ground, filled her head. Ashiol had fallen, like she saw in that vision. Velody knew what happened next. How could she doubt it?

How many of the devils were solid now? Too many. More and more. They were using the skysilver somehow, and Velody couldn't help thinking about the skysilver cage in Poet's territory, of the swords of dead sentinels hanging on the Haymarket walls, or the supply that the Smith must have. There was plenty more skysilver in this city and dust was still pouring.

Someone called her name.

Velody tried to resist it at first, remembering how the noxcrawl had lured Poet in with its deadly siren song. Mysterious voices were not to be trusted.

But then another voice joined the cacophony — one she knew almost as well as her own. A real voice, not an imaginary one.

Velody broke free of the battle and flew as fast as she could, tearing across the sky. She changed to Lord form as she streaked towards that voice, following it down into the lower city.

She found them at street level. It was cold, and everything was lit by that horrible red moon. Rhian stood waiting for her, standing taller than Velody had seen her since that awful Lupercalia that had turned her into a different person.

'You called me,' Velody blurted. 'How did you call me?'

Delphine leaned against a wall with her arms wrapped tightly around herself. The Duchessa stood close to her, as if Delphine was the only one she trusted. Crane was at their feet, broken but breathing. That was different. Velody had been so sure he wasn't going to make it through this nox. If the vision got that wrong, what else was wrong? A horrible hope shot through her that maybe it was different, maybe she wouldn't have to...

But then she saw Heliora. 'Saints,' she whispered miserably. 'Oh, saints.'

The Seer of the Court lay in the street, her body red-raw and twisted and so very still. Velody's first thought was that this would break Ashiol, and then she just let herself feel miserable for Heliora's sake.

And now you understand.

'She tried to hold on to the sword,' Crane said in a low rattle of a voice.

'Velody,' Rhian said. 'You must listen.'

'You need to keep moving,' Velody said shakily. 'Get the Duchessa to the Palazzo, or a nest, or — something. We're losing the battle up there. The devils are solid and we can't fight them forever. If they get under the city there's so much skysilver...'

Velody. You have to listen to me.

That was not Rhian. Velody stared at Heliora's fallen body.

You're dead, she thought clearly.

Not gone, though. Not yet. Hear me.

Rhian smiled, a sweet and steady smile that wasn't hers at all. The light in her eyes was hard to look at. 'I've seen the futures. Velody, if the Queen is sacrificed, they will go back where they came from. She's the only reason they are here. The wrongness needs to be stopped, now. Before dawn.'

'The Queen,' Velody repeated. 'But there are no Queens in Aufleur, there's only —'

The Duchessa cried out.

Velody whipped around to see that Delphine gripped the Duchessa's wrist in a tight hold. Delphine refused to meet anyone's eyes, but her fingers held firmly.

'No,' Isangell said in a low voice, tugging at the grip. 'You can't mean — no!' She sounded more affronted than genuinely afraid. That was probably a mistake.

Crane rose to his feet painfully, and drew his steel sword. He passed his knife to Delphine, who closed her fingers tightly around the hilt.

Don't blame Rhian; she's new to this, said the voice of Heliora. *You know, don't you? Your vision was clear. The Duchessa isn't the sacrifice.*

'No,' Velody said quickly. 'You've got it wrong. This isn't what you saw, Rhian.'

'She's the new Seer,' Crane said quietly. 'We have to listen to her, Velody. You said it yourself — we're losing the battle.'

Isangell had greater resources than Velody would have given her credit for. She ground her foot hard on Delphine's and tugged herself free, turning to run.

Crane slammed into her, catching her around the waist and pushing her against the brickwork. Delphine followed him, holding the knife as if (disturbingly) she knew exactly how to use it.

'This is not who we are!' Velody demanded. 'Crane, let her go! Delphine, what do you think you are doing?'

'Being a sentinel, finally,' said Delphine, on the edge of hysteria. 'Isn't that what you all wanted?'

Crane stared defiantly at Velody.

'Trust me,' she told him, trying to stay calm. She could rely on Delphine to hesitate over striking a killing blow, but Crane was another matter. His belief shone out of his face like a beacon. 'If I am really your Power and Majesty, trust me, this is not the way.'

Crane hesitated.

Velody took a step towards him, then another. She held out her hand. 'Give me the sword.'

He was hers, she knew that; more than the other sentinels. Macready was loyal as hell, and Kelpie believed in the service so deeply despite her hurts, but Crane was Velody's, body and soul. He would listen to her. Please, let him listen to her.

She held him with her eyes, waiting, hoping. Finally Crane let go of both the Duchessa and the sword in a rush. It clattered to the ground. 'Velody, we don't have time to mess about.'

You really don't have time, Heliora said inside Velody's mind. *Ashiol's coming; he will stop you.*

'Trust me,' Velody said again, and reached out her arms to gather Crane to her, holding him tight and pressing a ghost of a kiss to his cheek. 'This isn't your war to win, it's mine. I know how to fix this.' She turned her head and looked pointedly at Delphine. Her friend looked wary, but lowered the knife that she held.

Isangell backed away from them all, shaking with fear. She turned to run and smacked straight into the imposing, furious figure of Ashiol Xandelian. 'Ash,' she gasped, and then stepped back as if she wasn't sure whether to hug him or flee from him too.

Ashiol looked as if he had fought every step of the way to get here. Blood ran in a thin trickle down his face and one of his shoulders was badly twisted. He limped painfully as he walked towards the others. 'What is happening here?'

'A misunderstanding about a prophecy,' Velody said softly. 'It's all right. I know you all meant this for the best. It's not your fault.'

Crane looked apologetically in the Duchessa's direction. 'This is about Aufleur. We can't lose another city. She should understand that...'

'She *is* Aufleur, you fucking child,' Ashiol said thunderously. 'She's what we're fighting for. We do not sacrifice those of the daylight, we protect them. What was Heliora thinking —'

'Heliora didn't see the vision,' Rhian said miserably. 'Ashiol, I'm sorry. She's dead.'

Velody saw his face close over. From fury to — nothing, in only a moment. Had he known, or only suspected?

'Go on,' he said.

'She gave me the futures,' said Rhian. 'I don't pretend to understand it all yet. But Velody, the message is so clear, I can't see anything else. The Queen has to die, and all this will be over. The devils will eat our city alive if someone does not stop this.'

'We don't have Queens in Aufleur,' Ashiol said. 'What in the seven hells made you idiots think Isangell was the one that the vision meant?' He reached an arm out to his cousin but she shied away from his touch, keeping him between herself and Crane but otherwise not prepared to touch him.

'They belong to the daylight,' Velody said tiredly. 'Seer and sentinel they may be, Ash.' Oh, saints, Rhian and

Delphine both of them... she had done this, and she would not be able to protect them from everything the nox had to throw at them, not now. 'But they can't see beyond the daylight world, not yet. You're going to have to do something about that.'

She, apparently, had something else to do.

'It doesn't mean that either,' Ash snapped, guessing where her thoughts were going. 'Don't be an idiot, Velody.'

She smiled thinly at him. 'See, that's the trouble. I do see clearly. Rhian isn't the only one who's been having visions. I know what I have to do to save you all.'

'What are you saying?' Crane asked.

'Rhian's prophecy isn't wrong,' Velody said gently. 'But there aren't any Queens in Aufleur. Just the Duchessa — and the Kings.'

Crane stared at her. 'You can't be serious.'

'She isn't,' Ashiol growled, stepping forward and getting into Velody's space.

Don't let him touch you, Heliora hissed. *He would do anything to stop you.*

'How can you doubt me?' Velody flung at him, stepping back, keeping a distance between them. 'I did this. I was supposed to protect you all, lead you all as Power and Majesty, and I brought us here. With a dead Seer and a new vision of the futures.' She reached out to Rhian, who was close enough for Velody to catch one of her hands in hers. She felt only a slight flinch. 'Rhian, you've seen it. The sacrifice of the Queen will send the devils back where they came from.'

'I can't see all the futures, not yet,' Rhian said, eyes bright. 'But the sacrifice is necessary...' Her voice broke a little. 'I didn't see you at all.'

Velody nodded, and squeezed Rhian's hands before letting go. 'It's all right. I saw me. And so did Heliora.'

It was a relief, really. She felt so very calm.

'Velody,' Ashiol said warningly, and he took another step towards her.

'Sentinels,' Velody cried out, already moving. 'Rhian, if you love me, don't let him stop me!' She shaped herself into chimaera form and flew, hard and fast as she could, into the sky.

MACREADY HAD BEEN GUARDING Kelpie's fallen body, his eyes on the sky as the Lords and Court fought the dust devils. They were so fecking strong, relentless, and they were only getting stronger. One by one, the Lords and Court fell back, or were struck down, and returned weaker to the fight.

The dust kept pouring in through that damned crack in the sky.

'Mac,' Kelpie said finally in a whisper, stirring.

'Aye, lass, I'm here,' he said, taking her hand. She lay on her back, not moving, eyes on the sky. 'I don't see Ash, or Velody.'

'Me neither.' Her hand was so cold. Was she shivering? 'Wait, there's Velody. I see her now.'

Their Power and Majesty burst up out of the streets below, glowing black in her chimaera form, all speed and heat and claws, and then she wasn't black at all but the intangible colour of skysilver, blindingly bright.

Kelpie lifted herself a little on her elbows. 'What is she doing?'

'I don't know,' Macready said in a low voice.

The devils swarmed after Velody as she plunged furiously towards the crack in the sky, and kept going.

Macready realised a few seconds before the rest of the Lords and Court exactly what it was she was doing. There was no way he could reach her. No way any of them could reach her.

~

THE SKY WAS hot and dizzying, the faster she flew. Velody soared past the Lords and Court as they battled with the relentless devils of light and sand. As she passed, each devil peeled away from the battle and followed her. Oh, yes. It was true.

Poet yelled something after her, a question, a demand, and she ignored him. For once, being the Power and Majesty did not mean listening to anything the Creature Court had to say.

This is how it was always supposed to be.

Fire and moonlight crashed into Velody's vision as she approached the tearing wound in the sky. Hands grabbed her, the dust devils dragging her back.

If there are devils, why not saints and angels? she thought frantically. *Help me now, saints and angels. Let me fly.*

She was closer to the light, the burning cold of it. She could stop now. She could turn back. They could hold on until dawn, use the day to plan for the next battle... If the city survived this nox at all.

The closer Velody got to the sky wound, the more it burned. The dust was still pouring out of it, filling the world, and she choked on it, coughed at the hot dryness as it scattered through the air. The devils hung on harder, trying to drag her back, but they were no match for chimaera strength.

This was something the Creature Court had always fought against. The sky had no idea how to deal with a Power and Majesty who wanted to be swallowed. Velody seized the lip of the wound and tore at it. Not so bad. She could do this.

There was a relief in it. She could stop fighting, finally. She could make a difference. She could leave it all behind.

Are you there? she asked Heliora, suddenly not wanting to be alone.

Barely. Take us through, Velody. Time to go.

The heat scorched her fur and claws, made her teeth ache. Velody forced herself into Lord shape, glowing and floating but undeniably herself. 'Take me,' she said between cracked and blistered lips. 'Take us.'

The wound in the sky opened up, and she found herself falling forward, into its depth. Darkness would have been a blessing, but there was light, only light.

22

CIRCUS OF BEASTS AND SONG

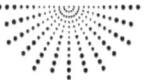

SEVENTH DAY OF THE LUDI SACRIS, ONE DAY BEFORE THE IDES OF FELICITAS

NOX

*N*o, this wasn't happening, not again. He couldn't stand it. Ashiol roared and let the animor inside him burst free. Rhian smacked into him first, her whole body reverberating as she hit his chest. Crane brought them both down, slamming Ashiol hard to the ground. He was shaking, eyes wet. Delphine threw herself on top of all of them, openly crying.

'She's going to kill herself, you fucking monsters,' Ashiol raged. 'You can't let her. We can't lose her.'

Rhian lifted her head, and he saw such fury in her face that even he was taken aback. 'You think we want this?' she demanded. 'Shut the hells up, Seigneur Ducomte. You have no idea what we just lost.'

Ashiol changed to Lord form and then chimaera, struggling and growling. He could destroy them all with a flick of his hand (burn them, freeze them, hurt them, cut them).

'You have to kill us to be free of us,' Delphine said in a

low, trembling voice. 'She wants you to save us. Which will it be?'

Ashiol's red eyes glowed at her, and he howled. What the hells made them think he gave a damn about any of them? He had already lost Heliora, and now Velody was abandoning him to the fucking Creature Court?

He growled between his teeth and threw animor at them, hot enough to scald the sentinels away. They gasped and gritted their teeth but hung on, all three of them.

Cool hands touched his forehead, holding him down. Isangell looked at him, face composed. 'Are you a subject, or a ruler?' she asked him calmly.

Ashiol closed his eyes. 'Subject,' he muttered.

'Then you don't get to make this decision,' she told him, and kept her hands there, soothing on his skin, until he stopped struggling.

The sky went calm. One moment it was raging with fire and battle and blood, and then it was a quiet nox. The moon was clear and creamy. The stars were twinkling, the little fuckers, like everything was fine. Ashiol lay in a pile of idiots, the cobbles cool under his back. 'Get. The. Hells. Off. Me,' he snarled.

Isangell moved first, drawing her hands away from him, stepping back. Rhian took in a shuddering breath and Delphine shifted quickly, helping Rhian to stand up and move away from them all.

Crane rolled off Ashiol, expressionless.

'Do you have any idea what you have done?' Ashiol accused them all, sitting up. He buried his head in his hands. That way, he didn't have to look at any of them. Might reduce the number of unnecessary deaths.

'What happened?' Poet demanded a few moments later, the first of the Lords to touch down near them. 'Where did the battle go?'

Ashiol got to his feet. 'Velody took it,' he said in a quiet, furious voice. 'The sky swallowed her. She let the fucking sky swallow her and every one of these bastards helped her.'

The sky was silent. Quiet. Taunting him.

Mars descended, one arm looped around Kelpie's waist. His courtesa Clara carried Macready. Both sentinels were in bad shape. The rest of the Lords and Court drifted down around them all.

Priest was the first to speak. 'What do we do now?'

'Velody's gone,' said Macready in a low voice. 'Swallowed — she sealed the rift in the sky.'

They were looking at Ashiol for the answers, and he hated them for it. He walked away, heading for the fragile, broken body of Heliora. His brave bright demme. He crouched down, taking her hand. Cold. Of course she was cold. Her cool blood came away on his fingertips.

'Ashiol.'

If it had been anyone else, he would have snapped, or hit them, but it was Isangell standing over him, sounding brittle and afraid. He looked up and saw that she was wearing Crane's brown cloak. 'Can I borrow that?' he asked.

Shaking, Isangell nodded. She let the garment slide from her shoulders, and passed it to him. 'Will you take me home?' she asked him.

Ashiol carefully wrapped Hel's body in the cloak. *Don't think don't think don't think.* He could fall apart later. Break things if he had to. Drink and scream and cry. But mostly drink. 'Of course I will,' he said, and swept the cloak-wrapped body into his arms. 'Let's go.'

'Where do you think you're going?' Poet called out, behind them. 'Ashiol, we need you.'

Heliora was dead. Velody was dead. He was the last King of Aufleur, and Ashiol was done with it all. 'I'm going home,' he said sharply. 'Any of you follow me, I really will kill you.'

Ashiol started walking, and Isangell followed him.

~

DELPHINE STARTED SHIVERING and couldn't stop. The atmosphere in the street was horrible. Everyone was broken, and miserable. 'She's really gone,' she said in a small voice.

Velody. She had sacrificed herself, and they had let her. They had helped her, and Delphine had no idea why she had done it, except that Rhian for once had seemed so sure, so confident, and Velody had asked, and...

Macready, barely managing to stay on his feet, reached out an arm and for once Delphine was prepared to forget how much she hated him. She leaned her body into him, trying not to cry. She never cried. Crying was for stupid little demmes who couldn't look after themselves.

'She made us different,' the one called Warlord said in a deep voice. 'How can we go back to what we were?'

Poet turned without speaking and flew from the rooftop, leaving them all behind. The weasel boy and stripecat man went with him.

'I'm not different,' Livilla said sharply. 'She was a bossy little demme who wandered in out of the daylight however she pleased. She wasn't *Garnet*.'

'No, she certainly was not,' Priest said gravely.

'We can rest,' Rhian said, not sounding at all like herself. 'We can rest and recover. That is what Velody bought us. Time. We should use it.'

'Sounds ominous,' Macready muttered, and Delphine could hear the vibrations of his voice through his chest. She resisted the urge to snuggle in closer. 'Is there worse to come, Rhian-my-lass?'

'Silence and calm,' Rhian said. Was it the confidence that was new in her? Or that odd sense that someone was talking

315

through her. Delphine didn't like it at all. This wasn't the old Rhian, this was something different. 'There will be further battles,' Rhian continued. 'But not soon. We have time to mourn, and to grow strong. The sky accepts our sacrifices, and it will be sated for a while.'

'We can't be strong without her,' Crane said, his voice surprisingly deep and loud.

'We still have a King,' Macready said heavily.

Delphine wondered if he had meant his voice to sound so despondent at the thought of Ashiol as their Power and Majesty. 'It's not fair,' she murmured into Macready's neck. 'None of you knew her. She was ours, not yours. And now you have Rhian too.'

And me, oh, saints. They have me. It's not going to end.

As if he understood her silent thoughts, Macready held her harder.

~

IT WAS RAINING. Ordinary rain — no threat in it — beat against the windows of the Duchessa's bedchamber. Ashiol sat in a corner, uncomfortable on one of her spindly demoiselle chairs, waiting for his cousin to wake up.

The city healed itself, when dawn swept over it. Every broken stone and brick slowly rolled back into place. Every shard of glass replaced itself seamlessly in a window frame.

That farce of a circus had worked. Ashiol couldn't feel anything about that — not glad, not relief. He couldn't feel much of anything.

Isangell was peaceful in her slumber now. She had woken twice with shaky, confused dreams, and he stroked her hair like a child until she went back to sleep.

He had only left her once, to go to the Temple of Thresholds, outside the city borders, and give Heliora over to be cremated. He returned with a small ivory box that he set awkwardly on the Duchessa's ornamental mantle, not knowing what to do with it. It felt like the worst kind of appropriation, to make the decision about Heliora's ashes.

Isangell might know. She was the mistress of etiquette, after all.

No more of this. No more conflict between worlds. The daylight was the daylight, and the nox was the nox. Ashiol should never have let this touch Isangell. Should never have let Velody continue to work for her. He should have listened to Hel when she told him she was going to die.

So many things he could have done differently.

'Ash,' Isangell said in a small voice.

He went to her, sitting on the edge of the bed. 'I'm here, gosling.'

Those blue eyes of hers that saw everything. Isangell was looking at him now, as if he was the one they needed to worry about. 'Is that what it's always like for you? Fighting and death, and always being afraid?'

'Pretty much,' Ashiol said, surprised into honesty. 'This not was one of the worst we've seen in a long time.'

Isangell smiled weakly. 'Mama just thought you drank too much and went to brothels.'

That coaxed a laugh out of him. 'Only when there's nothing better to do.'

The loss of Heliora was already a raw wound in his stomach. Ashiol couldn't begin to start thinking about Velody, how he had let her down. He built her into a Power and Majesty who thought it was perfectly reasonable to sacrifice herself.

'I can make you forget,' he blurted. Isangell darted back against the pillows, giving him a startled look. 'I mean — you're daylight, you weren't supposed to see anything of what you saw. I have the power to wipe it from you, if you

317

want. You needn't remember about the other world, about devils and sentinels and the Creature Court.'

Isangell gave him a stern look, reminding him that she was the Duchessa and not his baby cousin any more. 'Don't you dare. I want to know more, not less. This is my city, Ashiol.'

'You are daylight,' he repeated.

'You needed me for that wretched circus. What if you need me again? You are all my subjects, every bit as much as the — ribbon-sellers and bakers.'

Oh no, he couldn't afford to have her start thinking like that. 'We're not,' Ashiol insisted. 'We're not part of your city, gosling. We follow different rules. You'd be better off not knowing anything about us. Your job is to keep the festivals going. Sacrifice the sheep, read the entrails, walk in circles while the priests sing songs. Follow the traditions, Isangell.'

'You sound like you're going away,' she said, giving him a searching look. 'Is that true, Ashiol? Are you leaving me again?'

Power and fucking Majesty. He couldn't avoid it now.

'I don't know.' For the first time Ashiol thought he knew how Heliora had always felt, a thousand futures stretching out in all directions, hungry and noisy. 'I don't know what I'm going to do. Get drunk.'

'That's nothing new,' Isangell sighed. 'What then?'

Run away. As far and fast as I can.

Ashiol closed his eyes. He could hear Garnet mocking him, Velody scolding him. He didn't know which was worse. It was never a good thing, to hear voices of the dead.

'I don't know, gosling,' he said, and his voice cracked. He didn't realise how hard he was shaking until Isangell sat up in a rush, wrapping her arms around him like a mother comforting her child.

It's my turn to play the King for real. How long before I choose to be sacrificed too?

'So,' Isangell said quietly. 'Would now be a bad time to ask how exactly it is that you met my dressmaker?'

Ashiol laughed, a horrible sound that continued far longer than he meant it to. Isangell kept holding on to him until he could breathe again.

~

RHIAN WAS asleep and the house was otherwise empty. Not a sentinel in sight. Except, of course, Delphine herself. Ha, hilarious.

The kitchen table required to be stared at a great deal. Delphine was fulfilling a necessary duty.

The door opened. Had she forgotten to latch it? No Velody to remind her. Tears were hot in her eyes when she looked up to see Macready standing there. 'Lass,' he said, and then stopped.

'Oh, don't.' There were no words that could fix this. 'Tomorrow — later today, when we've had some sleep,' she said, 'will you take me back to that Smith of yours? See if he'll make me some blades?' Time to surrender.

Macready looked startled. 'Is that honestly what you want?'

'Don't ask me that,' she said helplessly. 'I don't have anything *left*.'

He nodded, and came forward a step.

Delphine sighed, and got to her feet. Standing up straight was an achievement. She would take what she could get. 'Bolt the door, will you?'

'Want me to stay down here, lass, keep an eye on things while you get some sleep?' he asked once the bolt was secure.

Men. Worse than thick sometimes. Delphine reached out,

taking his hand. The skin of his palm was rough and warm against hers 'I want you to come upstairs,' she said clearly, so there would be no misunderstanding. 'So that I can drown in you. Now. Unless you plan to turn me down again?'

She waited, long enough for her pride to sting. How was it that he of all men was able to do that to her, over and over again? Then Macready moved, a hand gentle on either side of her face and saints, he could kiss, at least. Their mouths came together, slow at first, then more frantic and wanting.

When he finally released her, Delphine felt like all the breath had been sucked from her body, heat sparking through her for the first time all day. 'Good,' she said shakily. 'That's a good start.'

What else could they do, any of them, but start as they meant to go on?

~

RHIAN:

I hear you, Heliora. Your voice pounds in my ears (not just yours, the others are there too; poor Raoul, he is so very sad) and I can see your story, unfolding behind me.

I don't know if my story will be any better. But for the first time I understand, actually understand something terrible that happened to me a long time ago. I thought I was crazy, flying apart. Thought I was broken forever, that I was damaged somehow, to see such things, feel such things. Now I know. I was waiting for you to make sense of it all.

Waiting for you to make me Seer of the Creature Court. I've never received a gift so bitter, or so important.

I will save them if I can. My turn to put the pieces together. You can lay your burdens down, now. Be free. Sleep.

Thank you.

PART II
SONGS FROM THE BESTIALIA CABARET

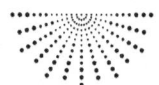

23

LUX DIANI

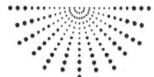

TWO DAYS BEFORE THE IDES OF CERIALIS

ONE MONTH LATER

*I*t was more than a year since Rhian last set foot on the docks near the Noces Gate, on the far side of the river Verticordia. Little had changed in that time. The same faces were here, the same strong arms and merry grins, and the usual hubbub surrounded the new boats, where the shipments of flowers and fruits from Orcadia and Atulia had just come in.

She was jostled this way and that as she made her way to the boat where they were unloading crates of fresh clematis, violetti and lilacs, perfect for the holiday of slaves that only the finest of families would be celebrating this nox, in memory of a time when slavery was common in Aufleur.

The pampered sons and daughters of the Great Families would wear purple garlands on their hair and pretend to serve a fancy meal to their servants, who themselves would have spent all day cooking and preparing the false feast.

Every time someone bumped against Rhian, she breathed deeply and held herself together. *No harm. No harm done. All is well.* She was not ready for this, but if she did not start now, when would she be ready?

Her head was full of so many horrors, but she was learning control finally, and there was a freedom in that.

All her old friends and workmates were here, many dames and demmes and fellows she knew from apprentice days, or when she and the others ran a market stall in the Forum.

Many of them seemed to know Rhian's story, or whatever version Delphine had spilled to them, because she saw pity on their faces, and overly bright smiles. *Yes, that's right, poor old Rhian finally found the courage to climb out from her walls and face the world.* No one knew about Velody, that she was gone. It was a pain in Rhian's stomach every time someone called out a greeting, or sent their love to her friends.

Rhian had not had time to mourn. She missed Velody so much, but there was work to be done. Delphine was rushed off her feet, struggling to keep up with the usual demand for ribbons as well as her new duties as a sentinel. Without Velody's commissions to keep them in grain and cheese, Rhian had to work.

She could do this. She was stronger now.

Rhian bought her blooms and walked across the city on steady feet, returning home. The autumn sunshine was bright in her eyes, and her cheeks were warm when she returned to the house with the sign of the rose and needle.

She took three steps into the kitchen, and the voices filled her head. Rhian staggered, dropping her laden basket. Flowers scattered across the floor as she pressed her hands to her temples, trying to make them stop.

Heliora's voice was the loudest. She had been there for

several market-nines already, reciting her own story like an old ghost in an empty room. If it was only Heliora, Rhian could cope, but sometimes it was all of them — every Seer who had ever lived — talking all at once, and when it got like that was just noise threatening to burst through her ears and nose.

Oh, but this time there were words that she recognised, one in particular, over and over, in dozens of voices.

Liar liar liar liar liar liar.

'Stop it,' she commanded, shaken. For a miracle, they stopped. Rhian paused to catch her breath, and then busied herself in collecting all the flowers, straightening their stems, and arranging them in the basket once more.

Of course the Seers could see into her head. How could they not, if they were trapped in there? They knew her greatest, most awful secret. The thing she had not lied about, not really, and yet... She let them all assume that they knew why it was so hard for her to leave this house, why the anxiety had swallowed her whole, ever since that awful Lupercalia more than a year and a half ago.

Rhian let them weep for her, and imagine the worst. Every time her friends looked at her like she might break into a thousand pieces, the lie burned on her tongue, unspoken but always there. Thinking back to that day, when it all began, she could no longer remember if there was a time when she could possibly have spoken the truth.

'Rhian, lass, is that you?'

She jolted in surprise as Macready sauntered into the kitchen. Of course he was here. 'I bought flowers,' she said.

His face lit up. 'Look at you,' he said so proudly. 'No trouble in the streets? I would have come with you if you'd asked, so I would.'

She knew that. Macready went out of his way to make

sure Rhian was as easy as she could be about him all but living here now. He had watched her baby steps into the world as if he were a protective brother.

Macready was making tea now — they had him well trained — chattering about how Ashiol had gone missing again, and he had been hoping he might be here, though he knew as well as she did that Ashiol had not set foot in this house since Velody died. No, if Mac was here without Delphine it was to check on her, for no other reason. Rhian wanted to be glad of his kindness, but instead she had acquired yet another person who would hate her if he knew the truth.

What would he do if she blurted it out in front of him right now, in the kitchen? *I was never raped.*

RHIAN WAS ACCOSTED by drunken men in the street that awful Lupercalia, but it was not an assault on her body that drove her to cut the hair from her head, to slice deeply into her skin and watch the blood well up through the wounds. Nothing so mundane.

Delphine and Velody had told the lie for her in their careful looks and silences. Rhian jumped at every sound back then, flinched at every touch for so long; she felt the world suck away into blackness, and she was so grateful that their assumptions gave her an excuse for that.

She would have broken entirely, had she been forced to speak the real truth aloud.

Later, when she felt stronger, the lie was already well in place. It was too late now to confess to Velody, and Rhian wished more than anything that she had. Velody might have understood. Delphine never would, and Rhian regretted her brief impulse to spill the truth to Macready. He was not hers.

She and the many voices of dead Seers in her head would have to keep their secrets to themselves.

DELPHINE FOUND the useless sot in the Pretty Princel, slouched in the corner of a bar. Of all people, it had to be she who found him. She had no wish to scrape a drunkard out of a bar in the middle of the afternoon, but this was the world she lived in now.

This was all Macready's fault.

She ordered a bitter lime, which would in no way sate her craving for something stronger, and went to sit beside the wreck of a man at the bar. 'Hello, Ashiol.'

'Delphine,' he slurred, eyes dangerously bright as he raised his glass to her. 'A pleasure, as always.'

She sipped, resenting that she was the one on her best behaviour. Falling apart in a sea of booze and potions was her own way of coping with the unimaginable, or even the everyday. Being the good one was just short of abominable. 'It's been a month,' she said finally, her mouth puckering around lime and salt. 'Don't you think it's time you sobered up?'

Ashiol laughed at her. 'Look at you, sentinel. Shiny swords on your back, shiny knives tucked into your bodice. I thought you wanted nothing to do with any of us. Or has Macready frigged compliance into you?'

Oh, this one was a charming drunk. Delphine loved her swords, even if she was still this side of rubbish when it came to training. She wasn't going to take any of the inebriated Ducomte's crap. 'I know that if we don't get a Power and Majesty who is up to the job, I'll end up as dead as the rest of you when the sky...'

She shut her mouth on the sentence, but he knew what she had been about to say.

'When the sky swallows Aufleur,' said Ashiol, lips shaping the words with great deliberation. 'Believe me, I'm looking forward to it. It will be like a family reunion.'

Delphine set her glass down so sharply that her drink splashed against the smooth wood of the bar. 'Why don't you stop acting like such a spoiled brat? All you lost is a chance to escape responsibility. I lost my *friend*.'

The thought of Velody, the fact that she was gone, the hurting space she had left behind, was enough to make Delphine fall apart all over again. But she couldn't. Everyone needed her to be strong, and she hated them for it.

Ashiol watched her like she was something he wanted to eat. He slid a small velvet bag out of his shirt and lay it on the bar between them, letting the contents spill a little on to the polished surface.

Delphine stared. She knew what that was. The tiny glittering crystals, like crushed moonstone and sugar. They called it Surrender. She'd only tried it once or twice, when a seigneur with more money than sense was trying to impress her. It was worth a small fortune, and she could practically taste it on her tongue.

Ashiol smiled that cat's smile of his. 'Want to share?'

Delphine was going to retort that the last thing he needed — they needed — was to get high. She had been good for so long. Instead, she found herself saying, 'Why not?'

ASHIOL NEVER HAD much of a taste for potions and powders when he was young. Animor was his drug of choice in those days. He needed nothing but that burst of blood under the teeth, that fierce light inside the chest when he swarmed over the rooftops as cats.

It was Garnet who needed more.

Tasha had encouraged it, using the prettier potions to reward her lions for good behaviour. Garnet, taking to the life of indulgence with glee, lapped up everything that came his way.

Ashiol remembered shouting at him, furious, more than once. The sky would be ablaze, their lives were on the line, and Garnet might be high on Surrender or Bliss, laughing like a madman as he threw himself into the fray.

I don't understand why you need it, Ashiol spat in disgust one nox when they were what, seventeen years old? *We have everything.*

Garnet looked at him as if he was a special kind of stupid. *You have everything*, he said. *The rest us cluster at your feet to lick at the scraps.*

Livilla had liked the powders too. It was something she and Garnet shared, even when she went through phases of preferring Ashiol as her bedmate. Sometimes she would come to Ashiol smelling of gin and mint and something else he couldn't recognise, eyes shining with a metallic glow. Sometimes she would make him taste fragments on her tongue, or a fingertip, and he would do it because... she was Livilla.

Garnet never minded that Livilla had that power over Ashiol. He would watch them with a sly smile. He had his own power over Ashiol, and he did not waste it on potions and powders. He used it to make him hold true to him; to give complete loyalty even when they were Lords of separate households, building their own power bases, and should no longer be friends, nor anything else.

Breaking the rules was what Garnet did best.

Ashiol arched his neck back now, letting the Surrender

crystals melt on his tongue. He lay on the rough tiles of the roof of the Pretty Princel, with a lithe demme beside him, her own lips reddened and wet as she sucked another pinch from her fingers.

It didn't matter that this was Delphine, who hated him, and not Livilla. The type was the same. She giggled now, shifting awkwardly, not used to dealing with the angles and planes of roofs in her knee-high silk sheath dress. Her cloak and sword-harness — still so new they squeaked — lay abandoned near a chimney stack. 'The sky is so sharp,' Delphine said, eyes wide and fixed upon the aimless stars. 'Like someone stabbed it. Over and over and over...'

Ashiol stretched his whole body out, wanting to be in cat shape. 'Makes it all better, doesn't it?'

'Mmm,' Delphine breathed, wriggling her shoulders, breasts half-spilling out of her low neckline. 'I'd forgotten what it was like to just *be*.'

Must be nice.

THERE WAS ONE DAY, five years ago, when Ashiol awoke on the floor of the Palazzo, completely drained, no memory of how he got there. Garnet had taken everything from him. Ashiol didn't know how to function without animor at first, without his cats, without the thrum of power that came with being a King.

(The sentinels had shared their blood with him sometimes, offering him a taste of mortality to allow respite from Garnet's tortures, and he had resented it every time.)

That day when he realised he was empty, Ashiol's skin hurt, everything hurt. He could feel scars burning into him, and then he hadn't been able to feel the scars at all which was worse, because it meant his animor was completely gone. He had nothing. He was nothing. He closed himself in his suite of rooms for three days, speaking to no one, not eating, barely sleeping. Eventually he climbed out a window and took to the streets, looking for something that would take the edge off. Crumbs and scraps.

Powders and potions had helped, then. Until they didn't.

'VELODY WOULD BE SO cranky about this,' Delphine said sleepily, her voice breaking into his thoughts. He had almost forgotten about her presence.

'Don't say her name,' Ashiol snapped, but too late. Everything he was trying to push away came crowding back. Heliora, grabbing at him. *I can't see past Saturnalia. I'm not going to live...* He ignored her, because he didn't want to think about it, didn't even want to consider the possibility. He entirely failed to give her any kind of comfort, and instead devoted all his attention to sniffing around Velody, selling her on the myth of how to be a hero. He hadn't saved either of them. He deserved to be alone, in the rubble of the Creature Court.

He still had Heliora's ashes. It was supposed to be bad luck, to hold on to them. Ashiol should have cast them from a hill, interred them in one of the city walls, or hurled them into the fires of any one of several dozen saints or angels. He couldn't decide, though. Couldn't let her go.

Neither had he checked on Livilla recently, no matter that she had suffered her own losses. He hadn't bothered to ask how well Mars had recovered, if Priest was hanging on to sanity, if Poet had killed them all in their sleep. He let Velody sacrifice herself, and he couldn't even pull himself together long enough to take her place. What was the sodding point? He couldn't be her. He couldn't even be Garnet.

He was not fit to be Power and Majesty.

Every time Ashiol passed a mirror, he had to turn his eyes away from it. There were shadows there. If he looked too long, he saw faces of the dead. (He never looked long enough to let that happen.)

'Where's the bag?' he muttered now, slithering on to his stomach to look at Delphine.

She smiled teasingly at him, withholding it. 'Mine.'

'I don't think so.' He pounced, covering her body with his own, searching her for the small scrap of velvet. Delphine wriggled under him, not seeming to mind his possessive touch. Her eyes were glazed and warm, and it would be so easy to just...

'I don't frig demmes I don't like,' he warned her, slipping his fingers between the small of her back and the hard curves of the roof tiles, giving her arse a squeeze. There the bag was, tucked under her. Little wench.

'I don't frig men I do like,' she said lightly, eyes fastened on his. 'Very important rule.'

She was Macready's, Ashiol reminded himself. Not that he had ever given a damn about those kind of rules. The Creature Court was hardly a haven of monogamy. 'Are we safe from each other, then?'

Delphine laughed. He didn't like her laugh. It made her sound like a spoiled child. 'Saints, I hope so.'

Ashiol poured a measure of glittering Surrender from the bag on to his fingers, and sucked it off, letting it melt sweetly against his tongue and the roof of his mouth, an explosion of light and colour. Delphine was rubbing against him now, or he was rubbing against her, not entirely like a cat. It would be so easy.

'Share,' she whispered, and he kissed her, tongue sweeping hard against hers.

She was so warm, and then cold, and then warm, and she tasted like skysilver.

The sky above them exploded into shards that stabbed his skin like broken glass.

~

IT WAS SUCH a relief to be free for once of being Good Delphine, responsible and careful and trailing around after the Ducomte d'Aufleur like she gave a damn about anything.

The sky was clear and free and Surrender tasted like everything good. Even sharing the glee with Ashiol Xandelian didn't spoil it.

Kissing him had not been in the plan, but this was the Delphine who didn't plan, who answered to no one, who slid home in a giggling heap in the early hours, and woke without remembering exactly what she had been up to.

Saints, she had missed this Delphine. Everything was so much easier in her skin. Ashiol's body was heavy over hers, it felt good, and it didn't matter who he was, or that Macready might...

Don't think about Macready, no no no.

Delphine had been clinging to Mac for a month or more now, since Velody threw herself into that sky. It got comfortable way too fast. Delphine didn't like comfortable. It was too much like belonging to someone, and she knew Macready had all these expectations that he never spoke aloud.

Ashiol's mouth was wet and hot on hers, and she didn't care any more about who he was, or why this was a bad idea. He didn't want anything from her other than this second right now, and that was good enough for her.

Then he threw himself away from her like she was on fire, hands pressing over his ears, face twisted up in pain.

'The sky,' he moaned. 'Broken into pieces, reflecting, bright, too bright...'

Oh, frig. Was it the Surrender, or was it — that other thing? Delphine tipped her head back, searching for some sign. The sky was clear. How could it be anything but clear? She had seen things since Dhynar Lord Ferax died, sparks and colours and hints of that other world. All part of being a sentinel, Macready told her, which made her want to smack him every single time.

She could see nothing but the blue sky now, fading into evening grey. Which meant that Ashiol was seeing things that weren't there. His eyes rolled in his head and there was a chalky whiteness to them that was most definitely not good.

'Calm down,' she said, reaching out to him. 'Breathe. You took too much. You need a drink of water or something.'

Ashiol clambered unevenly to his feet, staggering towards the edge of the roof. Delphine lunged for him, catching the edge of his leather coat and dragging him back. 'You can't fly, you know,' she warned before remembering that yes, he could, but maybe not right now, not with that much Surrender flooding his system.

Ashiol turned, looking at her with a sneer. No, not at her. Right through her, as if she didn't exist. 'The sky is coming for me,' he said in a vicious voice. 'It wants to cut me into tiny pieces. It doesn't matter if I can fly. One way or another, I'm going to fall.'

Oh, saints. 'You can't,' Delphine protested. 'I mean — you *can't*. They need you.' Macready and the other sentinels had shared enough harried conversations about it, taking up space in Rhian's kitchen, which they now seemed to view as their personal territory (Rhian never said a word of complaint, damn her). 'Velody's gone; you're all they have.'

'Better off without me,' Ashiol said, making each word slow and precise. And then the bastard stepped off the roof.

He was gone so fast Delphine could barely scream, the sound catching in her throat. She leaned dizzily over the edge to see his body explode messily into black, devilish shapes that scattered across the street in all directions. Not devils. Cats. Of course, cats. Everything was hot and cold, and Delphine couldn't breathe. Her hands clutched uselessly at the guttering. She pushed back finally, gasping for air as she felt solid tile under her. She hadn't fallen. Hadn't broken.

Ashiol, on the other hand... Oh, Macready was going to kill her for this.

24

LUX DIANI

TWO DAYS BEFORE THE IDES OF CERIALIS

DAYLIGHT

*M*acready had never been a superstitious lad. His ma believed in horseshoes for luck and bowls of milk for the pictsies, but he scoffed at it all until he sailed across the wide blue sea and came to this fair city, full of living saints and devils.

He came into his sentinel's gifts later than most, but he liked to think that made him stronger in some ways: quicker, less brittle. He saw it all clearer than the rest of them. The sentinels were used to thinking of themselves as less than the Creature Court, but the Silver Captain drilled home that standing between the nox and the daylight gave them a power no one else had. A strength.

They could choose their path, unlike the Lords and Court. They chose to be here, every day. It was loyalty, not blood, that kept them on the leash.

Walking the streets away from Via Silviana, Macready opened himself to Aufleur, letting his senses roam ahead of him. He could see and hear further than any daylight lad when he had a mind to it. The daylight was fading, but the sky was quiet. In that moment, an odd warning cracked through the air, scraping at his senses like a sound gone wrong. A disturbance, somewhere in the city.

Fecking saints, who was it likely to be but the man himself? *Ashiol Xandelian, the King of us. Saints help us all.*

Macready started to run.

～

THE SKY HAD NEVER DONE this before, never blazed so brightly. Even as cats, Ashiol couldn't escape it. Sharp as daylight, worse, it hurt his eyes, shard by shard stabbing into him. He pressed himself into the corners of the street, trying to hide from those colours, the fierce intensity of it. The sharp edges of a million pieces of sky, scattering around him. Pain, pain, pain.

Finally the light faded, and in the blessed dark he crawled back into himself, shaping his various cats into a human body again. He lay there on the cool stones, naked and struggling to breathe.

The sky was empty. Not just quiet. Where were the stars? The pale blueness pressed down over his body, smothering him.

'Ho there, laddie-buck,' said a wry voice above him. Macready threw Ashiol's own crumpled shirt at him. 'What are you doing to yourself now?'

Ashiol stared at the sentinel. 'What happened to the sky, Mac?'

To his credit, Macready at least glanced up, but seemed to see nothing unusual. 'It's quiet, my King. Barely evening yet. Nothing to see.'

'No,' Ashiol protested. 'There's something...' His whole body was trembling. Was it cold? 'Why won't it take me too?'

Macready sighed. 'Nothing more pathetic than a self-pitying drunk, *Majesty*.'

Oh, he was drunk. That explained a lot, really. Ashiol staggered to his feet, buttoning the shirt. Macready threw his trews at him next. Ashiol managed those somehow, but it wasn't good. The edge of his vision was starting to melt and lose colour. 'You can't see that?' he said, turning one way and then the other. 'You can't...'

There were spaces opening up in the sky, where the stars were supposed to be, bleeding out between the broken pieces of blue. This was different to anything that he had ever seen before. Ashiol tipped his head back up, staring at the long spiderweb of cracks. 'Something is happening,' he said in an urgent voice. 'We need to call the Creature Court together...' The broken fragments of sky spun and danced above him, and he could feel his heartbeat pulsing loudly inside his head. 'They're coming for us.'

Ashiol tried to run, but Macready got in his face, shoving him back against the wall. 'For feck's sake, man, what are you on?' he roared.

'Surrender,' said a tiny voice, far far away. Delphine appeared, bedraggled and barely holding herself together, and beautiful. She wore her swords again, the brown cloak thrown over one shoulder, but she had lost her shoes and her feet were bare.

Ashiol gazed at her. She had never looked like that before. 'You're glowing,' he said in awe.

'Am I?' she said uncomfortably. 'I don't feel glowing. I feel sick.'

'You really are, aren't you?' he said, turning his head this way and that, examining every inch of her.

'Really am what?' said Delphine, crossing her arms.

'One of us.' Ashiol turned to Macready, grinning like a maniac. 'Look at her. All blazing.'

'Took you until now to notice, did it?' said Macready. 'She's been a sentinel a while now, Majesty.'

Ashiol tore his eyes away from Delphine. She was too bright, and Macready was too dull, and there was something very important here that he was missing. Something caught between the sharp edges. He started to walk, back and forth over the cobbled street, feeling the shapes of the stones under his feet. Something missing.

Ashiol kept walking, though Macready shouted out behind him, and Delphine had the rest of the Surrender.

Missing something, missing something.

ASHIOL COULD COUNT on one hand the number of times he had really gone crazy. The first time was when he was seven years old, and his mother informed him that his father was dead. He didn't understand her words.

They went into mourning, which meant Ashiol wasn't allowed to play in the Palazzo gardens or be seen in the streets. He kept asking where his father was. His mother looked at him in bemusement the first few times. Later, she accused him of cruelty. She beat him once, only once, and stood there with tears running down her face.

He apologised, and never asked her again. He asked the servants, though, when he thought he could get away for it. Mostly they said nothing, and slipped him extra cakes.

Seven years old. Ashiol blinked, and the Palazzo was gone from under his feet. They were living in the country all of a sudden, and six months had passed, and his mother had a new husband who would answer to 'Baronne' or 'sir' or 'Diamagne'.

Ashiol moved from room to room, not understanding how he had apparently lived here for months and none of it was familiar. He made his way outside, and no one stopped him. Apparently they weren't in mourning any more. He ran and breathed the fresh air and lay on his back in the grass for ages, staring at the clouds. A face as small as his leaned over him, a bright-eyed, dirty-faced boy who said, 'Are you the one they say is mad as a hatter?'

'Yes,' said Ash in a gasp. 'I suppose so.'

The boy considered this thoughtfully. 'Want to catch tadpoles with me?'

Ash nodded. 'Who are you?'

'Garnet, of course.' He said it as if he had introduced himself a dozen times. Possibly he had, in that strange blank space before now. 'Race you to the river!'

THE SECOND TIME IT HAPPENED, Ashiol was seventeen, and Tasha was dead. That was not in itself enough to send him over the edge. Tasha being dead meant he was finally free to be his own self rather than her plaything. Garnet was now a Lord and took Livilla and Poet as his courtesi. Ashiol and Lysandor made a deal with Priest, choosing him as their Lord.

The whole arrangement was remarkably sane.

But then one morning a few months later, Priest was sleeping off a red wine binge and Lysandor was off cuddling his lover, and Ashiol stepped out of the cathedral to find Tasha waiting for him on Mayor's Bridge.

Lithe, wicked, dead Tasha. 'Miss me, kitten?' Ashiol stared at her. 'What happened to you?' 'I think you know exactly what happened to me,' she said sweetly. 'Darling Garnet cut me down and sucked me dry. Or did he tell you a different story?'

Ashiol's mouth was dry. Tasha had died twice already. He saw her body pale and bloodless on the floor of the den, and he was part of the crew that cleansed the city of her revenant after it dragged a dark plague through the city because she had died forsworn. A third death seemed unimaginable.

'Why are you here?' he asked. *Why me*, was what he meant. Garnet was the one who killed her, after all.

'I'm here for you, kitten,' she said sweetly. 'Didn't think I was really going to let you go, did you?'

'I AM NOT SEEING THINGS!' Ashiol roared at the sentinels who couldn't mind their own fucking business. Ilsa and Macready found him talking to "himself", not for the first time, as he wandered the Angel Gardens. They had no loyalty to a courteso like him; all they cared about was their Kings.

'Never said you were, laddie buck,' Macready said in a gentle voice. 'Put the knife down.'

Ashiol stared at the blade. He hadn't even noticed that he was holding it, let alone moving it back and forth in what could be a threatening manner. 'You know I could kill you without even touching you, knife or no knife,' he said quietly.

'That thought had not occurred to us at all,' Ilsa said without inflection.

'Come away with us now,' said Macready. 'We'll find you a fine nest to sleep in, so we will.'

'Stop patronising me, sentinel,' Ashiol growled. 'I know what you think of me. I am not mindsick.' He tossed the knife to Ilsa, who caught it neatly and stuck it in her pocket. 'Tasha's back. And she's going to make us all pay.'

'Aye, renowned for coming back from the dead, so are the Lords and Court,' Macready drawled.

'Ignore them, kitten,' said Tasha, standing with her hand on one hip. 'She was always jealous of me, and he's just a hick Islandser. Get rid of them.'

Ashiol tried not to look at her, but Macready had caught the flick of his eyes. 'Come away,' Mac said again, his voice annoyingly gentle.

'Don't trust him,' Tasha said fiercely. 'He's a sentinel, he's not *yours*. He has no allegiance to a courteso like you. Sentinels only care about the blood and love and protection of Kings and you, my cat, are not a Creature King. You never will be, unless you listen to me.'

Macready tried to use reason, but Ashiol couldn't even hear his words. Tasha pressed up against his chest, making sure he could see and hear nothing but her. 'What does he want from you?' she purred. 'Why is he pretending to care?'

'What do *you* want from me?' Ashiol demanded of her.

Tasha smiled her beautiful smile. 'What I've always wanted. Your heart. Your soul. And I want you to kill them all.'

Ashiol looked into her eyes. He never had been able to resist doing anything she wanted. He looked back at the sentinels, knowing how easily he could tear them apart without even a touch. 'Sedate me,' he said between his teeth.

'Sorry, what was that?' said Ilsa, blinking.

'Get the Silver Captain if you're not up to the job,' Ashiol snarled. 'I'm not fucking safe. Nettlebane for a start, something stronger if you can get it. If you can't, you're going to have to chain me up.'

'Is this you mad, or lucid?' Ilsa asked, still hesitating.

Ashiol turned and caught her by the face, hand squeezing her chin and cheeks together. 'Restrain me,' he said calmly. 'Or I will eat you alive.'

'You can't do this,' Tasha declared, her voice thin behind him. 'I need you!'

'I will not be your tool for revenge,' he yelled at her, and gave Ilsa a shove, letting her go. He met Macready's eyes, silently begging the other man to take him seriously. 'You'll get the potions.'

'Oh, aye, lad,' said Macready gently. 'You've made your point.'

'I can make you kill them,' Tasha said gleefully. 'Nothing you can do will prevent me from that.' 'Watch me,' Ashiol said between gritted teeth.

It took three market-nines and a cocktail of potions and powders so strong he could hardly keep his eyes open, to make Tasha disappear. Macready stuck with him every step of the way, guarding him from the others, wiping his sweaty brow. Ashiol never thanked him for it, but he never forgot, either. Macready was the one who had listened to him.

Within months of that, Ashiol was a Creature Lord. Within three years, a King. The sentinels were his then, body and soul. He never stopped needing them, and he had always known that if his mind broke again, Macready was the one who would catch him.

Delphine didn't want to meet Macready's eyes. She was chilly in her thin dress, where before she had felt nothing but numb and blissed out. She couldn't quite bring herself to wrap the brown cloak around herself. He gave her that when she received her swords; another symbol that she was one of them now. A sentinel.

The colour didn't suit her at all. She didn't deserve to wear it. 'Surrender,' Macready repeated, sounding tired.

Delphine could probably read "disappointed" into it if she wanted to look that hard. She really didn't.

'Anything else I should know, lass?'

She shook her head. His presence was like a splash of cold water on the skin. Her mind had a haze to it still, but the pleasure of the powder was long gone.

'Oi, where's he going?' Macready muttered. 'My King! Get back here!'

Delphine turned and saw that Ashiol was making his barefoot way down the street, mumbling as he paced erratically back and forth. 'What should we do with him?' she asked.

'Get him to a nest, sleep it off,' said Macready, taking off after their rogue Ducomte. 'You too.'

'I'm fine.'

'Is that what you are?'

He was so *reasonable*. Why didn't he yell, like a normal boyfriend? Why didn't he give her an excuse to cry and feel bad and run far away from either of them?

Ashiol was still muttering. Delphine kept up with Macready, following him down the street, but she couldn't hear what Ashiol was saying until he swung around and pointed directly at her. 'This is all your fault,' he said clearly.

'Come now, none of that,' said Macready in his "more reasonable than anyone else" lilt of a voice.

'Oh what, I forced you to take the powder?' Delphine snapped defensively. 'You bought it, Ashiol. You offered it to me!'

'Not the Surrender,' he said, smiling viciously. 'Velody. All your fault.'

Delphine felt as if she had been slapped. 'Don't you frigging *dare*.'

'She never belonged to us, not really. She was yours. You keep reminding us of that, but have you thought about what it means? She was tied to both of you. She gave up on the idea of defending herself, of being a part of the Creature Court, because she wanted to protect you.' Ashiol tilted his head, mouth twisting cruelly. 'Were you worth it?'

Delphine bit her lip. She would not let him get to her. He was lashing out, trying for some kind of reaction. She would not give it to him.

Why was it *him* trying to hurt her, and not Macready? She had given Mac reason enough.

'How does it feel to know that you killed her?' Ashiol said next, still with that horrible smile of his.

'He doesn't mean it,' Macready warned, his hand brushing Delphine's arm.

Delphine shook him off, along with any comfort he intended. 'The hells he doesn't.' She stepped forward, facing Ashiol. 'The only reason you're trying to pass the blame to me is because you feel guilty!'

'Oh yes,' he agreed with a snap of his teeth. 'I killed her too.'

'Delphine, shut up and back off,' Macready said in a low, worried voice.

She turned on him. 'Me? Why am I the one who has to shut up when he's spewing vile accusations?'

'He's not himself.'

'I think he's exactly himself, same old arrogant, spiteful, selfish —' Delphine gasped as Ashiol grabbed hold of her. She froze for a moment as his arms wrapped around her waist. One hand reached out, tugging lightly at her bobbed blonde hair.

'Pretty colour,' he crooned.

Macready's eyes were on Ashiol like he was dangerous. Saints, of course he was dangerous. He was probably the

345

most dangerous person in the city. 'Perhaps next time, lass,' Mac said in a steady voice, 'when I say someone is not himself, you'll be listening to me.'

'Let go,' Delphine said, hating how small her voice sounded.

'She's not the enemy, my King,' Macready said in a low voice, edging towards them, a little at a time.

'Oh, but she is,' said Ashiol directly into Delphine's ear. 'Can't you see how sharp she is? She'll cut you all to pieces, stitch you up like ribbons. It's what they do. We trust them, we believe them, and they smash us to pieces.'

Delphine slid her hand a little lower, and found the hilt of her knife. He was still holding her, too close, too close. Before Macready could call out to stop her, she drew her knife and slammed it hard into Ashiol's stomach.

'For feck's sake,' Macready cried out, diving for them both as Ashiol fell. 'That's skysilver, you stupid bint. It could kill him.'

Ashiol gasped, landing hard on his knees, Delphine's knife sticking out of his gut.

'I know that,' Delphine said calmly. 'Steel wouldn't have made him let go of me.'

Macready gave her a horrified look. 'That's not what the blades are *for*!'

The last month had been full of sentinels telling Delphine how great an honour it was to wear the blades, how much it meant, all the time quietly ignoring the fact that they were still mourning their own swords and daggers to the dust devils of the sky rift.

Macready's new swords had grey-wrapped hilts, and the balance was designed to take his missing finger into account, but he was evidently still uncomfortable with them. He never referred to them as 'lasses', though Kelpie had accepted her own new blades as 'sisters' all over again. As far as Delphine knew, Mac hadn't even named his new blades. Maybe that meant something, but she didn't push. It was none of her business.

'If he doesn't want to be stabbed he has to learn to keep his hands to himself,' she said.

Macready tended the wound, drawing the knife out despite Ashiol's cry of pain. He tossed it at Delphine without cleaning it first — a sure sign he was hacked off at her — and then drew his own steel knife to cut a vein for Ashiol. 'Should have done this anyway,' he said matter-of- factly as Ashiol closed his mouth over his wrist. 'Some of those potions and powders take them worse when there's animor in the mix. Mortal blood will quiet him some.'

Delphine cleaned her own knife and resheathed it. 'He's not a child,' she said bitterly. 'Why do you treat him like one?'

'Because I've seen him like this before,' Macready said. Still too calm, still not hating her. Obviously she hadn't tried hard enough to hurt him. 'I think there's more going on than the fecking Surrender. And I don't want to be right.' He drew his wrist back from Ashiol's mouth, oddly gentle, and lifted the bloodstained shirt to check that Ashiol's stomach had healed over. 'How d'ye feel, my King?'

'Lost,' said Ashiol in a distant voice.

'Well, then. Better be getting you back to the Palazzo, eh? Somewhere quiet to rest your head?'

Ashiol seemed to think about this, then nodded. 'Hel's there. I can talk to her.' He stood up in that instant and strolled away down the street.

Delphine stared after him. 'That's not right.'

'Aye,' Macready said grimly.

'It's not just the powder?'

'Hard to tell. Our man has not been all the way sober since Felicitas. But — aye. I think it's more.'

'So what do we do?'

347

'We, is it? Thought you were having second thoughts all over again.'

'I was weak,' Delphine said sharply. 'Don't be so frigging judgemental. We can't all be perfect.'

That at least raised a smile from Macready. 'Never said I was perfect, lass.'

'*It was implied.*' She shook her head. 'So what do we do — try to sober him up and see if he's still in one piece underneath it all?'

Macready patted her arm. 'Go home, Delphine. I'll handle this.'

'I can help!' she insisted without even asking herself if she wanted to. Damn it.

'Can you?' Macready asked, without judgement in his voice. Not even a little. How did he do that?

'I'm not Velody,' she said, sharper than she intended.

'I don't expect you to be.'

'Don't you?' She quickened her step until she was only a few steps behind Ashiol. 'I can help. I can be a bloody sentinel. Just don't expect me to be anyone other than myself.'

Macready gave her a skeptical look, but caught up with her so that they were both trailing Ashiol and his steady stride. 'You're in no danger of being mistaken for her, lass.'

Ha, and wasn't that the truth. 'You'd better do the talking if we run into the Duchessa,' said Delphine. 'Last time we crossed paths, I tried to help sacrifice her to the sky.'

'Eh, that was a month ago,' Macready said lightly. 'Sure she won't hold a grudge.'

She bit her lip, willing herself not to laugh, not now. She didn't want to laugh. She didn't want to feel warm all over with gratitude that Macready seemed to have forgiven her.

It was deeply irritating, the power he had to make her feel good, and safe. Someone should put a stop to it.

25
LUX DIANI

TWO DAYS BEFORE THE IDES OF CERIALIS

NOX

*J*sangell, the Duchessa d'Aufleur, had been fighting with dressmakers all evening; a ridiculous pastime. What did it honestly matter what she wore for the Volcanalia (except that she hated every idea they suggested, nothing felt right).

She was out of sorts with Armand, her mother and her maids. How hard was it for them to understand that she needed some minutes of each day to herself? She had taken to walking the corridors or slipping into the gardens to avoid them all; her rooms had long since ceased to be any kind of sanctuary.

There was so much to think about. Isangell circled her grandfather's rose atrium, wondering if she could risk hiding herself for a moment or two in the deep green shadows without being captured by one of her many tormentors. She paused when she heard a thump from within, and what sounded like muffled swearing.

Calling the lictors would be the sensible response, but instead she opened the glass doors and stepped inside the atrium.

Two intruders stopped suddenly, allowing a third — Ashiol — to slump on to the ground behind them. Isangell knew these people. The Islandser, and the blonde demoiselle named Delphine. What did he call them? Sentinels. The equivalent of lictors in that strange dreamlike nox world that had hold of Ashiol's heart.

These were the people who would have killed her, because one of their friends had a vision of the future. It was somewhat hard to look past that detail. Both sentinels were in a wretched state, flustered and dishevelled, though not as bad as her cousin, crumpled on the floor.

'Your ladyship,' said the Islandser, hovering as if he might be about to do something dreadfully awkward like bow or scrape.

'Seigneur,' Isangell replied with frosty politeness, and then nodded her head in acknowledgement to Delphine, who looked uncomfortable. 'I take it you have brought my cousin back to us?'

'Somewhat the worse for wear, I'm afraid,' said the Islandser with a weak grin. 'A little under the weather, as you see. He'll be back to his old self in no time, to be sure.'

Delphine muttered something like, 'Don't bet on it.'

'I'm afraid I have forgotten your name,' Isangell said, eyes fixed on Ashiol. He was pale and muttering and looked far beyond drunk.

'Macready, ladyship,' the Islandser told her. 'Just passing through, trying to make sure your man here gets home safely.'

The atrium wasn't an obvious thoroughfare. Isangell stared at them both and then looked up, to where sunlight streamed through the open ceiling. 'Did you come in by the *roof?*' Neither of them answered that and she was happy to let the question drop. 'Has he been drinking?'

'Among other things,' said Macready.

'I've never seen him in such a state.'

'You've led quite the sheltered life, then.'

'Not at all,' Isangell snapped, and then reconsidered. 'Well, yes. Obviously. But Ashiol has never lost control like this before.'

'As you say, ladyship,' Macready said, so polite that it hurt, even if he had no idea of formal terms of address and protocol. 'Could you see your way to pointing us in the direction of his quarters? Your man here needs to sleep it off.'

Isangell nodded slowly. Getting Ashiol out of the way before her mother saw the mess he was in was an absolute priority. 'I can take you there. It isn't far.'

'See, you're making yourself useful already,' Macready said with a lopsided grin. 'I knew it would be worth my while to strike up a friendship with you.'

Isangell led the way, while Macready and Delphine dragged along a muttering but compliant Ashiol. Luckily, they met no one in the corridor except servants low enough in rank to avoid the Duchessa's gaze and pretend they had seen nothing.

Once Ashiol was sprawled out on his bed, he quickly fell asleep, though that might have had something to do with a small vial Isangell saw a flash of in Macready's hand. Isangell sat on the edge of her cousin's bed.

He looked younger in sleep; less careworn and tense. She had watched him becoming more and more distant over the last few nundinae, and had hoped he would mourn and pull through his grief. Ashiol never wanted to speak of anything, the few occasions she had tried. 'This is about the woman who died.'

'Two,' said Delphine in a low voice, from where she stood

with her back to the window, putting distance between herself and the rest of them. 'Two women died.'

Isangell nodded. She remembered every step of that walk back to the Palazzo, with Ashiol holding the wrapped body of his friend. She still had no idea really who that demoiselle was, or what she meant to him. She now knew more about Ashiol than she ever had before, yet he was even more of a mystery.

'Right,' said Macready after allowing her only a moment of quiet reflection. He clapped his hands together in a businesslike manner. 'You're just the lass to arrange things for us. We'll be needing food and the like delivered here, though none of your Palazzo servants will be allowed beyond the outer door. We may be here a day or two, maybe a full market-nine.'

Isangell blinked. 'How long is it going to take him to sober up?'

Macready looked uncomfortable.

Isangell tensed, as the old fear returned to her. 'That babble, the look of him... that *was* the drink, was it not?'

'He's been drinking a long time,' Delphine spoke up, not meeting Isangell's eyes. 'We don't know everything else he's been taking. The only sure method is to let it all wear out of him.'

'And then we get to see what's left behind,' said Macready, sounding far too grave. 'I've seen him like this before, your ladyship. Chances are he's a wee bit broken. But he'll mend, never you mind that. The mind's not as fragile as people tend to think. It can mend clean.'

'Are you saying he's mindsick?' Isangell demanded. 'Mad?'

'Of course not,' said Macready, sounding outraged. 'Mad, the very idea!' He paused. 'He's not entirely sane right now, it has to be said.'

'A bit broken?' she repeated.

'Exactly.'

I will not hyperventilate. 'Our grandfather went mad,' Isangell said. 'The family complaint, we call it. It came and went, but in his last few years, the dottores could do nothing more for him and they locked him away.'

'Don't worry your head about it,' said Macready. 'We've seen your man through times like this before. We can do it again.'

Isangell looked to the demoiselle, hoping for some kind of reassurance or confirmation, but Delphine's face was flat and unmoving. 'How can I help?' Isangell asked.

'Look in from time to time if you've a mind to it,' said Macready. 'It will cheer him, right enough, to see that pretty face of yours. Make me climb mountains, it would.'

Isangell almost blushed — the flirting habits of the sons of the Great Families were nowhere near this good. 'You won't leave him alone?'

Macready shrugged and smiled. 'Aye, what's that servant that Lords have? The one who lays out your clothes and goes on the hunt with you?'

A bubble of laughter welled up in Isangell's throat. 'A valet?'

'Exactly. Think of me as your man's valet.'

'I'll do my best.' Honestly, a valet. Who did he think he was going to fool? 'Anything else?'

Macready turned serious. 'A couple of strong-armed coves on the door wouldn't hurt, lass. Make sure no one comes in here, no matter who they say they are. We've friends who will be useful — I can give you their names — but otherwise our man here should be kept away from the prying eyes of Palazzo folk, if you follow me.'

Mother, then, was not to be admitted. Not that Isangell hadn't already come to that conclusion all on her own. 'I will assign lictors to the doors,' she decided. 'Perhaps — some kind of password that you only share with those you trust to be near Ashiol?'

A shadow passed over Macready's face. 'Rose and needle,' he said sombrely. 'That will do, right enough.'

~

ASHIOL COULD NOT SUFFER MIRRORS. At first he covered every polished surface in his rooms. After the cloth slid off one by accident, he started breaking them instead.

Isangell quietly had them all removed, after that.

No one asked him why, but then no one was asking him much of anything these days. He had so many words in his head, and they spilled out at the slightest provocation, slashing and wounding and piling up until everyone else felt as crazy as he did.

At least, that was the logical explanation.

The sentinels took turns watching over him, as was their sworn duty. Funny word, 'duty'. Ashiol wasn't sure it meant what it used to mean. Kelpie watched him always, like he was something fragile made out of glass or spun sugar. Macready and Crane were more stoic. You couldn't see what they were thinking, either of them, though Ashiol could hear the tick tick tick of their brains in any case.

Delphine was the only one he actually liked to have there, because she wasn't treating him like some invalid. She would huff and pout about wasting her time on him, and if he was lucky he could goad her into some proper bitching and yelling.

Isangell never yelled. She was more of a ghost than any of them, a pale outline who jumped every time Ashiol said something remotely strange.

(It made him want to act extra crazy around her, every single time.)

'It's fer your own good,' Macready insisted, when Ashiol found the bars on the windows, wrapped in skysilver wire.

'Whose good?' Ashiol snarled, pacing back and forth, not wanting to stay still. 'I need to be out there. I need to breathe.'

'You need to heal,' Macready insisted.

The sentinels were putting their faith in the powder pills prescribed by the Palazzo dottore, but all they did was to bring down the mist. Ashiol could not move some days, after taking them. When he escaped the mist, he was exactly the same. Broken, and on fire.

'The cats do not want to be caged,' he said.

'We're trying to keep you safe, you fool.'

Ashiol waited. His time would come. 'Are you sure all the mirrors are gone?'

Macready sighed. 'Aye, my King. All gone.'

The first time since Velody's sacrifice that the sky woke up, Ashiol almost tore his hands off trying to get out of that fucking room. 'They need me,' he had snarled when Crane and Kelpie held him back.

'They need a Power and Majesty,' Kelpie snapped back. 'Can you be that for them right now? If not, shut up.'

He liked that; it was the Kelpie he knew and not the hesitant, protective creature who fluttered at his bedside in recent days. Much though he provoked her, though, he could not get her to repeat it.

Even with no mirrors in the room, he could not avoid his reflection. Not when it grew dark outside, and there was a lantern burning in the room.

Do you trust me? asked Garnet one evening, staring out of the reflection of the glass. The bars on the window made lines on his face, like the scars Ashiol once bore.

'Why even ask the question?' replied Ashiol, barely doing

more than mouth the words. He remembered this conversation. He remembered what it had led to.

Then trust me, his friend said, with exaggerated warmth. *I'll take care of it. I'm sorry the sentinels didn't feel they could come to me with their concerns.*

'They love you,' Ashiol said, remembering how afraid he had been of making Garnet angry, back then, when the world belonged to them. 'They are yours, absolutely. Their loyalty does not waver.'

Ours, said Garnet. *Sentinels serve the Kings, not only the Power and Majesty. And they never let me forget it.* His voice was chilly now.

Ashiol closed his eyes. 'You're imagining things.' He had leaned over and kissed Garnet then, years ago, the first time they had shared this conversation. Garnet had kissed him back, sincerely, as if he still loved him.

Only days later, Ashiol woke up screaming, his animor gone, gone, fucking gone, his skin bleeding from a thousand cuts. 'Give it back!' he howled. 'Give it back!'

He blinked, and he was back in his room, palms slammed against the cold glass, and Garnet's face still there in the reflection, smirking at him. 'You're not real.'

Can't get rid of me, though, can you?

This much was true. 'You should never have done that to me. Not me.'

Did you think you were special? Poor little rich boy. You couldn't give it up, could you? The fucking privilege you were born with that said you should be better than me. Stronger, taller. You didn't mind me having things as long as you had more.

Ashiol felt the despair all over again. Garnet was always angry, always had this kind of resentment bubbling at the surface. It was only at the end that Ashiol realised how bad it was.

'I always shared,' he said in a low voice.

Garnet laughed, an awful laugh. *Oh yes, you loved to share. Loved to be the magnanimous one, doling out rewards to the keeper's son. Demonstrating all over again that you were greater, I was lesser. Do you not see that? I only came to this city because of you. Everything I had in my life was owed to you.* His voice cracked on his final words. *I lost my last battle because I couldn't get you out of my head.*

'You were Power and Majesty, and I was not.'

You think I don't know that? Garnet banged his own fists against the glass, and it seemed to rattle under his blows. An angry ghost indeed. *I was Power and Majesty. That meant something, Ashiol, to everyone but you. Because you still saw the scraped knees and the beaten back. You still saw the boy so scrawny that everyone said: how can that little thing be the keeper's son? You knew my skeletons, and you never let me forget it.*

'No,' Ashiol said hoarsely. 'That's not how it was. You became Lord before me. King before me. You were the Power and Majesty. If it was all some kind of twisted competition between us, you won.'

Not yet, said Garnet. *Not until I take everything away from you. Everything. For a start.*

Fear shot through Ashiol, and he hated that. Even in death, Garnet was the person he loved most, and feared most. He slammed his fists hard against the window, wanting to break his hands, wanting to feel something other than this.

The glass finally shattered under his blows, and his hands smashed into the skysilver-wrapped bars on the outside. The pain shot through him, overwhelming everything else.

He could still hear Garnet laughing as the broken pieces of window fell away into the grounds below.

26

VOLCANALIA

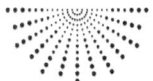

EIGHT DAYS AFTER THE IDES OF CERIALIS

DAYLIGHT

*M*acready wasn't one for the musette. Pomp and painted faces did little for him. The only songs he had a yen for were the Islandser drinking hymns that reminded him of his red-faced uncles and cousins back at home.

He felt like a fraud as he strolled into the Vittorine Royale under the guise of a messenger with a parcel of Volcanalia sweetmeats for the Orphan Princel.

Poet was on stage, playing at being a real person. Interesting. Macready slid on to one of the benches in the stalls, watching. They were rehearsing a large chorus number, with a dozen or so youngsters in bright, gaudy finery. Poet walked through all the dance steps, calling out instructions here and there, even exchanging a wry laugh or two as he demonstrated what each of them needed to be doing. After the second walkthrough he did it in real time, singing and dancing his number with the painted flowers in support.

Macready felt his blood chill. That lass — the one who joined in on the second chorus with a cheeky line or two about why floristers like their blooms stripped of thorns — there was something about her. A glow beneath her brown cheeks, a fierce light shining out of her dark eyes.

That lad, too, the tumbler. Both the tumblers, masked and near-identical, copying each other's moves, mimicking Poet's own choreography. No one had timing that good. It was as if they knew what he was going to do before he did it. Even when he performed the steps differently to the walkthrough.

Macready paid more attention after that, his gaze sweeping over each of the peacock children. Taking it in. Holy feck, what had Poet done?

They could sing, that much was for sure. But there was more to the song than there should be. He could almost feel himself being dragged into it, compelled despite the creeping worry that he had to get out of there before...

'Sentinel,' said a low voice behind him. 'Enjoying the show?'

Macready jumped. Poet was right there, leaning in from the bench behind, lips near his ear. 'They're all —' he said. 'Are they not?' Saints and fecking angels, every single one of them.

'Not yet,' said Poet, looking naked without his spectacles, face white with cosmetick. He was made up like a harlequinus, with a black-inked tear on one cheek. 'But they will be, I think.' He grinned fiercely, making a nonsense of the painted-on sad face. 'Show business is all about spotting potential, don't you know.'

Potential. A dozen or more children with fecking potential. Some could be courtesi. Some could be sentinels. The stage vibrated with their contained power. Not yet, not yet... How the devil had he found them all?

Macready's mouth was dry. 'I have a message from the

Power and Majesty,' he said. 'You and Livilla are to be on watch for the sky this nox.'

Poet looked at Macready far too long. 'Is that so,' he said finally. 'Our sweet Ashiol is still unwell, I take it? Unable to make his requests in person?'

It was an unconvincing lie. Macready knew it. The whole fecking Creature Court knew it. They didn't get sick. They did not take wounds for long. But how else to explain Ashiol's absence from the sky? There had been few battles since Velody's sacrifice, and those very small, but there was still no excuse.

'Won't be long now,' Macready said with false humour. 'He'll be back on his feet in no time.' The Creature Court had allowed this unbalance, because none of them had the powers of a King. It wouldn't last. Any day now, they would pounce.

'I'll be going, then. Leave you to your—'... *gang of children ripe to be swallowed up by the Creature Court as soon as they come into their own*. Bloody hellfire. If this was Poet's game, what might the other Lords be up to?

'I'll give the oath, you know,' Poet said mildly. 'Any time Ashiol asks for it.'

'Aye,' Macready sighed. 'You're a loyal cove, right enough.'

HER NAME WAS TOPAZ. She started out as Gemimy, but that was too ordinary a name for the musette. Every demme who started out in a joint like this had an eye to be a stellar someday, and you needed a name that gave you an edge. She reckoned 'Topaz' had to sit right with all them Rubies and Sapphiras in the company.

Topaz still couldn't believe she was here, that those bright, bonny costumes in the shared dressing room were hers, and she was one of the lucky dozen chosen by the Orphan Princel Himself to be his own personal cabaret troupe. The Princel's Lambs, the company called them, though everyone knew there was another term you used for a troupe of children in a theatre: cabaret of monsters.

Himself had spoken directly to Topaz only once, outside of the stage directions and choreography notes he gave to all the lambs. He met her gaze, eyes odd behind those funny spectacles of his, and said, 'Your voice is as good as any of them, but you need to use it harder if you want to stand out.'

Topaz sang herself raw in the next rehearsal, and swore up and down she saw him smile.

Bart made it through to the final dozen as well. He was a tumbler, so stretchy and twisty that it made Topaz's belly ache to watch him. He played the clown too much, and earned glares from the Orphan Princel more'n once for adding too much dumbshow to his act.

They had to know their place. The lambs weren't here to be stellars, not yet. They weren't masks or columbines or songbirds, not in their own right. They were here to make the Orphan Princel look his best.

'You're good enough to be one of the real songbirds, Tope,' Bart said lazily one afternoon backstage, in the shoebox of a dressing room they shared with the other lambs and casuals. 'Your voice is as fine as that Dame Violet...'

'Hush your mouth,' said Topaz, squeezing herself into the new costume for the Bestialia chorus. She was going to be a cat, which she rather liked, in tabby velvet that showed off her hips. She was finally starting to look shapely now she was thirteen and eating regular. 'I'm only a sprat.'

Topaz had her dreams, though, oh aye. Stellar dreams. The Orphan Princel was going to be the one to help her catch hold of them.

The dressing room filled up with the rest of the lambs, all

scrambling for their Bestialia skins, and there was no time for daft talk. A good thing, too; the last thing she needed was word getting around that she was getting Ideas Above.

Gussied up as all manner of critters, Himself's Lambs hurried out to take their marks on the stage. The stagemaster had declared that if they proved good enough, their cabaret of monsters would be launched in the Bestialia revue — in the main show, not tucked away as a reserve act for matinées like their previous turns on the stage. They had a month and a handful of days to show him they were worthy.

Topaz had a whole stanza to herself, in the middle of the song. Anxiety gnawed at her as she posed in cat stance, false tail swish-swishing. Bart crouched near her, a jot too round-faced and friendly for a ferax, though the red fur looked fine on him.

Her belly was tumbling inside as Topaz made her way through the group chorus and the dance steps, not wanting to put a paw out of place. Then it was her go, and she sang. She stared straight at Himself as she hit the notes she needed to, but he wasn't paying no mind to the stage. A lad Topaz had seen around a few times stood close to him, their heads bowed together as they muttered.

So much for making an impression on the lord and master.

Topaz sang anyway, putting all her blood into it, her best moves and voice trills. She finished by climbing cat-like up the false roof that was part of the set.

The rest of the troupe crawled and writhed on the stage, carolling together with their critter cries before they all launched into the final chorus. Not only Topaz's cat and Bart's ferax, but a panther, gattopardo, wolf, a real frenzy of birds and rodents.

Not only on the stage. As the song built up to its big finish, Topaz was staring out into the stalls, and she saw animals there, too. Right where the Orphan Princel stood, there was a mess of white rats draped over his skinny frame like a coat. They wriggled like anything, crawling all over him. The lad at his side was swamped in brown weasels. (Was that right? Were they clambering over him or was it something more — were they filling the space where he ought to be?)

It made no sense to Topaz. Another man came down the aisle, and she saw darkhounds snapping and snarling inside his skin.

Oh, yes. Inside his skin. No doubt about it.

Topaz lost her grip on the lightwood roof. She fell, and heard Bart cry out in alarm. A couple of the other lambs jumped up to grab her, while the others just stared like fools. She landed hard on the stage, and felt something snap. The pain hit her leg a moment later and she let out one long whimper.

She might have lost consciousness for a moment. When she awoke, Himself was leaning over her, making a show of concern. 'All right there, little one?' His cool hand brushed her forehead, and she shuddered at the touch.

Topaz could still see them inside his skin. 'White rats,' she said, and then screamed as the musette dottore tried to straighten her ankle.

'Interesting,' said the Orphan Princel. The last thing Topaz saw before the pain pushed her into darkness was his grin, biting and satisfied.

Why should her daftness make Himself so happy? It made no sense at all.

TOPAZ AWOKE to find herself in a sunshiney room with roses on the curtains. She shouldn't be in a place like this; it was too fine and she could never pay for it. When she tried to sit up, though, her ankle sent a jolt of pain all the way up to her knee. 'Cack!'

The sheets were clean and fresh. She'd never seen a room this nice.

'Ah, you're awake,' said a smooth voice as the door opened.

Topaz covered herself with the quilt, though she wore a respectable enough shift (no mends on the sleeve, it wasn't hers).

'Stagemaster,' she said nervously, recognising Himself (the latter name was what all the crew and cast called him, but never to his face).

Himself looked pale and washed out without his stage-paint, and wore clothes of white and bone. Not his regular clobber at all. 'How do you feel?' he asked her.

'Like a horse sat itself on my leg,' Topaz said honestly, and he laughed.

'Aye, I imagine you do. It was a bad fall.' His words were normal enough, but he watched her in a strange way, eyes darting over her with every syllable.

Was he going to try it on? Topaz knew it was a common thing for demmes like her, that the older blokes in the company expected a bit of slap and tickle if they fancied it, and you didn't get much of a chance to say whether it was to your fancy or no. Himself was a real stellar, though. He could have anyone. No one else had ever taken an interest in her growing curves. She thought her dark skin and eyes might give her some protection on that score, though there were demmes darker than her in the chorus who already had fancy men sniffing around.

'Where am I?' she asked.

'I hired a room for you with Mistress Nance,' her boss said, as if it was naught. 'Many of our dancers board here.'

He meant the contract columbines — demmes who had shilleins to spare.

'I don't have the purse for this place,' Topaz said quickly.

Himself gave her an amused look. 'I do. Your friend Bart tried to suggest you should rest up in that rat-nest you're all clustered into. Ridiculous idea. I need you near the theatre, for the dottore if nothing else.'

Topaz knew how this worked. If you picked up an injury bad enough to stop you doing your job, you were kicked out. She'd never heard of anyone being cosseted like this. Maybe one of the big names, but she was barely one of the company.

Demmes like her got fumbled in corridors, not seduced with lush lodging houses.

'What's so special about me?' she demanded and aye, she was being rude, but she needed it to make sense.

Himself smiled at her with that funny little face of his (mad as a box of frogs, him), and sat on the bed. 'Tell me about what you saw,' he said. 'On the stage.'

Topaz swallowed. 'I didn't see nothing. The lights made me dizzy.'

In an instant, the pleasant smile was gone. 'You won't lie to me,' he said, stating it as a fact. Oh, his voice; there was such a chill to it that Topaz could have sworn the daylight bled out of the room.

'Critters,' she admitted finally, in a broken sort of whisper. 'I saw critters. Rats and weasels and that. Only they weren't really there, were they?'

Himself relaxed, all smiles again. 'You'd be surprised.'

THREE MARKET-NINES PASSED, and there was no limit to the special treatment Topaz got from his high and brightness. A dottore visited her every couple of days, checking her bandages and covering her leg in goopy unguents that made her muscles ache while stinking out the rosy sunshine room.

She had coronets and fresh fruit for breakfast every day, and never got used to it.

A couple of coves came to the door of the boarding house every afternoon to make sure she got to the Vittorina Royale for rehearsal. Bad enough that the other lambs were already giving her funny looks and calling her the Princel's pet — if they knew she was carried there every day on a litter, they would never let her hear the end of it.

Then it happened. After a long, hard morning rehearsal, Himself sent the other lambs away to their dinner (oats and grease at Madam Bertha's, one centime a plate) and kept Topaz behind. 'I think you'll do,' he said, eyes roaming critically over her.

She shivered under his scrutiny. 'Do for what, seigneur?'

'For the song, of course.' His earnest expression broke into a grin, the cheery sort that was even scarier than his faraway dreamy grin. 'I want you to have your own song in the show.'

'You're cracked, you are,' she said without thinking, and then pressed her hand to her mouth in horror. 'I didn't mean —'

'Aye you did,' Himself said, enjoying her discomfort. 'I'm quite sane, you know, compared to most of my friends.'

Topaz decided then and there she never wanted to meet his friends. 'Really my own song?'

'Really,' he said, and his eyes were oddly warm. Usually he was cold as brick. 'You're the one I've been waiting for, Topaz.' He leaned in, and she expected a kiss or a grope, even after all this time of him keeping his hands to himself, but instead he was measuring her, noting the length of her arms, the width of her shoulders, the span of her waist. 'You'll fit the costume,' he said. 'Nary an alternation. Will you do it, lamb?'

'Aye,' she said. 'I'm not cracked. Even if you are.' If he claimed to like her cheek, she could give him plenty. 'What do I need to do?'

He handed her a crackling piece of paper. 'Learn the words. We start rehearsing this tomorrow, after the others have gone. Don't mind extra work, do you?'

Topaz shook her head wordlessly. Her own song. 'I can't stand on my stems without a stick,' she reminded him.

'Oh, the patrons will love that,' he assured her. 'I performed with a broken arm once — they felt so sorry for me, it made my career.'

BACK IN THE rosy room in the boarding house, Topaz tried to concentrate on Himself's scratchy handwriting. It weren't like a song at all, more a sort of children's skipping rhyme. Nothing so toffish she didn't understand all the words, thank the saints.

The landlady who brought her meals on a tray rapped on the door. 'You've a caller, lovey.' She stuck her face in. 'Normally I'd insist you see him down in the parlour, but with that leg I'll let him up here if you behave yerselves. Door stays open, understand?'

A pink, embarrassed face appeared at her elbow. 'It's only Bart,' said Topaz, shoving her new words under a pillow. 'Don't worry about him, Mistress Nance.'

'Best not give me any reason to,' the landlady said, but she was grinning a bit like they had a joke to share.

Bart came in, shuffling his feet and avoiding her gaze. 'Doing all right for yourself here then, Topaz?'

'Don't give me a hard time,' she sighed. 'I ain't done a

thing to ask for this, and you know it. He's bonkers, that's all, the stagemaster.'

'Aye,' said Bart, his face creasing into a bit of a smile. He looked at her finally. 'Reckon he is. You're all right, then?'

'Apart from a broken stem, and that'll mend.'

'Does it hurt?' He came over and prodded thoughtfully at the bandage.

'Ey, leave off!' she protested as a jolt of pain shot through her.

'Sorry. Just, you know. It's rum, all this.' Bart looked around the room like he was expecting to be chucked out at any minute.

'Won't last long, just til I'm back on my feet,' she assured him. Burning devils couldn't have forced her to tell him about the solo song, not right then.

There was plenty she couldn't tell him. Like the dreams she had, nox and day alike, all rats and mice painted with cosmetick and draped in satin flounces, dancing madly across the stage.

He'd reckon she was as cracked as the Orphan Princel if she spilled a word about that.

'Not long to go till the Bestialia season starts,' Bart said with half a grin. 'Reckon we'll kill the audience dead?'

Topaz's first thought was 'Bloody hope not', but she had the sense not to say that aloud. 'Course we will,' she said, thinking of the song under her pillow. 'We'll be stellar. Try and stop us.'

27

FIRST DAY OF THE LUDI AUFLEURIS

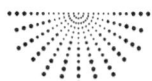

THE NONES OF LUDI

DAYLIGHT

*T*ell me about the lie you told, said Heliora.

Rhian worked hard to keep the voices of the Seers out of her head. She was able to quiet most of them, keeping the cacophony of troubled souls from overwhelming her, except for first thing in the morning and last thing before she went to sleep.

One voice stayed, though. Now that the others were quiet, Heliora was sharper and clearer than before.

'This isn't really you,' Rhian told her as she made her bed and swept the floor. 'You're dead.'

Of course I'm dead. Don't get distracted by details. I want to know about Lupercalia.

'No.' Rhian pushed and pushed until Heliora's voice was a small leaf, drifting alone on a wide, dark lake. 'Go away.'

She had spent so long working to forget that day, and thanks to the false Heliora in her head, the memories kept swirling back at her.

I'll tell you mine if you tell me yours, said Heliora, bobbing to the surface of her mind again as Rhian laid armfuls of flowers out on the kitchen table for garland preparation. Another set of Sacred Games were here, and it wouldn't be the Ludi Aufleuris without roses by the bucketload — red to throw to the gladiator you loved, white to compliment their skill, the rarer purple and gold blooms to offer patronage or sponsorship, and the powerful-smelling common pink to hurl at the arena just because.

Rhian trimmed the stalks savagely, one by one. 'You're not here. I don't owe you anything. Go away.'

She felt the former Seer shift within her mind, and felt a shiver like invisible fingers had stroked her hair. *Tell me.*

∽

RHIAN:

I should never have gone out alone, not with the streets awash with drunkards and lechers celebrating the Lupercalia. I knew it at the time, though I could think of little but the council contracts and what they meant to us. The courier's lateness was not our fault, but we'd still be fined or dropped to make room for some other favoured team of garlanders.

I delivered the garlands, just in time. On my way back, I was followed by two louts in wolf skins who teased and taunted me along the Forum. I didn't manage to shake them off until I reached the Lake of Follies. I crouched by the lanterns and the water, gasping for breath, waiting to recover my sensibilities.

Fool, I was such a fool. At the very least I should have told the others I was going, given them a chance to join me or force me to stay home. Hidden by trailing strands of bunting from the dancing revellers and the stink of honey wine, I let myself feel safe again. A little longer, and I might have the courage to walk home with my wits about me.

I did not hear them coming until they were on top of me, voices laughing and cruelly mocking, hands biting into my hands and legs, forcing me forwards until I lost my balance.

The hands pushed me into the cold water of the Lake of Follies, holding me under.

Then you were there.

The voices of the Seers, for the very first time, jeering voices crowding my thoughts (inside my head, inside my head) even as the hands pushed me down again and again.

Visions unfolded before me, of blood and horror, of people I loved doing terrible things, of blades and pain and buildings crumbling to dust. I screamed to see myself wielding a blade, cutting a man into pieces as if he were a goat ready for sacrifice. I was too calm in that other place. Untouchable, carved of ice. Roots burst out of my feet and hands, holding my victims in place. Water dripped along my skin, earth crumbled out of my nose and mouth, and the winds whipped hard and fast around us.

I was a monster, and a murderess.

I saw myself hold that knife, cutting the flesh away as easily as stripping thorns from stems. He twitched and writhed beneath my hands, so afraid of what I could do. I felt what it was like to be her, that other me. Felt the glee and the glory. She — I — enjoyed making him scream. She took satisfaction from it. It thrilled in my veins. More visions came, thick and fast, more versions of myself, each worse than the last. I coughed and choked on the water of the lake. I killed and maimed. I was chained and beaten.

Thorns dug into every inch of my body. Hands bound me to a stake and set me alight.

I could still smell the smoke when I rocked back on my heels, beside the lake. My hands were shaking wildly, and it was a long time before I could stand. My clothes and hair were dry. There were no hands, no people around me. No one had pushed me in the lake.

I was going mad. That much was obvious.

I walked home slowly, barely noticing the capering men in their animal suits, or the thick smell of wine and vomit and sweaty leather. The wind was cold, but I had left my shawl beside the lake. I could not think of anything except my own madness. The visions clung to me.

What was causing this? What had I done to deserve it?

I was three streets from our home when the men grabbed me. It was a jest at first. They laughed as one of them spun me around, dancing to the music of a nearby flute. Another grabbed my hips, ground himself against me, his false phallus digging into my stomach. Then there was a whiff of sour breath, and I realised they were not letting me go.

They backed me against the nearest building, four of them, maybe five, still laughing, talking amongst themselves, slurring obscenities, laying claims as to who would have me first.

I felt strangely passive, outside myself. They thought they could hurt me? I was already broken. How could they do more... Then one of them shoved his hands between my thighs, and I snapped to attention. That woman, the cold-eyed Other Rhian with the knives who sacrificed men like beasts. She would never let this happen to her.

Drunk men in Lupercalia goatskins, shrugging aside their costumes and false phalluses to free up their real erections. A demme's body was just another festival token to them. I knew what they intended to do to me. They didn't fear me. Why should they?

I saw, though. I saw everything. I saw their futures. One man watching the birth of his daughter, face gentled with shock and love. One man slapping his wife to the floor. One man coughing blood from his lips as he lay of a wasting illness. One man proud of his new business, opening for customers. One man... saints, I knew that one, I had bought timbers from him to build our kitchen table, he had been inside our house...

I took their futures away from them.

Something burned brightly inside me, went through me... and the smell of honey wine and sour leathers was overpowered by burning flesh.

The men started screaming, clutching at their own skin as if they could claw it out of them. Heat washed over me as they collapsed to their knees. They were alive through it all, their screams swallowed by the noise and madness of the crowd. There was not a mark on any of them; no sign of the flames.

I tried to end it. They stopped screaming, at least, but they lay so still on the ground. When I found it in me to touch them, their skin was chilled, and there was nothing left of them that was human. Their twisted limbs and agonised faces were sculpted in stone.

I walked away, stepping over their granite limbs and frozen faces, leaving them behind in my haste to escape what I had done. But the visions I had, the futures that those men would never see, they stayed with me. They are with me still.

As are you all.

I WAS A MONSTER, I was a victim, I was broken, I was crazy. I cut my braid from my scalp. It was all I could do not to cut deeper, dragging every hair from my head. I was dirty, I was filthy, I was a killer. Blood, blood, I couldn't get it out of my head, couldn't concentrate on anything but cleansing myself, scrubbing away the horrors, letting it all drip out of me. I couldn't kill myself, I didn't deserve such a release, but I could make myself hurt and bleed. That was how my friends found me, cuts welling in my skin. I was a demon, I was a witch, I was...

Now do you see? Now do you see what I have been hiding from, what I have been trying to prevent from happening again? There were times I managed to convince myself it had just been a strange turn, that it hadn't happened, that the heat had just stirred my imagination into something ridiculous and cruel. That I was raped, by four men, or five, and the rest was a crazy dream I had made up, an elaborate revenge fantasy to hide the truth of it from myself.

Then Velody brought them home, one by one, the Lords and Court and Kings and Sentinels, speaking of animor and cats and power and the sky falling. It was real. Anything was possible. These people would not blink to hear of a person who could burn men from the inside or turn them into stone. Nor would they hesitate to put me down if they thought I was a danger to them. They had their own power, their own monstrous abilities. They were like me.

I knew the truth then.

Can you honestly say that Delphine or Macready would forgive me for what I have done, for the lie I allowed them to believe? That Velody would have forgiven me? I can't even forgive myself.

DELPHINE LEFT the Palazzo after spending half a day ignoring Ashiol's attempts to pretend he was sane. Having left Crane in her place, she was surprised to find Macready waiting for her on the road. He fell into step beside her as she walked down the hill.

They had been avoiding each other for the most part since that day she took Surrender and Ashiol's mind was broken once and for all. It was only the business of being a sentinel between them now, or at least Delphine assumed so.

It was best that it was over. She couldn't stand sleeping with someone who was so damned good about everything, and she absolutely hated anyone having expectations of her. She was bound to be a disappointment to Macready.

It wasn't like he was that great in bed.

Delphine was tired. If he had something to say, he should say it now. She didn't want to fight when they got home. She didn't want to fight at all. She wanted to sleep. Halfway along Via Cinqueline, Macready reached out and took her hand. 'Let me show you something.'

She frowned as he led her into a narrow alleyway between two shops. 'What are we doing here? There are spiders!'

'I spotted this place a while back,' he said lightly. 'Thought it would make a fine nest, so it would.'

'So? What's that got to do with me?' Macready looked at her. She looked back, waiting. The centi dropped. 'You want me to make a nest? I don't know how!'

'I wasn't going to stand here and watch you make it up as you go along,' he said, rolling his eyes at her. 'I'll teach you, if you've a mind to it. Now, take your blades out, the skysilver sword and knife. Just so.'

He turned Delphine gently to face the wall. She could hear the clank and rattle on the other side of dishes being washed, and the acrid scent of pulses on the boil. 'There are people in there.'

'It's of no matter. That's not where you're going.' His voice was low, and his breath tickled the back of her neck. 'A nest is a new space. It's not entirely of the city. Now, lay your blades against the wall.'

She did so, first the knife blade and then the sword.

'Imagine a space opening up, a room, a place of safety,' Macready told her, still in that low, firm voice that had her heating up from the inside out. Delphine did as he told her, for once. She felt the prickle of the skysilver against the skin of her hands, and imagined a safe place like the first nest that Macready had taken her to.

She gasped as the skysilver came awake under her hands, and she could feel the wall opening up at her command.

Macready kept with her, murmuring encouragement and instructions as Delphine stretched the city wide open, creating a nest for herself.

Finally, exhausted, she fell through into a small and lopsided space full of new air which tasted of skysilver. She gasped in the air, laughing. She had done it. She had no idea what she had done, but it was hers, and it felt safe in a way nowhere else had felt safe in a very long time.

Macready stood above her, grinning all over his stupid face. 'You can seal it with a blade, or with your hand once you're accustomed —' he said, and probably would have said more if she hadn't lunged herself at him, kissing him to shut him up.

'Is that what it's like for them?' she said breathlessly, still bathed in the afterglow of what she had done. 'When they use animor?'

Macready's eyes were a little unfocused from the kissing. 'It's better,' he said, holding her hips steady so that she did not twist away from him. 'Because it's ours.'

She smiled, and pulled him down on to the floor of her new nest. They tugged and fumbled at each other's clothes, grinding possessively against each other.

Yes, all right then. This probably counted as a relationship.

SOME TIME LATER, Delphine and Macready reached the little courtyard behind her house. She felt sore and dishevelled, and deliberately didn't invite him in, pretending not to see the disappointed look on his face.

Rhian sat at the kitchen table, with armfuls of hacked-apart roses spread out on the table before her. She was still cutting them, slicing through ruined flower heads, spreading them out into messy patterns. There were colours every-where, bruised and slashed petals tumbling off the edge of the table and on to the floor.

'Are you all right?' Delphine asked, letting the door fall closed behind her. Rhian looked up and there was something awful about her eyes. 'Mac!' Delphine screamed, and he was there in moments, slamming back the door and crossing the threshold.

'Lass?'

'There's something wrong with her.' Delphine was trying not to panic, but this was Rhian, and they'd all gone through so much. (She couldn't lose Rhian too, she just couldn't, she would fall to a million pieces.)

Macready went to Rhian's side, neatly disarming her and placing the knife further along the table, out of reach. 'Now then, my lovely, how are you doing? What a mess you've made here.'

Rhian turned to look at him, but her eyes were sightless. 'I can hear them singing,' she said in a frantic voice. 'They keep singing at me.'

'Is she...' said Delphine, and choked on the rest of the question. First Ashiol, now this. 'Is she broken too?' She couldn't do this, couldn't look after a crazy Rhian by herself. She needed Velody, and that thought was enough to make her chest twist into knots.

Velody was gone, and they were on their own.

'Not like Ashiol,' Macready said in what he probably thought was a comforting tone of voice. 'But she's the Seer now, lass. It could take her hard.'

'She has to give the power back,' Delphine blurted. 'She can't do this; she was already so fragile.'

'Is that what you think?' said Macready, his hand hovering as if he was going to touch Rhian's hair, before he pulled back without making contact. 'I always thought she was the strong one, so I did.'

Rhian grabbed out at his hand, squeezing his fingers tightly between hers. 'He's making them sing, Macready! Cover the mirrors, quickly, before they come through.'

'Aye, lass, we'll see to it, but you must draw out, now. No getting lost in the futures. Trust me, there are no kind ways to bring you back.'

Delphine watched as he soothed Rhian with his voice, responding to her as if what she said was normal. He kept it up for far longer than she would have had patience for. What kind of a thimblehead was she, trying to push this man away?

Finally Rhian was calm and herself again. 'Thank you,' she said to Mac in a soft voice.

Delphine tidied away the ruined flowers and then made mint tisane for them all with shaking hands, forgetting as she always did how many scoops of the fine dried leaves she should use, and she almost cried with relief when Rhian chided her for making it too strong. Normal. Somewhere near normal.

'Well now,' said Macready a while later. 'We've had a narrow escape here, so we have. So busy working on Delphine's training, we never gave a thought to yours.'

'I —' said Rhian and then stopped, darting an anxious look at Delphine, as if whatever she was about to say could be worse than anything else Delphine had put up with lately. 'I hear them. The other Seers, the ones from before. I hear their voices. I think they are the ones who are supposed to teach me how to do this.'

'Aye,' Macready said grimly. 'I thought it might be something like that. They won't always be able to help you, my lovely. There are some things about being a Seer that — will be a problem for you.'

'Like what?' Delphine interrupted.

Rhian broke her cup. They both turned to stare at her, but she was lost again, staring at the tisane as it dripped over the edge of the table, her eyes locked on the broken pieces. 'He's coming back,' Rhian wailed. 'He's coming back, he's coming back, and you're all going to *burn!*'

MACREADY WATCHED Rhian as she babbled, eyes glazed over by the futures only she could see. *My poor sweet lass.*

He's coming back, she had said. He. Not Velody, then. It couldn't be good.

No time to dwell on that. Rhian was lost again, deeper than before, and feck it. He might not be able to talk her down this time.

Macready remembered how hard Heliora railed against all this when it first crashed in on her. She loathed being a Seer, and it swallowed her up whole and hard. She was a tough wee fighter, though, right from the start. For all he said that Rhian was strong, there were clearly some things she couldn't deal with, and this damned role was going to hurl them all at her.

'Make it stop,' Delphine said in a high, panicky voice, dragging Macready back to the here and now. 'Do something. How do we make it stop?'

Well, one of us could frig her against the wall. How would that be?

Saints and devils. Rhian was tumbling over herself now, barely able to speak the prophecies as they fell from her mouth. She was losing herself. 'He'll break us in pieces, all over again, he can't come back, we can't return to what we were, we won't survive it...' She was trembling, and the words burst out of her as if she was trying to hold them in.

'Rhian,' Macready said urgently. 'Don't let them take you. We can't bring you back. You have to do it. Stay strong, lass.'

'Help me,' she mouthed, pushing herself back from the table so violently she almost fell back on her chair.

Macready made his decision. He got up and dragged the table against the wall, making space.

'What are you doing?' Delphine demanded.

'Give her one of your swords,' Macready ordered her, drawing his own, the steel blade that still didn't feel like his. (The loss of his lasses was an ache he hadn't come to terms with yet.)

'Are you kidding me? She can't *fight* you.'

'Physical reality — it's the only way to snap the Seer back when the futures take them,' he said, wishing he didn't have to spell it out. 'Sex, lass. That's what Heliora always used. Given a choice between fecking and fighting... which do you think we should force on your lass here?'

Delphine hesitated and nodded, tugging Rhian to her feet and closing her fingers around the hilt of her own sword. 'Don't hurt her.'

As if he would. Macready leaned in, flicking his sword against Rhian's in a stage trick rather than a genuine fighting move. 'Play,' he said firmly.

Rhian had been silent for some time, though her eyes were still glazed with the unmistakeable look of someone lost in the futures. She looked at him blankly.

'Play,' he said again, and rapped his blade harder against hers. Maybe she didn't have much experience with a sword — but she had a multitude of Seers in her noggin, and Hel surely wasn't the only one of them who had started out sentinel.

Rhian's eyes narrowed, just a little. 'The children will sing and he will return and the sky will fall,' she burst out. 'It happens that way a thousand different times, different events, different deaths, but they always sing and he always returns and it's going to be a bloodbath.'

'Good to know,' Macready said steadily.

The third time he rapped her blade with his, she started fighting back. Her moves were slow at first, as if she was relearning something she had known instinctively as a child, but when he pressed his advantage she began to fence him like someone who knew how to use a sword.

Some of Rhian's moves were classic Heliora, picked up from the Silver Captain, and it stabbed Macready's gut every single time she used them. He hadn't thought about how he missed having Heliora around, until now. How much of her was inside Rhian's head?

All of them. He missed all of them. The rowdy family of sentinels he had once been part of. The Creature Court was not the same place without them.

Finally Rhian stepped back, out of breath, and lowered the sword. 'What — what are we doing? I was making dinner.'

Delphine squeaked and threw her arms around Rhian from behind.

Macready shook his head. There had to be an easier way.

28

ELSEWHERE

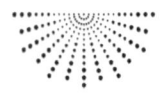

THE FIRST DAY

*S*he was cold. Cold was a good thing, surely. It meant that she was somewhere. Not blown into random threads across the sky.

Velody opened her eyes, and found herself lying on stone. She was naked, and as a matter of habit she reached inside herself for that familiar glow of Lord shape. It was not there. She breathed deeply, calling upon her animor, and found her skin empty of it.

Maybe that was why she was cold.

Silence spread across the air in front of her, reaching in all directions. Velody had spent most of her life within city walls, and had never heard a silence so deep or all-encompassing as this.

Heliora?

But no, even the last remnant of the Seer that clung to Velody in those moments before the sky swallowed her was gone now. Velody made the sign for swift passing, hoping that wherever Heliora was now, it was peaceful.

This did not address the question of where Velody was. The stone was part of a street. The cobbles were a dusty yellow colour, not the usual brown or black or grey she knew from Aufleur. And yet it was familiar.

She walked out into the main street, and there was no sky. It was not nox, nor daylight. There was no ceiling or pavilion roof covering it, and there was no cloud. The sky was merely absent, as her animor was absent.

This was a city, Velody realised, as she followed the empty street down to a crossroads. A wooden saint was skewered neatly in the centre, as was normal back in Aufleur. This was not her city, though. The stone was golden yellow, and the buildings of a different age and style.

She turned another corner, and was swamped by a wave of memory, so intimate that it almost turned her stomach. This *was* her city. She was two streets from the Greater Dockyards of Tierce. She was home.

Velody began to run. How could she not? Twelve years ago, she stepped into the carriage that would take her away from here, to an apprentice fair that would change her life forever. It was only a few months since her memories returned, and they came in fractured pieces — her papa's arms, kneading the dough he would make into crisp bread rolls. Her mam's apron. Her sisters, squirrelling over who would wear the best dress. Her brothers, shouting and tumbling through the busy house until they were put to work in the yard, or at the ovens. Her grandmother's swift fingers as she spun yarn in starlight colours, to sell to the local weavery.

Her grandfather's stiff back as he lectured them all (even the babies) on the proper handling of flour.

Velody stopped, finally, because she knew this lane. There was the bakery, whole and exactly the same. Smaller, perhaps. Humbler than the palazzo of yeast and rye that resolved itself as a memory in her head after so long away. There was no scent of baking bread. The shop was as empty as the rest of the city. It smelled like death, or the cold stone of an abandoned home. Where were they all?

She hesitated on the threshold, wanting and afraid at the same time that she would see nothing but the empty spaces left behind by her family. Where had they all gone? The bakery was never empty. There was always new bread. The scent of it infused everything. Velody breathed in, and smelled nothing but stone and dust and the absence of everything she craved.

There was nothing here for her, and yet she could not resist going inside to see the emptiness for herself. The ovens in the bakery were cold. The house upstairs was full of things, but no people. No food. Nothing that felt as if it belonged to *now*. Velody couldn't bring herself to step into the room she had shared with her sisters, not yet, but she went into her parents' room and found a soft grey dress, well-mended, folded in a chest. Mam's funeral dress. What could be more appropriate for Velody to clothe herself with upon her homecoming?

She didn't stay. Being here was too painful. She emerged from the bakery and sat on the top step, staring out at the desolate street. Utterly alone.

Five minutes later, someone started singing. Velody wasn't sure of the sound at first and then she was on her feet, running, trying to find the source of that odd, lilting sound. She wasn't alone here after all.

The docks made everything sound wrong (water, there was no water lapping against the pier, just more of that nothingness that hurt the eyes), and it took a long time before Velody could make sense of the echoes.

She found herself at the entrance to the bathhouse at the corner between the docks and her home, and yes — the singing was coming from in here. Velody walked nervously through the frigidarium, and the demoiselles' pool, finally ending up at the caldarium. Here, among the stone arches, there was water. It steamed, and how was it possible to have this source of heat when there was nothing else in the city?

The song had stopped, leaving her with no trail, but as she stumbled forward into the hot and clammy room, she saw him.

A man half-floated lazily in the water, naked and muscled. As Velody watched, he turned his head. The wet hair made it look darker, but his skin stood out, pale and bright beneath the red.

Now would be a really good time to start breathing again.

He smiled a slow smile of recognition. Maybe a flash of hunger. It made her shiver. 'Velody,' he said. 'I've been waiting for you.'

Garnet. Holy saints and angels. It was Garnet.

TIME PASSED. Velody regretted now that she had done nothing to mark her days here, but what exactly was she supposed to record? There was no daylight, no nox. No waterclocks, nothing but her heartbeat.

She wasn't even sure that her heartbeat could be trusted. Some days, she couldn't hear it at all.

It felt like she had been here a long time, but perhaps it was one of those dreams which gave you an entire epic story in the time it took to blink asleep and awake again.

Velody had considered marking the wall of her old room above the bakery every time she slept. But time went on and she didn't sleep. Sometimes when the weariness overtook her she would lie on the cool, musty covers and remember the room as it had been, full of the giggles and whispers of her sisters, but somehow she never managed to slip into any kind of darkness. She was relentlessly *here*.

She could record the number of times she avoided Garnet; that might be worth remembering.

This was her life now. She avoided Garnet when she could. Spent her time walking the canal paths of the city. She had no hunger, no thirst. No animor.

One of Velody's favourite places to wander was the city museion, an edifice of stone and pillars that she had never even known existed in her old life as a baker's daughter in Tierce. She could spend hours (minutes? days? no way of knowing) walking through the many grand halls, looking at the paintings and statues and costumes.

The hall of costumes almost broke her heart. So many lovely dresses, fine suits, representing decades and centuries of history. Velody touched the fabrics, the edgings and bindings, telling herself that as long as she could feel the difference between silk from Isharo and silk from Camoise, she was still a real person who actually existed.

On her third visit, she stripped off the grey funeral dress and slid an antique emerald-green gown over her body, fastening the clasps with shaking hands. Why not? The city was empty of everyone but ghosts.

She still felt like a thief as she walked out of the museion.

Garnet waited for her, legs dangled casually as he lounged on the plinth of a great granite statue. 'That colour suits you,' he said lightly. 'You look like a King. If Kings wore frocks.'

'They do these days,' said Velody.

'So they do.' Garnet surveyed her thoughtfully. Her skin prickled under his gaze. He wasn't the long-limbed boy she had dreamed about for so many years. There was nothing romantic about him. He was lean; all angles and taut muscle. His skin was pale, and his hair a coppery shock. She had expected it to be longer — in her visions he wore it back with a ribbon.

She remembered it falling loose around his shoulders as

he kissed Ashiol, mouth dragging down his neck and teeth fastening on to his collarbone. But that wasn't Velody's memory and she forced it away, before Garnet could see it in her face.

'Why do you keep running away from me?' he said. 'I can't hurt you now.'

That 'now' was significant — a reminder that when they were alive, he would have hurt her without a second thought.

Velody lifted her chin. 'I don't need anything from you.'

'Not even company?' he said mournfully. 'Aren't you a little worried that you might go insane with no one to talk to in this broken dead city of ours?'

'Is that what happened to you?'

Garnet flashed his bright white teeth at her in a grin. 'Not yet.'

'Then I'll take my chances. It's a fair bet that my mental state was better than yours to begin with.'

'You make a good point.' He swung his legs back and forth. 'What do you miss the most, ladyking?'

Home, my friends, my hearth, my work...

'What do you miss?' Velody flung at him. 'Ruling the Creature Court? Torturing your friends? Fighting for your life every nox? I don't want to talk to you, Garnet. You should have stayed dead.'

He shrugged as if giving up, and slid down off the plinth to land neatly on his feet. 'Sadly, that's harder than it sounds. Trust me, little mouse. A few more endless days of this and you'll be wishing for your own death, not mine.'

'Something to look forward to,' Velody said unsteadily.

She walked away, and made it to the edge of the courtyard before Garnet yelled after her: 'You're just like me!'

Not that, never that, no, no, no.

~

VELODY STARTED SMASHING GLASS. There was something satisfying about it. The city was so damned silent, and the noise cut through everything, harsh and clear and perfect.

She broke every window in her family's bakery, watching the arc of smashed glass fly out into the street, or the canal behind the house. When there were no windows left, she went to the next house, and the next. So many windows, so little time. For the first time in forever, she felt something pulsing through her; not quite a heartbeat, not quite animor, but something.

She felt alive.

When she was done with that street, she worked on another, and then another. The destruction was compulsive, and what else did she have to do? She made her way out of Cheapside and into more affluent districts, leaving a streak of damage in her wake.

Broken pieces of everything.

Some time later, she found a street she had never set foot in before. It was an avenue lined with trees (no leaves, just bare branches, nothing was allowed to live here); the kind of place where Delphine and her fancy family might have lived.

Every window was broken. The street was awash with glass. She stared at it, knowing she had never been here before, wondering how... but of course. She wasn't the only prisoner in Tierce.

You're just like me, Garnet had told her. Apparently, it was true.

Glass crunched under her shoes. Velody crouched down, picking up a long sliver. It had an edge to it, like a knife.

She thought of Rhian, of that horrible Lupercalia, blood dripping from her slashed wrist. Velody had always thought that there was no despair, nothing that could make her do something like that to herself. Even when the Creature Court had driven her to the edge, she had never thought of this.

But she had to do something. Had to remind herself that she was real.

Velody held the glass against her wrist, pressing it brutally against the skin.

'I wouldn't,' said that voice, coming out of nowhere. She looked up and found Garnet lounging against a wall as if he had been watching her for some time.

(Well, what else did he have to do?)

'Wouldn't you?' said Velody.

'Believe me, little mouse, you don't want to know the answer to that particular question.' He sounded calm and reassuring, which was disturbing beyond belief.

'I don't trust you,' she said clearly and stabbed down at the skin.

She didn't bleed. There really was nothing in her veins. Velody stared at the ragged gash in her wrist, wanting some sign that she was alive. Even the pain was dull, and the moment she stopped concentrating on it, it was nothing at all.

Garnet came to her, one hand wrapping around the empty wound on her wrist, another taking the glass from her hand. She let him. 'Fancy a reason to live?' he asked in a low voice.

That made Velody laugh. 'Think a lot of yourself, don't you.'

Garnet laughed too, and for once she didn't think it was an awful sound. 'You should be so lucky. I'm offering something better. Almost as good as breathing.' He leaned in, mouth on her ear. 'Break all the windows you like, but keep the mirrors in one piece. We're going to need them.'

MERCATUS

SEVEN DAYS BEFORE THE
KALENDS OF BESTIALIS

DAYLIGHT

*R*hian loved the swordplay. There was a pleasure in reminding herself that she was physically strong, and that she could do something other than bind flowers and ribbons together. In another life, she might have been a carpenter or a builder, someone with clever hands and muscular arms who worked with the sun beating down on her head.

For now, she had this.

Macready came to train Delphine every other afternoon, and every single time Delphine would act surprised that he had turned up, and claim some work that had to be finished first. She liked to make him wait — her way of keeping him in his place. Delphine never did like anyone thinking she was at their beck and call.

Macready never let on whether it bothered him; not to Rhian, anyway. He just grinned and asked her out into the yard instead. They could usually get in a good hour or so of a lesson before Delphine made her grudging appearance.

Rhian tried not to resent that the best hour of her day was contingent on Delphine's borrowed sword and her borrowed man.

'Stay with us,' Macready called as Rhian headed for the house.

She shook her head and smiled. She had promised an old friend she would supply two trays of cupboard wreaths and nosegays for the final day of the Great Market, and that was as fine an excuse as any to close the door on their banter and flirting.

You worry too much about what people think of you, said Heliora as Rhian shut herself away in the workroom again.

'It matters,' Rhian said impatiently. She only ever replied to the dead Seer's goading when she was tired or melancholy. The rest of the time, she could shut her away. 'Of course it matters. Velody and Delphine are all I've ever had.'

That's not true, said Heliora. *You had a brother. Parents.*

'I don't remember them,' Rhian said quickly. 'You know I don't remember them.'

Interesting, that, Heliora mused. *You were touched by animor and Court before Velody ever was. Why don't you remember Tierce and your family? Maybe if you opened yourself up to your powers, you could see them again. Let them back into your memory.*

Rhian took down bunch after bunch of roses and lilacs she had dried on hooks and laid out her tools, concentrating on staying here in this moment. She must not allow Heliora's voice to push her into the futures. 'So I can hurt with the losing of them? No. I don't need those memories. I don't need any of this. I don't need anything but —'

Delphine and Velody was her usual answer, but Velody was gone, and Delphine was unreliable as all hells, and Rhian had never felt more alone in her life.

She won't leave you alone, Heliora said softly.

'She doesn't know what I've done,' replied Rhian.

I know what you've done and I'm not going anywhere.

'Very reassuring,' Rhian sighed.

∽

LATER IN THE MONTH, when Delphine and Macready were training in the yard and Rhian had no work to busy herself with, she shut herself away in her room, ignoring the clash of swords and laughter from below.

Heliora asked her: *What frightens you most?*

'You know what frightens me,' Rhian replied. She hated the end of the month, when there were rarely festivals to keep her busy. She needed to work.

Apart from Delphine finding out that you're a bloodthirsty murderess who can turn men to stone.

'It's not a joke,' Rhian said furiously. 'It's not funny.'

I died before my twenty-seventh birthday, Heliora drawled. *How's that for a joke?*

'Don't make this about you,' snapped Rhian. 'You're not even real. The real Heliora died in the street with a sword in her hand. You're an echo of her.' There was silence after that, and Rhian jumped up almost in fright at the thought that Heliora might have left her alone. 'Are you there? Come back!' More silence. 'I need you,' Rhian said wretchedly.

Of course you do, said Heliora, sounding smug.

Rhian sighed and flopped back on her bed. 'Don't do that again,' she chided.

You care about what Macready thinks, Heliora went on. *You let him put a sword in your hand. You let him get closer to you than any other man. You think he won't burn? He's not a Lord or a Creature King. Just another man. Or is it that you trust him not to touch you, not to take advantage? Do you think he'll never make you angry enough to be a danger to himself?*

Rhian wished Heliora was really here, so she had someone to direct her glare at. 'I hardly think about Macready at all,' she said flatly.

Interesting, said Heliora, in a tone so knowing that it made Rhian's cheeks flame red. *Shall I tell you who my favourite lover was?* she continued out of nowhere.

Was this Rhian's life now? Gossiping with a dead person who had taken up residence in her head? 'I think I can guess.'

Oh, not Ashiol, I grew out of him years ago. He's good — no denying it — and I spent my younger years adoring him like an idiot. But a demme gets tired of frigging a man whose head is else-where. Half the time I wasn't sure if he remembered which one I was.

If Rhian needed any further evidence that this voice was something she was not imagining, there it was right there. 'You're so blunt.'

Well, I'm dead, said Heliora matter-of-factly. *That tends to knock a few corners off.*

There was a long silence after that, during which Rhian most definitely did not ask Heliora to identify her favourite lover.

Macready, volunteered Heliora.

Rhian put a pillow over her own head. Smothering herself was a valid option at this point. 'I don't want to discuss this any more.'

Because it's about frigging, or because it's about Macready? You can't avoid it. Sex is deeply tangled in the power of the Creature Court — for the Seer most of all.

Rhian clenched her hands into fists. The rules had to be different for her. There was no other choice.

Heliora continued as if she had voiced that thought aloud. *Haven't you got it by now? There are no rules. So why does it bother you that I used to frig Macready?*

The shift from one topic to another bothered Rhian.

Heliora was trying to trick her into an admission of some kind. 'It doesn't bother me. It's irrelevant.'

Is that what it is?

'He's my friend. The first male friend I've let myself have since... I don't want to think about him that way.'

Worried that if you do, you'll end up frying him to a crisp?

'That's not funny. Why do you joke about that? Why do I let you?'

It's been nearly two years since all that happened, Rhian. If you can't find humour in tragedy, you'll end up as crazy as the rest of us. Jumping at shadows, overreacting to every male glance, living some kind of half life... oh, wait!

Rhian was angry now, so angry she could almost hear the crackle of flames. Was that smoke she could smell? Where was it coming from? 'Don't laugh at me. Don't you dare laugh at me.'

Mockery is all I have left.

'I want you out of my head!' Rhian cried. Saints, her hands — what was happening to her hands? She fell on her knees beside the bed, staring at her fists. They were grey and rigid, like the stone she had turned those men into. As she watched, water ran over her stone fists, and she could move her fingers again. The water dried from her skin rapidly and when she opened her hands wide, dust fell from her palms to shimmer across the floor. 'Heliora!'

It's no use asking, said the Seer, sounding far away now. *That never happened to me.*

'It's not part of being a Seer?' There it was — the only hope that she might finally have an answer to who and what she was, gone on the wind. Rhian's hands felt like flesh now, but they were still far too cold.

I don't know what you are, said Heliora.

Could she hear the noise Rhian was making as she fought

to stifle a sob of terror? Could she feel the tears run down her face? Rhian did not know. But Heliora kept talking, as if nothing had changed, filling the room with words until Rhian had recovered enough to stand again, and breathe.

I didn't tell you why he was my favourite. He was the most honest of any of them — never said a word he didn't mean, never pretended to care about things he couldn't be bothered with. We were barely even friends, just convenient to each other. But when he was in my arms, he was really there. He paid attention like I was the only person in the world, and he didn't let up until we were done. There was an intensity to him — the same thing you see when there are blades in his hand and a battle in the wind...

That was better. Nothing to do with Rhian. She could stand tall and pretend that they were two ordinary demmes, talking about some fellow, as if the world was not a darker place than it had been only a few moments ago. 'You're saying he makes love like he fights?' she said lightly, some time later.

All duty and detail, said Heliora, and Rhian could hear the smirk in her voice. *Believe me — in bed, dutiful is a long way from dull.*

Macready brought Rhian a sword. He produced it as if it was nothing special, an afterthought. 'This should make things easier, love.'

Rhian stared at him.

'It's just a sword,' he went on, mistaking her expression. 'Nothing to do with the Creature Court. I bought it at the Basilica. Thought you'd be better with one suited to your height — borrowing Delphine's has done you no favours.'

He looked at her with those wide, guileless eyes of his.

Rhian couldn't find the air to breathe. She turned and ran, hurrying back into the house, bolting her bedroom door, panic crashing in on her from every wall.

Too much, too much, too much, too much.

She heard his baffled voice, some time later, and Delphine's voice beneath her window saying blithely, 'She does that sometimes, when she's happy. Don't worry about it.'

Happy. Was that what she was? Rhian's pulse was beating so hard that she thought she was going to fly into pieces.

～

SOME TIME LATER, they came upstairs together, and though they tried to keep their voices low, she heard every murmur and moan through the walls.

Only the memory of charred flesh and cool stone under her fingertips calmed her thoughts, and what did that say about her?

I really am a monster.

It's nothing to be ashamed of, said Heliora. *Wanting to be loved is the most natural urge there is.*

He loves Delphine, thought Rhian, not daring to speak aloud in case they heard her.

Ha! I don't know what the hells is between those two, but I can bet you half a shillein it's not love.

He's good for her. They need each other.

Are you so used to giving and hiding that you've forgotten how to want anything for yourself?

I don't matter.

That has to be the stupidest thing you've ever said.

I don't look at him. I never look at him.

Of course you don't. If you did, you might have noticed how often he looks back.

Rhian stretched out on her bed, trying to sleep. They were silent in the room next door, at least.

I lied, Heliora said, some time later. *Macready wasn't my favourite. It was always Ashiol.*

Rhian felt her mouth curve into a smile. 'I know,' she said in a murmur. 'I may be crazy, but I'm not stupid.'

30

FIDES

THE KALENDS OF BESTIALIS

DAYLIGHT

*O*ften it was Rhian who sat with Ashiol, when the others were sleeping or occupied elsewhere. She always brought some busywork with her — letters to write, or socks to darn. She was knitting a scarf, and he watched it grow over a series of days, ruddy dark wool the colour of blood.

'You're not afraid any more,' he said once, eyes on the clicking of her needles.

Rhian smiled faintly. 'Oh yes I am,' she said. 'I'm afraid all the time. A door opens and my mind slams shut until I'm so panicked I can hardly breathe. The sheer effort it takes to come here leaves me exhausted for days afterward.' She raised her eyes and looked at him. 'Keeping my hands busy helps.'

'But you're here.'

'Yes, I'm here.'

'Is Heliora with you?' It was the first time Ashiol asked Rhian about her new powers as the Seer. Even with his mind running at a million miles a minute, he could tell she was calmer and less prone to anxiety than when he first knew her. The influence of the other Seers, perhaps? Heliora had always hinted that they were in there, inside her somehow, their voices tangled in her head along with the millions of possible futures.

'I hear her often,' said Rhian. 'The others too, though she has the strongest voice. It's not like you're hoping for, though. I think it's just memories. The real Heliora is long gone.'

Well, yes. He knew that. How could he not know that?

Ashiol paced back and forth, his energy sparking off his skin, off the walls. 'I need to get out of here.'

'You should go then,' Rhian said helpfully.

He stared at her. 'You'd let me?'

'I don't see how I'm supposed to stop you. Besides, the dottore's advice isn't doing much for you. You need to find your own path.' She smiled that sweet smile of hers. 'Want me to send the lictors away?'

Oh, he had underestimated this demme. 'Yes,' Ashiol breathed. He could run on the rooftops, be himself in the open. 'Stay away from mirrors,' he told her firmly, one piece of help before he fled and left her in major trouble. 'If you hear the music, cover your ears. That's how they'll get us, you know.'

Rhian nodded. 'I'll remember that.'

Strange, that he felt he could trust her more than any of the others. Ashiol waited impatiently while Rhian sent the lictors on an errand, and then he slipped out into the Palazzo corridor to make his escape.

He passed six mirrors on the way out, and turned each of them facing inwards. He only hoped it could be enough.

~

THE CATS that were Ashiol streaked across the grounds of the Palazzo and away, yowling down streets, knocking loose tiles off roofs, terrorising rodents as he went.

His jaws were bloody and paws aching when he finally shaped himself back into himself, on the roof of a temple. He was still hard and hot and hungry, but the important thing was that he had his freedom. His mind was racing a mile a minute but clear. He could see in all directions. He wanted to change into chimaera, to tear the sky into threads, to remind himself that his wings were intact instead of the bloody stumps they still were when he managed to sleep deep enough for dreams, but right now he just lay back, body heaving with the sheer exhaustion of having run himself to pieces. The sun was warm on him and he slept, naked and sprawled out in the bright heat of it, purring.

When he awoke, Ashiol was not alone. He smelled the perfume and cigarette smoke, and knew it was Livilla before he even opened his eyes.

'Back in the game, are you?' she asked in a lazy voice.

'Never left,' he growled.

'The sentinels have done an almost competent job of hiding the fact that they think you're broken,' she observed, using her absurd cigarette holder to create a flourish.

'We're all broken.'

'That's certainly true.' She smiled at him, inhaling the smoke. 'I like you broken. Always did. Just like the old days.'

The old days. Lithe young bodies tangled together, kittens and cubs. The absence of Garnet was an ache between them, a silent space. *No, no, not that. Don't think about that.* Ashiol had to keep his head calm or he'd go spiralling off again, and he couldn't afford to lose control. 'What do you want, Livilla?'

She twirled her cigarette holder around, making patterns of smoke in the air. 'I want what Tasha wanted, and never thought she could have. I want to be Power and Majesty.'

He laughed at her honesty. 'You'll have to eat a few of us to get there.'

'Oh, I can live with that. Don't you think Priest would taste delicious?'

'Poet's too stringy. Lennoc's too young, barely seasoned. And you're sentimental about the rest of us.'

'You might think so,' she said. 'I don't think I'm sentimental about anything any more.'

Ashiol rolled on top of her, his hands pinning her arms back against the tiles, keeping the cigarette holder pointed well away from him. The smoke made him feel ill, but he could smell her underneath the haze and it made him want to lick her.

'You'd miss me if you quenched my animor and let me die,' he said in a growl.

'I lived without you for five years,' she said, painted red lips only inches from his. 'I think I could cope.'

He leaned into her neck, nuzzling. He had always loved her neck. Somewhere underneath the warpaint and the perfumed smoke was his Livilla, the first demme who really got under his skin.

She loved Garnet more, but that wasn't a problem at the time. Ashiol loved Garnet more too. Now they were the only ones left. 'Did he ever hurt you?' he asked, purring into her neck. 'Like he hurt me?'

Livilla stiffened under him. 'Let go. Get off me.'

He lifted his face, looking into her eyes. 'You don't like the question?'

'I don't like you. Get off me, Ashiol. You're not a cub any more.'

He rolled off her slowly, letting go of her arms.

Livilla sat up, cupping the cigarette holder in both hands (trembling, she was trembling) and inhaled, then blew out a long breath of smoke. 'Everything's different now.'

'That's one way of putting it.'

She wouldn't look at him. 'I mean it, Ash. If you can't get your act together to rule the city, I will.'

'That's quite a threat.'

'Being crazy shouldn't stop you. It never stopped you from doing anything before.'

She had a point there.

'I don't know if I have anything left,' he said. 'I can't be Garnet, and I sure as fuck can't be Velody.'

'No, you can't,' she said flatly. 'But no one's asking for that. We want to stay alive. We need some hope.'

Ashiol breathed out, slowly. 'How's your new courtesa working out?'

'Bree. I think she hates me,' Livilla sighed. 'I kind of like it.'

That made him laugh. 'You're so twisted.'

'Right back at you, darling.' She leaned in unexpectedly and gave him a ripe, smacking kiss on the cheek. The kiss of a jolly aunt, not a former lover. 'Next time the sky falls, I want to see your crazy self in the air. No reason why you should have special treatment.'

He wiped the cosmetick off his cheek. 'I'll do my best.'

ASHIOL STOPPED TAKING the pills and potions. The sentinels and Isangell didn't notice at first. He became an expert at hiding them, slipping the pills into his hand or under his tongue, and pouring the potions into vases or out the window. The first thing to go was sleep, but that was fine with him. Who needed sleep?

He faked sleep until whichever guard was sleeping themselves, and then he would shape himself into cats. Cats could squeeze through the bars on the window — the skysilver burned but it was worth it for the escape.

Outside, he killed and ate warm bodies, crunching the bones with glee, then rampage across the roofs. His cats could nap, at least; small bursts of sleep that kept him going.

Cats were easier than humans. When he needed to fuck, he sent out the call, and every female cat in heat would flock to him, anxious to be mounted and rutted. The worst danger was having boots flung at them for making so much noise, and his reflexes were still good.

In his rooms at Isangell's, when he was pretending to be human, Ashiol would pace the walls, exercising his body as much as he could in the space. Press-ups, sit-ups, anything to make his muscles work the way they were supposed to.

When Delphine was on duty she watched him shamelessly. Somehow he always managed to do more when she was there — nothing like an admiring pair of eyes for incentive.

He kept his mind as still as he could without the influence of the pills, making sure the jumble of words and thoughts in his head did not spill out on to his tongue and betray him. As the month of Bestialis wore on, he convinced them all that he was entirely sane.

Then it came, on the nox before the Ides, the prickling sensation that told him the sky was falling, and he was needed elsewhere. 'I'm going,' Ashiol told Macready in a firm voice. 'I need to be there, and they need me. You know they do.'

The sentinel regarded him suspiciously, but agreed.

The sky was alive with fire and ice and scratchlight and gleamspray and crackling bloodstars. Ashiol felt his heartbeat quicken as he saw the state it was in. *What did Velody sacrifice herself for if here we are, all over again?*

The Lords were already fighting the sky, and he watched them, trying to imagine himself as their Power and Majesty, giving orders, leading from the front. Would they let him now? Would they ever have let him?

He shaped himself into Lord form, bright and shimmering with animor. There was a security in that. The sky wouldn't press down around him, crushing the breath out of his lungs, when he was a Creature Lord.

Except of course that it did. Shapes blazed out of the darkness, and Ashiol found himself twitching, hands clenching and unclenching. Where had his battle-strength gone? He was thinking too much.

He could hear Garnet's voice in the back of his head, mocking and jeering him, pointing out all his failings. A dark shadow swished over his head, and he almost obliterated it with a wash of animor before he realised it was Livilla. She slammed into a cloudweb, burning it from the inside out, surrounded by a cloud of sparrows. She and her new courtesa tore down the cloudweb in a matter of moments, and moved on to new meat.

The Court were doing fine without him. He should be angry as hell about that, not relieved. Ashiol swayed, watching the scene. There was a beat in his head that wasn't his heartbeat. It was some kind of jazzy musical number and wasn't that exactly what he needed? Musical interludes inside his head.

The moon was swelling, almost full. Tomorrow would be the Ides.

'Joining us, kitten?' carolled Poet, sweeping over his shoulder. 'We've got devils to crush and eat. Tasty bones!'

Ashiol whipped around as he saw dust devils converging on Poet. He lashed out without thinking, his animor bursting out of his fingertips and smashing into the figures. They exploded into dust.

Poet swung around in surprise, laughing. 'Sweetheart, I didn't know you cared.'

'They weren't solid,' Ashiol muttered.

'The solid ones haven't come back,' said Poet. 'She saw to that.' He was looking at Ashiol carefully, as if he expected to see something or someone else behind his eyes. 'You up for this?'

'Always,' said Ashiol, grinding his teeth. He couldn't let it beat him, couldn't let the jumble in his head take him over. He had things to do.

The sky burst forth anew with burning light, and Ashiol pulled himself together. He went chimaera and found security in the dark, violent shape that only the Kings could wear.

Last one, you're the last one left. Velody left you here to do this alone.

Up here in the sky, he couldn't avoid thinking about Velody the way he could on the ground. Flying and fighting had once reminded him only of Garnet, of the good times and the bad. But these last few months with Velody, teaching her how to be a King, showing her how she could lead the Creature Court as Power and Majesty...

Wasted now, all wasted. Garnet, Heliora, Velody, all dead and gone.

It was down to Ashiol, and he couldn't do it. He didn't have the strength, or the will. He didn't even have the balls to run away. Better to let a deathbolt or the screelight take him out, give his animor to the rest of them.

Better to let it end.

Ashiol hovered in the middle of the firefight, no longer watching the flickering figures of the Lords and Court as they battled the sky. He released the chimaera form, becoming Lord again, pale and glowing. He extended his arms towards a hail of warlight, not moving from its path.

Let it take him.

A weight slammed into him from the side, and he fell helplessly, straight down. Self-preservation took over in the last instant and he used animor to cushion himself and his rescuer as they crashed into the roof garden of a private residence.

'None of that, kitten,' Poet said, the words muffled against his chest. 'Court rule. You stay out of the sky if you're feeling suicidal.'

'You could quench me,' Ashiol said in a gasp.

'Promises, promises.' Poet's eyes were serious behind his wire-rimmed spectacles. 'Would you trust me with this city?'

'Do you trust me?'

'Mostly.'

Ashiol laughed at that, tilting back his aching neck. 'Madness.'

'That too.' Still resting against Ashiol's chest, Poet raised himself up on his elbows. 'Come to the Vittorina Royale tomorrow.' The light show of the skybattle above threw colours and sparks against his hair as he looked down at Ashiol.

Ashiol tried to laugh again, but it turned into a dry cough. 'You're inviting me to your musette?'

'What better time? Assuming we survive this nox, tomorrow's is bound to be clear and fine.' Poet smiled sweetly. 'You love a good Bestialia Cabaret.'

Ashiol's smile faltered. That song he had been hearing. It was a Bestialia chorus, without a doubt. 'What are you up to, Poet?'

'Me? I'm as innocent as a newborn babe.' Poet's smile, however, was far from innocent.

'The sentinels and Isangell only let me out to fight the

sky, and that's under sufferance. They won't let me play theatre patron.'

'Oh, I'll break you out of your cell, kitten,' Poet promised him. 'Believe me, you want to be at this show. An unforgettable spectacle.'

Ashiol shook his head as Poet climbed off him. 'I've always loved your sense of priorities, ratling.'

Poet blew him a kiss. 'Style, sweetheart. It's all about style.'

The battle was over. Ashiol had been little use, he knew it. Macready would have a good case for preventing Ashiol from ever leaving the Palazzo again. What was the point if he couldn't fight the sky? Every time the bolts fell, or the sizzle of flame shot past his head, he was overwhelmed. The past burst inside his head, and he could no longer tell what was a memory and what was a genuine hallucination.

He wasn't safe. Not for anyone.

Ashiol needed to walk away through the gates, out of the city. He needed to go home to Diamagne, to the stern mother who looked at him with that slightly puzzled expression, to the mostly grown gang of half-brothers and one sister who adored him like a pile of puppies looking for a hero, to empty fields and a sky that stayed where it was supposed to, every single nox.

No. Not that. He had to be here. He had to suck it up and take whatever pills and potions he needed to keep steady. For Isangell, for the Court... He had to heal, and be healed. There was no time for weakness.

Ashiol nodded grimly to the lictors who stood at his door, knowing that he was about to be their prisoner all over again. Fuck it. It wasn't like he had anywhere else to go. He walked inside, heading straight for the little table where the glass vials were laid out for him. Two potion doses, one vial of pills, all different colours. One was basic nettlebane, to ease his sleep. Another was supposed to still his anxiety — it was the potion that made him feel numb for days, as if everything was a few inches out of reach. The pills were odd, misshapen gobbets of something green and oily. They were supposed to rid him of the hallucinations.

'You are going to take them now, I hope?' said a quiet voice. Ashiol looked up, and saw Heliora.

She seemed different, but only slightly. Her rough-shorn hair had grown out a little. She was taller, or maybe thinner. But it was his Hel. Not dead. Warm and ordinary and here. He had missed her so much.

Ashiol's bones ached with weariness. 'I have to warn you. Seeing visions of dead people has never worked out well for me.'

Heliora cracked a smile at him. 'Story of my life.'

31

ELSEWHERE

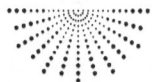

SOME TIME LATER

*T*he sand-coloured Palazzo at the heart of Tierce was a far more modest building than the grand edifice of Aufleur, but it still had high walls and towers, decorated with dormice and turtles. Those creatures Velody remembered — they were stamped on every canalboat in the city. Velody would never have set foot inside the Palazzo in her old life. That demme, the one who lived above the bakery and had to fight her sisters for the best cast-offs, would never have thought she would ever see anything so grand.

'I still don't trust you,' she said as their footsteps echoed through the empty entrance hall.

'No reason why you should,' said Garnet lightly.

'Why are we here?'

'Mirrors.'

'I have a polished glass at home at the bakery.'

He laughed. '*Home*. Trust you, little mouse. You've set up home in this place, taken a tiny nest for yourself when you could own the whole city.'

'Half the city, surely,' Velody said. 'You don't strike me as the type to share unconditionally.'

'Ah well,' said Garnet vaguely. 'I won't be here forever.' He stopped in one lushly carpeted corridor, outside a set of beautifully carved doors. 'Other mirrors work, once you've seen the truth, but these are better. Clearer, somehow.' He pushed the doors open. 'In you go.'

Velody didn't like him, and sure as the seven hells didn't trust him, but what else did she have? She was trying so hard to hold on to herself. She couldn't stand being on her own, and like it or not, Garnet was the only other person here.

She stepped into the room.

The walls were scarlet, the covered in century-old murals. Painted women circled them, dancing and holding trays of foods or urns of wine. Some posed with snakes or other sacred objects. Several baked honey cakes.

'This is a hall of mysteries,' Velody said, surveying the murals that adorned the walls. 'You shouldn't be in here. It's not for the eyes of men.'

Garnet shrugged. 'Do you think anyone cares now?'

'The saints and angels might.'

'Let them punish me for my transgressions. A touch of religious judgement might cut the boredom.' He made a sweeping gesture with his arm. 'Further in, little mouse.'

She kept walking, through the mysteries to the next room. The light inside blinded her momentarily before she realised what she was looking at. The walls were almost entirely made from polished glass. Grey light streamed in through windows on the far side of the room, which only made the mirrored walls glow harder, more intensely.

Velody stood in the centre of the room, staring at many different versions of herself. Strange. She wasn't sure she had ever seen herself so clearly — and at the same time it was hard to be sure who she was looking at. Her skin was paler than she was used to. Perhaps the light here in the sky-Tierce was different. Her eyes were still grey. Her dark hair was tidy, her body sturdy as ever, her fingers long and slender. The dress she stole from the museion was the only splash of colour, but even the green silk looked muted and wrong. She was a child playing dress ups, lost in a city she no longer belonged to.

'What happened to them all?' she asked in a whisper.

Garnet came to join her, standing almost close enough to touch. He was pale too, greyer than she was. His shirt and trews were almost colourless. His hair — his hair was still bright, but hadn't it been brighter when she first saw him? She couldn't even see his eyes properly. She had thought blue or green, but now they seemed grey like hers, pale and washed out. 'They forgot,' he said simply. 'Some of them were still here when I arrived. Ghosts and echoes, holding on to who they used to be. Walking around in circles, keeping up their routine. But they faded, one by one. I think we're not meant to be here. Once we lose who we are, we drift away.' He shrugged. 'Finally they were all gone, just the city left behind. At least the city seems to remember what shape it's supposed to be.'

Velody stared at the hundreds of Velodies reflected in the many mirrors, the hundreds of Garnets. 'So you come here to stare at yourself and remember who you are?' she said softly.

'Ha,' he said, amused. 'I suppose it has that benefit. Dull, though. I find it very unlikely that the outer shell is the be all and end all. I always wanted to be taller.' He gave her a friendly jab in the waist with one finger, like he was one of her brothers. 'Look more closely, little mouse. There's more in these mirrors than you and me and this fucking shadow of a city.'

Velody couldn't get away from the thought that he was out to trick her or trap her. She looked past the many Velodies and Garnets to the reflections of the windows, and then she saw it. Moments of darkness and light, of faces and hands — of movement.

She whipped around and stared through the windows themselves. She saw nothing but grey light, yellow stone and an empty city, then turned back to gaze into the reflections. 'That's not Tierce, it's...'

'Aufleur,' Garnet said calmly. 'Well, not always. All kinds of places flicker into view from time to time. But the more you concentrate on what you need to see, the more likely you are to see fragments you care about. People, even.'

Velody looked hard, but it was still just shapes and flickers. For now. 'You do this a lot?'

'Whenever I can. This is how to hold on to yourself. Remembering who you were, who you cared about. Seeing pieces of them — knowing what's happening in the world outside. Talking to them, if you can. Sometimes it's all there is.'

He sounded so lost, and Velody had vowed she would not do this, not start feeling sorry for him or thinking of him as a person. 'Why,' she said. 'Why hold on? Why not just let it happen? The sky swallowed us. We're supposed to be dead.'

Garnet smiled sadly. 'And I thought you were a fighter.'

'I don't know what I am. But we can't go back there. Why torture ourselves?'

'Because there's still a fucking battle to be fought, and a war to win,' he said, his voice harder than she had ever heard it. 'If we don't stay alive, if we don't do everything we can, then what use are we?'

'I didn't think you cared about all that,' she said, surprised.

'You don't know me,' he snapped. 'All you've ever known is what they said about me.'

'You're the one wso keen to point out what a monster you are,' she commented.

'Of course I'm a fucking monster. We have to be. It's the only way we'll win.' Garnet had never reminded her more of Ashiol, his stance aggressive, a scowl on his face. They must have been astounding together when they were young and strong and undamaged.

'You still think we can win?' Velody echoed. 'I mean, not just survive, but *win*.'

'More than that,' Garnet said, teeth gleaming at her in a wicked smile. 'I think if we work together, we can get back there.'

'To Aufleur.'

'Aye, to Aufleur. That's what the mirrors are for. You think I'd stand here staring into nothing out of nostalgia? You think I'd waste my last days of energy taunting Ashiol fucking Xandelian? These mirrors are our way home.'

Velody swallowed. She had been so sure there was no way out of this but a graceful letting go. Fading away as her family must have, long before she got here. The thought of returning to them all, to Delphine and Rhian and Ashiol and the sentinels, rose up in her as a sudden desperate hope. She had to do it. If it was possible, she had to try to get back.

Even if it meant unleashing Garnet on Aufleur all over again.

'Convince me,' she said finally.

Velody could not remember the last time she had returned to the bakery. It was not like she needed to sleep. The more she sat and gazed into the ever-reflecting mirrors, the closer she came to seeing what she wanted to see, back in Aufleur.

She thought once that she saw a piece of Via Silviana and she gazed at it until her eyes began to hurt (so rare to feel pain, or anything else in this false and empty Tierce), hoping for a sign of Rhian or Delphine.

Every now and then, she caught the dark flash of a cat's tail or a rat's paw and wondered if it was Ashiol, or Poet.

Sometimes Garnet joined her. She was getting used to his presence. Hate made so little sense when there were only the two of them here. The old rules did not apply.

'There,' she said one day, after finding a corner of the mirror room that looked directly into one of the main thoroughfares of Aufleur. 'I see Macready.'

There was no mistaking that stocky figure, the way he walked, though she could only really see a shoulder, part of his back and one boot.

'Aye, the old bastard,' said Garnet, sounding almost admiring. 'Indestructible.'

There was a gleam of light against a sword or a knife, just for a moment. Velody leaned back on her heels, remembering all over again that Garnet was an enemy rather than an ally. 'I gave them back their blades.'

'Good for you,' he said evenly.

Velody swallowed hard. 'We can't go back. I can't let you go back.'

Garnet blinked, looking almost amused. 'So you will deprive them of yourself, of their greatest one and only, the Power and Majesty who saved their souls, because you don't want to share them with me?'

She stared at him. 'I never said anything about being the greatest Power and Majesty.'

'You are, of course. That's how they see you. Saint Velody, that's how you are remembered. I suppose you're afraid of losing that, if you're back among the mortals. They might realise you're as flawed as any of us.'

'How much have you seen through these mirrors?' she demanded.

'Oh, I see more than you think.' Garnet stood, and left her alone in the room. 'You'll change your mind.'

～

ANOTHER TIME, the mirrors opened up and Velody saw the gardens of Trajus Alysaundre at nox. She watched for so long, certain that she would see some sign of how the Creature Court were continuing without her.

The nox sky was quiet, though, and they did not come. 'Have patience,' said Garnet from the doorway.

'You don't strike me as the world's most patient person,' Velody said, turning away from the mirrors in frustration. 'This isn't getting us anywhere. I don't believe we can step through the mirrors at all. It's just a game you invented to pass the time.'

Garnet laughed. 'To keep us sane, you mean? That doesn't sound like me.'

'I'm not convinced it's keeping me sane,' said Velody. 'More like the opposite.' Their hands brushed as she tried to step past him to leave the room, and they both recoiled.

'Don't touch me,' he snapped.

'You're cold,' she said in surprise. It wasn't just the ordinary cold that seeped into everything in Tierce. He almost burned with it. 'Are you sick?'

'We don't exist here. You think we can get sick?'

'Then why —' Velody stepped closer even as he backed away from her. 'You're losing the battle, aren't you?' she said softly. 'You're fading.'

Garnet gave her a cynical smile. 'Don't pretend it's not what you want. With me gone, you can return to Aufleur without bringing the fiend with you. Happy endings all around.'

'I don't believe we can go back,' said Velody. 'We're not real any more. We don't have a place there.'

Garnet threw up his hands. 'Oh, by all means, let's embrace the reality where Ashiol is Power and Majesty! Is that really the best future you can imagine for them all?'

'Don't talk about him like that.'

'Should I not?' His eyes burned with a deep intensity. 'I've known Ash longer and deeper than you ever could, little mouse. If one of us doesn't get back there, he will destroy Aufleur all on his own.'

'I'm supposed to believe you care about the city, that you care about them?'

Garnet gave her an odd look. 'It's all I've ever cared about. How can you not know that?'

'I don't know you,' she reminded him. 'I have no reason to trust the words that come out of your mouth, and every reason not to.'

'Because of what my lovely Ashiol told you about me?'

'Not just him. All of them. They hate you.'

'They feared me. It's not the same thing.'

'Believe me,' Velody said with fervour. 'They *hate* you.'

Garnet took it in that time, though his face was still devoid of emotion. He was so different to Ashiol, she thought. Ashiol wore everything on his face, every flash of rage or fear. Garnet kept his emotions so far inside that you only saw what he wanted you to see.

'You put your trust in a madman,' he said finally. 'You let yourself see the world through his eyes.'

'Ashiol isn't crazy,' Velody retorted.

Garnet looked amused. Well, that was almost an emotion. 'Which Aufleur were *you* living in?'

She reached out again, her hand brushing his. 'You're trying to distract me with all this talk of Ashiol. But you're dying, or whatever passes for dying in this place.'

'That is a distinct possibility,' Garnet admitted.

'Don't leave me alone here.' The words tumbled out before Velody could stop them.

Garnet laughed, pulling his hand away. 'I wouldn't worry, mouseling. You'll have company soon enough. If you don't make your way back, Aufleur will join Tierce in the sky... you'll have plenty of playmates then. For a while.'

He walked out of the hall of mirrors. Velody expected him to come back after a moment or two. He never could stay away from her for long.

But this time, he did not return.

Velody waited at the bakery, at the hall of mirrors, but there was no sign of Garnet. She did not even know which parts of the city she might find him in, should she wish to look.

Why would she look for him? Ashiol could be Power and Majesty. She knew he could. He was the one who had taught her. He was perfectly capable of accepting his place. Garnet was wrong. He had a nerve, suggesting that Ashiol was unstable, or that he couldn't be trusted. Look what he himself had done with all that power.

Once she gave up on Garnet, Velody spent most of her time lying on the bed in her old room, gazing into the polished bronze hand-mirror that had been her grandmother's and thinking of home. When she finally saw a part of Aufleur that was familiar to her, it was nothing like what she wanted to see.

She saw Ashiol raving, Delphine crying, Rhian on the point of collapse, the sentinels bleeding, falling, dying. She didn't know if it was the past, present or future, but she knew now what she didn't want.

Garnet was right. Velody had to go back. There was no way she could do it without him, without his belief in how it could be done. She needed him for her very survival.

417

He still did not return.

~

VELODY SEARCHED the city for Garnet. The Palazzo first, then other buildings in areas where she had seen him in the past. She returned to the baths regularly and saw no sign he had been there. She scoured the streets for more broken glass.

(He could be gone, really gone; she might be alone here.)

In the end, of course, the most obvious place came to mind, and she could not rid herself of the thought that maybe, if he wanted to be found, he would be there.

Velody returned to her mother's bakery, inhaling the dust and absence of bread as she entered, and found Garnet lying wanly on her sister's bed.

She smacked him on the shoulder, and the cold burned all the way up her skin. 'Is this your idea of fighting for Aufleur?' she demanded.

Garnet opened his eyes and looked at her. 'You judge me for giving up? I've fought my whole fucking life for Aufleur. You've had a few months of it, and you claim to be the expert.'

'I would have had longer if you let me,' she hissed. 'If you hadn't stolen my animor when I was a child.'

'Why yes, you would,' he said cynically. 'Maybe then you'd be as tired as I am. This is it, Velody. You're on your own.' His skin was practically translucent, and his voice didn't sound like him any more.

'You can't give up,' she said, but it sounded pathetic, like begging the sky not to fall.

'Of course I can. I'm the selfish one, remember? You're the saint.'

She opened her mouth to snap at him not to call her that, but Garnet's eyes were closed. He was still — well, not breathing, neither of them breathed here — but still present, even as he faded in and out of colour.

Velody was not going to wait around and watch him fade away. She went out of the bakery, slamming the door behind her. She began to walk for the sensation of doing something, of being *here* instead of fading into nothingness like everyone else.

She was so angry at Garnet she could spit. Where was that fire and venom that took control of the Court? Where was the man who conquered Ashiol and stolen his powers? Seven hells, she would settle for the boy who kissed her on a balcony twelve years ago — he at least had an ounce of daring in him.

This Garnet would let himself disappear into the sky, and she hated him for it.

As she stood there, not knowing what to do next, Velody heard a breath of a sound across the silent, empty city. She stood still and listened, acutely aware of how silent she could now be without breath in her lungs or blood in her veins.

She thought she had lost it, but then it came back, again and again. Music. It was music. Not Garnet, this time. Something else.

Velody followed the tune along the docks, then up the slope to the familiar temple that she remembered so clearly from her childhood. The temple of the Market Saints. It was a smaller, homelier temple than its equivalent in Aufleur, but she knew now why she had always felt so safe when she and Rhian and Delphine went to make their sacrifices.

The grand, carved doors at the front of the temple did not open — they were steam-powered, she remembered, and there was no water here, so no steam.

(Even the baths where she first met Garnet were empty now.)

She had to walk around and let herself into the temple by

419

the back way. The music was louder in here. Velody could hear the voices, children's voices singing. Even a word or two was familiar.

Cats and mice, creatures that crawl...

There was no fire, of course. A temple should have flames, but there was nothing in the public hearth but old ashes and fragments of bone or burnt cloth. Velody circled the stone pillars of the inner sanctum, looking at each of the scarlet murals she remembered from her childhood. Finally, she stopped to sink her fingers into the dry ash.

Ferax, bat, come one, come all.

Sensations of any kind were a luxury in this strange and empty version of Tierce. There was no heat in the ashes, but they felt scratchy and soft against her palms. Velody pulled her hands out and drew grey smudgy lines up and down her arms, then across her cheekbones, nose and forehead.

As nox grows dark, we come, we feast...

Velody could not say whom she was mourning with this ritual. Not Garnet, who deserved no pity from her. Not herself — she was still here, still present in her mind and body, though neither of them felt overly familiar any more.

She combed her fingers through her dark hair, streaking it with ash, and then plunged her hands into the grate again.

This time, she felt something. Her palm brushed against a nub and she seized the object, pulling it out and blowing the ashes from it.

Dance with the cabaret of monsters, dance with the beasts...

It was grey and charred and old and stale, but as Velody scratched at it with her nails she saw dry crumbs the colour of gold. When she brought it close to her face and inhaled, she almost smelled it.

A honey cake, thrown into the fire for sacrifice.

Velody walked back to the bakery, the stale and ash-covered honey cake pressed into the folds of her silk skirt.

The song had faded, but when she concentrated she could still hear snatches of it in the still air. She walked so fast that she could almost hear her heart beating, could almost feel the rasp of cold air in her lungs.

(Almost, almost.)

She had found no other food in this city, in all this time. Hardly surprising; they had no need to eat. The bakery was empty of flour or grain or yeasts or sugars. It all faded away as surely as the people of Tierce faded away.

Why had it faded? If they had no need of food, why should it not be here, lying around as pointlessly as the clothes or the blankets? Velody opened the door of the bakery with a loud rattle, and took the stairs as fast as she could. 'Garnet!'

Was she too late? (Did she want to be too late?) Velody hurried into the room she had shared with her sisters, and he was there, the outline of him still grey and visible on the bed. She flung herself at him, straddling his narrow chest with a leg flung on either side of him. 'You can't go yet,' she insisted. 'Not if there's a way we can be real enough to fight this.'

She drew out the honey cake and broke it in half. Crumbs and ashes fell on to Garnet's unmoving face.

Velody bounced impatiently. She could feel the ridges of his ribs beneath her. He was here, and he was real. No excuses. 'Open your eyes, damn you. Or you're exactly the coward Ashiol always said you were.'

Garnet's eyes came open, and she shoved half the honey cake to his mouth, even as she brought the other half to her own.

It was like eating grit and woodshavings. The cake was so dry that it scraped her mouth and tongue, and she could barely swallow. She had not eaten or drunk a thing since she came to this place.

(Water, they had taken most of the water too, whomever

brought them to this place. She had no doubt that it meant something. Water was life, wasn't it? So many of Aufleur's rituals were about blood, water, fire, food.)

Garnet coughed, and struggled to swallow. 'You're crazy.'

'I must be, since I'm trying to save your life,' Velody said, cramming more of the stale cake into her mouth, forcing herself to chew and swallow. She felt different. Almost alive.

Garnet's eyes flashed and he took another bite of the cake, chewing slowly, licking crumbs from his lips.

Velody thought that she actually could hear her heart beating this time. Or maybe it was his heart. Garnet ate obediently, even the parts of the cake that were covered in ash, and then he tipped his head up to lick Velody's fingers clean. Velody stared down at him, and he gave her a lazy look. He wasn't grey any more, or translucent. He looked like Garnet.

He sat up in a hurry and she jolted, realising too late that she was sitting in his lap. Garnet smiled, and for the first time Velody seriously imagined what he looked like in his Creature form, with the pointed teeth of a gattopardo. 'You have no idea what you have done,' he said in a low voice.

'Don't make me regret it,' she warned, but barely got the sentence out before he pounced, mouth dry on hers at first, and then warm and wet.

Velody kissed him back. Never mind that this was Garnet, the bright-eyed boy who had been in her dreams since she was fourteen (damn him). Never mind that this was the tyrant who took Macready's finger and Ashiol's heart, who made the Creature Court so fearful.

To feel anything for the first time in so long was warm and amazing, and her body wanted more of it. They kissed messily, hands touching each other everywhere, and yes. There was blood in her veins. Saliva in her mouth. Her breasts ached, her stomach twisted up in cramps, her feet began to hurt from all the walking she had done today.

'You've undone me,' Garnet breathed. 'I was ready to let go.'

'I need you,' Velody told him. 'We're going to get back there, and I can't do it alone.'

'Ashiol will hate you forever,' he said with a tight smile.

'I'll risk it.'

Garnet kissed her again, and Velody's blood cried out for him. Oh yes. Heat sparked between them in the places where their skin touched.

They felt it in the same moment. Garnet looked at her, eyes wide in triumph and exultation. Velody mirrored it right back at him. Whole, they were whole.

Animor, pulsing through their veins, better than food or blood or sex. The essence of everything.

Velody exploded into little brown mice, scampering across the bed and floor and walls. Paws and tails and fur and oh, it was glorious. She wanted to run forever, to climb and bite and fly.

Finally she returned to herself, naked and gasping for breath (breathing, she was breathing). She sat on the floor, leaning back against the bed, and once the sheer novelty of breathing had worn off, she saw that he was watching her, and that he was not Garnet any more.

The gattopardo crouched on one of the other beds, his tail swinging slowly back and forth. A large, spotted cat with eyes like liquid amber. Velody found herself lost in his gaze, almost hypnotised by that deep colour. He stood and stretched, then stepped down towards her with an easy gait. Did wild animals swagger? This one did.

Velody stayed perfectly still as the gattopardo crossed the floor and placed one paw on her thigh. She braced herself for the impact of claws, but he was gentle. A second paw

TANSY RAYNER ROBERTS

followed the first, and the gattopardo nestled his face against the heat of her body.

She should move. She really should move because he was licking her now, that rough scarlet tongue lapping its way over her stomach, up to her breasts. Velody gasped once as the gattopardo grazed her nipple with that tongue, hot and scratchy.

She took hold of him by the sides of his neck, dragging the large powerful cat face up to hers. 'Change,' she commanded. 'Now.'

The gattopardo smiled with all of his teeth, and then he shaped himself back into Garnet, mortal and lean and every bit as naked as Velody.

She was still holding his face in her hands, and dragged him in to kiss her, generating that heat again. Her heart beat louder in her head. Her pulse sped up. Oh, yes. She could feel her animor racing to every inch of her body. What Ashiol had said about sex and the Creature Court was entirely accurate.

The song was back, filling her ears. Velody knew it now, an old Bestialia rhyme, though the voices and beats of the music gave it more the air of a musette number. It felt real, calling her home.

Everything was real.

Garnet growled against Velody's mouth and pressed her more firmly against the bed. She could feel every plane of his body, every muscle against her softness, the hardness of his cock pressing urgently against her thigh.

Velody let out a sound, wanting him.

Garnet pulled his mouth from hers and kissed down her throat, leaving sucking bites there, and across her breasts. She writhed under his touch, letting him play, revelling in the fact that this was her body, it was here and real and no one was fading into the sky.

424

Not today.

He mapped out her body with his tongue and teeth. Velody rolled over, arms braced against the bed, and felt him cover her body with hers from behind, teeth grazing her neck, shoulders, spine. His fingernails traced the softness of her stomach, dug more fiercely into her hipbones, and finally parted her legs.

Velody cried out once as he thrust into her from behind. She was so wet by now that he slid in easily, long and hard, filling her entirely. She pushed back against him, and he fucked her with the ruthless efficiency of the animal he was.

The animals they both were.

Her power lit up inside her body like a temple fire, the dry honey cake churning in her stomach, and it didn't matter that they were trapped in an empty city without even ghosts to show them the way home.

They had this. Blood and animor and sex and life. It would bring them home.

32

BESTIALIA

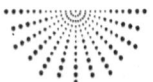

THE IDES OF BESTIALIS

DAYLIGHT

*T*hey talked for hours, well into the morning. Ashiol lay on the couch and Heliora sat beside him, just out of reach, her eyes steady on his. He told her everything; most of it she had heard before, but it tumbled out as he tried to make sense of it all. Losing her, losing Velody, losing Garnet, losing himself.

The world was new. Ashiol didn't know if he should take the potions or not. He didn't know if it would make a difference. He sure as hells didn't know if he could make it as Power and Majesty.

'I always thought you could,' said Hel. 'You were the one who wanted to run and hide. Everyone else believed in you.'

Ashiol hadn't thought of it that way. 'Don't you think it will break me?'

'It breaks us all, sooner or later. I think I broke a long time ago, and it's only starting to make sense to me now.'

'But it will make sense? Eventually?'

'I hope so. Sometimes hope is all we have.'

Ashiol rolled the vials around his hand. 'If I take these, will you disappear?'

'Try it,' Hel suggested.

He swallowed both potion doses, then the three sticky green pills. Nothing happened straightaway, but when he tried to move, his hands felt slower than usual. It took him a long time to make it to the bed, and once he was there it was pretty clear he wouldn't be going anywhere for some time. 'Stay with me,' he said, panicked when he couldn't see her.

'I'm here,' said Hel, stepping into his line of sight again. 'I'll stay as long as I can.'

ASHIOL DREAMED OF MIRRORS, of broken glass and singing children who blinked bright-eyed behind animal masks. He woke with a dry, rasping throat, and the first thing he saw was Heliora. The old Hel would have curled up in that fancy chair beside his bed, bare feet tucked under her. Death had brought a new sense of gravity to her. She sat straight-backed, holding her body as if poised to flee at any moment. Her eyes were on him as he awoke.

'You're still here,' he said, not quite believing it.

'Someone has to be,' she said, hands folded oddly in her lap.

'I thought I made you go away.' His voice cracked a little. 'Don't leave me again.'

She looked confused and hesitant. Was it wrong to tell a ghost they were dead? Would it make her vanish? He was desperate to hold on to her, to make her stay. Ashiol reached out his hand, and she took it. 'I should have saved you, Hel,' he whispered.

She let out a breath in a heavy sigh. 'Oh, Ashiol,' she said, and it was wrong, all wrong, because why did she sound sorry for him? Was he so pathetic that even a dead demme took pity on him?

The outer door clicked closed and one of Isangell's mousy maidservants came into the suite. Ashiol could hear her bustling around, tidying and primping the outer sitting room. He looked at Hel, wanting to say so much more, but it was important now that he pretended to be sane. The maids were spying on him for Isangell, obviously, and she would give everything she knew to Macready.

He had to hide Hel from them all, or they would find a new mix of potions that really would make her go away.

The maid entered the bedchamber — he knew her by sight; there were only a few whom Isangell trusted with his care. In truth it was probably more likely that only a few were willing to enter the rooms of the mad Ducomte.

'Coffee, seigneur?' she asked.

Ashiol nodded abruptly. It had become habit not to speak to them. Anything he said would be taken back to the precious Duchessa, and that might be the last straw, the final piece of evidence she used against him. Animor or not, being in this place made him so fucking powerless.

The maid brought in a tray, and poured coffee silently into a fine cup. She knew not to add honey or spices to it, so she must have served him before. She met his gaze briefly as she handed him the cup. 'And for the demoiselle?'

Ashiol stared at her. 'What did you say?'

The maid flicked her eyes in the direction of Hel, and then stepped back, made nervous by the tone of his voice. 'I meant no offence, seigneur.'

'Thank you, no,' said Heliora, speaking clearly.

The maid nodded, bobbed her head again, and fled the room.

Ashiol's hand was shaking so hard he barely got the rattling cup to his dresser in time. 'She can see you?'

Hel looked uneasy. 'There's something I have to tell you.'

But he was up and out of bed, kneeling at her feet. He laid his hands on one knee, and then the other. She was warm. 'You're really here.'

'I know it pleases you to think so —'

'She saw you.' Ashiol pulled her to the ground in one swift tug, pinning her body to the chair with his own. 'Do you know what it's been like? I can't taste food in my mouth, I can't set foot outside these fucking walls without thinking I'm going to die, but every day I stay trapped in here makes me feel like I have to scrape my skin off just to keep breathing. I don't feel real in my skin, I'm lost, and you're dead, you're dead...'

Hel let out half a sob and pressed her mouth to his. He kissed her, and she tasted raw and warm and wrong; not like his Hel at all. But she wasn't cold — that was the main thing.

There were tears on her face. 'I have to go,' she gasped. 'Macready will be here soon.'

'I don't give a frig about Macready,' said Ashiol, hands in her short hair, gripping her tightly. 'I need you.'

'Not me,' she whispered, but he kissed her roughly, drowning out anything she had to say. She was dead, after all. What were the chances it was something he would want to hear?

They took it slow. Hands and mouths and heat; so much heat Ashiol couldn't believe it. He laughed at one point, because if he was going to frig a dead demme Tasha would be furious it wasn't her, but he got tangled up trying to explain the joke and Hel kissed him so sweetly to shut him up that he stopped talking and let himself fall into her.

Death smelled like roses, or maybe he was just getting

sentimental in his insanity. Hel grasped him as he slid into her, and he swallowed her moans into his own mouth.

Finally they were sated, their bodies pressed together under the sheets, and only then he thought to wonder if the maid had left, or if she was still plumping pillows in the other room, closing her ears to their cries.

'You still haven't disappeared,' he said, mouth busy on her shoulder. She wasn't cold. Shouldn't she be cold? 'Fine ghost you are. Anyone would think you wanted to stay.'

Hel half-turned under him, her fingers sliding through his hair. 'Ashiol, I have to tell you...' She sounded sad.

The door opened and Macready stood there, startled and angry. 'What the feck —' he demanded.

'Get out of here,' Ashiol growled. 'This is none of your business.'

'Like hells it isn't,' Macready spat. 'What the saints and devils do you think you're doing?'

'Macready,' said Hel, her voice sounding broken. 'It's not what it looks like.'

The sentinel's voice was rough. 'Is it not, lass?' He glared at Ashiol. 'You should be ashamed of yourself, you selfish sod.'

'Who do you think you are?' Ashiol roared. He rose up out of bed, ready to force Macready out if he had to.

'Less of a monster than you, apparently.'

'Stop it,' said Heliora, covering herself with a sheet. 'Both of you. You don't have to protect me, Mac. I make my own choices.'

'This isn't like you,' said Macready, sounding strangled. 'I don't understand.'

'What are you talking about?' The buzzing was back in Ashiol's head, and nothing made any sense. Macready and Heliora had a history, didn't they? 'You never had any qualms about us frigging the same demme before.'

Macready hit him. Ashiol didn't expect it, and the blow was a fierce pain hard on his jaw. He lunged for Macready, not even bothering to summon animor. He could beat him with his bare hands, no other powers required.

Hel thrust herself between them, sheet still wrapped around her body. She pushed Macready back with one hand flat against his chest. 'Mac, stop it. He thinks I'm Heliora!'

Time froze. Ashiol stared at her, but she only had eyes for Macready. 'Oh, lass,' the sentinel said quietly. 'What have you done?'

It was his Hel. How could it not be? It looked like her, sounded like her (the way she held herself was wrong, he knew that from the start). If it wasn't her, that meant she was really dead.

Ashiol roared, lunging at the woman, hands tight around her throat. 'Who are you?' If this was one of Livilla's games, he was going to kill her. Right here, Isangell's carpets be damned.

'My King, no!' yelled Macready behind him, and his hands closed over Ashiol's, trying to pull him back.

Ashiol was giving no quarter this time. His hands burned with power. He squeezed her neck hard.

There was a scream, but it came from behind him. Another demme joined them, sharp nails digging into his wrists. Delphine.

'Ashiol!' she shrieked like a fishwife. 'Stop it. Are you crazy? It's Rhian!'

Ashiol rocked back on his heels, hands still on her neck. Heliora stared back at him, wide-eyed and shaking. Not Hel. He forced himself to see past the hallucination, to acknowledge that this demme was taller, differently built, in no way the same as the one he had loved. He reached out slowly and touched her hair. Red. It was red.

431

'Yes,' he said in a low voice. 'Apparently I am still quite mad.'

'What did he do to you? What did he do to her?' Delphine was shrill enough to drill holes in his skull with her voice.

Heliora was dead and there was nothing for him here. Ashiol dropped his hands, stepped back, and shaped himself into cats.

'No, wait!' Macready called out, but it was too late.

The gang of black cats swarmed out of the room, out of the Palazzo, and away.

WHILE DELPHINE and Macready chased after Ashiol, Rhian dressed slowly and left the Palazzo. No one tried to stop her. No one even noticed her.

She walked down the side of the Balisquine hill, heading home, for once not stopping to wonder at what might happen if someone accosted her; if she might kill again, just to be left alone.

Well, said Heliora, in her head.

Don't talk, Rhian thought numbly. *Not a word.*

I didn't see that coming.

Rhian couldn't think. She couldn't breathe.

That good, was it?

It occurred to Rhian that if she used the main roads, it would be easier for Delphine and Macready to catch up with her. She veered off into a side street, and then another, and found herself climbing the Lucretine hill, surrounded by houses she did not know. 'It was you,' she muttered beneath her breath. 'He saw you inside my head. He wanted *you*.' But Heliora had not been there, not in that moment, when Rhian chose to let him believe in his hallucination. 'I don't know what I was thinking,' she said finally.

Heliora's voice sounded different in her head, now. Ugly, and accusing. *Who's the rapist now?*

Rhian slipped on the gutter and stumbled. 'Don't say that! You don't understand.'

A couple of children stood in the street, staring at her. Of course they were staring. She was talking to herself. Rhian pulled her shawl over her head and hurried her step, desperate to get home.

Heliora was silent in her head.

ASHIOL KEPT RUNNING until his paws ached. He dug rats out of a rubbish heap somewhere near the Alexandrine, chased them down one by one and tore them to shreds, licking the blood from his furry chins. He scrambled up the hillside, among the old abandoned terrace gardens. He collapsed finally, a blur of black shadows spread out in a wide patch of hot morning sunshine.

When he woke, he was human and naked and the sun wasn't warm any more. He wasn't alone, either.

'I thought it was going to be hard to spring you out of the Palazzo for our date,' said Poet, his legs dangling aimlessly from an overhanging tree branch. 'You're not even making me work for it, kitten.'

'Sorry I'm not more of a challenge,' Ashiol rasped in a dry throat. He closed his eyes again, tipping his hair back. 'The sentinels have gone completely fucking insane.'

'This is a new development?' asked Poet in mock-astonishment.

I've been seeing Heliora,' Ashiol confessed, and opened his eyes. He could just see Poet's face leaning forward out of the draping tree-fronds. There was nothing there but mild curiosity. 'I talked to her. Touched her. Frigged another demme, thinking it was her. How's that for insane?'

'You've been crazier,' suggested Poet. 'Not lately, but still. I find it *fascinating* that you're so wrapped up in guilt and grief for what happened to our late lamented Seer, but you don't show a scrap of remorse about Velody.'

Ashiol leaned up on his elbows, pushing down the anger that was his first response. 'Velody made her own choices.'

'She sacrificed herself to save this city.'

'And Hel didn't?'

'What is it that broke you so badly, kitten? Not losing Heliora. Did you think about her for a minute, in the five years you were exiled? I think you don't want to admit how angry you are that the little mouse threw herself into the sky.'

'Glad that's cleared up,' Ashiol grunted. 'You should moonlight as a dottore, with insights like that.'

'I can't help being brilliant. Come on, sweetpea. We have to get you dressed for the theatre. Naked is not the new velvet.'

'I'm not going to your fucking show,' Ashiol said darkly.

'Don't be such a tease. It's the Bestialia Cabaret, the darkest and most sinful season of the theatre year. Everyone will be there, and I'm not talking about the so-called Great Families.'

That surprised Ashiol. He looked at Poet strangely. 'How did you talk the rest of the Creature Court into that?'

'How else? I told them they could frock up.'

'You're planning something in that devious head of yours.'

'When am I not? Come on, kitten. Admit it. You're curious.'

As Ashiol hesitated, clothes fell around him. A silk shirt. Trews with beaded cuffs. One shapely boot, and then another. 'This is just an excuse for you to dress me,' he muttered.

Poet laughed, sounding genuinely happy. 'As if I needed an excuse.'

33
BESTIALIA

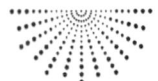

THE IDES OF BESTIALIS

NOX

*T*he simple act of choosing a dress made Delphine
feel as if she was living another life. A life in which
Velody had not let herself be swallowed by the sky. It seemed
wrong to be dressing for the theatre — the Vittorina Royale,
no less — without Velody at her side.

Delphine put on a sapphire-coloured frock that dripped
with seed pearls, knowing that if Velody was there, Delphine
would beg her to add a trim to glam it up — a little fringe, or
some ribbons. Velody would do it, even if they were running
late. Nothing was more important than the dress being perfect.

Delphine's hands shook as she tried to fasten the buttons
at the back. She stepped out of her room, and saw Rhian's
closed door.

It didn't make sense. How had Rhian ended up tangled in
Ashiol Xandelian's bedclothes? She could barely even look at
a man. It was Ashiol's fault, it had to be. If he hadn't forced

her, it was something else. Potions, perhaps? Something to hurl Rhian's inhibitions to the wayside.

It was enough to make Delphine bite through the walls. Men like him got anything they wanted, anything, no matter who they hurt along the way.

Rhian couldn't have changed so much in so little time. Could she?

Velody would know what to say. Velody would listen to Delphine rant about this for hours until she let her out in the world again. Velody would be able to ask Rhian for her side of the story without sounding like a demonic fishwife.

'I need help,' Delphine called down the stairs. Macready came up from the kitchen and fastened the back of her dress with hands far steadier than hers. 'Ready to go?' she asked him, and he shrugged.

Neither of them knew why this exhibition of Poet's was so important, but the invitations were inked in Poet's own hand. They were all expected to be there — sentinels, Lords and Court. Seer.

'Thinks he's Power and Majesty or something,' was what Kelpie had said about it.

Crane had shrugged. 'No one else is doing the job,' he replied in a low voice, the only thing any of them had heard him say in days.

Now Ashiol was missing, and none of the sentinels had any excuses to be elsewhere. Turning up to the theatre might be their best chance to track him down again. Delphine's private opinion was that he was best lost, for good. It wasn't likely to endear her to the other sentinels, so she kept her trap shut.

But, *Rhian*.

'I'll meet you downstairs in a minute,' said Delphine. Macready nodded, and headed back down. He had been uncharacteristically sombre since the scene at the Palazzo. They were all in shock.

Delphine hesitated at Rhian's door. Barging in was against the rules of their carefully balanced household. But apparently there were no rules any more, and there was sure as hells no balance.

Delphine pushed the door open without knocking. She expected the bolts to hold true, jarring her arm, but the door opened easily.

Rhian sat at the window, straight-backed in the chair. She did not turn her head.

'Are you coming?' Delphine asked, though Rhian was hardly dressed for the occasion.

Rhian made a small sound that might have been a laugh. 'Because attending the theatre is such a normal activity for me.'

'I thought —' Delphine bit down what she had been about to say. 'You're part of this now.'

'Velody's dark little world of imaginary beasts and toy soldiers. Yes, I am part of it, despite my best wishes. And I'm cured now, right? So everything is different.' Rhian sounded so bitter.

'I didn't say that.'

'You thought it.' Rhian did turn now, and there was such an awful look on her face that Delphine drew in a breath. 'Ask me, Dee. Ask me how I knew what you were thinking.'

Delphine shook her head, refusing to play that game.

'I have voices in my head. Did you know that? All the Seers who ever lived. I can't hear all of them clearly, but that makes it worse. It's like having people standing right behind you, whispering. I can step outside the house now, but it costs me. Every time.'

Anger poured out of Rhian until the room filled with it. Delphine didn't know if it was her new sentinel senses that made her feel the fury all the more strongly — or the sheer weight of Rhian's emotions. She wanted to reach out and hold her friend. She wanted to rip a hole in time and go back to the days when they were three hard-working apprentices, with time for laughs and honey cakes. She wanted to run until her feet bled, drink herself stupid and dance, dance, dance. More than anything, Delphine wanted to go back to being the screwed-up one, the careless one, the irresponsible one. Caring and trying led to utter badness.

Rhian continued, speaking in that awful voice. 'I hate Velody for this. I hate her for bringing this world to us. The futures — you have no idea what it's like. I can't turn it off, can't make it go away. This is what I was hiding from, all this time, and I didn't know until she brought it home...'

She broke off, as if that had been one secret too many.

Delphine couldn't help herself. 'Where does Ashiol fit into this?'

Rhian was very still after she asked that. 'Another form of self-harm?' she said finally, in the kind of voice that could be joking, only not.

'I want to understand. For nearly two years, ever since... you've barely been able to be in the same room with a man. Even when you're training with Macready, you don't let him touch you. How do you go from that to —' Delphine swallowed, not wanting to say anything hateful. Could Rhian read her thoughts this time, too? It was Ashiol Xandelian, for saints' sake.

'I wanted to see how much it had changed me,' said Rhian. 'The Seers, the futures. Am I still the same person? I don't even know.'

'But why choose him?' Delphine blurted.

'Heliora is in my head,' said Rhian. 'Louder than the rest of them. I have *conversations* with her. He could see that, for some reason. He saw through my skin and he thought I was her. It was easy to — be her for a while.' She let out a long breath. 'For once, I wanted things to be easy.'

Delphine couldn't help making a face. 'So what — Heliora wanted to frig him and you let her?'

'That would be a nice excuse,' said Rhian. She sounded so sensible about it. 'But it wasn't her, it was me. I chose him because — with him, I didn't have to be afraid.'

'You should be. He's more powerful than any of them. And more broken. He's dangerous, the baddest of bad news.'

Rhian nodded. 'Exactly.' She dropped her gaze for a moment, drooping in her chair. 'Damn. I have to — *damn*.' After a moment, she stood and went to her wardrobe. 'I have to wear a dress.'

'The futures told you that?'

'Whatever is going to happen this nox, I have to be there.' Rhian looked grim. 'We all have to be there.'

A chill went over Delphine. 'Not just dinner and a show, then?'

Rhian pulled out a dress Delphine hadn't seen her wear in years — soft green fabric, something from their apprentice days. 'When is it ever?' she said wearily.

Well, yes. She had a point.

MACREADY KNEW CRAZY, but this was a special kind of crazy. The streets were thick with masked people, celebrating the Bestialia. Cats and hounds, panthers and dragons. Real creatures and those of distant myth clashed together in false faces of paper and leather.

Bells. Everyone wore fecking bells, ribboned to ankle and wrist. The streets sang with the shrill, unhappy sound, ting ting ting ting.

Delphine caught the pained look on his face. 'I used to

make those damned things,' she said with a hint of that impish smile of hers. 'But I decided they were a crime against the city. Now I don't work the Bestialia. Let someone else torture the masses.'

They escaped off the street, and into the relative sanity of the theatre. The Master of the House accepted their tickets without a word. 'Only the dress circle,' said Delphine, still pretending this was some kind of lark. 'We've come down in the world, a sad state of affairs.'

Macready looked from her to Rhian, who was following them like a shadow, her arms held stiff and tense at her side. 'You're full of laughs this nox,' he said to Delphine, and it came out more cranky than he meant it to.

Delphine tossed her head at him. 'I could scream or wail if you would prefer,' she said, with a hint of genuine upset in her voice. 'Don't think I haven't considered it.' Then she was back to smiling and faking it, her best skills of shiny denial on display.

Macready's collar was scratchy. He didn't want to be here, dressed up and playacting. He didn't want any of them to be here.

Something bad was going to happen. That much was obvious.

They took their seats in the dress circle. Crane was already there. 'Kelpie wouldn't sit still,' he said, pointing the out other sentinel. She was on her feet between the stalls and the standing-room area known as the pit, looking around the theatre as if she expected murderers to leap out of the shadows. Perhaps they would, at that.

Macready knew how she felt. He wished he hadn't let himself get hemmed in here, between Delphine and the silent Rhian. He looked up, and saw every inch of the theatre reflected in a thousand mirrored tiles. Mirrors were creepy. He never liked the idea that something like you (but not quite like you) could look back out of them. Then there was the fact that their mad King had gone out of his way lately to cover or shatter every mirror he came across, ever since the sky and devils took Heliora and Velody.

'Quite an entrance,' said Delphine under her breath.

Macready followed her gaze and saw Livilla making her way through the theatre in a trail of pearls and black feathers. It was odd seeing her without her lads at her beck and call, but the courtesa she had wrangled from Priest was frocked up to the nines, in a baby version of Livilla's own costume.

Livilla was escorted to a box, and found herself sharing it with Warlord. They were obviously in a fighting stage of their relationship; both were stony-faced as they took their seats.

Nice, Macready couldn't help thinking. Trust Poet to cause trouble with the seating arrangements before the show even started.

The other private box held a sombre-looking Priest, his courtesi, and Lennoc. No sign of Ashiol yet.

The show had started already — some random act of tumblers and columbine dancers in gaudy petal skirts. The daylight audience were watching and cat-calling like it was any other performance. Half of them wore Bestialia finery, which gave the impression that the audience was full of creatures instead of demmes and coves.

'It's not right,' Macready said over Delphine's head to the lad. 'All of us here, among them. Poet's gone out of his mind at last.'

'Poet's up to something,' said Crane, chewing on a chestnut from a paper cone. 'But we have to be here, don't we, to find out what it is?'

Oh, aye. They were sentinels. This was their task — to

wait and watch, and be there to rescue their beloved King from the jaws of the seven hells.

Regardless whether he wanted their help.

∽

ASHIOL SAT up high in the wing, legs dangling from the struts that crossed over the stage. From here, he could see every piece of scenery, every scurrying stagehand, and even half the faces of the audience, if he craned his neck. A good position, and one he could leap from at any moment, should the need arise.

Also, the ceiling above him here was wood, not mirror, which meant he didn't have to scratch his own skin off to get away from it. 'I gave you an actual ticket,' said Poet, amused as he joined him on the wooden strut.

'Seats are too comfortable,' Ashiol said shortly.

'And besides, you're hiding.'

'I never said that.'

'I'm not judging you, kitten. As long as you watch my show, I'm satisfied.'

'Well, as long as *you're* satisfied.' Ashiol was bored with the banter. 'Why are we here, Poet?'

'So I can show off my lambs, of course.' Poet placed one finger to his lips. 'The rest is a surprise for you all.'

Ashiol peered out at the audience. He had a fine view from here of Livilla and Warlord, sitting in a formal box and not speaking to each other. He could practically feel the cold from where he was. 'Because we all deal so well with surprises.'

∽

DELPHINE HAD CHOSEN the wrong frock for the theatre. It was a fine thing to wear while standing upright, but it slid in all the wrong directions as soon as she was seated. The neckline flopped awkwardly, and she had to keep wriggling to stop it completely exposing her breasts.

Also, the boots she had chosen specifically to hide her knives in were dreadfully uncomfortable. There was no way to bring her swords, as she refused flat out to wear that ugly brown cloak to the theatre. Macready had helped her conceal them nearby — though he disapproved of her not wearing them.

Delphine shifted back and forth, not really paying attention to the tumblers and columbines. She had seen it all before. She wanted to walk out of here, taking Rhian with her. No good could come of this.

Every lamp guttered and went out, making it as dark as the Shambles. Delphine reached out to take Macready's hand, then remembered they should be battle-ready, and reached down to take hold of her knife hilts instead.

'It's part of the show,' Rhian said in a barely perceptible whisper.

Delphine did not let go of her blades.

The whispers started. Creepy whispers, children imitating animal noises. Cats, mice, hounds, birds, more predatory beasts. Delphine shivered. The whispers were everywhere. As her eyes adjusted to the darkness, she became aware of shapes slithering and creeping through the audience, heading for the stage.

'Mesdames, demoiselles, seigneurs,' said a rich voice, bursting out of the blackness. 'Pray let me introduce the Cabaret of Monsters!'

The lamps flared and were lit again in an instant. How had he done that, Poet or the Orphan Princel or whatever he called himself? Had he used animor, or was it a stage trick?

The stage crawled with children. They were trained dancers; you could see it in the way they held themselves, in the awful accuracy of their animalistic poses. But children.

Delphine turned her head, as Rhian and Macready reacted in the same moment to what they saw on stage. 'What is it?' she asked in an undertone.

'They are the future,' whispered Rhian.

'Poor bastards,' Macready added. Then the song started, building up to a mighty chorus. It seemed familiar in that nagging way of children's rhymes, as if Delphine had been hearing it for days already. Not that she paid much attention to skipping chants, or children in general.

She did, however, pay attention when the theatre shook for the first time; the ground was quaking under their feet. 'What the hells is that?'

'It's the song,' said Macready in a grim voice. 'Feel it?'

Every time the children's voices came together, the theatre shook in response. The audience was beginning to notice, hissing and whispering in alarm, but the children's chorus only rose to drown them out.

Delphine gripped the arms of her seat, only allowing her muscles to relax once the caterwauling was over, and the children were taking their bows. 'Is it over?'

'When have you ever known Poet to stop before he went too far?' grated Macready.

Sure enough, the children on the stage were still in character as a mess of creatures, all ears and paws and tails. It was grotesque, but no more so than any other Bestialia show Delphine had ever seen.

A young demme in a cat costume came forward, one leg dragging as she took her place in the centre of the stage. There was silence for a moment and then she began to sing, a rich adult voice flooding the musette. The old theatre bowed and creaked around them.

'We need to get out of here,' Macready said urgently. 'We need to get everyone out of here.' Kelpie was shoving her way through the crowds in the pit. Crane was on his feet. Rhian had her hands over her eyes, making a wretched keening sound.

The cat demme's voice rose, impossibly loud and rich around them. Delphine tried to concentrate on the words, looking for some kind of clue about what madness was coming next, but it was just a song, lost love and secret destinies; it could be any song on any day.

The glass beads of the chandeliers rattled so loud they sounded like teeth, but still the song would not be drowned out. Delphine looked up just as a wind whipped through the theatre, guttering half the candles in one go. Cracks appeared like flung ribbons across the mirrored ceiling. Too late, too late to stop it.

Delphine forgot about swords and knives and animor. As the mirrored ceiling broke open, bringing a storm of broken glass falling straight down on the audience, she screamed and shielded her eyes.

ASHIOL WAS FASCINATED by what Poet had done. Every one of those child performers — his lambs — had animor under their skin. It was bright in some, skimming close to the surface. With others it was buried deep, not due to fly free for months perhaps, or years. He must have searched far and wide to bring this crew together.

Above the stage, Ashiol could ignore the music, even as it rattled the rafters under him. He raised himself on the balls of his feet, poised to leap free if he had to, and watched the audience.

Daylight folk and the Creature Court, mixed up together. Why would Poet do this? What was his plan?

When the little lame demme began to sing, Ashiol felt a rush of recognition. Her animor wasn't close to the surface, it was bubbling free. She was a courtesa waiting to happen, and soon. It would be soon.

He heard the cracks in the ceiling before he saw them, and oh, fuck. The theatre was coming down around them. Ashiol leaped down into the wings, safe from the blizzard of glass and blood and death, though the scenery was crashing and falling around him. 'Poet!' he yelled as darkness and destruction descended. 'Where are you, you mad bastard?'

A hand caught his sleeve, pulled him away from the screams and the shaking stage floor. 'Can you feel it?' Poet whispered, mouth close to his ear. 'Can you feel them?'

Ashiol shook him off. 'Are we absolutely sure I'm the crazy one of the family?'

Then he did feel it, waves of something else, a different familiarity, so intense and well known that it almost slammed him into the floor. Oh. *That*.

Ashiol shaped himself into chimaera and flew out above the audience, ignoring the cries of pain and urgency below him.

34

ELSEWHERE

THE MORNING AFTER, IF
MORNINGS EXISTED IN THIS PLACE

The city of Tierce sighed.

Velody awoke naked and tangled in Garnet's arms. She ached all over, in the best possible way. Without moving her body, she reached out with one arm to the shelf by the bed, picked up the polished bronze hand-mirror and held it in front of her mouth, watching her breath pool across the surface. Alive.

Garnet stirred against her, his face pressed into her back. He was warm too, undeniably so. No fading today.

Velody pushed him away and sat up. For a moment she thought her vision had blurred, and then — no. It wasn't her eyes, it was the house. She could see straight through the wall as if it was no more substantial than a shadow. The crenellations and golden brickwork of the buildings across the street jutted out clearly, visible through the hazy edge of the bakery.

'Garnet, wake up,' she hissed, jabbing him with her elbow.

'Hmmph?' He flung out one arm, stretching lazily. 'We're real. More real than before. Clever old you. Let's sleep in.'

'We might be real,' said Velody. 'But Tierce is fading from under us.'

'What?' That had Garnet's eyes open at least. 'Seven hells!'

'Will we die if we lose the city?' Velody asked.

'I don't know.' Garnet scrabbled at his face with the back of his hand. 'I think we're not supposed to be alive. Maybe we took too much from Tierce when you made us real.' He held his chin out to her. 'Feel that.'

She touched him and felt stubble under her fingers. 'You need to shave. Is this a first for you?'

'Funny. First time since I woke up in this shell of a city.' Garnet stood up, pulling his trews on in a hurry. 'I don't think we're going to be real and alive for long once we lose the city from under our feet. We're not designed to float through the sky.'

'We have our animor back,' Velody argued, reaching for her dress. 'We can fly.'

'Fly where? How far? Do you know how deep into the sky we are? Which direction is Aufleur?' Mostly dressed, he looked at her. 'We have to move fast.'

'The room of mirrors?'

Garnet nodded, then grinned suddenly, his face looking ten years younger, like the mad boy on the balcony all over again. 'You make a very good point, demoiselle Velody. We can *fly*.'

THE RUSH of air through her lungs was incredible. Velody's whole body glowed with animor and cold as they soared over the flickering city. It was greyer than before and was growing insubstantial. That couldn't be good. When they landed in the grounds outside the Palazzo, she saw that the trees were colourless, just pale shapes approximating branches. 'It's getting worse.'

'So move,' Garnet said impatiently, already ahead of her, his feet making muffled sounds against the fading pavement.

Velody caught up with him, matching his pace. They charged through the entrance hall of the Palazzo, statues crumbling into nothingness as Garnet and Velody passed them. Half the walls were missing.

Her heart beat loudly in her head. She stopped at a window which had once held a view over the whole city. Technically it still did, though half the city was gone. She couldn't see the docks any more, or Cheapside. Her family's bakery really was beyond her reach this time.

It was lost long ago. It meant nothing.

Velody drew a deep breath, grateful at least that she could breathe after so long barely existing, and ran after Garnet, who had not waited for her. He flung the doors open and teetered on the threshold of the mirror room, only just stopping himself from falling inside. He turned around, eyes bright against his pale face. 'Too late.'

Velody reached him and looked past his narrow frame to see a gaping hole where the mirror room should be. The Palazzo simply broke away, stone wall crumbling into nothingness. Below them was a shadow that barely resembled the ornate gardens that had surrounded the building.

'No,' she said, breathing hard. Still a luxury to breathe, even if it hurt her chest. 'There has to be a way out.'

'The mirrors are gone, Velody,' Garnet barked at her. 'Everything we were working towards.'

'You were ready to fade away not so long ago,' she said angrily. 'Stop giving up! There must be a mirror somewhere in the Palazzo.'

'By all means, I'm sure any other mirror would work fine,' Garnet said sarcastically.

Velody was furious at him. 'Do you want to argue with me, or do you want to go home? Where's the ruthless baby-eating torturer who used to rule the Creature Court? I need *him* right now!' She turned and ran in the other direction. There was most of a staircase intact and she tore towards it, taking the steps two at a time. Bedchambers. Bedchambers were likely to be higher up. The Duc of Tierce had five daughters, she remembered that much. There had to be mirrors.

The children were singing again. Velody could hear their voices bright and steady, all around her, getting louder. She had to believe that they were coming from Aufleur. They did not fit in this pale and fading city.

In the upper corridor, Velody flung doors open until she found a bedchamber that had to belong to one of Tierce's many young Ducomtessas. It looked like a pink lace crinoline had exploded against the furniture and walls. Every available surface was crowded with china shepherdesses and blown glass pigs.

There were no looking glasses on the walls but when Velody looked up, she saw a vast mirror stretching across the length and breadth of the ceiling. The song grew louder.

'The staircase is gone,' said Garnet, close to her. 'And for the record, I hardly ever ate babies.'

Velody reached out and took his hand, not taking her eyes off the mirrored ceiling. 'You can clear up that rumour yourself, once we get back.'

Garnet tipped up his chin, and they watched each other in the mirror.

Come on, come on. There must be something in there. Some hint of Aufleur. A shadow, a face. A hand. Something other than that wretched song.

Velody should be searching the mirror rather than just staring into Garnet's eyes.

'He will hate you for bringing me back,' he reminded her. As if she didn't know that herself.

There. Oh, there. As the walls crumbled around them, Velody saw familiar shapes looming in the glass. The Basilica. The mausoleum in the Gardens of Trajus. Oh, saints, the Vittorine Royale. *Home, home, home.*

Velody and Garnet fell forward into nothing, into crumbling walls and a city that didn't exist any more. Into the mirror.

HUNDREDS OF THOUSANDS of Velodys gazed at each other, facing out of so many mirrors. She reached out one hand, and every hand echoed her movement. 'Garnet!' she called out, and heard nothing but echoes in response. Where was he? She had been holding his hand, but could not feel him now.

She started to run, twisting and turning down corridor after corridor of glass and silver and her own face, her own body, her bright green gown and antique buttoned boots.

'*Garnet!*'

Velody teetered on a precipice of shining glass, only just preventing herself from falling over the edge into — what? Liquid glass rushed past her ankles and poured down a sheer drop, disappearing into a pool of darkness.

She stared into its depths, and for a moment she almost saw what she had been looking for, that world beyond the sky. Not Aufleur, with its cathedral roofs and gothic spires. Not Tierce, empty and pale yellow and fading from view. Something else.

'Velody.' Garnet's hand wrapped around her wrist, pulling her back from the brink. 'We're out of time.'

'How do you know?' She looked at him, really looked at

him. 'What do you know about any of this?' How was he so sure this was the path home?

The children were singing, louder and louder, all around them.

'You didn't think we were going back without an invitation, did you?' Garnet let go of her wrist only to take hold of her hand.

Velody felt a jolt inside her skin, as if her animor wanted to burst free of her body. Garnet tugged her against his chest, and the mirrors exploded around them into a dizzying storm of broken glass.

THE VITTORINA ROYALE was in chaos. People were screaming, hurting, dying all around Delphine. She had lost track of Rhian and the other sentinels in the crush and was half-dragged down a staircase by a crowd of bloodied, frantic theatregoers. It was all she could do not to be swept out through the main doors. Instead, she struggled her way to the stalls, heading for the stage.

The theatre was broken. Not only the glass of the mirrored ceiling, or fallen chandeliers. Half of the dress circle had buckled, and one of the formal boxes was caved in.

Glass pierced arteries, dug into faces and limbs. There was still screaming and crying in the near-darkness, punctuated by coughs and sickening gurgles. Some of the fallen glass had been sharp and large enough to kill. There was dust everywhere. Delphine choked on it.

Where were the frigging Creature Court? That was what she wanted to know. What was the point of their ridiculous powers if they couldn't stop things like this, if they couldn't save people?

Delphine pulled herself up on the stage and screamed.
'ASHIOL! POET! WARLORD!'

Useless bastards.

'Help,' begged a voice near her. 'Please, help us!' Delphine
found her way to a demme who was desperately trying to
move a broken stone column away from... oh. A lad, trapped
underneath. He was moaning, but it wasn't a hopeful sound.

It was too heavy for both of them. The demme was crying
softly. 'Bart,' she said once. 'Hold on, please.'

It was enough to break Delphine's heart. Her nails
scraped the heavy piece of stone as she renewed her efforts
to roll the thing off him. It was grainy and strange under her
palms, leaving a residue of grit on her skin.

Cool hands brushed against hers, and the swish of a
familiar cloak. When he spoke though, it was not Macready,
but Crane. 'Delphine, stop,' he said gently. 'It crushed his
chest. If you move this off him, he'll die faster.'

'Do it,' the lad managed in a whisper. His friend made a
noise of protest. 'Don't mope about it, Topaz. Just — hurts.'
The demme rocked back and forth for a moment, then came
forward and kissed his forehead, all in a rush. Crane and
Delphine rolled the stone column aside, and the lad's air
whooshed out of him. It was fast, and then he was gone. The
demme, still crying, slipped off into the darkness and away
from them.

'Delphine,' Crane said in an urgent voice.

She dashed her own tears away with an impatient hand.
'What now?'

'This pillar is sandstone. Yellow sandstone.'

'So?'

'So, there wasn't any sandstone in this theatre before the
ceiling broke. There's hardly a brick of it anywhere in this
city.' He drew in a breath and pulled her hands across to feel
the shape that sat atop the column — a squat, carved creature

of some kind. It was familiar, like an old story she couldn't quite remember, settled in the back of her mind.

'How do you know it's yellow?' was all she thought of to ask, since it was still too dark to see more than outlines and different shades of black and grey.

'This came from Tierce,' said Crane, squeezing her hand.

She drew in a breath. 'How can you know — that's impossible.'

But she could see them, the pillars of the city, surrounding the magnificent Palazzo, just as they had in her dreams. She had never been allowed inside, but her eldest sister Petronelle had been invited once, for her coming-out ball. Delphine had been so jealous she broke the arm of Petra's porcelain doll...

Oh. Oh. Oh. Sandstone columns with fat sculpted dormice sitting atop them.

'Tierce,' she said softly.

'Aye,' said Crane.

They clung to each other for another moment, fingers pressing together. Then both sentinels turned to the moans and cries around them, trying to help as best they could.

Nothing else to do, for now. Delphine's mind was racing. Tierce. How had parts of Tierce crashed into the Vittorina Royale?

THE CEILING WAS CRACKED and damaged, with only a few pieces of mirrored glass still clinging to the wood and plaster. Ashiol flew up at it, scrabbling at each fragment, searching. Finally he found a large fragment of mirror which had not fallen. He pressed his black-clawed hands to it, gazing into its depths.

She was there, he knew it. He could feel her, so close but

out of reach. Then, finally, a face swam into focus. Pale skin, dark hair, grey eyes. Power so fierce he could taste it in the back of his mouth. *Velody*.

She reached out her palm and placed it against the surface of the mirror. Ashiol matched her gesture, palm to palm, and something gave.

It felt soft, sticky against his palm. Warm, not cold as glass should be. Ashiol shifted from chimera to Lord form, pressed his glowing hand experimentally into the odd substance, and felt her skin against his. Slowly, their fingers linked.

He could hear the cries and muffled sounds of the rescue effort below him. It didn't matter, none of them mattered. Ashiol was holding Velody's hand. She had found her way home.

Another illusion, of course it could be. He hadn't been seeing straight in months. But this felt like Velody. When he touched her, he could all but taste her familiar animor, sparking off his own.

He took a firmer hold of her hand. Velody mouthed his name, and smiled that warm, cynical smile of hers.

Ashiol tugged on her hand, trying to pull her through. Velody screamed, her face rippling and shuddering behind the piece of mirror. A thin rivulet of blood ran down her face. He almost released her, but she shook her head at him impatiently.

She wanted him to try again.

Ashiol braced himself and pulled harder this time. Velody gritted her teeth, not screaming, though her image wavered and he could see pain in her face. Slowly, slowly, she slid out of the mirror.

Glass stuck to her skin like cobweb. Between them, she and Ashiol prised it away from her. Then she had one arm hooked around his neck, and he eased her body out of the glass. She wore a long, bright green gown, the torn shreds of the skirt wrapped around them both as he supported her.

Velody's breath was against his cheek, her heart beating against his, and she was here, really here. Whole except for one hand which was raised above her head, still buried in the mirror.

She made a noise, half a laugh, and then her weight lifted from his chest and she was floating under her own power. 'I hope you've been taking care of my city,' she said in a scratchy, hoarse sort of voice, not quite hers.

Ashiol kissed her.

There were other things to think about, like freeing her hand, like telling the Court that their real Power and Majesty had returned. But for now he was just kissing her, his hands holding her against him as if she might fly away at any moment.

There was precedent, after all.

She kissed him back, her mouth warm and welcoming, and then she drew back. 'Don't hate me,' Velody said breathlessly, and drew her hand out of the mirror, clasping someone else's.

VELODY'S BODY felt as if she had been beaten. The final burst through to Aufleur was more painful than she had imagined. But she was here, and how had she really thought she was breathing, back in that empty and soulless version of Tierce? Aufleur was real, and she sucked it into her lungs. Tierce had smelled of nothing but artificial dust, but this place had the unmistakeable odours of old sweat and pomade, soaked into the very stones of the theatre. There was blood, too, fresh and stinging in the air around them.

Velody only had eyes for Ashiol. She clung to him longer

than she should, when really she had to stop, had to explain before it all got too messy for words.

Then the time for explanations was past, because she could feel Garnet drifting in the void. Tierce was gone; there was nothing left for them but here. She pulled fiercely on his hand, dragging him through the remnant of mirror that still clung to the ceiling. Garnet emerged, shirt and trews torn, lines of blood tracing his arms and chest and face. His hair hung too-long into his eyes.

For one moment the three of them hovered there together, an odd little triangle, joined by her hands. Garnet had that smile on his face, the one that was nothing but cruel twists. Ashiol stared, breathing hard.

Velody opened her mouth to speak, but really, what was there to say?

Look what I found on the road, sweetheart. He followed me home. Can I keep him?

3 5

BESTIALIA

THE IDES OF BESTIALIS

NOX

*M*acready helped the survivors. Most of the audience had fled — those who could walk or run or be carried. The whole fecking place was drenched with blood.

The whole time, Macready kept thinking: *this is it. They can't deny this. Finally the daylight folk will see what's right in front of their faces.*

But the nox did its usual work. Macready set a wounded demoiselle down in the street outside and listened to the mutters around him. They were rewriting their own immediate history, one thought at a time.

Even the worst of the shocked and wounded told each other that the theatre had simply fallen apart, the old boards collapsing and the weight of the mirrored ceiling creating the tragedy. One or two remembered the tremors beforehand and suggested it was some kind of earthquake that had brought the theatre down around them.

They spoke of complaining to the Vittorine proctor, of demanding compensation from the Duchessa herself. None of them spoke of magical children or flying animals or monsters. Perhaps they hadn't seen Livilla and Mars leaping free of the box in Creature form, or Ashiol taking to the air as a fecking chimaera. Perhaps they hadn't felt the power of that damned song.

How was it so easy for them to remain in ignorance? Macready wanted to smash them in their miserable faces.

Delphine and Crane came out through the main doors, herding out several of the children in stage costume, all wearing animal masks. Macready opened his mouth to suggest they hang on to the children until Poet came around to explain himself, but too late. The lads and lasses were off, scurrying like rats into the shadows of the brightly moonlit street.

Delphine swooped at him, not even glancing around to see her lost charges making their getaway. 'Macready, did you see them? *Did you see* her?'

Crane's eyes were practically glowing. 'She's back, Mac. She made it back.'

'What the feck are you going on about?' Macready demanded, then stepped back as he saw Kelpie make her way out of the theatre. She was limping, a makeshift bandage of someone's shirt sleeve wrapped around her calf, bright with blood. 'You all right, Kelps?'

'No,' Kelpie said, half-falling on him. If Crane looked like all his birthdays had come at once, she looked like someone had walked over her grave. 'He's back, Macready. The stupid wench brought him with her.' She was shaking. Shock?

Macready slid one arm around her waist, keeping her upright. 'Easy there, my lovely. What are you on about?'

'Velody,' said Crane. 'Velody came back to us.'

'Don't thank her for it yet,' Kelpie snarled. 'She brought Garnet right along with her.'

Macready almost dropped her. Velody. Garnet. All their pretty Kings, lined up in a row. 'Feck,' he breathed.

'You said it,' said Kelpie.

'Don't look so startled, my cat,' said Garnet. 'You must have known I would come back to finish what I started.'

Velody felt the anger well up inside Ashiol's body. His animor burned with it, even as his eyes showed what he was feeling.

'Please,' she said, hoping for some kind of truce, even a momentary one, to allow her a chance to get her bearings. Ashiol snarled and went chimaera, hurling himself directly at Garnet's chest with unbelievable force. The two of them smashed through the wall of the theatre, scattering splinters of painted wood outwards as they soared out into the nox. Velody wanted to chase them down, to beat sense into both of them. *The city needs you alive, damn it. Both of you.*

'Leave them,' said a voice.

Velody spun around in the air and saw Poet, painted up in his Orphan Princel costume (hard to think of it as anything but a costume). He hovered a few feet from her, watching. She was not sure if she should defend herself or give him a hug. Poet's blank cosmeticked face creased into a smile, which didn't go anyway towards answering that question. 'You've made quite a mess of my theatre,' he said.

Velody looked around, realising for the first time where they were. The Vittorina Royale was dark and broken, with moonlight shining in through the hole Ashiol and Garnet had made in the wall.

She could smell the blood. There were bodies littered

here and there around the banks of seats, some pale from blood loss, others trampled in the crush. Pillars, stone and broken glass had fallen across the pit and the stage. 'I did this?' she whispered.

'Well,' said Poet. 'Let's say it was a co-production.'

'You don't look surprised to see me.'

'I pay attention to the way the wind blows.'

Velody didn't have any time or patience for this. She had to get out, had to stop Garnet and Ashiol from killing each other. She pushed her way through the jagged, broken hole in the wall and stood on the edge, searching the skies for her boys.

'You could say thank you,' Poet's voice came from behind her. 'You didn't open that door by yourself, my Power.'

Velody ignored him, and leaped.

It was all too much for Rhian. There was glass everywhere, and broken stone, and blood, and the futures had crashed in on her, tumbling around her senses.

She dug her way down through the broken stage, curling her body tight into a ball. The future was awful, every future, and she couldn't stand it. Closing her eyes made the futures whirl faster around her.

Everything's broken, falling down, crumbling, broken, they're coming, he'll kill us, he'll break everything, the sky is falling, it's over, it's over, it's over.

Shhh, said Heliora, a comforting voice in her head. *Help is coming.*

No. No one can help me. No one is coming. I'm lost.

I'm here. I'm always with you. I can hear footsteps. Voices. They wouldn't leave you alone.

I'm scared. I can see my future like one silk ribbon unfurling in the street. I don't want it. I don't want to be that.

There's always another future. Another choice.

No. Not this time. There's just me. I am the seed of destruction. I'm the reason that everyone is going to die.

~

VELODY SOARED through the bright moonlit sky, searching for the two men. It was surreal to be back in Aufleur, to have real air in her lungs, to have made it back alive.

She closed her eyes and let her animor explore the city, ribbons of power sliding under doors, over walls. She listened to the heartbeat of every mouse under floorboards, in tiny nooks or midden heaps. Her own heart started pounding louder as she recognised familiar shapes and sounds. They were at the Lake of Follies.

She flew down in a rush, tumbling out of her Lord form as she reached the edge of the lake. Her antique green gown swept into the water and she tugged it out, but not before the hem was well and truly soaked.

'Ashiol!' she cried over the lake. 'Garnet!'

The lake was strung with lanterns and beast-masks, and the bright Ideslight illuminated them all. Two black beasts fought in the water, smashing and snarling and ripping at each other. Both were streaked with blood, and pulsing with animor. Velody felt ridiculous, like some damsel from a newspaper serial, watching from the side while two fops fought for her honour.

She was not fooling herself that this fight had anything to do with her.

Are you Power and Majesty or not? she asked herself. But no, not even that. She didn't have the right to that title. She left Ashiol behind to rule the city. He was the one who should take the lead, instead of scrapping in the lake like a butcher's boy with a grudge.

Ashiol and Garnet fought for an hour or more, neither of them getting the better of the other. Finally they fell out of chimaera shape, naked but for a few ragged threads of clothing, bleeding from various bites and claw marks. They were both shaking from exhaustion, but that wasn't enough to stop them throwing punches and staggering around like circus wrestlers.

Velody sighed and waded out into the water, pushing herself between the two of them. They were too weak and battered to resist her. She reached up, one cool hand on the back of Ashiol's neck, one on Garnet's. 'Stop now,' she said, and she didn't even have to use animor to reinforce her words. They came to the shore with her, and lay on the grass, breathing heavily, one on either side of her.

'What the fuck do we do now?' Ashiol said finally.

Garnet just laughed, that knowing sarcastic laugh of his. It had become so familiar to her.

'We're all in this together,' said Velody, wanting to close her eyes, wanting to sleep forever. She had tried that. It hadn't worked out. Time to do something different. Time to live.

It wasn't even late. The full moon was high above them, but there were many hours of nox still to come. Velody shivered as the cold of the lake seeped into her skin. Here she was, lying on the bank of the Lake of Follies with a naked man on either side of her. This was not the destiny she had imagined so many years ago, when she arrived in Aufleur as a wide-eyed hopeful for the apprentice fair.

How long had she been gone?

'Velody.' She raised herself up on her elbows and saw a small group approach from the general direction of the Vittorine. Macready. Crane. Kelpie. Delphine.

Saints, Delphine was dressed like one of them, brown cloak over her theatre dress, and she had swords, two of them. When had she gotten swords? Velody stared for a moment, and then she scrambled to her feet, wet skirts slopping at her ankles. She threw herself at Delphine, who let out a squeaking sound and dropped both swords. 'What have you done?' Velody whispered as they clung to each other.

'I don't know,' Delphine said in a rush. 'It all made sense at the time.'

Velody turned to the others. She held out her hand to Macready, who clasped it in his, a moment of real warmth. She moved to Crane, cupping her palm against his cheek, and received a sad smile in return. Then Kelpie, who hesitated before holding out her arm to be grasped, comradestyle. Velody looked back and realised that Ashiol and Garnet no longer lay on the grass where she had left them.

'They'll be back,' Macready said in a low voice. 'Not easy to get rid of, those two.' He shook his head, and she could hear the bemusement in his voice. 'Only you, lass, would collar and leash Garnet to bring him back to us.'

'I'm not so sure there's a leash,' Velody said.

Would Macready hate her for this? Would the rest of them? Would bringing Garnet back to Aufleur be the greatest mistake of her life?

'Aye, well,' Macready said heavily. 'We'll see, will we not?'

36

BESTIALIA

THE IDES OF BESTIALIS

NOX

*T*opaz sobbed so hard she could hardly breathe.
Bart was dead; he was empty underneath that slab
of stone. The other lambs had scattered. The whole theatre
smelled of blood and animals, and she had to get *out*...

She ran backstage, squeezing herself through the narrow
gaps in the scenery, the shortcuts that all the lambs used.
Finally she emerged, limping out into the alley behind the
theatre. It was near as bright as day, the moon was so high
and full. The Ides, it was the Ides.

It was almost winter, and the nox should be cold, but
Topaz was hot all over, about to burst out of her skin. She
clenched and unclenched her hands, staring at them like they
belonged to someone else.

As she watched, the skin of her arm buckled and bubbled.
A shape was crawling around in there. She made out a head,
a long back and a tail. She shook all over, but couldn't tear
her eyes away. There was a critter of some kind, inside her.

She nudged at the moving bump under her skin with one fingernail. It felt warm, and real.

Two figures flew out of the theatre over her head, scattering broken bits of wood over Topaz's head. She looked up and saw them smash into a nearby stone wall and fall to the ground, punching and clawing at each other, rolling on the ground of the alley.

One snarled — and then they both transformed into huge creatures, black shadows and gleaming claws, and flew straight up into the sky, still tearing at each other.

This, then. This was what Himself had brought them to. Topaz knew it was him, with his promises and his high and mighty manners. She had known from the moment she opened her mouth to sing that song, the one she was so proud of, with all the lambs clustered around her. She had felt it, the power running from one of them to the other, building up around her, and when the mirrored ceiling came down, guttering the lamps and candles, she knew.

It was her: her song, their power, and it was all the stage-master's fault.

The skittering crawling thing moved from her wrist to her elbow, stretching the skin, and Topaz could almost make out the shape of its feet, its little legs. Like a dream, but not a dream. Very much not a dream when you could feel a critter tickling you from the wrong side of your skin.

Topaz picked up one of the broken bits of wood that had splintered off the wall when the two beasties crunched through it. It was a long shard with a good old point right at the end. She thought about stabbing the Orphan Princel through the belly or the chest, maybe gouging an eyeball. None of these things made her feel better about the fact that Bart was dead and it was half her fault.

She ran the point of the wood up and down the inside of her arm, where the crawling thing was still moving. She jabbed hard enough to bleed, and the pain was good. Something simple to think about. She jabbed again, wondering if she could kill the thing, or if she even wanted to.

She wouldn't be alone, if she let it live.

Blood welled over the wooden point, and something greyish pushed its way out of the ragged cut Topaz had made in her own arm. Small black eyes stared unblinkingly at her in the moonlight. It was cold and slithery, like a snake, only it had feet that it used to clamber out.

The critter eased its back legs out of the wound in her arm and ran up to her shoulder, along her chest, those little black eyes still staring, staring.

Her arm wasn't bleeding any more. That wasn't right, but there was plenty not right here to worry about.

'Are there more where you come from?' she whispered. The crawling thing gazed at her, and Topaz felt a push against her mind, almost like it was talking to her, showing the way. 'Oh,' she said in a small voice, and then she did it, all on her own. She changed.

Topaz was crawling, crawling, up walls and clinging to ceilings. She was a horde, lots of little pattering feet and she was hot, so hot, though everything she touched was cold.

She sure wasn't Topaz any more, and here was another thing to hate Himself for.

She was not a lamb, not a demme, not even a person.

Finally she found her way back, and lay on her belly, naked and sweating, crazy itchy in her own skin.

Hot, cold, she didn't know what she was. Topsy turvy upside down, confused about everything except for hate and misery. She liked it better crawling. You didn't care so much on all fours, with a tail to lash out at the world. Topaz could smell smoke. It tasted bad in the back of her throat, and she coughed as she pushed herself up.

'Your first time?' a voice said sympathetically. 'Poor chicken. I remember that.'

Topaz sat up, staring wildly around the alley. It weren't one she knew. She could be anywhere, far from the theatre.

A lady stepped out of the shadows so that the moonlight fell on her just so. She wore a frock that shimmered, and her hair was all glossy in that way that a stellar would take hours to get right. Her mouth was bright red with cosmetick, like blood. She smoked a cigarette in a fancy holder, and her eyes burned into Topaz.

At first Topaz wanted to cover herself with her hands, so this lady couldn't see her naked. Still, the look was snooty enough that she'd feel naked even if she was head to toe in a bearskin, so she didn't bother. 'What you talking about?'

'Don't play games with me, brat,' said the lady, as pleasantly as before. 'I saw you change. I know what you are.'

'I didn't do nothing,' Topaz said, desperately afraid. 'I didn't ask for this. It's not my fault. He made me!'

The lady moved, her pearls rattling and her heels clicking against the stone. She reached Topaz and held out a hand, so pale and smooth that Topaz didn't dare touch it. A fine lady like this shouldn't even know she existed, lest she was on stage entertaining her. 'I want to help you,' said the lady. 'Let me help you. My name is Livilla. And do you know what? I'm just like you.'

'I don't believe you,' Topaz said in a shaky voice, but then the demme's eyes went sort of yellow. Hound's eyes.

She didn't know she'd voiced that thought aloud until Lady Livilla corrected her: 'Wolf.'

Topaz was a city brat; she didn't know nothing about wolves. 'I want to go home,' she said, but there wasn't a home. There was the fancy boarding-house room bought and paid for in Bart's blood. There was the grotty rat nest that wouldn't be home without the other lambs — and Topaz

469

didn't want to see any of them if they had made it there. They wouldn't want to see her, neither.

They'd know, wouldn't they? Himself had used them, but it was *her* song that brought the ceiling down. It was her fault.

'Let me look after you,' said Livilla, and the smoke was rough but her voice was smooth and inviting. 'Are you hungry?'

Topaz's belly turned over before she could even think about the question. 'Oh, aye,' she breathed.

Livilla smiled, and if that was what wolves smiled like, then all the songs about them were true. 'I have meat,' she promised.

Topaz took her hand.

TOPAZ HAD SPENT several recent market-nines sleeping in a rosy room much nicer than anything she'd had in her life — clean cotton sheets, fat pillows, and space to herself. But this den was something else. She was now wrapped in a quilt so soft that it slithered against her skin, and the room was draped in black and scarlet, like a stage setting for a foreign boudoir. It smelled of smoke and perfume. She'd been fed a cup of ciocolata before she slept, and it still felt warm and sweet in her belly when she awoke.

'There you are,' said a voice. Topaz turned in a hurry, almost sliding out of the prissy bed. It wasn't the fine lady, but another demme dressed in grey who sat on a similar bed all draped in silks and gauze.

'Who are you then?' Topaz asked rudely.

'Bree,' said the demme, eyeing Topaz as if she wasn't impressed with what she saw. 'I was here first, and don't you forget it. There's rules to these things. I'm top courtesa. If milady wants something, I'm the first to her side. You fetch and carry for me. Got it?'

Topaz blinked. What, was she in service now? There were worse fates for a theatrical that left the stage than becoming a maid — stupid she'd been, not to ask what Lady Livilla wanted of her. She might have ended up whoring just as easily.

'Mind you tell the others that, too,' Bree added firmly. 'I was here first.'

'Others,' Topaz repeated.

Bree rolled her eyes. 'Go on, then. Go see for yourself.' Topaz looked around for her clothes, but remembered too late that she had been wearing none when she arrived. There was a dress like Bree's lying across her bed and she pulled it on, gasping at the high grade of the linen — not even stellars in the Royale wore anything like this, it was so fancy.

Bree flung the door open and then stood back to make way for Topaz. Holy blooming saints. Lady Livilla stood there, her arms and legs covered with all manner of critters. Birds, mice, rats. The room was full of them. Feraxes, hounds, even one bear that could have escaped straight from the Circus Verdigris.

'Ah, Topaz,' said Lady Livilla serenely. She shook all the critters off her arms and they clustered into groups, mice with mice, rats with rats... as Topaz watched, they shaped back into people. Small, naked, shivering forms.

Not people. Lambs. Her lambs. Ten of them, all miserable and scared. Sarah, Merrick, Belinny. All of them, cept for Bart, had made it here to this strange place, with this lady and no windows. Why were there no windows?

'Isn't it wonderful?' Lady Livilla said. 'Between us, my lambs, we shall take the Creature Court once and for all.' She smiled at Topaz, looking all sympathetic. 'It doesn't make any sense yet, my sweetling, but it will. I am going to rule this

471

city. Let the daylight have their Duchessa. I want the nox, every inch of it, and you are going to help me take it.'

~

THE ARCHES WERE EMPTY. Ashiol climbed down via the Eyrie and made his way silently through the tunnels and streets. He had visited the Palazzo first, creeping in cat shape and walking out again, unchallenged, dressed respectably and carrying a ceramic urn.

The ground down here was softer than above, except for the concrete slab of the Haymarket. Ashiol was happy to pad barefoot through the undercity, making his way to the Angel Gardens.

Once upon a time, this place was where the people of Aufleur grew their fresh food as they hid from the skywar that rained down upon them, before it disappeared into the nox and the daylight folk thought it safe to venture back above. There was animor in the earth here, rich enough that you could taste it on the back of your throat. Had to be, to let grass grow underground, let alone vegetables and the like.

There were no vegetables now, just grass and pale silver roses. The Angel Gardens had been a graveyard for as long as Ashiol could remember. Stones littered the place, each marked with a symbol of import. A cluster of them bore crudely sketched swords, the mark of the sentinel. Some had eyes, the mark of the Seer. The rest of the stones had creatures on them, all kinds of creatures, one for every fallen courteso, Lord or King.

There were no bodies here. In Aufleur, you burned your dead. The daylight folk were interred in the walls outside the bounds of the city. Most of the stones here in the Angel Gardens were placed to mark where ceramic urns full of ash and charred bone were buried. Some stones marked with stars had been put there to honour those who were swallowed by the sky, and left no remains behind.

No one had put a stone down for Garnet; or if they had, Ashiol never saw it. Too glad the bastard was dead, the lot of them.

And now he was back.

Ashiol hurt all over. He could use his animor to heal the wounds and bruises from his fight with Garnet, but he wasn't ready for that yet. (Didn't want to stop feeling it.) Priorities.

He found a stone with mice and stars carved into it and realised someone had set it here for Velody. They wouldn't be needing that. He shoved the stone out of the way and dug his hands into the earth, pushing viciously at it with animor until the dirt churned under his fingers, producing a hole.

Once he buried the urn, Ashiol took the stone into his hands and poured power against the smooth surface until the mice faded, and the stars were gone. He should carve an eye into it, because Heliora was the Seer, or swords because she had been a sentinel. He couldn't bring himself to do either. Instead, he glared at the stone until it broke into pieces, crumbling under his hands like dry bread.

A cairn of broken stones seemed appropriate. It was not as if he was ever going to forget her.

'Are you here?' A voice broke through the silence. Ashiol darted back to hide behind a ridiculously huge boulder with a bear carved into its surface. He recognised Garnet's voice, and was not ready to face him yet. If he concentrated, he could dampen down his own animor, so that no one would sense his presence.

'I've been waiting,' said another voice. Poet.

Ashiol went from rock to rock, searching for them. Finally he spotted two silhouettes in the near-darkness, standing near an arbour of silvery roses and the lioness stone that marked Tasha's passing.

Garnet wore a flashy suit of red velvet with a bright silk kerchief around his neck. 'I had to dress appropriately. It took time.'

Poet laughed shortly. 'Did the owner of that put up much of a struggle?'

'Hardly at all. See, not a drop of blood.'

'Yes, I can see that.' Poet dropped the pretence of being casual. 'My Power — do you have any idea what I have sacrificed for you?'

Garnet smiled that gorgeous smile of his, the one that made you forget how much you hated him. He reached out, touching the back of Poet's head, ruffling his hair a little. 'Beautiful boy. Do I seem ungrateful?' Poet leaned forward with a broken sigh, and Garnet held him. 'You don't need to be the Orphan Princel any more,' he whispered. 'You don't need that pretty theatre, or your fancy clothes — any of it. You have me.'

Poet tipped his face up, and Garnet kissed him, on the forehead and then the mouth.

Ashiol watched, stunned. This, he had not seen. This, he had not known.

'Thanks to you,' Garnet whispered, 'I made it back in excellent time. We have two months, and there is much to do. Your sacrifice was worthy.'

Poet slid to his knees, looking exhausted. 'They will try to stop us,' he said softly. 'Velody, Ashiol... I didn't know I would have to sacrifice my theatre!'

Garnet stroked his hands through Poet's hair as if he was a child. 'Velody is mine already. Leave Ashiol to me as well. He's weaker than anyone knows. Don't fret, love. This will be the finest Saturnalia that the Creature Court — and Aufleur — has ever known.'

Ashiol shaped himself into cats and slid away into the shadows, as silently as he could go. His mind was racing with all that he had heard. Velody and Poet were in thrall to Garnet. No one could be trusted, not now.

He had a choice. He could leave the city in their hands, let the sky fall as it might. Or he could take it back. He could really be the Power and Majesty.

He wanted Heliora desperately, craved to hear her voice the futures. She could give him the hope he needed to survive. But Hel was gone for good; he knew that now. If he was going to take Aufleur back, Ashiol was going to have to do it alone.

If Garnet, or Velody, or Poet or any of the rest of them tried to stop him, the answer was simple.

He would have to kill them all.

THE BATTLE CONTINUES IN
THE CREATURE COURT BOOK 3
Reign of Beasts

THE CREATURE
COURT CONTINUES

BOOK 3: REIGN OF BEASTS

With three kings at war over the title of Power and Majesty, someone's going to bleed. A final battle is coming, and the Creature Court must learn from their past to save their future, before they lose everyone.

Saturnalia will change the Creature Court and the city of Aufleur forever.

Get your copy of *Reign of Beasts* today. You can pick up a signed copy at the Teacup Magic Emporium.*

CABARET OF MONSTERS

A PREQUEL NOVELLA TO THE CREATURE COURT TRILOGY

Saturnalia in Aufleur is a time of topsy-turvy revels, of the world turned upside down and transformed before your eyes. The city's theatres produce an annual display of reversals, surprises and transformations. In Aufleur, flappers can transform into wolves. Even the rats are not what they seem.

Evie Inglirra is on a mission to infiltrate the theatrical world of Aufleur and discover what lies beneath their glamorous cabaret costumes and backstage scandals. What secrets will she uncover?

Get your copy of *Cabaret of Monsters* today. You can pick up a signed copy at the Teacup Magic Emporium.*

---

* tansyrr.com/collections/dark-divine

CALENDAR NOTES

The Ammorian calendar, or Fasti, has three named days —
the Kalends (first day of the month), the Nones (nine days
before the Ides) and the Ides (full moon — which falls more
or less in the middle of the month). Generally people refer to
days in relation to these, e.g. "four days after the Ides," or
"two days before the Kalends."

The day after each Kalends, Nones and Ides is considered
nefas/unlucky.

Market-nines or nundinae are the closest thing they have
to the idea of weeks — these refer to the markets held in the
city every 9 days regardless of other festivals.

MONTHS OF THE YEAR:

Venturis (winter)
  Lupercal (winter)
  Martial (spring)
  Aphrodal (spring)
  Floralis (spring)
  Lucina (summer)

Felicitas (summer)
Cerialis (summer)
Ludi (autumn)
Bestialis (autumn)
Fortuna (autumn)
Saturnalis (winter)

GLOSSARY

- **Alexandrine Basilica** — once the largest church in the known world, constructed by the fourth Duc d'Aufleur, mad old Ilexandros. His successor, Duc Giulio Gauget, declared the Basilica to be an unholy abomination and stripped its rich furnishings to ornament his own Palazzo. The hollowed-out and falling-down Basilica is now used as a marketplace, and a merchant's lot here is worth a small fortune.
- **Ammoria** — a principality once consisting of three duchies: Silano (capital city: Bazeppe), Lattorio (capital city: Aufleur) and Reyenna (capital city: Tierce). When the city of Tierce vanished, Reyenna became one of the baronies of Lattorio.
- **Animor** — the energy/power contained within the bodies of all full members of the Creature Court. Seers and sentinels do not hold animor, though they are touched/contaminated by it, which gives them a status between the nox and daylight worlds.

- **Ansouisette** — a fashionable cocktail of aniseed and lemon liqueur.
- **Arches, the** — ruined city that exists below Aufleur, where the city's inhabitants once lived after being forced underground during the old skywar. Now inhabited by the Creature Court. Also known as 'the undercity'.
- **Artorio Xandelian** — former Ducomte d'Aufleur, son of Duc Ynescho Xandelian and Duchessa Givette Camellie. Artorio refused to marry in his youth, but at age thirty-three was prevailed upon by his father to marry nineteen-year-old Eglantine in order to produce an heir. A year later Isangell was born. Artorio died of the Silent Sleep when his daughter was thirteen.
- **Ashiol Xandelian** — Ducomte d'Aufleur, son of Augusta and Bruges, stepson of Diamagne. Cousin to Isangell, Duchessa d'Aufleur. Member of the Creature Court; rank: King; creature: black cat.
- **Atulia** — region to the north of Ammoria.
- **Aufrey** — one of the twelve Great Families of Aufleur.
- **Aufleur** — capital city of the duchy of Lattorio in the principality of Ammoria. Ruled by Isangell, the daylight Duchessa.
- **Augusta Xandelian** — second child of Duc Ynescho Xandelian and Duchessa Givette Camellie. Married Bruges Lanouvre and had one son, Ashiol. A year after Bruges's death, Augusta married the Baronne di Diamagne and retired to his estate. She and Diamagne had four sons: Bryn, Keil, Jemmen and Zade, and a daughter, Phage (Pip). Now widowed again, her official title is the

Dowager Baronnille though she is technically entitled to use the title Ducomtessa.

- **Avleurine** — one of the hill districts of Aufleur; location of the Temple of the Market Saints.
- **Bree** — member of the Creature Court; rank: courtesa to Livilla, formerly to Priest; creature: sparrow.
- **Bridescake** — ornate wedding cake traditionally covered in spring flowers.
- **Bruges Lanouvre** — late husband of Augusta Xandelian; father of Ashiol (died when Ashiol was seven years old).
- **Burnplague** — a spreading sky pattern of blisters that spit motes of light and acid.
- **Camellie** — one of the twelve Great Families of Aufleur.
- **Camoise** — country to the far east of Ammoria. One of many cultures that trades extensively with Aufleur. Providers of the exotic and expensive 'real tea', the best of which is Camoiserian leaf.
- **Carmentines** — bright scarlet flowers with long stems.
- **Cathedral of Ires** — place of worship dedicated to the Crone Ires, who is venerated by the Irean Priestesses. Place where wills are lodged for safekeeping.
- **Celeste** — former Lord of the Creature Court who left with Lysandor during the tyrannical reign of Garnet as Power and Majesty.
- **Centi opera** — portable stalls featuring puppet shows. Sometimes a young female performer, an ingénue, performs among the puppets.
- **Centrini** — affluent mercantile district in the centre of Aufleur.

- **Cheapside** — part of the market district of Tierce, where Velody's family own a bakery.
- **Chimaera** — a monstrous dark shadowy shape with claws, teeth and scales; an amalgam of every devil and forbidden creature imaginable. Only Creature Kings are able to take chimaera form; used in battle.
- **Church Bridge** — traditional starting point for festival parades; finishing point is the Forum. One of two city bridges across the River Verticordia, the other being the Marius Bridge.
- **Ciocolate** — a very expensive delicacy brought over from Nova Stella. Served as a fondant or as a hot, spicy drink called ciocolata.
- **Circus Verdigris:** a central arena in the city with a grass surface, used for public games.
- **City Fathers** — the members of the City Council, who meet in the Curia: this group is made up of the Duc's Ministers, a Proctor for each of the city districts, and the three senior priests who between them form the ruling body of the city, under the hand of the Duc or Duchessa. The three senior priests are the Matrona Irea of the Irean Priestesses (the only woman allowed to be a city father), Brother Typhisus of the Silver Brethren, and the Master of Saints.
- **Clara** — member of the Creature Court; rank: courtesa to Warlord; creature: greymoon cat.
- **Coinage** — the coins of Aufleur are divided into gold ducs, silver ducs, copper shilleins and copper centi.
- **Columbine** — a female dancer who performs in musette and theatre revues.

- **Coronets** — delicious lemon-glazed breakfast pastries, shaped like crowns and unique to Aufleur.
- **Courtesi (courteso: male; courtesa: female)** — the lowest rank of the Creature Court; must ally themselves with a particular Lord for protection. Too vulnerable to exist alone.
- **Crane** — youngest of the surviving sentinels. Weapons: blue-hilted daggers and swords.
- **Creature Court** — the courtesi, Lords and Kings who hold animor within their bodies, belong to the nox and have the ability to fight the sky. Ruled by the Power and Majesty, the highest ranked of their Kings. Peripheral members of the Court include the sentinels and the seer, but they often consider themselves separate from the Court.
- **Crossroads** — any part of the city where two streets meet is considered sacred to the protective spirits or household gods of Aufleur. Casual sacrifices (for example chickens or honey cakes) are often made here for greater effect.
- **Curia** — slope-roofed building in the Forum that houses meetings of the City Council.
- **Cyniver** — brother of Rhian and lover of Velody; lost when Tierce was swallowed by the sky.
- **Damascine Virgins** — an order of priestesses in service to Damascus the war-angel. They sacrifice to him on the eleventh day of Martial.
- **Dame** — appropriate form of address for a respectable matron, diminutive of 'madame'.
- **Damson** — member of the Creature Court; rank: courtesa to Priest; creature: gull.
- **Delphine** — friend to Velody and Rhian; ribboner and garland-maker.

- **Demoiselle** — unmarried (young) woman; 'demme' for short.
- **Duc/Duchessa d'Aufleur** — ruler of the city of Aufleur.
- **Dhynar** — **member of the Creature Court**; rank: Lord; creature: ferax.
- **Diamagne** — farming and wine region south of Aufleur; part of Lattorio. Also the name of the Baronne di Diamagne (now deceased), who married Augusta Xandelian (Ashiol's mother) as her second husband.
- **Donagan** — reputed to be the finest tailor in Aufleur, a master craftsman.
- **Dottores** — medical practitioners, mostly male. The only women allowed to practise in Aufleur as dottores are those registered as midwives, although many of them dispense other forms of medical advice on the side.
- **Edore** — region to the north of Ammoria and Atulia.
- **Evander X** — a popular writer of newspaper adventure serials, pen-name for Evanderline Inglirra.
- **Farrier** — member of the Creature Court; rank: courteso to Warlord, formerly to Dhynar; creature: slashcat.
- **Fionella** — member of the Creature Court; rank: courtesa to Priest.
- **Floralia** — six-day festival commemorating the glory of spring and the fertility of the coming summer. It begins in the month of Aphrodal and ends in the month of Floralis. Honours maidens, sweethearts, brides, household gods, passion and abundance, each on a different day. The first day

(maidens) is celebrated with a public parade by the Spring Queen (the highest-ranking female in the city) and her Spring Consort, both dressed in pink and white.

- **Flame-and-gin** — common bar drink.
- **Florister** — artisan who works with plants and flowers; often works in conjunction with a ribboner or garland-maker to produce festival garlands.
- **Fornacalia** — festival from the sixth to the seventeenth of Lupercal in honour of the harvest saints, and the baking of the corn. Citizens wear ceremonial baking aprons for the rituals. Overlaps with the Parentalia, Quirinalia and Lupercalia.
- **Forum** — the public centre of Aufleur, a large area lined with temples and public buildings such as the Alexandrine Basilica and the Curia. The city market is held here every nine days, events such as the apprentice fairs are held here, and this is the traditional climax of most public parades and pageants. The Duchessa's Avenue connects the Forum to the Lake of Follies. Other cities, such as Tierce, also have a Forum, though the Forum of Aufleur is unusually large.
- **Gardens of Trajus Alysaundre** — gardens covering one side of the Lucretine hill in the centre of Aufleur; built over the top of the decadent public baths established in honour of the third Duc d'Aufleur, Trajus Alysaundre. The gardens face on to the Lake of Follies and the Forum.
- **Garnet** — member of the Creature Court; rank: Power and Majesty; creature: gattopardo (mountain cat). He is the son of the cook and the

groundskeeper on the Diamagne estate, and was Ashiol's boyhood friend.

- **Giacosa** — bustling merchant district at the southern end of Aufleur.
- **Giulio Gauget** — fifth Duc d'Aufleur. Known for excessive modesty and piety in contrast to his predecessor, Ilexandros Alysaundre.
- **Givette Camellie** — the Old Duchessa, wife of Duc Ynescho, mother of Artorio and Augusta, grandmother of Isangell, Ashiol, Bryn, Keil, Jemmen, Zade and Phage. Became Regenta when her late husband was mentally incapacitated; pre-deceased him after a long illness.
- **Gleamspray** — a rare and lethal element of the skybattles which is known for killing daylight folk; victims appear to succumb to the 'Silent Sleep'.
- **Grago** — member of the Creature Court; rank: courteso to Warlord, formerly to Dhynar; creature: stripecat.
- **Great Families** — the twelve Great Families of Aufleur: Xandelian (ducal), Leorgette, Lanouvre, Gauget, Paucini, Aufrey, Alysaundre, Vittorio, Giuliano, Camellie, Delgardie, Octaviano.
- **Halberk** — member of the Creature Court; courteso to Poet; creature: bear.
- **Harlequinus** — a sad dancing clown, main male role in the harlequinade, a regular feature of musette revues.
- **Haymarket** — located in the Arches. Formerly a packing and storage facility; now a large space where the Power and Majesty resides. A canal runs water from the River Verticordia right through the Haymarket and down through the Arches, emerging at the Lock in the side of the

Lucretine hill, which is the main entrance to the Arches.

- **Heliora** — member of the Creature Court; rank: Seer. Joined Court as a sentinel; became Seer during Ortheus's reign as Power and Majesty.
- **Ilexandros Alysaundre** — fourth Duc d'Aufleur; also known as 'mad old Ilexandros'. Built the Alexandrine Basilica, largest church in the known world, in the Forum of Aufleur.
- **Imperium** — a distilled alcoholic beverage made from fermented grain mash.
- **Inglirrus** — a small country across the strait from Orcadia.
- **Irean Priestesses** — powerful priestesses who venerate Ires the Crone, otherwise known as Saint Grandmere. The priestesses wear white and are said to have communion with the dead. Wills are lodged with them for safekeeping, and the priestesses are responsible for public readings of said wills. Their chief priestess is the Matrona Irea, one of the three priests included in the City Fathers.
- **Ires** — the Crone, or Saint Grandmere, worshipped in the Cathedral of Ires and venerated by the Irean Priestesses.
- **Isangell** — Duchessa d'Aufleur (full name/title: Duchessa Isangell Xandelian d'Aufleur, First Lady of the Silver Seal); daughter of Artorio Xandelian and Eglantine; granddaughter of previous Duc d'Aufleur, Ynescho Xandelian, and his Regenta, the Duchessa Givette.
- **Isharo** — an island country to the Far East, a trading partner with Aufleur, particularly for flowers and fabrics.

- **Islandser** — a person from the Green Islands, to the west of Inglirrus, with a distinctive accent.
- **Janvier** — member of the Creature Court; courteso to Livilla; creature: raven.
- **Jardin Falcone** — editor of the Aufleur Gazette, a popular city newspaper.
- **Kelpie** — sentinel. Refers to her swords as her 'Sisters' and her daggers as her 'Nieces': hilts are wrapped in dark leather.
- **Lanouvre** — one of the twelve Great Families of Aufleur.
- **Laudinon** — the capital city of Inglirrus
- **Lemuria** — festival during Floralis to placate the shades of dead ancestors and lost loves.
- **Lennoc** — member of the Creature Court; rank: courteso to Poet (formerly to Lief and then Dhynar); creature: brighthound.
- **Leorgette** — one of the twelve Great Families of Aufleur.
- **Librarion** — Aufleur's city library.
- **Lictors** — honour guard that protects ranks of Duc, Duchessa, Ducomte or Ducomtessa, as well as select City Fathers, priests of high status and the Chief Minister. Lictors travel in multiples of three, carry ceremonial rods of state, are armed with axes and wear black and scarlet.
- **Lief** — deceased member of the Creature Court; rank: Lord; creature: greathound.
- **Livilla** — member of the Creature Court; rank: Lord; creature: wolf.
- **Lucian** — one of the districts of Aufleur, known as the theatre district.
- **Ludi** — as well as being the name of the first autumn month, this word means 'games'.

- **Ludi Aufleuris** — fifteen-day series of games held during the first month of autumn, Ludi. Women traditionally wear scarlet shawls when attending these games and wave the corners of the shawls to favoured gladiators and performers.
- **Ludi Megalensia** — Games of the Great Mother, held in the month of Aphrodal. Unlike other Ludi, there are no fights, animals or mock battles; instead, the games feature theatrical performances.
- **Ludi Sacris** — Sacred Games, held in the month of Felicitas. On the chief day of sacrifice (day four), everyone in the city makes a sacrifice to their chosen saints or gods.
- **Ludi Victoriae** — Victory Games, held in the month of Cerialis, in which favourite historical battles are re-enacted in the Circus Verdigris by gladiators and actors.
- **Lupercalia** — one-day festival in Lupercal during which men carouse in the streets wearing goatskins, goat masks and fake phalluses. Not unheard of for their real phalluses to hang out, for extra authenticity.
- **Lysandor** — member of the Creature Court; rank: King. Fled with Celeste during Garnet's tyrannical reign as Power and Majesty.
- **Macready** — sentinel. Original weapons: Alicity (steel sword), Tarea (skysilver sword), Phoebe (steel dagger), Jeunille (skysilver dagger); hilts wrapped in green leather. New weapons: hilts wrapped in grey leather.
- **Margarethe** — one of the lower districts of Aufleur, run- down and poor.
- **Market-nines** — every ninth day (nundinae) is a public market day, regardless of other festival

constraints. The phrase 'market-nine' refers to these nine-day groupings. Market-nines fall on different days each year.

- **Mars/Warlord** — member of the Creature Court; rank: Lord; creature: panther (Khatri zaba in Zafiran). Born Maziz dal Sara, he was the son of the Zafiran ambassador.
- **Mask** — an actor who performs with their face covered in musette and theatre revues.
- **Matralia** — festival during month of Lucina, when mothers and maternal relatives everywhere are crowned with silverbreath and ivy.
- **Mercatus** — grand city-wide market festivals held in Cerialis and Ludi, the two months with the most sacred games.
- **Musette** — a theatrical establishment or performance, usually in the style of a music hall, variety show or pantomime.
- **Nefas** — means 'unlucky', particularly in relation to a day; for example the day immediately after the Kalends, Nones or Ides of each month is nefas, and business transactions are rarely performed on these days.
- **Neptunalia** — a winter festival held on the Kalends of Saturnalis, celebrating the ancient Seafather with sweetmeats, sacrifice and rituals involving paper boats.
- **Nova Stella** — a land far to the West of Ammoria, discovered and colonised two hundred years previously by explorers from Stelleza. Source for ciocolate and tobacco.
- **Nox** — the opposite of day.
- **Orcadia** — north-western region, known for its gentle climate and bubbled wine.

- **Orcadian Strait** — a body of water between Orcadia and Inglirrus.
- **Orphan Princel** — Poet's theatrical alter ego, stellar and stagemaster of the Mermaid Revue.
- **Ortheus** — former member of the Creature Court; rank: King; Power and Majesty (before Garnet). Creature: serpent.
- **Palazzo** — home of the ruling ducal family, located on the Balisquine hill and surrounded by other opulent residences. A former palazzo, now abandoned, is located on the Avleurine Hill.
- **Parentalia** — nine-day festival from the thirteenth to the twenty-first of Lupercal, during which all citizens of Aufleur travel to place flowers and sweetmeats on their family tombs and grave markers. White silk garlands are traditionally worn.
- **Paucini** — one of the twelve Great Families of Aufleur.
- **Piazza Nautilia** — public square at the conjunction of three major streets in Aufleur: Via Delgardie, Via Leondrine and Via Camellie; location of Triton's Church and the best public baths in Aufleur.
- **Poet** — member of the Creature Court; rank: Lord; creature: white rats. Moonlights as the Orphan Princel, a famous musette performer.
- **Power and Majesty** — leader of the Creature Court; must hold the rank of King.
- **Priest** — member of the Creature Court; rank: Lord; creature: pigeon.
- **Proctors** — public officials elected each year; one for each district in Aufleur. Included among the City Fathers.

- **Quirinalia** — One-day festival on the seventeenth of Lupercal, overlapping with the Fornacalia and Parentalia. Bunches of myrtle are exchanged and worn at the belt to ward off ill-luck for soldiers. Vigiles and lictors are allowed this day off public duties for religious observance.
- **Raoul** — former Seer of the Creature Court, who passed his powers on to Heliora upon his death.
- **Reyenna** — formerly one of the three duchies of Ammoria. After the disappearance of its capital city, Tierce, Reyenna became known as one of the baronies of Lattorio.
- **Rhian** — friend to Velody and Delphine; florister.
- **Sage** — Velody's brother, who was lost along with the rest of her family when Tierce was swallowed by the sky. Originally a dock worker, he was injured in an accident and ended up taking recreational potions for many years before cleaning up his act and getting factory work.
- **Saints** — worshipped by the daylight folk through rituals and festivals. 'Saints and angels' and 'saints and devils' are two common swearing phrases heard throughout the city.
- **Samara** — legendary former member of the Creature Court; female Lord who took in too much animor and blew apart. Cited as evidence that women cannot be Kings.
- **Saturnalia** — an eight-day festival, held from the seventeenth to the twenty-fourth of Saturnalis, in which masters and servants traditionally swap roles, men and women wear each other's clothing, etc. Also sometimes known as the Feast of Fools, it celebrates all things topsy-turvy. Traditional refreshments include hot cider, bean

syrup and roasted chestnuts. An important theatre season.

- **Scratchlight** — weapon used by the sky in battle; kills one in fifty mortals it hits — not as effective as the rarer shadowstreak or gleamspray.
- **Seer** — member of the Creature Court, outside the usual hierarchy. The seer has the ability to look into the future and pull out visions of what is to come.
- **Seigneur** — a polite term of address for men, which gets politer the higher in rank they actually are.
- **Sentinels** — the loyal armed servants of the Kings of the Creature Court. Each bears blades of steel and skysilver to represent the thin line they tread between the nox and the daylight. They are ready to give up their blood to their masters at a moment's notice.
- **Seonard** — member of the Creature Court; rank: courteso to Livilla; creature: wolf.
- **Serenai** — patron saint of gamblers and good fortune. Friendly bets often include promises for the loser to sacrifice to Serenai or other saints and angels on the winner's behalf.
- **Shade** — member of the Creature Court; rank: courteso to Poet (formerly courteso to Lief and then Dhynar); creature: darkhound.
- **Silent Sleep** — a fatal illness that tends to affect the very young and the elderly. A side-effect of skybattle, but to daylight folk a mystery illness that attacks without warning and leaves no contamination trail.
- **Silver Brethren** — a chaste order of male priests, who wear silver chains and shave their heads. They

never speak once they have taken orders, only sing and chant during their street processions.

- **Silver Captain** — Nathanial, former leader of the sentinels. Died on the eve of Vestalia, three years before the return of Ashiol.
- **Silverstorm** — shards of skysilver generated by the sky during battle.
- **Skybattle** — when the sky opens and attacks the city, using all manner of deadly phenomena. Only happens at nox, and only the Creature Court and their allies, such as the seer and sentinels, are aware of this. The Creature Court exists to battle the sky and protect the city. Any damage to buildings or other parts of the city is repaired at dawn, and any daylight folk affected by the sky's weapons recover and return to normal. Occasionally there are fatalities if a person has suffered a direct hit, particularly if they are very young or elderly. Such fatalities are referred to by the daylight folk as the Silent Sleep.
- **Skyburn** — the effect of some sky weapons on the sentinels. In its lightest form it is similar to sunburn; more serious symptoms include deeply reddened or bruised skin, fever and weakness.
- **Skyfall** — to be swallowed by the sky. Death by skyfall means a Court member's animor goes with them into the sky and is lost forever, instead of being shared among the survivors of the Creature Court. 'The sky is falling' is an expression often used to indicate that a skybattle is beginning.
- **Skyseed** — a red cloud that is the seed of a deathstorm. Deathstorms bring flaming hail, 'devils' (violent animated dust clouds) and 'angels' (poisonous bursts of steam)'. A skyseed can be

destroyed by lancing — similar to lancing a boil, only a million times more disgusting.

- **Skysilver** — a metallic substance that falls from the sky. The Creature Court believes it comes from the stars. All skysilver is the property of Kings and given to the Smith, who forges it into weapons for the sentinels.

- **Slow rain** — a force of destruction from the sky, liquid that can burn a hole right through a member of the Court and give a sentinel skyburn. Usually occurs a couple of times a month, often heralding worse to come.

- **Smith, the** — a figure who is both part of and apart from the Creature Court, only accessible for an hour at noon each day. The Smith crafts the skysilver into weapons for the sentinels, and has been around since before Aufleur was built.

- **Songbird** — a singer who performs in musette and theatre revues.

- **Star tar** — hideous black muck that oozes through the cracks in the sky during the worst skybattles.

- **Stellar** — the most prominent and popular performer in a musette or theatre revue.

- **Stelleza** — an affluent country to the west of Ammoria, known for its adventurers and explorers. Strong trading partner with Aufleur.

- **Surrender** — a party potion that makes the user high and giddy.

- **Sweetheart Saints** — patron saints of romance and sweethearts.

- **Tanaquil** — mistress of birds, one of the ancient saints of Aufleur.

- **Tasha** — former member of the Creature Court; rank: Lord; creature: lion. Recruited Ashiol,

Garnet, Lysandor, Poet and Livilla as her courtesi. Died forsworn, and returned as a shade who dragged corruption and disease through the city before she was stopped.

- **Temple of the Market Saints** — located on the Avleurine hill. The Market Saints are the patron saints of all traders and merchants.
- **Tierce** — capital city of Reyenna, and where Velody, Delphine and Rhian come from. When Tierce disappeared, Reyenna became a barony of the duchy of Lattorio.
- **Trajus Alysaundre** — third Duc d'Aufleur; see also 'Gardens of Trajus Alysaundre'.
- **Velody** — friend to Rhian and Delphine; dressmaker. Sister to Amber, Thaya, Iris, Sage (all deceased). Member of the Creature Court; rank: King; Power and Majesty; creature: little brown mouse.
- **Vestalia** — a rural festival on the ninth day of Lucina in which people dress up in milkmaid costumes, aprons and other 'peasant' attire. Other features are green paper lanterns and sacrifices of honey, cake, bread and salt. The day is sacred to bakers and millers.
- **Via Ciceline** — a vibrant shopping strip in the heart of the wealthy Centrini district.
- **Via Silviana** — a narrow street crammed between the affluent Vittorine hill and the shabby, bustling Giacosa commercial district. The shop belonging to Velody, Rhian and Delphine stands at the halfway point between Vittorine and Giacosa, under the Sign of the Rose and Needle.
- **Vittorine** — one of the hill districts of Aufleur; also extends below the foot of the hill into an

upmarket shopping district that meets the thriving merchant district of Giacosa.

- **Vittorina Royale** — a theatre in the Vittorine district, currently managed by the Orphan Princel, and hosting the Mermaid Revue. Current and former performers at this theatre include Christophe, Sunshine, Ruby-red, Zephyr, Topaz, Bart, Adriane and Madalena.
- **Warlord** — member of the Creature Court; see 'Mars'.
- **Xandelian** — one of the districts of Aufleur. Also the name of the current ruling ducal family, whose members include Ynescho, Augusta, Artorio, Isangell and Ashiol. One of the twelve Great Families of Aufleur.
- **Ynescho Xandelian** — the Old Duc, grandfather to Isangell, Ashiol, Bryn, Keil, Jemmen, Zade and Phage, father of Artorio and Augusta. Ruled with an iron fist until his wits gave way; his wife, Duchessa Givette, took over as his Regenta.
- **Yvette LeBeau** — former mistress of the Old Duc and former columbine; in her retirement she owns a house on the corner of the Marius Bridge over the River Verticordia and entertains theatricals.
- **Zafir** — an eastern country rich with culture, source of the popular 'princessa and djinn' plays that are a regularly revived trend in the Aufleur theatres and musettes.
- **Zero** — member of the Creature Court; rank: courteso to Poet; creature: weasel.

ABOUT THE AUTHOR

Tansy Rayner Roberts is an award-winning Australian science fiction and fantasy author who does not make her own gowns, or run across rooftops. She lives with her family in Tasmania and has been known to pick up the occasional embroidery hoop.

Listen to Tansy on Sheep Might Fly, a podcast where she reads aloud her stories as audio serials.

What tea is Tansy drinking? Find out at when you subscribe to her excellent newsletter.[*]

Follow TansyRR at:
tansyrr.com

Visit the Teacup Magic Emporium[†] to get signed paperbacks, bundles, magical merch and bonus content direct from the author!

---

[*] tinyurl.com/tansyrr
[†] tansyrr.com/collections/dark-divine